JEDDER'S LAND

by *Maureen O'Donoghue*

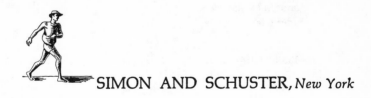

SIMON AND SCHUSTER, *New York*

Copyright © 1983 by Maureen O'Donoghue

All rights reserved
including the right of reproduction
in whole or in part in any form
Published by Simon and Schuster
A Division of Gulf & Western Corporation

Simon & Schuster Building
Rockefeller Center
1230 Avenue of the Americas
New York, New York 10020

SIMON AND SCHUSTER and colophon are registered trademarks
of Simon & Schuster

Designed by Irving Perkins Associates

Manufactured in the United States of America

10 9 8 7 6 5 4 3 2 1

Library of Congress Cataloging in Publication Data

O'Donoghue, Maureen.
  Jedder's land.

  I. Title.
PR6065.D594J4   1983   823'.914   83–473
ISBN 0–671–47044–2

To
my good friend
Jo McCurrie

CHAPTER ONE

The master was smiling. His face was puckered, cheeks bunched into his eye sockets and lips tucked back under the ragged moustache to reveal long, yellow teeth. Rachel Jedder had never seen him smile before.

Staying close to the doorpost, she slid her eyes toward his wife, and those features, too, were goffered by an iron grin. The girl focused abruptly on the flagstones to conceal her apprehension.

When the parish overseer had ridden up to the farm that morning, she had remained hidden in the barn, wondering whether he had come about her or about young Sam. Squinting through a crack in the timber, she had torn absently at the hunk of bread left out for her breakfast and muttered, as his tethered horse turned its hindquarters into the morning wind and sagged to rest one leg.

Minutes skimmed by and still the man did not emerge from the house to be gone. A thin cat stole across the yard, coaxed into courage by an open door to shelter at the other side. It was nearly an hour since she had stirred rennet into the milk. Now the curd should be broken. Much more delay and she would catch a beating. Crouched in the straw the girl had begun to rock slightly with indecision when her name was shouted.

"Rachel Jedder!"

The pulse stopped in her throat. He had come about her.

"Rachel Jedder!"

They were standing in the kitchen. Smiling. She did not dare to look at him, but she could see his boots and remembered how they had thudded into her back, sending her tumbling onto the stone track, over and over again, that time she had been caught in Shaltam. Big, bluff, beefy as the master's bull, and just as dangerous, William Styles knew how to treat runaway paupers.

"Now, girl. What would you say to a change in your situation?" As he spoke, he raised a hand and she jerked. "What would you say to becoming a daughter in this house?"

Rachel Jedder watched the hand and stayed completely still. She did not understand the words, but the smiles bit warningly at the edges of

9

her sight. Water bubbled in the cauldron over the damp wood fire, filling the dark room with noisy steam as they all waited.

"Well, wench? Your master and mistress would make you their daughter instead of one of the wretched poor. Well?" The overseer thrust out his fleshy jaw with impatience.

She shifted uneasily, trying not to let the sound of her breathing escape. There was still a mark on her face where the farmer's wife had flicked a wet cloth across it the day before because her skirt had trailed a few dead leaves into the dairy. Daughter. What did he mean, they wanted to make her a daughter?

Mister Wame, the master, was staring at a jumble of parchments on the table between them, as though they were slices of game pie. It was the same expression he unwittingly wore while selling off a barrener as an in-calf cow, and the smell of trickery was as thick as pig dung.

"Curd needs breaking, mistress," she said at last.

"Curd! Is the pauper simple?" William Styles glowered at the farmer and his wife, then stepped aggressively forward, his whiskers risen like hackles. "Did you not hear me, wench? They would take you into their own family, make you the child of the house."

The handle of the door dug into Rachel's spine as she pressed against it. Mistress Wame was making alien gestures, stretching out arms, as though to clasp her to a suet-hard bosom, and promising, "She'll sleep in a proper feather bed and not out wi' the cattle no more."

"Hear that? A feather bed an' all. You oughter be down on your knees with thankfulness, wench," blared the parish overseer, seizing her arm and pulling her to the table with a vehemence that made her head snap back. "You only need put your mark on the document here and 'tis done."

The master, already close against her side, pushed a goose quill swiftly into her hand and directed it to a space at the foot of a paper. Surprised, the girl dropped the pen and stared at the features almost touching her own. His eyelids had tightened around pupils so dilated that all trace of the irises had been sucked into them. The skin over his cheekbones was loose and damp, and a fleck of spittle bubbled in the slack corner of his mouth. It was the unmistakable face of pure and rapacious greed. Beer-heavy air blew into her lungs and a pair of crows suddenly cackled past the window. She twisted away from the two men.

Workhouse children received no education and the only book she had ever seen was the Bible. Even the indenture by which, at the age of nine, she had been apprenticed to this farmer, would have been incomprehensible to her. The one piece of knowledge Rachel Jedder had about writing and documents was that, no matter what befell, you never put your mark to them. Matthew Manby had been taken unwilling into the Militia only a month back after giving his mark while drunk, and Meg Caley's husband had lost their common rights through making his mark on some paper. There were many other like tales, all ending in misfortune, for everyone knew the only time you put your mark was in church after you were wed. A barb of anger scratched her mind.

"No," she mumbled and then, loudly, "No! I'll not make no mark."

There was an astounded pause before Mistress Wame drew in a scalding gasp and her husband, breathing coarsely through angry nostrils, stooped like a hawk, his eyes bloodveined and protruding.

"Wait you there, Mister Styles. I'll whip the ungrateful hussy into obedience. Won't take but five minutes, sir, afore she begs mercy." He grasped a fistful of her long hair and reached for the horsewhip hanging on the wall. "You'll not say 'No' again, girl," he bellowed.

It was as though a torch were being set to her scalp, and water coursed through her tear ducts as the matted black stands strained agonizingly against their roots. She could feel the scream in the back of her throat, like a bone, and clamped shut her teeth as he dragged her forward, scrabbling uselessly to maintain balance.

"Wait now, Mister Wame. There can't be no beating," William Styles interrupted in ponderously official tones. "Gold's been paid to end the apprenticeship and she must sign freely."

Rachel fell through the open door into the passage as the farmer released her; she was blinded by her own hair for a moment before she saw the chance to run across the yard to the buildings, with their secret, cobwebbed corners behind stored tools and lengths of wood and barrels, where a small, thin creature could crouch beside the rat holes in safety until dusk.

The master and the parish overseer were growling at each other like dogs. Ready to flee, she hesitated against all her instincts, half conscious of being part of some fateful riddle. Money had been paid and the beating had been stopped. Something was happening to do with her life; something she had to understand.

"Tell 'er, then," she heard his resentful voice agree and, when the terrible William Styles called her name again, she tautened for an instant before drawing back very slowly from the daylight and returning to the kitchen to face him.

"It seems you have not been without relatives all these years, Rachel Jedder," he began, then stopped to sit himself back in the large wooden chair by the dresser and watch her with spiteful amusement. The farmer sulkily poured and passed over a tankard of ale and he drew on it deliberately, still holding her in view over the pewter rim.

She could feel her body begin to tremble. Every pauper child lying under a shop counter, or in a draughty barn, or by the cold millstone, had the same nightly dream, of being discovered by an unknown aunt, loving and sweet-smelling, of being carried away to a real home with beds and log fires by an all-powerful uncle, or older brother, or cousin, after years of searching. Each and every one knew that his poverty was a mistake.

11

But the girl was too old to believe such nonsenses. She forced her muscles into rigid discipline and William Styles read the reaction with malicious accuracy.

"Aye, that's right, wench. You *had* a grandfather, but not now; not since threee months past," he taunted, winking at the farmer's wife. " 'Cos he died, see?"

Rachel stared ahead, unseeing, lapped by an unexpected misery. Pictures of homely rooms and good hot food and pretty gowns and caring adults and fat, kissable children, relatives, her own people, *family*, had invaded her unguarded mind in those few seconds. She had not been too old to believe after all.

William Styles honked with laughter, snorting into his drink and thumping his thigh with his fist at the sight of her face. It was a short while before he could continue.

"This grandfather of yours lived in Devon, where your wretched mother come from," he went on, exploding again, as though it was the funniest tale ever told.

Rachel barely heard him. She wished they would let her go away to her work. There was no longer enough time left to complete everything by the end of the day, which meant a certain thrashing at evening.

"It would appear when he died he left you a hovel and a patch of rough ground there." After making this last choking announcement, William Styles abandoned himself to total mirth.

Mistress Wame glared at him. Any more fuss and the baggage would forget her place. She crossed the kitchen to confront the girl.

"Now, Rachel Jedder, it's decided to do right by you, to bring you into the house and make you our daughter," she said peremptorily. "And Mister Styles here is to sell off that bit of old land to pay for your keep."

Rachel felt confused and did not know how to respond. "Where is Devon?" she wondered, with effort. "Is it in England?"

The farmer's wife shrugged and looked questioningly at her husband, who grunted and waved a directionless arm.

" 'Tis in England, but 'tis hundreds and hundreds of mile away, wench," he answered vaguely. "And what matter *where* it is? Git along and make your bloody mark on the parchment so Mister Styles can carry out the business."

Rachel's fingers picked at her skirt as she looked at each face in turn, forcing herself to concentrate on what had been said. A hovel meant a cottage . . . a cottage . . . and land. . . . There was a cottage and land belonging to her . . . somewhere in England. They were her own.

"That I aren't, master," she said finally, through numb lips. "I'll make no mark I'll niver make no mark, niver."

They moved in a rolling wave of menace, buffeting against her and roaring, their features fragmented by the torrent of anger, their hands clenched and very near. She was frightened and hunched her shoulders;

but, for all their squalling, not one hit her. So she dipped her head and wriggled between them, snatching up the papers from the table and darting to the open door. The shouting stopped, as though she had jammed an apple in each mouth.

"I'll have my land," she said flatly, clutching the documents to her. "And no one will sell what's mine."

Then she was through the door and racing across the cobblestones as the voices rose again behind her, blustering and cursing and braying her name, until, rusty as a guinea fowl above the male grumblings, Mistress Wame loosed the accusation screeching into the air.

"Witch! Witch! A witch!"

It reached Rachel by the wooden five-bar gate and she shied automatically from the footpath beyond to duck between the mushroom-shaped staddle stones, which supported the new granary, and crawl to the stables on the far side, scrambling up to the loft and over its lining of hay to the nestlike hollow of Sam's bed. Curling to fit the contours, she pulled down a thatch of dried grasses and lay motionless under its protection.

The word repeated in her head. *Witch. Witch.* She had heard it all her life, after every error or oversight, as her face had turned anxiously to the angry men and women in whose care she had been placed after the death of her mother. They had each looked into those strange particolored eyes and stepped back, hissing of witchcraft and the Devil's mark.

Rachel Jedder had always been an undersized child, with knees and elbows too big for her emaciated legs and arms, and rabbitty shoulder blades jutting beyond the pebble ridge of her spine, as though small, dark wings were about to sprout from them. Her hair was lank and hung like string because it was rarely washed. Its blackness accentuated the paleness of her skin and the bony structure of her small face. These aspects of her appearance were not unusual in one of the poor of the parish, which would have disapproved vociferously of a well-covered pauper, the burden of whose support by the small community was far too heavy to permit more than subsistence feeding.

Puberty had come late and caused little outward change. Now, at sixteen, the girl was still flat-chested and boy-hipped, with only the first shadow of body hair and a new fullness about her lips confirming maturity. To the village she was just one skinny waif among many—except for her eyes, the irises of which were abnormally wide and each composed of two distinct bands of contrasting color, an inner circle of light green and an outer rim of deep brown. Their effect was startling, disturbing. Concealing the human feelings behind them, they spoke of the unknown and, therefore, of the fearsome. Less that fifty years before, the burning of witches had been forbidden by law, but folk still believed in sorcery and looked into Rachel Jedder's extraordinary eyes and were afraid.

13

The door below cracked open and the men's boots squelched through the stable muck and knocked on the wooden rungs of the ladder to the loft.

"She ain't there, I tell you," the woman called after them. "You saw thet, how she disappeared afore our eyes, vanished into the air. 'Twas a black spell and Satan's work. She's gone back to the Devil, where she come from, and it's no good a-troubling after her."

The hay swished under their heavy movements as they climbed through the hatch in the floor, muttering doubtfully. Rachel lay as though dead while they argued over whether the wife could be right, the farmer convinced by the great bird he had seen rise from where the girl had stood, and fly away over the gate; but William Styles was less prepared to admit it, for fear of being made to look foolish later and so damaging his reputation as a public figure.

"That wench was always a rum 'un," the master said, nervously. "Mistress Wame has been plagued with the rheum and a weak belly ever since she were sent here, and not decoctions of rue nor rose-hip cordial bring ease. And I recall near fifteen yews dropped dead lambs last year after Rachel Jedder walked by the flock on Lady Day."

"Come now, Mister Wame. 'Tis said by folk that knows that there ain't such things as witches." The parish overseer tried to sound convincing, but his feet twitched to be off.

"Well, I niver see eyes like they in any mortal," maintained the farmer, then lowered his voice to impart a confidence. "And I tell you, Mister Styles, a demon comes to her by night. I swear I see him myself once afore dawn in a storm. 'Twas too small to be the Devil himself, but sloe-black and cat-nimble leapin' from her bed and into the lightning. I swear it, sir."

The parish official cleared his throat loudly and squared his shoulders. It was perilous to speak of such ungodly matters and the discussion had made them both uneasy. They peered warily into the gloom of the loft, then backed down the steps and left the building, their voices lifting in bravado, to disguise secret relief that the girl had not materialized again. The shuffling sounds of their retreat carried to her hiding place, grew distant and then beyond the cast net of her hearing, which caught only the fidgets of the hay as it settled back into place.

The parchments had lost their ribbons and were now crumpled and torn. Rachel sat up and stared at them in dismay. Some of the writing was smudged with dirt. She spat on her finger and tried to rub it off, but that only made it worse, because the ink smeared and the shapes of the lettering changed. She blinked worriedly, wondering whether this would matter to those who could read. There was a great deal of writing, and suddenly she realized that each word was divided from the next by a space. Perhaps it was not so hard to learn to read. Pleased, she bent forward to examine the curlicues slowly, wishing she knew which of them

14

made up her own name. The papers concerned her, so her name had to be there. Rachel Jedder.

One of the horses nickered in its stall below and the metal of a harness chinked. Rachel hurriedly rolled the documents into each other and bound them with a length of twisted hay. Someone talked to the horse as the leather ridge pad slapped onto its back, and she crabbed quickly across the cushioned surface to spy through the hole in the floor.

"Sam! Sam!"

The boy started and instinctively glanced under the horse's belly to the open door before looking up at her smiling face and whispering, "They've been a-calling you everywhere, Rachel."

"Come up!" she beckoned and, when he reached her side, showed him the parchments and told of her grandfather and the miraculous inheritance.

"I'm leaving here, Sam, forever. I'm going to find Devon and I'm niver coming back."

He drooped a little and she patted his arm. Ten years old, he had been foisted upon his reluctant master two years previously by the church-wardens, who considered the farm sufficiently prosperous to maintain two pauper apprentices. Like the girl, he was thin and slight, but Mister Wame demanded a grown man's work, and so he had spent from before dawn until nightfall of every day since then struggling with huge horses and forkloads of manure and wild young steers, and pitting his feather-weight hopelessly against sacks of grain and loads of logs and cast-iron tools and wood barrels of stinking pig swill. The hired farm servants helped when they would, but Rachel was his friend, who would let him creep at night into her warmth on the chaff-filled mattress in the barn and shelter his punished frame in her own aching arms.

"I got to go to Devon, Sam." She caught sight of his wet eyes and gave him a shake. "They'll send another girl 'prentice from the workhouse. You won't be on your own—and maybe you'll find a grandfather, too." But she knew he would not. "Listen, now. You niver saw me today, not once, when they asks." His expression was pathetic, and she stood up decisively. "But I'll make you laugh afore I leave, Sam Hiskey. You'll see." She slid through the hatch and found the top rung of the ladder with her feet. "Goodbye, Sam."

The boy held her hand. "Rachel?"

She looked up, the green inner bands of her eyes bright in a shaft of light from a gap in the weatherboard.

He looked stricken. "You're not a witch, are you?"

" 'Course not, goose. Else I'd have left this place long afore now—and turned the master and mistress into toads."

She disappeared below and he heard her tap down to the ground, across the stable and hesitate for a watchful minute before edging round the outside to the back of the building by the stack yard. Then all was quiet. The boy freed his tears as he slowly climbed down to complete harnessing the horse.

Isaac Wame was proud that his farm was the most modern in the district. Quick to see the advantages of enclosed fields, he had set up, with the aid of the local commissioners, fences, gates and stiles across wide areas of common land, where the village had previously grazed its sheep. Where there had been scrub, his wheat, turnips, barley and clover now grew in rotation and fattened his bullocks and maintained his dairy herd throughout winter, when once half of them would have gone for slaughter.

As some of his neighbors began to follow his example, the "wastes," which had supported the few stock and communal crops of the cottagers, were being quickly and forcibly reduced.

Wame's granary and three-stead barn had been constructed to the very latest design within the past five years, and he was the first man in the parish to bring his hogs into a specially built enclosure with shelter.

Rachel waded through the gravy of their smell to look over the low wall. The sows pricked up their ears, raised their snouts and hurried over, grunting. She leaned to them and scratched a bristly, spotted back, slid the catch on the gate and pushed it open. A piglet trotted out, squealing, and was immediately followed by its siblings, its mother, and then by all the friends and relations. The herd scattered happily between the haystacks.

At the next gate she wasted no time but simply unfastened the catch and stood well back. Twelve-hundredweight of ill-humored boar trundled out, caught sight of the last piglet and trumpeted irritably after it with amazing agility for such a boulder of a beast. In passing, he rubbed against a wagon, which rocked splintering onto its side. There was the clash and clatter of destruction as the herd swerved into the open-sided cart shed and plunged through the farm implements, oiled and stored so neatly there.

Rachel returned, running, along the back of the farmstead, to a solitary door on the cold north side. As the unexpected light attacked his darkness, he grunted, and she slipped inside. The air was steaming with his breath. Their eyes met through the iron bars and his were red and mad, and she felt her heart flap and hands shake as he lowered his head and flexed knotted shoulders and pawed the ground until the whole shed shuddered. It was like facing a crashing oak and, in her mind, she was already hooked into its savage branches and flung skyward.

Her muscles strained to flee. Instead, she crouched to the heavy bolt near the floor and slid it back. The bull lunged. The metal-bound door jarred, but the other two bolts held. Rachel Jedder stretched her arm like a swift snake to the top bolt and clanged it open. The animal groaned and heaved his massive body against the partition.

She remembered him as a chestnut calf, born soon after her own arrival at the farm, and suckling his dam on the common land all that first summer. Then, before he was a year old, they had shut him in the coffin-black box and, except for a few weeks each spring, he had been there ever since. It took half a dozen men with iron stakes and chains to bring him in from running with the cows, and, despite all their sweating caution, he had still managed to trample one to death. No one else would have dared to enter the shed alone as she was doing.

Hatred vibrated from him, hot and tangible as a forge fire, and setting alight her own memories of all the cruelties, the hurts and bruises and injustices of the years. She gripped the last bolt tightly and jerked it back with such force that the door recoiled out of control and slammed her against the wall.

The bull stared out in confusion. Rachel Jedder stood transfixed in the shadows, hypnotized by the danger, certain he would see her and turn. But he only stood, gazing into the space beyond. At last he stepped gingerly forward, swinging his heavy head and drawing in the message of the outside world through flared nostrils. He moved faster, rising on his toes, ears rigid with anticipation, tail stiff and straight out behind, through the gap and into the open.

William Styles was mounting his horse at the door of the house, and Farmer Wame, who had followed him out, had just heard the noise from the cart shed and was about to investigate when the bull rounded the corner of the yard.

The animal was dazzled by the light and excited by the noise of the wind and strident birds and the growing plants stretching and shifting all around. The smell of living grass and the fresh water of the Broads intoxicated after so many months of dusty hay and sour drinking buckets. His nerve endings quivered at the touch of the air and his breath came in loud, pulling sobs.

The horse whinnied and reared, and the unexpected movement turned the exhilaration into ferocity. William Styles's coat fluttered as he hopped around trying to mount the frightened mare, and men shouted.

The bull floated forward, head dropping low and muscles bunching, horns like white cutlasses, eyes of lit glass, power building up smoothly, inexorably, with a precision perfected over centuries of bloody ancestral battles. He paused, catching the familiar smell of their panic, incited by open wounds inflicted only days before by their pikes. He lowered his poll and charged.

The horse shrieked and bolted, her master only half in the saddle and hanging on desperately to her mane. The bull veered after them without breaking pace or lessening speed. The wall enclosing the farmstead was five feet high. The mare rose to it, shedding the burden of William Styles and soaring to safety. The parish overseer fell in the direct path of the bull, which tilted its head, caught him with inevitable accuracy on its pitchfork horns and tossed him, like a sheaf of corn, after his horse, before galloping off beyond the buildings.

The man lay writhing on the footpath and howling for help, but Wame had run in the opposite direction and his wife had locked herself in her kitchen. Only Rachel Jedder was watching from beneath the granary, and she made no move.

At last he rolled over onto his knees, crawled painfully to the five-bar gate, pulled himself to his feet and stumbled through, holding his back and weeping with shock.

Rachel looked after him, remembering how young Sam had clumsily dabbed cold water on the swollen, discolored skin of her own back after Styles had returned her from Shaltam.

"You must be feeling the kidney ache yourself now, Mister Styles, though 'tis nothing a bit of hog's grease and betony won't cure," she said aloud, and, grinning, walked out through the gate he had left ajar and along the path which led to the mere. Bushes closed around the farm behind her.

The wind was blowing across the water, turning the sails of the wind-mill a steady eight times to the minute, the rumble of wheels and grind-ing stones underlying the ebb-and-flow whisper of each rushing sweep. The sounds were so much part of her life that she no longer noticed them, for the Norfolk wind was as persistent and unrelenting as her own breath. Under the cathedral dome of the night skies, it swelled like a great pipe organ, with stops for the voices of martyrs and hellhounds and parting lovers and swarming wasps and dying babes. By day, it scored wrinkles in young skins and tied knots in the hair of the women and leered lasciviously up their skirts. The corn was flattened under its rolling game, doors and shutters prized off by its teeth, and washing and bonnets snatched away.

Now, without warning, it changed direction, throwing grit into her eyes. The spinning sails faltered and the miller and his sons hurried out to the primitive pulley-and-block at the tail pole of the mill, to haul the entire construction back into its eye. Rachel drew behind the last of the shrubs and watched them struggle, their calls blasted back into their throats and dammed there by the plangent creak of the timbers. The outdated contraption staggered on its axle and seemed about to topple before setting, at last, into the wind again. The men wiped their fore-heads and returned inside, panting.

Reed beds crowded in on the narrow way and the marsh was cut by half-hidden channels draining from the mere, which lay on the left. Rachel's eyes crossed its tufted surface to sweep the flat landscape be-yond. Cold and bleak, disturbed only by clumps of frayed trees marking out hamlets sucked of color by distance, it was the only view she had ever known, and yet it did not attract her.

A long, high ridge of sand dunes stood, as though man-made, between soil and sea a few miles away. She had been sent with a cheese to her master's sister at Malling once and had climbed to the top to see the ocean, hoping for magic. The water, gray, and boundless, had been like a wet sky. She had turned her back and gazed inland, but there only the windmills and one or two curious round towers far, far away had broken the monotony. After that, she had accepted that everywhere looked the same.

Only the days of the sun, opening in rose and dying in blood, brought richness and beauty to the place, unwrapping the early earth from a muslin mist, casting a thousand mirrors upon the Broads, raddling dull pantiles and brick, and varnishing leaves and stems and grasses with light. The sun, setting in tangerine and mustard, mulberry and moss, forced tired heads to lift, kindled hopes and persuaded there was God.

Rachel pulled her rough cloak about her against the morning chill and wished for its warmth. She wore a coarse wool chemise beneath her one dress, and in her hand she carried the precious documents. These were all her possessions.

Ahead, the track branched in two, one way leading to Shaltam and the other across country to an unknown end. The runaway horse was cantering home along the righthand fork, whipped to speed by flying stirrups and reins, still racing in fright before its master's spirit. She stared after it, then turned resolutely to the untried path.

The mere and the post-mill and Wame's farm remained visible behind her for many miles, but Rachel Jedder did not look back.

CHAPTER TWO

A flight of wild duck took off from Ricklene Broad and flew in victory formation toward the round tower, which stood like a thick chimney some way ahead. Solid and important against a background of stunted trees, it did not look like a farm building and was far enough from the parish for her to be unknown. Rachel decided to make it her first destination, too, and hoped that someone there might be able to read and explain the documents.

Instinct had driven her through the past two hours. Although there had been no choices in her life before, each decision had arrived in her mind readymade, requiring only physical action to implement it. Now she thought back and her skin pricked with gooseflesh and the thump of her heart showed against the long muscle of her neck and in the fine blue lines at her wrists as she gradually realized what had happened and what she had done. She was walking away, away from Wame's farm. Even the air changed its texture, becoming as explosive as gunpowder, and the rain fizzed against her face.

A small flock of sheep was grazing the pasture beside the footpath, each solemnly concentrating upon the task which filled every waking hour. Rachel spread her arms and rushed at them, whooping, her billowing cloak turning her into an eagle before their vexed eyes. They bleated plaintively and rolled away like snowballs across the grass, leaving her prancing and laughing behind.

She was free. She belonged to no one but herself. No woman could slap her face again, no man would ever again kick her or load burdens on her back. No workhouse prison waited. No master could claim her.

The rain fell steadily, dripping from the ends of her hair, soaking through her clothes and trickling down her breastbone, until only her feet inside the heavily greased leather boots remained dry. Ricklene Broad puffed into a huge, soft cloud, obscuring the tower, but Rachel kept up the pace, lost in thoughts luxurious beyond dreams, past a reed boathouse on stilts and a fisherman in a wherry near the shore, who kept on staring long after she had gone.

Her steps ticked by two more hours of miles. The lake fell back in the downpour and the tower was there. Rachel saw with surprise that it was a church, although nothing like the small thatched church of her parish with its roof lining of reed behind the rafters and the graveyard guarded by yews and roses. This church had a long flintstone body, like a barn, which looked as though it had been added to the fat tower as an afterthought. It stood at a point where several routes met, with cottages straggling along their verges. Its appearance was so unexpected that Rachel came out of her reverie to a feeling of doubt, but, knowing that the local parson would be able to read, she drew the roll of documents from under her cloak and began to walk toward the door.

"What are you doing there, girl?" A hard voice made her swing round. "Who are you?"

He had come from his parsonage across the footpath and was striding over, stern in his severe black coat and tricorne hat. "Come here, pauper! What is that in your hand?" He sounded annoyed and his face was pinched with suspicion.

Rachel's new sense of security was instantly crushed by his expression and by the memory of the vicar of Sauton's regular sermons on the idleness and sinfulness which had undoubtedly brought the poor to their wretched condition. In her experience God was not known for His sympathy, and this hostile cleric might even take the parchments and not return them. She covered them again quickly, but he saw the movement and put out a hand to seize her arm. Rachel wrenched away and began to run along the broadest of the four tracks, the sound of his voice only spurring her the faster.

The new track was obviously far more frequently used than the one which had led past the Broads. Its surface was grooved by wagon wheels and pockmarked by hooves. She had traveled ten miles from Wame's farm and was now hungry, cold and wet. Running was an effort, but as she slowed down after some minutes and glanced over her shoulder, she saw a horseman start out from the crossroads by the round tower. The angry parson was sending a man to catch her. Rachel sped on wildly, stumbling over the uneven clods, her mind full of terrors. Soon the sound of approaching hooves crossed the borders of her hearing, grew louder, closer, and hammered upon her. She gripped the irreplaceable papers with both hands and stopped, sobbing and snarling.

Mud spattered her all over as the horse galloped straight past, its rider not even glancing down.

Rachel gaped stupidly after them for a few moments and then, gathering her breath and shaking a little with reaction, she laid her papers on the wet turf and took off her cloak. Stitched to its right shoulder was a red cloth patch on which were sewn the large roman letters P. S. They were the only two letters Rachel Jedder recognized and they stood for Parish of Sauton, the statutory badge of all paupers in receipt of parish relief. Rachel tore at the threads with her broken nails and then with her teeth, and finally ripped the rag from the garment and threw it into the mud. Putting on her cloak again, she walked a few steps and then wheeled back to grind the hated red cloth into the silt with her heel until it blackened and drowned.

For the first time she surveyed the new track and realized it was the width of several wagons and must lead to a large town. Her spirits rose. She sheltered the roll of documents again and set off. The rain diminished to a gray dampness and the land developed a lilt, which filled out its flat body and lifted the yellow-flowered gorse onto crests. Light and shade exaggerated the slightly dipping surfaces of the plowed fields, and mounds of sandy heath obscured the approaches of the numerous small lakes and ponds which were the final inland claims of the Broads. More trees grew, singly, like outriders, then grouped in spinneys and coverts, ahead of the blue smoke of their approaching armies. They were bigger and stronger than the trees near the coast, their dignified boles signifying great age; and the prevailing wind had not warped their sturdy boughs, which were sprayed with traceries of twigs, fine as web.

Stepping-stones crossed the River Ant alongside its ford and Rachel used them carefully to keep her feet dry, although all her clothes were now clammy against her skin. The bank on the far side bordered a wood, still rattling with water dripping onto the leafmold of its floor, and the track tunneled through the dimness, snaking to avoid the oldest oaks and becoming a mire in places. On either side, ash and chestnut and birch and willow congregated and tangled over undergrowth as dense as a wall. Rachel, who had known only horizon-wide prospects across the open commons and sheeted waters of Sauton, felt nervous. The winter afternoon was growing so dark that it was becoming difficult to see, and the place seethed with unfamiliar sounds, snapping branches and raucous birds, disturbed brushwood, scuttlings and breathing and the humming wind.

She tried to move quietly, in case the wild boars, which must be waiting in the thickets, heard and charged, but her feet slithered in the mud and when she put out a hand to save herself, it was scratched by angry briars. For the first time that day she was near to tears, spasms of cramp gripped her empty stomach and her hard little body ached under the rain-weighted clothes. She had eaten nothing since the hunk of breakfast bread, and she began to understand that without money she might even starve, for who would help a ragged girl with no possessions other than a few crumpled papers signifying a piece of rough land in some unknown county? She wanted to sit down and rest, and only fear of the deep wood drove her on.

As evening crossed the sky and blotted out the last faint outline of the track, Rachel lost her balance and fell into a deep puddle, treacle-thick with mud, which oozed over the tops of her boots and soaked her feet at last. Swearing loudly, she scrambled out and rushed blindly into the darkness, and suddenly there was a light in a cottage window, lucent as a moon. The wood was gone, left behind, and the small hazards of stones and shrubs along the way were made visible within the little halo and by other glowing cottages which lay nearby.

Released from the trees, the track had become even wider, and there were people ahead. Rachel hurried to walk behind them and share the rays from their rushlights, and then large houses rose in blocks against the navy sky and a long line of packhorses plodded past, and men, pushing empty handcarts, jogged in the opposite direction, and a laden wagon, hauled by a pair of straining oxen, jolted by to its own concert of drumming wheels and shouting driver and cracking whip, and there was a thronged brick bridge and a cobblestone street with houses squeezed tightly together on either side, more houses than Rachel Jedder had ever seen.

Candles flickered in the windows and lamps burned in the doorways making the narrow way bright enough for the faces of the crowd to show up quite clearly. Rachel stopped and gawked, amazed by the townspeople, their smart clothes and bustling movements and oddly rapid speech. Sometimes one appeared to be in even greater haste and elbowed past the others, who grumbled and pushed back, and every now and again the entire mob gave way before an oncoming cart or a group of horsemen; but no one noticed the thin, dirty waif standing entranced against the flintstone terrace.

A girl of about her own age was standing, with a basket of ribbons,

22

on a corner where the street was crossed by another, and Rachel edged nearer. Two women paused to finger the colorful strands and the seller's head bobbed as she talked eagerly and displayed the goods over their fat white hands, until they chose a length of purple and moved away. Then, while the girl packed the rest of the ribbons into the basket and closed the wicker lid, Rachel reached her side to shyly ask the name of the town.

The other gave her a long, slow look, which took in her farm boots and torn skirt, and filthy cloak and hands and face, and uncovered head and uncombed hair.

"Norwich," she replied contemptuously, and walked away.

Rachel, made aware of her appearance for the first time, was filled with shame. She had heard of the city of Norwich and remembered how the master and mistress had once dressed in their best clothes just to go there, because it was the most important place in Norfolk and one of the most important places in the whole of England. Now its flurry and variety lost enchantment and she wanted to hide from the smart, scornful citizens. There was a great stone arch over an open gateway at the top of the street, beyond which no lights shone. She gathered her cloak around her and fled to it and through into the darkness.

There was grass under her feet and space around her. Trees rustled again close by, and, growing accustomed to the night, she saw stars reflected in glass, so high above that it seemed like a window in the sky, and she realized that the intense blackness ahead was not shadow but an immense building. From far behind the window came a glimmer, a hint of fire, and Rachel was suddenly overcome by such a craving for warmth that all sense of caution was lost. There was a small entrance cut in beside the huge main doors and it opened easily. Sick with cold and hunger, she went inside.

Hundreds of candles made the air dance with their flames and turned her eyes into moths, mesmerized sightless by the massed brilliance. She leaned against the wall, her head reeling, and, as her hands touched the stone, an unimaginable temple revealed itself. A forest of mighty pillars thrust through the flagstones and soared heavenward, higher and higher, until they exploded into a glory of fanning trumpets far above, and there were arches built upon arches, each as deep as a room, as rugged as a dungeon, yet all rising to taper at last into delicate gold-tipped fingers of stone overhead. Down each side of the edifice the arches and the pillars marched in long columns and with thundering steps, past the bank of lights and the tall, canopied seat and the sculpted screen and through a chiming cave to vanish in the distance behind a glint of stained glass.

Rachel's mouth had dropped open and her head tilted back to gaze up at the gilded roof in wonder, and she did not hear anyone approach until he said, "Evensong is over."

She shrank back to the door as a man in priestly vesture walked quietly toward her from the aisle through the nearest archway. He was elderly and stooped, but white hair bounced healthily from beneath a small cap and his gray eyes were lively and shrewd. As they searched hers, Rachel felt herself crumble, and the wave of fear she had refused to admit for the past hours broke and engulfed her. Top-heavy tears spilled down her dirty face.

"Have you run away, child?" he asked, but she could only shake her head dumbly in answer.

"You have come to the cathedral burdened," he observed, placing a hand on her shoulder and covering the mark where the pauper's badge had been. "Tell me what troubles you."

She rubbed a dirtier hand over her cheeks and looked at him damply. He met her strange particolored eyes and did not waver.

"You *must* put your trust in someone, child."

Slowly she drew forth the battered roll of documents and held them out. The rope of hay was still knotted and smudges of mud also stuck them together. Their edges were badly frayed.

"I cannot read, your worship," she whispered.

"I shall read them to you," he promised gravely, leaving the papers in her hands. "But first, tell me what you are called."

"Rachel Jedder, your Worship."

"Well, Rachel Jedder, I think you have journeyed far and that you are hungry and tired. Follow me and you shall eat."

The old man turned the way he had come, moving soundlessly and seeming in her blurred vision to appear and disappear through bands of fluttering light and perhaps not even to touch the floor. He did not look back or wait, and after only a moment's hesitation she stumbled to follow.

They left the cathedral by another way and crossed the night-damp grass to a large house, where a servant opened the door and another stood by a flight of stairs. Rachel was taken quickly down to a long kitchen and seated at a scrubbed wooden table before a trencher of hot mutton and a mug of frothing beer.

People spoke, but she did not really hear and was only vaguely aware of them around her, but her belly stopped nagging and grew warm and the air from the open fire thawed her hands and arms and then the rest of her body beneath the steaming, wet clothes, until only her feet, encased in the impenetrable boots, remained cold.

Hams and a flitch of fat bacon swung in the wide chimney and the wrought-iron crane squeaked as the cooking pot suspended from its hook quivered above the red-hot logs. The room smelled of all that was best, roast meat and burning wood and vegetable-oil lamps, smells from which dreams were created and ambitions manufactured. They were the last sensations Rachel remembered.

Daylight wakened her to a small attic. The events of the previous day filled her mind instantly and she sat up, searching around in panic until she saw the roll of parchments lying safely on the floor nearby. Then she saw that she was wearing only her shift and sitting in a low, wooden bed on a mattress filled with flock. She had never slept in a real bed before, nor in a room on her own. In the workhouse there had been rows of straw pallets full of bugs on the dormitory stone, and later, at Wame's farm, a corner of the barn had been allocated to her, together with the cats and the scuffling rats. She fingered the homespun linen sheets and wool cover tentatively, excitement making her muscles tingle, until, unable to restrain herself any longer, she jumped to the floor and ran to the window.

Across the precinct, the cathedral stood in the pale silk of a winter dawn, its spire and pinnacles creamy, as though newly built above windows of beaten silver, and the rays of the first sun played with the saintly figures among its buttresses. Nothing in her life on the flat lands of the Broads had prepared Rachel Jedder for its splendor and she stood, unconscious of the morning chill and wholly spellbound, until the door of the room opened behind her and an angular gray-haired woman brought in a wooden bucket of cold water and an earthenware jug of hot water, which she put on the floor beside a table on which rested a wide bowl.

She glared at Rachel with obvious dislike and released a loud sigh to show how heavy the bucket had been.

"You are to wash yourself," she instructed, bringing a lump of soap from a pocket in her apron.

Rachel looked down at her hands and saw, with surprise, that they were no longer smeared with dirt. "But I'm clean," she protested.

"No you're not," the woman replied rudely. "That was all we could get off last night, what with you lolling about asleep, but you are to wash proper now and use that hot water for your hair."

Her hair! Rachel was scandalized. Once she had been held under the farm pump and almost drowned in its freezing gush as punishment for some misdeed. Everyone knew that if you put your head in water you could die of the agues.

"That I will not," she said stoutly, looking around for the rest of her clothes and her boots. But they were not there, and for the first time she noticed that the documents were no longer tied with hay but with a thin scarlet cord.

The woman had turned back to the open door and was calling through it to the passage outside, "Mary! Amy!"

Two well-built girls girls appeared, their sleeves tucked back and their hair protected by muslin caps. Without a word they marched across the room, gripped Rachel Jedder by the arms and hauled her, hollering and kicking, toward the basin. Her shift was torn off, and the old woman emptied the jug and pushed her head unceremoniously into the scalding water. Rachel shrieked and struggled so that water slopped over all of them, and she was given a blow which made her ears pop before her head was shoved under again and the stone-hard soap scoured her scalp.

25

The water cascaded over her neck and stung her eyes and found its way up her nose as the foam was sluiced off. Then her head was ducked straight into the cold bucket and, while she still spluttered and sneezed, they scrubbed at her breasts and buttocks, rinsed her down with more icy water and left her standing naked, soaked and shivering by the bed.

A few minutes later, the old woman returned with a clean shift and underskirt and a plain brown robe, which she pushed into Rachel's arms, dropping the dried and freshly greased boots on the floor at the same time.

"His Reverence has sent for you," she snapped. "You will put these on, wench, and make haste."

Rachel stroked the dress almost lovingly. It was as soft as rabbit skin. Its skirt alone seemed to contain enough material to have made a second one. It had no darns or tears or patches to show that it had belonged to someone else. It even smelled unworn, although she knew it could not be, and there was a white linen chemise to go under the bodice and overlap at the neck. She looked speechlessly at the old woman, whose withered mouth compressed into an indignant scratch as she stamped from the room.

The Dean of Norwich was sitting at an oval table in a room lined with books. Although he did not smile when Rachel knocked and entered, he waved her courteously toward the fire and she felt tranquil in his presence, willingly handing over the parchments.

"I read these documents last night while you slept, Rachel Jedder," he said, loosening the red band and unrolling them. "You have been uncommonly fortunate, although there may be many hardships ahead."

Rachel forgot the discomfort of her wet hair and her eyes widened in anticipation as he smoothed out the top paper with veined, opaque hands and began to speak.

"This is the indenture by which you were apprenticed as dairymaid and servant to one Isaac Wame on the twenty-ninth day of the fifth month of the thirty-second year of the reign of our late Sovereign Lord, King George II, by the Grace of God, and it was signed, witnessed and sealed by your master and by Jonathan Emmerson, Justice of the Peace, and William Styles, Overseer of the Poor in the parish of Sauton. This document bound you to Isaac Wame until you reach the age of twenty-four years."

The next paper was small and flimsy and, although written only the day before, was already tattered and stained.

"This is also signed by Isaac Wame and William Styles, the parish overseer, and certifies that the sum of ten pounds has been paid to your master out of the estate of Penuel Jedder to release you from your apprenticeship," the churchman explained, glancing at her over the paper. "Are you warm enough, child? You may sit on the carpet near to the fire to dry your hair."

Rachel, who had been shivering with excitement, nodded impatiently and sat down. The heat from the ingle scorched her back and made her cheeks red as the dean methodically placed the first two documents on one side and perused the third.

"This last is a copy of your grandfather, Penuel Jedder's will, and it is a sad document, in which he regrets having withheld aid from your mother in her need."

He read, " 'I, Penuel Jedder, of Yellaton, on Beara Moor, do die in sorrow, having turned away from my only child, Grace Jedder, abucted by Michael Connell, itinerant Irish, and later deserted in the county of Norfolk. I bequeath my house and fifteen acres of land and rights of common on the moor for fifty sheep and all my possessions to her issue, male or female, and do instruct my life savings, the sum of thirty-two pounds and seven pence, be sent forthwith to cover the expenses of the journey of this child to bring him to his inheritance.' "

Only the numbers emerged distinct from the confusion of words. Fifteen acres. Fifty sheep. They mixed with a little stab of thought for her mother, whom Rachel remembered as haggard and red-eyed and who had died when she was four years old. Fifty sheep could graze, and fifteen acres belonged to her.

The Dean saw her lip tremble and her skin brighten. Her hair had dried and it shone before the fire, and the brown dress emphasized those extraordinary honey-dark-and-green eyes. She looked much younger than her years and there was unquenched hope in her face which alarmed him.

"It is three months since your grandfather died, Rachel Jedder. News travels slowly. He was a poor man and there is no money," he said, bluntly. "This fourth paper is a letter from the attorneys stating that their fees for the handling of his will and for tracing you have expended his savings, and your release from apprenticeship cost the sum set aside for your journey. Fifteen acres is very little land and there may be no stock on it by the time you reach there."

He saw that she did not believe him and understood that to someone who had owned nothing, his words could mean nothing, yet the unconscious strength in the steadiness of her look and the slight uplift of her head touched him, for he knew that a big spirit in a child's body would not be enough to see her safely across the breadth of England. She would surely perish from exposure to the elements, or starvation, or she would meet with vagabonds, or become lost in one of the vast, uncultivated wastes which almost straddled whole counties.

And so he continued, "You would be wise to stay here and instruct the lawyers to sell the property. I will place you in a respectable household and, with the proceeds from the sale, it will not be difficult for you to find a good man to marry before long."

Rachel Jedder was not listening. She was trying to imagine the house and her land and could see a mud-walled, earthen-floored dwelling of two rooms, with a thatched roof, and surrounded by a stretch of flat pasture bordering rough grazing, like that she had left only yesterday. Then it had been bleak and ugly. Now it seemed that nowhere could be more beautiful.

"Please, your Reverence?" she asked, after a long pause, "would you read the will of my grandfather to me again?"

This time he saw her lips move as she memorized every word, and he knew she would not stay.

She was given breakfast and grimaced over the unfamiliar taste of sweet tea, brewed from thrice-used tea leaves; then she snatched and gnawed at the hot buttered white bread in a way that trussed up the faces of the dean's servants with sneers. It was impossible to remain oblivious of their resentment, fired at her through slamming doors and dishes and their choppy body movements.

". . . I, Penuel Jedder . . . bequeath my house and fifteen acres of land and rights of common on the moor for fifty sheep . . ." marked her heart like a prayer and enclosed her within the impregnable aura of its protection. She smiled at the old woman and the two sullen girls who had washed her. Deeply offended, they turned their backs.

Within the hour, the dean had arranged her official travel pass for the journey and his seamstress had made up a cloth bag to be attached to her person by a cord and to hold the documents secure under her skirts. Her cloak had been washed and repaired, and a basket containing bread, cheese, a hunk of ham, pickles, apples and an oak bottle of ale was put into her hand, together with a little pouch containing a shilling in coins.

Rachel stared at the money in disbelief, never having held so much as a farthing before; and then she experienced a surprising sensation. She wanted to cling to the old man and feel his arms go round her, the way her mother's arms had once done.

"May God go with you, Rachel Jedder." He placed a hand on her head in benediction.

She remembered that he was a fine gentleman and curtsied clumsily, muttering inarticulate thanks before turning to the open door, where she stopped and looked back.

"Please, your Reverence?" She had blushed a deeper pink, believing he would think her simple. "Where is Devon?"

"It is a great distance, Rachel Jedder, three hundred miles or more, and lies in the west," he answered.

She blinked and looked even more embarrassed, and he read her ignorance, gently.

"The west is where the sun sets, child."

Norwich in daytime was more pleasing than it had been the night before. There were many orchards and the river wound through in such a way that Rachel crossed several bridges and thought each spanned a different water. There were fine new houses and elegant churches. The streets zigzagged and curved and her attention was drawn so often to marvels that she became confused and passed the same point more than once without recognizing it, and the walk to the flintstone city wall took nearly two hours instead of thirty minutes.

Beyond it, a bridleway unwound between gnarled and jagged hawthorns connecting hamlet to hamlet and copse to copse. The sun shone without warmth in the pellucid sky and gave the morning a crisp vigor. Rachel, wrapped in soft wool, sang all the way to Thetford, and there sat on a boulder to eat an apple and take out the coins the dean had given, examining them with care. There was a penny for each finger of her right hand, a halfpenny for each finger of both hands and farthings for all except the smallest toe on one foot. They made a very satisfying clink as she dropped them back into the leather pouch.

It had been a holiday, a whole day spent without labor or hunger and, although she had walked all day, she felt lusty enough to lift a hog singlehanded.

Ahead, the ground rose much higher than the sand dunes at Malling and hid the countryside which followed. Intrigued by this steep hill after the miles of level land behind, she attacked it with swinging stride and climbed until her calves ached, to reach the top, panting, and lean against a tree, closing her eyes.

Moments later they opened on a humbling view of primeval England, for the forest of Thetford covered all the crouching land beyond, like a pelt, brown in its February shagginess in the foreground, thickening to maroon and then to a distant horizon of purple. From her position it appeared unbroken by clearings and the path ran down the hill to disappear without a gap or furrow between the treetops to betray its direction thereafter. Mounds and hollows were lost beneath the prodigious growth. It seemed as limitless and as impassable as the ocean, and she could sense that, like the ocean, it was predatory and alive, neither sleeping nor waking, but eternally dying and being born, an absolute and indifferent being. Its muscles twitched under the wind and it threw up the scent of resin and decaying vegetation. The sun had slipped across the sky and turned crimson. Before her eyes it was poised to sink through the forest, down to her waiting land in the west. She could feel the tube of documents in the bag against her thigh, and yet she hesitated. Then a spiral of smoke rose from not far within, signaling the presence of others, gypsies perhaps, or even a cottage, and soon it would be too dark to reach them. She hurried down the slope and almost ran into the growling shadows.

The trees were more widely spaced than she had imagined and the path made easy progress for over a mile before it met up with a cart track and changed direction imperceptibly, pushing the glowing cinders of the

29

sunset to one side, so that Rachel Jedder, unknowing, was now walking away from where the smoke had leaked.

Damp vapors rose from the earth and condensed into a low-lying fog, which spread with the dusk and penetrated her wool gown. And then another moonless night imposed its curfew, sealing off all routes, and she crawled philosophically under a bush, wrapped the cloak tight as a sausage skin around her and lay down.

The mist settled like dew on her face and formed drops in the web of hair round the edge of her hood and, after the brisk walk, it felt cool and not unpleasant. But gradually the few stars visible between the leaves grew hard and bright, glaring down with glittering soullessness, and frost streamed from them to glaze the earth with a brittle sparkle and plate the branches with rime. The ground cover of mossy cloud turned into snails' trails of glass, and icicle talons were unsheathed on the twigs. Rachel's cloak stiffened into a crust. She could feel grains of ice forming around the rims of her eyes and her own breath turned solid on her lips. The air became raw as a wound. The owl stopped calling. The secret scurryings in the forest ceased. Small birds fell from their perches and hibernating bats hung frozen in the cocoons of their wings. Rachel, too, stopped shivering and struggling as all feeling deserted her limbs and a paralyzing pain clamped over her lungs. There was infinite silence and the cold intensified to a terrible purity.

Her blood thickened and slowed and her breathing became too shallow to mist a mirror. It was too late now to move. The compulsion to close her eyes and yield fondled her dazed mind, replacing the vision of destiny with the seduction of death, soft and safe and everlasting. Just to imagine its down-filled cradle stirred a fancy of warmth so deep within that it seemed to exist cats' lives away in another body and to reach her minutely through a needle point. And then it spread in little hot runnels and trickles, which sprang from the extremities of her hands and feet and coursed through the channels of her veins to meet finally in a great pool of gut warmth in which all the pain drowned deliciously; and Rachel Jedder fell asleep at last.

Sam was shifting restlessly at her back, forcing her awake with his knees. She grunted warningly and dug him with her elbow, but he would not be still. Irritated, she opened her eyes to an alien, white-frozen place and turned over in shock. A large hairy face lay close to hers and she caught a glimpse of two rows of fangs and a chasmal red throat before she catapulted, screaming, from the bush. The wolf lazily thumped its tail and then, seeing her back away in terror, climbed reluctantly to its feet, barked, and emerged as the biggest dog in the whole of England. He was the size of a small pony and covered with a long, wiry gray coat, so thick that it almost concealed his jutting hipbones and rib cage. He tucked up one side of his muzzle into a lopsided grin and sat down. Rachel threw a heavy stick and it cracked loudly against his head, but he did not move and his eyes stayed on her hopefully.

"Clear off! Clear off, varmint!" she shouted, making sure of keeping her distance at the same time. Then she saw the basket. It was lying overturned and empty under the bushes and all that was left of its mouthwatering contents was a mangled apple and the pickles. Rage flashed through her.

"Dirty-arsed hog! Filthy, wart-nosed trash! Pissabed varmint!" She screeched all the wickedest words she knew, completely forgetting her fear of the animal and grabbing frost-touched stones to fling at him.

"Thieving, guzzling brute!" As the first two caught him accurately on the rump, he stood up, startled, and, when more followed, he retreated to beyond her pitching reach and sat down again.

Rachel snatched the basket from the ground and hurled it after him, sick with disappointment, savage over having refrained so prudently from starting on the hoard the night before in order to make it last as long as possible, and now finding none left.

Then, sniffing as the icy wind made her eyes water, she retrieved the wicker container again and returned to the car track, her face set in an expression of grim stoicism. As she trudged off, the dog kept pace by slinking along behind the bordering undergrowth and, although she yelled at him once or twice and threw a last stone, he did not go away.

There were many indications that the route was often used by travelers, and during the first hour she kept stopping to listen for the sounds of approaching hooves and wheels, but the forest remained abnormally quiet. The weals of mud had frozen so solid they dented the soles of her boots and made her feet sore, and sometimes she slipped on puddles of ice, sending sound rasping metallically against the trees. Even walking as quickly as possible did not prevent the penetrating chill from crystallizing every muscle.

When it seemed to be about the middle of the day, she sat down, quaking, on a marble log and ate the pickles and the remains of the apple. The dog stole close on his belly and watched every mouthful. She wondered how far the forest stretched. The terrain had remained undisturbed by cultivation for an eight-hour march, densities of silver trees, canescent glades, crowds of waxen saplings, clearings of dead bracken and broom frozen to lather, more and more trees. The long finger of smoke which had beckoned her in had not risen again, and hoar-rime hid the charred circles where other fires had blazed. She thought ahead to the coming night with dread and then remembered how she had grown so inexplicably warm the night before and awakened warm that morning. The gray dog was sitting nearby, looking at the bitten apple in her hand.

All at once, Rachel Jedder knew he had saved her life. Had he not crept to lie at her back and enveloped her in his great matted coat, she

31

would certainly have died in the bitter cold of that night. She held out the apple core, still well-covered with flesh, and he stepped forward and accepted it with dignity.

After that, they walked together. Sam, she called him, after young Sam at Wame's farm, and time passed the faster for his being there. Before long she was talking to him, telling her life story, and she had just reached the part where the bull was chasing the parish overseer across the yard when the trees ended and the winding track straightened to cut directly to a village lying in the center of a broad, flat plain.

A woman with tired and angry features was drawing water from a well beside the inn. Although she looked middle-aged, several infants brawled around her and the arrival of another child was obviously imminent.

"Mistress . . . ?" Rachel began.

"Begone, slut!"

"I need work," the girl persisted humbly.

The woman yanked the full bucket from the pulley and turned away without answering. As she crossed the yard followed by the untidy trail of children, a man appeared in the open doorway and spoke sharply. She mumbled a reply and he pushed her roughly inside, then shouted to Rachel.

He was a broad man and stood with legs apart and hands on his hips as she came toward him. He had a florid complexion, with fleshy, red lips, and hot, slightly bloodshot blue eyes which ignored her face but examined her body as though the cloak and the brown dress were not there.

"There ain't much of you," he commented, reaching out and pulling her close to press against him. The gray dog growled and he kicked it viciously in the head, making it yelp and run off. Rachel felt his fingers pinch at her almost flat chest and heard him give a humiliating grunt.

"I suppose you seem clean enough," he said grudgingly. "So you can have your keep, if you work willing, but I like my customers kept happy, wench. Any complaints and out you go. Now get to the kitchen."

She hurried through the door to the passage beyond. Her first thought on seeing the inn had been to buy food, but then it had seemed foolish to part with any of the coins in the leather pouch so soon, and on impulse she had asked for work instead.

Several times over the past year, Farmer Wame had given her the same look as the innkeeper and had once pushed her against the inside wall of the barn, put his callused hand up her skirts and fumbled about her thighs, until the sound of his wife's voice outside had made him start guiltily and slouch away. After that, Rachel had stayed closer to the dairy and the house and had tried to avoid being alone with him.

She knew how women were bedded. At harvest, the village girls, tying sheaves and gleaning, talked of adventures in the rushes with local boys and the quick weddings that followed. The farm animals had illustrated the rest. But men liked wide-hipped and full-breasted women, so the eyes of the farm servants had dismissed her bony frame just as the innkeeper had done, and Rachel herself felt little interest in the matter.

The innkeeper's wife, still with averted face, put a bowl of thick soup and a chunk of bread on the table and urged her to eat quickly and start scouring the pile of iron pots by the fire. Before long, two more girls arrived from the village to help and then horses sounded on the cobblestones outside and the room steamed with flocks of hungry children and bustling barmaids and evaporation from cauldrons full of broth and stew. Men in the parlor began to sing. Travelers ordered gargantuan meals and demonstrated unslakable thirsts, gallons of ale sinking through their sandy throats to swill round their stomachs, marinade their livers and gush forth to form a beery puddle in the clay behind the inn.

Rachel, hurrying with full platters and dripping mugs, felt her smile stiffen into a rigid ache as the clumsy elbows and fists of the crowd buffeted and bruised her and their boots trod on her agonized feet. On the way back to the kitchen she walked more slowly, surreptitiously cramming their leftovers into her mouth and then, when she was no longer able to eat another bite, storing them in a piece of sacking behind the door to the stairs.

At last the noise diminished. The village men went home, followed by the girls from the kitchen, and a few travelers dispersed to the bedrooms above. Children slept in heaps near the kitchen fire and the innkeeper's wife let her ballooning body into a stout, wide-armed chair and closed her eyes, although her features refused to relax. She had not looked at Rachel Jedder once.

The innkeeper came in, eyed his wife and spat on the earth floor before handing the girl a glass of hot spiced punch on a small tray.

"There's a proper gentleman in the main bedroom, rich and paying good." He bent to talk hoarsely into her ear. "Take him this and see to his comforts and there might be a copper in it for you."

The stairs were narrow, each step sagging in the center and creaking with age. The corridor at the top dipped unevenly past a pair of closed bedroom doors and echoed with the snores and grumbles of their sleeping occupants. There was no answer when she tapped the brass knocker to the main bedroom so she went in. The fire was burning merrily, as though it had recently been made up, but the curtains were drawn closely round the box bed.

"Your hot punch, master," she said, placing the glass and the tray on a small walnut table. "Master?"

There was no answer and no sound and she leaned forward to part the curtains. Strong fingers gripped her wrist and hauled her through, to land face down on the bed with her skirts over her head. Several hard, playful slaps smacked her bare buttocks and a man's voice emitted a huntsman's halloo. Thoroughly frightened, Rachel squirmed around to catch a glimpse of a shiny, bulbous face under a bedcap before her bodice was seized and a hand as large as a cottage loaf attached itself to her left breast like a poultice.

She squeaked with shock and jerked back with such force that she found herself free and rolled to the far side of the mattress.

"What's this, wench? Would you turn down the sport of Venus?" His light eyes stared from between reptilian folds, which made them both attractive and repulsive, and Rachel received the warning with experienced clarity.

"No, sir." She gave a scared smile. "Oh, no."

"What is it then?" he demanded, and then an expression of hopeful lechery made the eyes heavy-lidded. "Is it the first time, maid? The first time at the altar of love, eh?"

"No!" Rachel lied hastily, and tried to laugh. " 'Tis my dress, sir. I have no other and I'm feared it will be torn."

"Oh, very well then." The man looked disappointed and bored. "Take it off yourself, if you must, but be quick about it."

She slid to the floor and faltered to the other side of the room, her arms crossing her body in a gesture of self protection. The threat of violence which had shadowed all her actions since infancy had trained her to think and move fast, but this was different. The stranger's hands on her body had forecast a more fundamental danger. Without fully understanding, she sensed a menace far more sinister than a beating and was shaken by a spasm of panic. If she ran out, the gentleman would certainly follow, shouting, and bring the innkeeper. She began plucking nervously at the buttons on her dress, as her mind darted about the problem.

"Now what keeps you?" The curtains rattled back as he swung off the bed and took a pugnacious stride towards her, his big-calved, hirsute legs visible below the nightshirt as he stood over her, proud of his corporation and his weight and his bull neck and the blue stubble on his jowls, sure of the authority and potency of his maleness.

And Rachel, with acute and frightened perception, read his vanity like an instruction. She gave him a sly grinning glance and let her bodice slip from one shoulder and fall low enough to reveal a small pale-pink nipple. His moustache lifted above a row of wolfish teeth and she sidled away, giggling.

"I ain't never been with no gentleman afore, but I've heard aplenty." Her eyes glinted green and gold in the firelight and mocked him.

He swaggered and gave a raffish leer. "What have you heard, hussy?"

"Why, sir, 'tis said among wenches that the laboring man has the arrow." The tip of her tongue curled over her top lip as she focused deliberately on the suggestive bulge beneath his shirt. "But the gentleman needs hide under his linen, because he has no more than a dart."

The man recoiled, his mouth slack with indignation, and then a bellowing laugh pulled back its corners and tossed his head and rolled his body about so violently that it was a full minute before he could speak.

"Why, baggage," he gasped, wiping his eyes delightedly, "you need have no fears on that account." And with an easy movement, he peeled off his nightshirt to display an extravagant member beneath a girth of impressive area.

Rachel was so astonished by her first sight of the rutting human male that she lost a valuable second staring and was almost caught when he reached to claim her. Just in time, she whirled away, shrieking with laughter, to dive through the curtains to the bed. As he followed joyfully, she leaped out of the other side, snatched up the discarded garment and his breeches and coat from the chair and fled from the room.

At the head of the stairs she could still hear his voice roaring and then the noise stopped and she knew he would not chase naked and foolish after her through the inn.

On the last step, she paused long enough to retrieve the store of left-over food from behind the door, sped to the passage where her cloak hung and silently let herself out to the yard beyond.

Just past the end house in the village, on a bridge about half a mile from the inn, she stopped running to pull up her dress and fasten on the cloak. Then, rolling the man's clothes into a bundle, she dropped them into the stream and began to laugh. A big, dark form broke away from a clump of bushes close by and bounded to her. Sam. She laid the leftover food on the ground and watched it disappear in a gulp. The scythe of a new moon sliced through a cloud and they started into another night together.

CHAPTER THREE

Rachel felt different. It was as though she could hear sleeping moths and the leaves of next spring stirring in their winter chrysalides, feel the breath of watching stoats and smell hunting vixens and crouching hare. She could see in the dark, secret dreys and sets, luminous white hawks and the moonshot, frost-sealed umbilical cord securing her to her own far-off piece of earth. It ran across the flats beyond the village and, as she was pulled along it, the exhaustion which had throbbed in her muscles was replaced by a nervous energy and the conviction that she could walk all night.

All at once, her life was more than just a series of unconnected experiences. She had refused the gentleman at the inn, and the encounter had propelled her out of childhood into a sudden realization of herself as a person with control over her own prospects. Her brain raced between past and future, comparing, discarding and selecting with an intensity which surprised her, because these were no longer simple fantasies of a cottage and field, but actual plans for crops and stock, and the unexpected knowledge of what she wanted and would build, and what she expected from others.

Systematically she began to recall and store every aspect of husbandry she had ever noticed or overheard, or practiced, the seasonal tasks, talk of costs, lambing, seeds, weather lore, quantities and measures, the failures and their reasons, the orderly and immutable rotation of beasts and plants over the land. It was a conscious decision to make the bitter apprenticeship at Wame's farm pay and to waste nothing. Rachel Jedder had discovered an unshakable purpose.

The outlines of freshly planted quickset hedge spiked the sides of the road blackly and, behind them, the plow-turned clods disintegrated under the heel of the frost. The night crackled as the soil crumbled and settled, ready to thaw into a rich, friable seedbed for April. And in the wood-fenced pound, stray cattle and ponies bellowed and snorted and clashed their horns and lashed their tails and jostled and stamped their hooves against the cold, as bewildered by being herded off the recently cordoned land as their owners. They crowded to the rails as Rachel went past, and the great gray dog shied to her other side. She clouted him and called him a coward and his long tail flapped in friendly agreement.

When they found an empty shelter near a shepherd's cottage and huddled into a corner for the rest of the night, her thoughts were still whirring and her senses remained abnormally acute, so that the faint tang of sheep seemed to fill the air with acid and the coarse hair of the dog felt spongy as a fleece. She tried to ignore the sound of marching spiders and closed her eyes to shut out the fiery sky, but the pictures in her head were even brighter, those of her future life as clear as those from the past, and all jumbled together out of sequence: the children dying in the workhouse, as sadly and quietly as old men, tomorrow's births, quick and hot and tender on the moor, the coming summer's milk, thick, yellow and balanced in buckets on the end of the yoke, huge bags of flour bringing her to her knees on the way to Mistress Wame's ratproof storeroom. They would not weigh heavy this year. Harvests cut and tilling next spring. Rachel Jedder, parish pauper. Rachel Jedder, freeholder. For a long time she could not sleep, and then, at last, her busy ideas turned without pause into identical dreams.

For the next days of her journey, Rachel remained inspired. It was the first opening of her mind and the first pleasurable realization of her senses. Such indulgence had been impossible when faced with a future without hope and while living in a present so full of drudgery that it had allowed little more than the repeated experiences of hunger and tiredness. Demoralized and without expectation, there had been no point until now in thinking about herself or wondering what would become of her. Total effort had been needed to complete each day and stay alive.

The road through Cambridgeshire imprinted its every detail on her, the peculiar, milky soil and heather-covered commons; stark enclosures, still cut and patterned by the half-acre strips of the old open fields, where each village family had had holdings on which to grow wheat and rye, oats, peas and beans, and then feed cattle on the stubble after harvest. Flocks of lapwings wheeled and drifted over them, their gleaming breasts like constellations of stars. The east wind swooped in from Sauton, howling curses, but catching in her cloak and bowling her onward. Along the prehistoric Icknield Way, treading where so many visionaries and seekers of fortune had gone before, she picked up the wisps of their inspirations and wove them into her hopes. No longer sure of the line between reality and her own imagination, she had removed to another dimension and walked there, talking loudly to herself, and untroubled.

In this abstraction she showed her signed travel pass to a skeptical church warden, who followed her on horseback to the borders of his parish to ensure that she did not tarry, and she bought a tinderbox in a village of a single street of overhanging, half-timbered houses. Another night was spent in a stable, carelessly left open and unguarded by dogs, and another in the ruins of a deserted village, sleeping soundly behind the last fragments of the church among the ghosts of plague victims. At Royston they gave her cheese and ale, paid for out of Parish funds set aside for poor travelers, and at dusk the gray dog caught a thin rabbit; she carried it quickly to the nearest wood and cooked it to leather over an open fire, which warmed them till dawn.

That same morning, a man driving a wagon loaded with stone offered a laboriously slow lift to St. Albans and then grew so frightened by her witch's eyes and absentminded mutterings that he pushed her off outside the Bull Inn at Wheathampstead. The square, heavy cathedral was just visible from there, crouched on a distant hill like a griffin protecting the town below.

Far to the right, a river wound across common land flecked with sheep and, beyond it, to the west, lay a range of hills. Rachel decided to skirt St. Albans and aim directly for them.

The sky was blue and the countryside was brightened, although not warmed, by sun, which had hardly melted the overnight frost. Clumps of snowdrops, so fragile that a bird's foot could have destroyed them, had magically withstood the brumal cold of the past week. They breathed of spring with delicate scent when she picked a few and held them against her face.

She followed a stream until it joined the river in a marshy meadow armed with platoons of rushes and lined by poplars. There was a wooden bridge to the opposite side and a worn path led from there toward the foothills of the Chilterns. The river branched away, and soon she was climbing knolls, then slopes and hillocks and heights, and then a long descent to a group of new cottages near the imposing entrance to an estate, to discover more activity than she had seen since Norwich.

Three long wagons piled with bricks waited in a line against the park boundary, and around them pack ponies rested in rows as six magnificent black horses and numerous men hauled a fully grown oak, complete with all its roots, through the wrought-iron gates. The muscular beasts staggered and groaned. The women and children of the hamlet were gathered to watch and everybody shouted. Rachel joined the crowd.

"Oh, aye, oh, heave! Oh, aye, oh, heave!" they chanted, and the mighty tree inched forward, chains rattling and branches sweeping the way like a giant broom.

"Why don't they saw it up first?" Rachel asked a woman.

"Sir Francis Dashwood would have 'em all transported, that's why," she answered. "That there tree has been brought near a mile to be planted in what they call the new landscape, because his head gardener says that there tree has the right shape for his worship's view."

There was a loud crack as a main branch broke, and Rachel laughed, a bold, infectious sound which made the children look around and join in. An angry, sweating man left the struggle to threaten the little group, and her neighbor turned on her aggressively.

"Who are you then, coming here asking questions and causing trouble?"

Rachel stopped laughing, her eyes flaring a little and she heard the familiar hiss as the other women saw the green-and-brown bands of her irises and stepped back, putting protective hands on their infants. A roar went up from the men as the tree was finally pulled like a cork from the gates, and during the brief diversion she slipped away.

After about a quarter of a mile, she noticed that the gray dog was no longer there. She stopped and called, coming out from the scattering of trees to scan the area, but there was no sign of him. She wondered if he had lost her at the hamlet, or whether the people there had chased him off, too, but in another direction. She did not dare return, and so, for about half an hour, she walked on very slowly, shouting his name every few minutes and pausing to listen and search; but he did not appear.

The estate lay below in the angular outline of its walls and hedges. The great house could be seen, reduced to the size of a rich child's toy, cased in wooden scaffolding and infested by miniature workmen, and the oak tree was now being dragged across a meadow toward a prepared pit.

Rachel, feeling depressed by the loss of the dog, stopped to watch.

All at once, there was a commotion on the south-facing terrace and she could see people running to it, their voices borne clearly over the still combe. A gray form bolted across the lawns and a fowling piece was fired, its explosion repeating over and over in ricochets against the walls of the valley.

"Sam! Sam!" Rachel screamed, but the dog was racing to the woods to the left, and she watched abjectly as he dived into them.

"Thieving bugger!" she thought resentfully to herself, shrugging her shoulders when he did not emerge again and turning back to the path, damning him as she puffed on uphill with joyless steps; but then there was a crescendo of rustling ahead and he suddenly crashed through the thicket and dropped his victim on the ground before her.

It was a marvelous bird, such as she had never seen, with a tail at least four feet long, and still warm when she bent to touch it, and plump. She lifted the first long feather and the tail unfolded into a screen of ferns hung with butterflies, iridescent greens and blues in ovals of peach. Rachel was delighted and pulled out some of the shorter fronds to hold against her skirt, wanting to wear them, to stitch them all into a magnificent gown. She pointed a toe and preened, her eyes darting from quills to bird. The gray dog yawned, unimpressed by her parade, and then his body stiffened and rumbled with a threatening growl and the woods below filled with the noise of people blundering through.

The bird lay fatly on the ground—some kind of game fowl belonging to the lord of the great house—and Rachel knew that the gallows waited for those caught poaching. The lovely tail fell from her hand to fold like a closed fan. She stepped forward and stood on it, seizing the bird's horny legs and jerking them upward with a quick, hard tug. The body left the tail with such force that she lost her balance and dumped back on the earth.

Sitting there, she worked quickly, pushing the body under her skirt and hooking the head and feet through the cord securing the parchments to her waist. The pursuers were only yards away, beating through the undergrowth. She spat at the dog and chased him off with a stone, before running on up the path, away from the incriminating feathers. There was a shout as they found them and then the scuffle of feet hurrying after her.

"Stop, wench!" The keeper was carrying a cudgel of blackthorn.

Rachel Jedder faced him warily, her hands clasped on her bulging belly.

"Have you seen a great gray hound pass this way, girl?" he asked.

She nodded, panting a little, and pointed behind her. " 'E were carrying summat blue in his mouth," she offered. "And traveling fast as a buzzard."

"Aye, that's him, the varmint! Stolen one of Sir Francis's peacocks, he

39

has," said the keeper furiously, and then glowered at her. "What are you doing here, wench?"

"My husband died, your honor, of the flux, and I walk to Yellaton, to my mother for my laying-in," Rachel answered, her eyes downcast.

"I ain't never heard of no village by that name." The keeper was suspicious from habit, but she guessed that, like most country folk, he had never been farther than the nearest market town.

" 'Tis many miles, a five-day journey, sir," she replied. "And I must reach the next village for shelter before nightfall."

"Begone then!" He waved her on and turned back to his men sourly. "We've lost him and that bird'll be in his belly by now. We'd best get back."

Rachel waited until the sounds of their tramping boots had grown muffled and then slipped quickly behind a bush, pulled the dead peacock from beneath her skirts and plucked it with fast, expert fingers. In less than fifteen minutes there was a confetti of blue on the ground around her and an appetizingly spit-ready bird in her hand. Tying its feet together with a tuft of dead grass, she attached it to her wrist and returned to the footpath, where the gray dog was sitting, looking as though he had been waiting there all afternoon.

"I won't be fretting over you no more, Sam," Rachel assured him.

There was an hour or so to go until dark, sufficient time to reach beyond the news of his crime and to set about cooking the exotic bird. The layer of fat visible under its skin would keep it juicy and rich, unlike the leather rabbit of the previous night, and the prospect of hot meat put them both in high spirits. They left the trees to stride across the smooth haunches of the hills, the girl singing and chattering and the dog tirelessly hunting.

As day dimmed, Rachel saw a cluster of carts and wagons gathered near a large shed on the edge of open wastes below and surrounded by a crowd of people. More people, herding sheep and leading horses, were coming and going along footpaths and her face smoothed and flushed with excitement.

She had never been to a fair, but she had heard of them often enough, occasions of abandonment and thrills, the hiring fairs of Lady Day and Michaelmas to which farm servants went to find new masters, and the goose fairs, and the special fairs of Easter, May Day and Christmas.

The promise of fun and company diverted her downhill to where sheep bells and flute music chimed and the track cut across the common, past tethered piebald ponies waiting for the sale, toward the chaos of tents being erected on poles, and booths hung with flags and placards.

Clutching the peacock under her cloak, she pushed through the people, just as the citizens of Norwich had done, and then, without warning, a man with legs twice as long as a seventeen-hands-high horse walked slowly by, his head level with the loft entrance above the open cart shed.

Rachel gave a little scream before her hands clapped over her mouth, and her eyes almost burst from her head. The man looked down and winked and *raised his hat*. She almost fainted with pride.

Lanterns and candles were already being lit as the dove-gray clouds filtered to charcoal. She gazed at the painted pictures illustrating the extravaganzas contained within each booth; jugglers, a man eating fire, jointed wooden dolls on strings, dancing bears and more men standing row upon row on each other's shoulders. She wandered, enthralled, between tarpaulins and wooden kiosks until she reached the edge of the fairground where the largest wagons stood.

From overheard bits of conversations she learned that the place was Christmas Common, where the important Shrove Tuesday Fair was due to open next day. One or two late carts were still pulling up on the outskirts of the gathering, their occupants bustling to set up their side-shows before it became too dark to see.

So much had happened since she left Wame's farm. The reflective mood which had shielded her for the past few days had worn off. Rachel suddenly felt very tired, and she stopped beside a canvas-covered wain. After so long in the open, its interior looked homely as a hearth and she climbed in to rest for a few minutes.

"Well, here's a pretty dormouse to find in my nest," an oddly accented voice said.

Rachel opened her eyes and sat up with a start, but could not discern the man's face behind the swinging lamp held in his hand.

"I was only sitting out of the wind," she mumbled guiltily.

"You were fast asleep, maid." There was a grin in the words, and the sky, showing black through the opening in the canvas, proved him right.

"Your pardon, your honor," she apologized nervously, preparing to jump to the ground.

"Your honor!" he mocked from behind the light, and he took her arm firmly to prevent her from leaving.

The cloak slipped back revealing the fat plucked bird still attached to her wrist. The stranger leaned forward and whistled and Rachel, alarmed, received only an impression of young features and curly hair before her supper was snatched away and his silhouette flew from the vehicle.

She let out a yell and followed, but then jolted to a stop, blinking and staring as the figure seemed to turn over and over in the dark, running alternately on hands and then on feet. It was impossible to believe what she was seeing as he revolved faster than a top and somersaulted and leaped to run along the edge of the sky, then twisted, turned, bucked and skipped like a flea, vaulted over man-high cart shafts and danced along a rope strung from the side of the shed to a pole and hung with washing. *A demon!* She had met with the Devil. Rachel Jedder felt her skin prick and

41

go cold and heard her own breath hiss with the same fear she generated so often in others. She backed against the wall of the shed and the fiend swooped past, so close that the breeze of the movement blew chill on her face, and she caught a glimpse of the peacock swinging in his hand, and he laughed. It was a very human laugh, and Rachel had been looking forward to that meal.

She flung herself on him and they both fell to the ground, her fist grabbing back the bird on the way down; but before she could get away, his arms were round her waist.

"Stay, maid. 'Twas only a jest. I'll not steal your fowl. Stay and roast it at our fire."

She stopped struggling and he released her. A few yards away, a fire burned on the common, and he stood up, smiling in its flickering light, and held out a hand. The smell of food thickened the night and the peacock lay, succulent and meaty, on her lap. She took the hand and went with him.

Jack Greenslade was not much older than herself. He was dark-haired and brown-eyed, but not handsome, because his nose had been broken and his mouth was quirkily lopsided. It was the way he moved that held Rachel Jedder's attention. Other men strode or slouched or trudged or strutted. Jack Greenslade had a fluid, feline walk, so relaxed it seemed to use no muscles, so quiet he might have been hunting.

He impaled the peacock on an iron rod and hung it over the flames on the hooks of a pair of metal dogs. He was an acrobat, he told her as they waited, and when she asked what that was, he turned a double somersault in the air and then chuckled loudly at the sight of her awe-struck face. Later, as they ate, he kept breaking off to greet other performers, who slapped his back or playfully cuffed him in passing.

"That's Alan Tucker, the tightrope walker. I haven't seen him since last Pack Monday at Sherborne. And that's Bob Harris, the strong man. He's just spent a year at Bartholomew Fair in London, and there's Harry Stuckley, and those are Thomasin Tripp and Philip Bidmead and Sarah Hellet, the players. I always travel with them, because they draw a crowd."

He pointed out the firelit people, who were quite unlike anyone Rachel had ever seen before. They were astonishingly shaped, giants and dwarfs, wizened and muscular, radiant actresses in brilliantly colored clothes, and then the man with the long, long legs.

"Stilts," explained Jack Greenslade. "Show the wench your legs, Amos Weston."

The man twitched back the flap of the ground-length coat, which concealed the slender wooden props and footrests, and doffed his hat to her again.

"And there's Ben Cottle, the tooth-puller, who joined us at Barnstaple Fair, last September in Devon."

42

"Devon!" she interrupted breathlessly. "You have been to Devon?"

"Of course, maid, to Bampton and Widecombe and Barnstaple and more. Did I not tell you I'd been everywhere?"

"Tell me of Devon," she pleaded.

"Why, 'tis a fine county. Not so fine as Somerset, which is where I come from, but still a fair county, ever pleasing to the eye."

Then he talked of the moors. Dartmoor, where a man could sink into bright-green grass and never be seen again, or stray only a short distance from one of the few narrow tracks to become lost in a wilderness of tors and wastes, or lie down on a placid evening, only to meet his fate within hours in an unexpected convulsion of the elements. And Exmoor, seemingly milder, but with more subtle dangers, deep and secret pools in which to drown, treacherous bogs, soft, floury winter snow building to sudden drifts high enough to smother complete houses and barns and countless herds of beasts.

His words were like a Bible reading and left Rachel Jedder joyful with renewed faith in her stars, and that night it seemed most natural to lie on the straw-covered floor of the actors' wagon near the man who had been to Devon.

The fair was due to travel south and, after a day of reveling and glee spent watching the dancing dolls and Punch and Judy, and entertainers doing incredible tricks with chairs and ladders, and Harry Stuckley standing up on the backs of a pair of galloping horses, she agreed to go with it. Jack Greenslade assured her that it was easy to turn west from Sussex, and he promised to teach her to stand on her head.

That evening, the drama of the Siege of Troy was performed by the players in the cart shed and she shrieked at the battle scenes and screamed warnings of the perfidy of Paris to Achilles and gaped at Helen's loveliness, but booed her faithlessness. By the time she curled up in the straw for the second night, her mind was revolving in a maypole dance of magic happenings, and, for the first time in her life, Rachel Jedder was experiencing the contentment of belonging. Everyone knew her name and accepted her presence without resentment or doubt—and not one of the fair people had flinched from her witch's eyes. Jack Greenslade even thought them beautiful.

Lent began and brought with it a depressing heaviness, which affected both weather and traveling people alike. The prospect of forty damp and colorless days without work took all impetus out of the journey. The company crossed country far more slowly than Rachel had done on her own, often taking ten hours to cover as many miles. They lumbered through villages, subdued by the pall of religious abstinence, and the wagons stuck in the mud traps set in every track by the thaw and ensuing rain. Food grew scarce and tempers short as they ground out of Oxfordshire and into Berkshire, harried by parish wardens and officers, and gradually reducing in number as individual peddlers and mountebanks left for routes leading to other prospective Easter fair meetings. The actors began begging, surreptitiously and with little success, and everyone became lethargic and weak from lack of food.

Only Jack Greenslade remained cheerful, rising before daybreak each morning to go off quietly with the gray dog and usually returning with an egg or pigeon from someone's dovecote or even a chicken, just as Rachel opened her eyes.

For the hour before they all moved on again he worked at his routine, his body, whippy as willow, turning cartwheels and handsprings, back somersaults and twisting into impossible contortions, each figure leading harmoniously to the next through a series of arcs, sinuous as a circling, silver fish. He could ride a wheel and balance on one hand on top of a pole and juggle eight balls and stand on his head with his arms folded. He could even drink a tankard of ale while hanging upside down.

Rachel watched him every day with admiration and a strangely uncomfortable sensation. Although she sat quite still, it was as though she were running, the way her heart pumped and her face turned hot and red. When their eyes met, she felt clumsy beside his artistry, and if he went off with Sam during the day, she found herself continually watching and listening, unable to concentrate on anything else until he returned. As they settled to sleep on either side of the floor of the canvas-covered wain, she would have liked to move closer to him, and each night became a restless waiting for some unidentifiable, momentous adventure.

March sprang on them from the northwest like a madwoman, ripping tents and wagon covers and smashing the flimsy stage properties. From the open hill, where they were caught, the whole earth looked as though it were being lifted and shaken. Trees crashed across roads, entire roofs were peeled off and dispersed as scatterings of straw. The horses refused to walk head to the blast and the gray dog kept up an incessant howl, stirred by the pack call of the gale. The miserable travelers, unable to continue their journey, huddled behind what little screening growth they could find.

Jack Greenslade and Rachel lost the protection of the tarpaulin and so crawled beneath the wain to sleep fitfully, and in the eye of the night she felt his mouth on hers and his hand lightly touching her breast, spreading rings of bright-blue flame, and she heard herself gasp as her lips opened and her startled body arched to him. He undid her bodice while the wind fanned her scorching flesh and she was rocked by a violent pulse drumming in the well of her belly. It was as though a complete skin had been torn off, leaving her exquisitely sensitive everywhere. His fingers teased and fawned, urged and played, finding each need and creating more, agonizing little fevers rushing into one uncontrollable current. He wound round her, letting her hips quiver and push instinctively against his, bending her back, like a bowman, into a straining curve, and she felt herself overcome by a frenzied impatience, which changed her kiss into a wailing, desperate, convulsive bite.

"Be still, Rachel Jedder," his voice ordered, his arms tightening, and then, at last, she was soaring with him, carried on rhythmic wings into the beating grace of his dance, curling and entwining, spinning and tumbling, melted beyond human shape, skimming over a sheet of glass until the glass shattered into a thousand images of herself, spiraling away across the night sky, slower and slower, hovering, before fluttering down like spent leaves to a long and lazy stillness.

The moon caught in Rachel Jedder's wide-open eyes and they glittered gold and emerald, as hard and unseeing as precious stones. Jack Greenslade leaned up on his arm to look at her and a perplexed expression crossed his face before he smiled down uncertainly, and she stroked his curly head with an absent-minded gesture, more for a child than a lover. She felt released, triumphant, as though a great victory had been won.

In the morning he was gentle, concerned that he might have hurt her, disbelieving that she had felt no pain, and she accepted his cosseting with some surprise. It was as though he imagined that he had been brought to maturity while she had been left behind in childhood, instead of realizing that the night had made them both grow up together.

As he insisted upon her remaining seated while he fetched beer from the communal barrel, Rachel felt a trace of irritation, until he began the daily practice of his fairground act and his skin glistened in the early sun and the electric charge of his beauty hypnotized her once more. As she watched, her eyes grew heavy under the spell of his eroticism and her body began to glow and grow restless, until, hardly knowing what she was doing, she uncoiled over the ground from their sheltered resting place, reaching into his circle with outstretched arms until her hand caught his and he was beside her again with his mouth on hers, and she was wondering dazedly if this was love.

But within a few days, unexpected restrictions were being imposed on her, in a kindly, protective way, as one would harness a young colt: so subtle that at first she barely noticed; a hand helping her over obstacles she could have managed alone, and restraining her when she wanted to ride one of the performing horses. Although she had laid fires since early childhood, he showed her how to do it his way, and once sent her to fetch water while Sarah Hallet was recounting the plot of "The Fall of Bajazet." She was petted extravagantly for producing a singularly tasteless broth from a rabbit carcass but expected to stay with the other women while the men played dice.

Most alarming of all was the way assumptions were made by all the company that Rachel Jedder belonged to Jack Greenslade, that Jack Greenslade possessed Rachel Jedder. What was more, he did not keep his promise to teach her to stand on her head.

After each half-recognized lick of annoyance she would press to him

45

and pour pleasure over the doubt, until, at last, even their lovemaking began to take on the flatness of a regular demand, its ripe sensuality spoiled by the ebb of resentment.

When she awoke that day the ground was warmer against her cheek and the sun from beneath the horizon was rising to a sky as pale yellow as a field of half-ripe corn. Standing up from her bed of pine, Rachel saw a new country, densely wooded, and pleated with hills which wrapped around farmhouses, cottages and villages like eiderdowns. A green haze softened the harsh outlines of its trees. New blades were cutting through the tangled dead grass. Shoots shook the winter soil from their tips and buds split open and birds stripped Old Man's Beard from the bushes and snatched at the combings of fleece caught on the bramble thorns with an urgency which seemed powered from the center of the earth.

One or two unsteady early bundles bobbed at the heels of their black-faced dams in the flocks below, like puffs of white smoke, and their reedy demands tugged at Rachel Jedder more than the cry of any infant could have done. She stared westward with sudden longing. Perhaps there were sheep belonging to her, uncared for and lambing without aid. The blinding disc floated over the rim of the world and the land sighed and surrendered to it, like a sunbather. It was almost time to plant.

Jack was returning from one of his early-morning forays with a hare and a wood pigeon dangling in his hand. He was whistling, and she stared down to avoid his eyes. Fragments of fur and the bones of small mammals lay at her feet, disgorged there as indigestible pellets by the owl which perched nightly on the branch overhead. She stirred them into the skeletons of last year's leaves with her toe and did not look up.

"I'll be on my way today, Jack Greenslade," she said.

The merry tune stopped, leaving only the light sounds of the gray dog's running paws and the man's heavier, more hesitant tread.

"Not yet, Rachel." He was beside her, protesting. " 'Tis Easter week. The fair opens and there's to be money again. It'll all be different, you wait and see."

He sounded stricken. Nearby the actors were waking up, noisy as always, clattering about and shouting to each other. She looked across the lush Sussex landscape as their chatter rattled over its stillness like a dogcart, and Jack's arms gesticulated jerkily, as though manipulated by strings. She wanted to be alone again, to walk along the edges of virgin fields and through frowning forests and down little-used tracks unaccompanied, and hear the living word of nature and feel the magnet of the land again.

"I can't stay no longer," she answered. "I been here too long already."

She looked into his face at last and it was crumpled, like a boy's, like Sam's had been at Wame's farm.

"Come now, Jack Greenslade," she said tenderly, standing on tiptoe and pulling his head down to kiss him on the lips. "Will you not be at Barnstaple Fair this autumn?"

"And you'll meet me there, upon oath?" he pressed anxiously.

"Can't be no problem to a wench what's crossed all England to find her way to such a famous fair in the same county," she assured him cockily. "O' course I'll be there."

"Swear it!"

" 'Pon my honor, Jack Greenslade."

He walked to the foot of the hill with her and stood watching and occasionally raising his hand as she crossed the common to the footpath, which ran through a spinney, where she did not have to look back any more, because the trees hid her from his sight.

The sounds of Harry Stuckley making ready his bony nags and the players' squabbling buzzed for a short distance before shrinking to mere insect bites on the quiet morning, and finally, she and the gray dog were on their own, strolling through a tunnel of overhanging branches.

The sunlight hung in green streamers from the new leaves, and the banks rising on each side of the lane were patched with clumps of primroses as thickly bunched as posies. The clean, heady smell of humus seeped from the ground and Rachel was clutched by happy tension and a feeling of anticipation, as though this were the beginning of the real love affair. She skipped a few steps, then began to run and jump and shout, the gray dog barking and bounding in circles around her until they emerged onto a close-cropped pasture.

A chestnut tree, its girth age-scarred and warped with knots and growths and old, deserted dreys, grew there, its trunk divided near the base into low-spreading limbs nodulated with fat, sticky, bee-covered buds. Rachel, with no hand to check her now, hitched her skirts above her knees, tucked them under her waistband and began to climb. Her heavy boots skidded over the ridges of the bark until, sitting astride the first bough, she undid them and dropped them to the ground, before continuing the ascent in bare feet. Each hold led easily to the next, and soon the branches thinned and swayed more under her weight, until there was only one slender shaft left, reaching higher than the rest, and she was clinging to it, tipping dangerously forward.

It was such a beautiful day. The whole of England was primed for spring: cows, heavily in calf, dipping over the meadows like fleets of sailing ships; nests, lined with breast feathers, waiting for eggs; the adder and the queen wasp waking; the grasses braced for their phenomenal first thrust. The black soil was slowly releasing its stored fertility ready for the seed, and under her hand she could feel the sap begin its swift upward surge. Her own blood sped with the same passion, and the compulsion to create and grow dominated all other instincts. If she did not reach her own land in time, all would start without her and the year would leave her behind. She scrambled down the tree so quickly the branches seemed

47

to close in and spin and the bees took off in a shocked froth, and she arrived quite breathless and dizzy on the ground. The tinderbox, a mug and a small, heavy cooking pot were wrapped in a cloth bundle, which she swung over one shoulder before starting out once more, parallel to the sun.

Sussex, cloistered behind the fastness of the South Downs, was full of secret places, streams and paths winding under dense rhododendron, deer trails threaded through the bracken, small churches curiously apart from the homes of their congregations in isolated fields, or on the edge of the world. Rachel remembered how, only a few weeks before, she had believed that all England must be like the hostile district around Wame's farm, monotonously flattened by the iron of the east wind; but this was a mellow county, where even the thatch was thicker and pulled down lower over the cottages, making them as pretty as bonneted girls, and the people had wool-soft voices, so deep and curly it was often impossible to extract their individual words. Her mental picture of Jedder's land changed as she walked from a mud hovel in bleak scrub to a lattice-windowed house of the weald, with small pastures cut from the surrounding woodland.

In the thirty hours after leaving Jack Greenslade, she met with no one, and was glad. Her life as an apprentice had been remarkably solitary, the mistress giving orders each daybreak and appearing only occasionally to scold in a crow-harsh voice between then and nightfall. Living communally with the people of the fair had left her feeling bombarded by action and noise, and although they had traveled slowly, there had been no time to stop and absorb the cambers and scrolls and angles, the tooled reliefs and planed contours making up the sculptured scenery ahead. Their presence had somehow dulled the senses, so that the smell of the badger and the sight of the fluttering kestrel went unnoticed and the first February song of the skylark had been made commonplace.

Now, as she crossed heaths and uncultivated commons and sidestepped the camouflaged bogs of Hampshire, coltsfoot and winter aconite suddenly sprang through the loam like yellow flames, brimstone butterflies posed on every holly bush, and a film of blossoms turned the elms dusty crimson in the sunlight. The lambs' tails on the hazel wiggled and wagged in the breeze. The first small toad crept across the melted earth with his news that the frosts were over at last, and Rachel felt deliriously alive again.

The bawling of cattle reinforced by a drone of bleating was the first signal that her isolation was almost over. The cacophony charged over the bank of peace like a pibroch and proclaimed great herds ahead. After a few more miles, the network of cart tracks and footpaths finally met at a hostelry beside a very wide and straight green lane, which ran due west. The heaving, clamoring beasts were crammed into two stances behind the inn, outside which stood a number of men with tankards in their hands. Dressed in sleeveless leather jerkins over wide-cut shirts and breeches, they did not look like ordinary village laborers, but they grinned and cheered boisterously at the sight of Rachel approaching.

In turn, she was inquisitive, because it seemed such an odd place to hold a market, so far from town or village, and she saw that some of the men were carrying packs, as though they, too, were traveling.

When they called again, she joined them and they filled her cup with ale from their jug and shared out fat bacon, telling that they were on their way to the cities with the first fresh meat of the year. The bullocks and wethers were unimpressively scraggy after the long hunger, but they would fill out fast on the succulent spring grazing along the way, and the city dwellers would pay well for a change from the winter diet of salt flesh. Already the herdsmen were celebrating the gold to come.

Rachel was on the drovers' road from Salisbury Plain, which, if followed the way they had come, would take her straight to the West Country. They made it sound only a few miles on.

The bacon was cut in brown-skinned, cream-colored chunks, each with a seam of lean along the inside edge. She stuffed them into her mouth, wiping the grease off her chin and giggling as the men pinched her cheeks and stroked her hair and discussed her strange eyes solemnly among themselves, because they were too drunk and it was too fine a day for fear.

The innkeeper sold a body-building ale, strong and nutty, which fulfilled the nostrils and resounded against the roof of the mouth and fired the maw. Rachel drew great gulps and held out for more, and more again, becoming quickly and enjoyably so befuddled that the faces of her companions developed second pairs of eyes and double noses, and when eventually they pointed her on her way, smothering her in kisses and proposals, the broad lane felt like deep, green sand, into which her feet sank groggily.

"Come with us, pretty. 'Tis as bad to walk alone as to bed alone."

"I'll take 'ee to London town, maid. You'll not find another like I in Devon."

"Put wake-robin beneath thy head to dream of me, and I'll come to thee, wench."

"Remember John James."

"And Robert Woolsey."

"And Robin Ashkettle."

She waved and stumbled, turning and turning to keep them in sight, until a hill rose between them and she was left on a surf which swept her forward on its crest and tossed her onto beaches of chalk over and over again. Sometimes she lay winded and mumbling, wondering how the gray dog always arrived before her, and as she picked herself up, another wave would lift her to its back and rush on.

Without warning, it became dark and the ground stopped flowing, and to her terror, a towering gathering of black ogres suddenly appeared ahead, formless and menacing, standing astride the road. Rachel blenched, and before her eyes they turned into colossal monoliths from which came ripples, like ridges on the night, drawing her inward until she was at the center of two concentric circles, which began to revolve with measured tread, flipping the moon over their fingers like a coin, so that its light beamed on and off, hypnotically, until she became giddy and fell on the waiting slab. The gray dog was howling a long way off as she lost consciousness.

Rachel Jedder could see herself standing in a small field of newly sown barley, looking over its harrowed surface, pleased that the job was done. A man was coming toward her and, some distance behind him, a callow boy. They were walking against the sunlight, with their faces in shadow, yet they were known and loved, and she turned to meet them; but the crop spurted up, fully grown, a march of gilded spears driving the man back, until he disappeared beneath the advance and the boy ran off, and she was left crying.

The sun blazed down and the swaying corn cast gleaming reflections over her face as though she were looking into a lake of molten copper, and the growth spread, like a torch set to the woods and heath around the field, until everywhere was covered by its tall, full-eared glory, and its color deepened from flaxen to flashing gold; a harvest beyond imagination, which brushed Rachel Jedder with a rich dust until she also changed to gold.

Then trails like veins brought her to the foot of a long, wide flight of steps bordered by balustrades of turned stone, and the corn closed like a metal wall as she began to climb. The steps were shallow and yet she was breathing with difficulty and bent with the strain by the time she reached the top, to be faced by a brass-studded, carved-oak door. It opened slowly and a girl with black hair and translucent skin and eyes parti-colored brown and green stood before her. Herself.

Rachel was clearly aware of her spirit returning to her body as first sun drew back the cast umbrage of the monoliths. She felt stiff and her head ached when she opened her eyes. The sorcery of the rings was over and the rough-hewn stones stood lifelessly grouped in the center of a flat plain. Yet she had not slept and dreamed it all. She had been brought to this place and given hints and clues she did not understand. For a few minutes she lay thinking it over, but the slab was uncomfortable and cold, and Sam was running around the perimeter, not daring to break through, but whining insistently. It would all be revealed one day, she decided, and joined him.

Drovers' roads avoided towns and villages and ran deliberately through remote parts where the herds could progress undisturbed and without causing damage. Rachel met some shepherds driving a scattered, tinkling flock, and begged some sheep's milk and a little more bacon, but after that she passed no one. At the top of each light rise she expected to see a farmhouse ahead, but only another incline lay beyond.

The next days and nights were cloudy, revealing neither sun nor stars. The plain was wild and bare, almost treeless, a tiring, frightening place for any traveler, and she became very hungry indeed and began to despair of coming to cottage or hamlet again. Until that time she had managed to survive on the generosity of charitable parishes and the spoils of the gray dog's hunting. Sometimes, with an armful of withered grass, she had crept to a small bunch of cows in a lonely field and milked one as it nosed the bribe, and in desperation she had twice bought pies at taverns. There were still threepence left in the leather pouch, and after thirty-six empty hours she would gladly have spent them all on food. The time with the fair people now seemed safe and merry in retrospect. There had been little to eat, but there also been no danger of dying of starvation alone in a ditch.

The gray dog lagged at her heels. A stray hind, surprised downwind, sprang into the air and winged away with bounding flight, which he was too weak to pursue. Hawks hovered over them ominously. It was as though they had walked beyond the last human outpost and were nearing the edge of the world. Rachel wondered if she had missed the way and somehow passed Devon. The drunken herdsmen at the inn had made it sound so near, but that was three days ago. She began to consider turning back, and only the knowledge that she had not the strength to retrace the track kept her moving forward. At last she labored to the brow of a low hill and saw a rose stone house ahead, surrounded by flintstone buildings and a wooden barn.

The farmer's wife there talked with the eagerness of one who misses company. She was young and pregnant, and Rachel was careful not to look directly at her, in case she became afraid for the unborn child and drove her away.

"Don't you let on to my husband. He won't have none of beggars," the young woman warned cheerfully, bringing out bread and salt pork and even a bowl of peelings and scraps for the gray dog. "Them vittles is meant for the chickens. I'd let you heat by the fire, indeed I would, but 'twould be against his wishes. You can sleep over the stable, if you get off afore he rises. Where are you going? No one but drovers travels this road. Be you lost? Or be you a runaway pauper? You're no gypsy, are you?"

Rachel shook her head and concentrated on the food. The other wondered if Devon lay beyond Bath and then fetched a large wedge of cheese and some soft apples for her to eat the next day.

It was the first warm and comfortable night the girl and the dog had passed for a week and they arose strong and full of hope, which carried them swiftly to Taunton and on to the borders of Exmoor itself.

By then, a thick fog was lying, but as soon as her feet began to tread the heather-covered floor of the moor, Rachel Jedder knew she had reached her homeland. The place even smelled different, harsh and smoky, and she did not mind that the wet air soaked her clothes and hair. Yellaton lay waiting only one more day away.

It was tempting to hurry on carelessly in spite of the weather, but she remembered Jack Greenslade's words and tried to keep strictly to the tracks. There was supposed to be a highway, but, being unfenced, it was not easy to follow. She passed pack ponies up to their hocks in the mire, and once she heard a man's cries and the scream of a horse not far off, but when she groped toward them, the road suddenly ended and the stone she threw clattered down a steep drop before reaching bottom.

An ostler at the Cuckoo Inn let her stay the night in the stables in return for a cuddle and a kiss or two; then, being discontented with the limits of the bargain, he gave her little chance to sleep. When she ran off from him it was still night, but the fog had lifted and the moor was floodlit by the moon, the black swath of the route cutting between its silvered slopes.

Before noon she was surveying the square in South Molton with interest, because this would be the market town closest to her new home and the attorneys who had drawn up her grandfather's will had offices here. She wondered if she should take the documents to them first, but her cloak and gown were torn and caked with dirt and both she and the gray dog reeked of stagnant bogs and dung, and, worst of all, such an appointment would delay her arrival at Yellaton by another whole day. A passerby pointed the way south and she did not rest again before reaching the Black Mantle five miles on.

As she was sitting on the mounting block there, eating the last of the cheese, two well-dressed young gentlemen left the inn, collected their horses and came over, laughing. She hastily jumped out of their way.

"Ten guineas to the mill!" shouted the taller of the two, swinging into the saddle.

"Done!" cried the other.

"Start the race, girl!" The first turned and threw twopence down to her. The horses tossed their heads and pirouetted nervously.

"Ready, your worships," called Rachel. "Go!"

Spurs dug, whips cracked, the horses leaped, mud sprayed, the ground shook and the two riders careered away, jostling each other and hallooing and growing perspectively smaller.

"Maized young rakes!" growled a voice. "And old squire not yet cold."

An ancient man stood behind her, smoking a clay pipe and glaring after the gentlemen through rheumy eyes.

"Who were they, then?" Rachel asked, quickly hiding her coins.

"Young Squire Waddon of Beara and one of his fine friends from London," the old man replied. "They bin in liquor and a-wenching since the old squire died not six months past, Lord rest him."

Rachel felt her fingers begin to tremble and she clasped her hands tightly together. "Beara Moor? Yellaton on Beara Moor? How far is it?" She tried to sound casual.

The old man puffed noisily and thought for quite some time before commenting, "Depends, maid, whether 'ee be going by horse, or whether 'ee be a-walking."

"On foot! On foot!" It was hard not to sound impatient.

He gazed into space through the haze of his own smoke until she began to wonder if he had forgotten the question, but at last he muttered vaguely, "Yellaton? Yellaton, you say? That be where Penuel Jedder do live to."

Her heart bounced at the sound of her grandfather's name. "Yes," she whispered, suddenly hoarse. "How far?"

He gave her a knowing look, mischievous and unexpectedly sharp. "Could be as far as a lifetime, wench, if you was my age and a poor man. How much gold did young squire give 'ee?"

She reluctantly held out one penny, which he snatched with the speed of a magpie, bit, and dropped into the pocket of his smock.

" 'Tis one hour to High Chilham village and near half another westward of there, up on through Moses wood to the hare's leg field at the top of Beara. That be Jedder's land."

Rachel hardly noticed the countryside on these last miles of her journey, and the clutter of houses at High Chilham left no impression other than that the village was the final landmark.

Rain drizzled and the air was drafty with gusts and swirls blowing round the ends of the thickets and between the trees, but it did not matter, nor that she tripped to her knees over a mat of briar and once stepped ankle-deep into an overgrown ditch. It did not matter that the stony track ended in a charcoal-burner's clearing in the woods. No path was needed to show the way. She knew exactly where she was, as though all her life had been spent there, and she walked without hesitation upward from the valley, through the deep heather, beyond the last elder and out onto Beara Moor, where a wild mare stared but did not move as she passed, and the warm southwest wind met her like an old friend. A familiar hedge ran along the ridge ahead. The field it enclosed had a wide, strong thigh and tapered to a slim running foot. The hare's leg. Jedder's land.

For a long, long time Rachel Jedder stood by the wooden gate looking over at her own land. Three irregularly shaped fields, dug spit by spit out of the wilderness by Jedder men and women over centuries and, on the highest point of the moor, a long, low, sturdy house, built facing the prevailing weather and sheltering the few old buildings behind.

The day sank soundlessly, pulling night in an ever-widening band across the sky, and the stars came out in their countless billions, timeless and brilliant beyond light, and still Rachel stared, tears trickling down her face.

At last she opened the gate and bent down slowly and scratched up a handful of earth, rubbing it between her fingers, clenching it into a wet and crumbling ball, warming it in her palms, and then, holding it like a fledgling, she walked across the grass.

The back door of the house was open and she went inside.

CHAPTER FOUR

It was too dark to see, but Rachel guessed that the door in the passageway led to the kitchen. She opened it and the straw covering beneath her feet told her she was right. The room was surprisingly warm.

She fumbled in her bundle for a rush taper and the tinderbox, which had been carefully filled with dried fragments of silver birch bark, and, as she began to rasp the flint with the metal striker, sparks turned arcs into these shavings and she breathed on them lightly, but they went out. The gray dog had wandered off outside, but there was a rustling somewhere nearby. She struck the flint again and blew, hoping to fan the bark alight. It was a frustrating task, which could take as long as half an hour, but this attempt was lucky. A weak flame bubbled from a splinter of wood, just enough to fire the taper.

Its miserly light showed up the dirtiest kitchen Rachel Jedder had ever seen. Hens roosted on chairs and shelves. A table and a dresser were piled high with farm tools and harness, wooden casks and heaps of logs, a milking stool and a pair of cartwheels, unwashed platters and an iron cauldron full of evil-smelling hash.

Taking a step forward, her foot touched something soft and yet unyielding, and she yelped automatically at the sight of a half-chewed dead rat. A cat yowled and shot from a corner. The door at the other side of the room opened and a heavily built man strode in.

Disconcerted, they stared at one another for a few seconds and then, before she had time to think, he pounced, seizing hold and pinning her arms to her sides.

"Come thieving, have 'ee?" he snarled. "Come thieving in my house, hussy?"

He shook her until her feet left the ground and the waxed rush taper dropped into the straw, where he stamped quickly on its flame and left them both in pitch blackness.

"Is this not Yellaton?" gasped Rachel. "Where Penuel Jedder lived?"

He was already hauling her behind him in the darkness through the door he had entered.

" 'Tis that," he agreed, striding into another room, in which a candle was burning. "And what's that to you? Penuel Jedder's bin gone near six months. This be my house now."

"Oh, no, sir! I don't know none of thee, but this is my house and my land," Rachel stated aggressively.

The man let her go and stared down in astonishment. "Yourn? This land be yourn?" A grin spread over his face. "And who be 'ee then, mommet? Not content wi' robbing me of my vittles, you would rob me of my house as well!" He laughed loudly. "Harken, wench. For the sass of 'ee, us'll let 'ee go, but . . ." He held a thick warning finger close to her face. "Don't never let I see 'ee no more."

"My name is Rachel Jedder. Penuel Jedder was my grandfather and he left all Yellaton to me when he died." In the candlelight she looked like a child of no more than ten years, so spindly and undersized. The man's laughter gave way to a look of bewilderment and then, slowly, to disbelief.

"Penuel Jedder didn't *have* no chillern, but one as disgraced him, so's he wouldn't have no more of her," he growled.

"Grace Jedder was my mother," responded Rachel, standing straight and daring to meet his eyes. "And before he died, he forgave her and left the land to me."

The face above her bloated and the arteries in the man's neck filled and swelled as he looked her over with fierce eyes and then jerked his head contemptuously.

"He niver done that. Him and my father was first cousin and you're no more than a bit of a maid. I knowed Penuel Jedder all my life and this land be mine. You're no blood of 'ee. You be lying, wench."

"I can prove 'tis mine," shouted Rachel, furiously. "There's proof."

He grabbed her arm again. "What then? What proof?"

The parchments were still concealed under her skirts. She had grown so accustomed to wearing the cloth bag attached to her waist that she no longer noticed it, and now for a moment imagined them lost. In the electric charge of fear, her hand moved instinctively to touch them and then stopped halfway. Suddenly she knew they must not be shown to this stranger but must be kept hidden until she herself was safe.

"Things," she muttered lamely.

He pulled her across the floor and opened the door to a deep stair cupboard.

55

"You'll hang for this night, hussy," he promised grimly, and threw her in.

The bolt grated into its slot and Rachel huddled on the floor, trembling. The situation seemed so unreal that she could scarcely bring herself to believe it. Her feelings during the long struggle to reach Yellaton had often been pessimistic. Many times she had pictured the disasters which might await there—the house in ruins, the livestock dispersed or dead, the holding ransacked and empty. Once, at the end of a particularly sodden and solitary march, she had even imagined that no such place existed. But it had never seemed possible that there could be any doubt about her ownership—that Penuel Jedder, her grandfather, had left all his possessions to her. Now, palsied with shock, her ideas slipped and collided out of control, leaving only an overpowering sense of hopelessness.

Her captor was clumping around in the room beyond—a big young man, Devon born, with family and local friends. The many times Rachel Jedder had been refused help or been driven from individual villages or had her travel "pass" scrutinized resentfully had taught her how unwelcome outsiders were. No one from Beara or High Chilham would come to her aid in this. They would whip her from the parish, as they did any vagabond without a certificate of settlement, and the next village would do the same, and the next, forcing her back across England until she died of starvation, or crawled back to the slavery of Wame's farm. Her thoughts screamed in panic, smashing the golden mirage of Yellaton, which had been her inspiration and strength through all the hardships and hungers of the great journey. Her lips moved over her catechism, as though reciting a spell.

". . . And I pray unto God, that he will send us all things that be needful both for our souls and bodies; and that he will be merciful to us and forgive us our sins; and that it will please him to save and defend us in all dangers ghostly and bodily. . . ."

The thin line of light around the door from the candle went out. At last, the man had gone away. Despair turned her breath into sighs and left her body slumped, until utter exhaustion finally blunted the edge of her fear. It was less uncomfortable in the cupboard than lying in a cold, wet wood, and in the end Rachel slept, a night full of tearful dreams.

When the men's voices woke her, the ill-fitting door was framed by daylight and she climbed silently to her knees to press her ear against the crack.

"That's what she said. Old Jedder was her granfer and as how he'd left the place to her. So you got to do summat, Uncle Walter." It was the man who had locked her up the night before.

"Suppose she's right?" The second man sounded doubtful. "Suppose her has Penuel Jedder's written word?"

"No. She'd have showed it last night. There be no paper." The other dismissed the idea. "I'll take oath as how she was stealing bread, and 'twill be simple to be rid of her. You're parish warden."

"Very well, young Matthew Claggett. Like you say, Yellaton be right-fully yours," the other agreed. "Now, fetch the woman and we'll take her afore the Justice."

The cupboard door opened and Rachel was dragged, blinking, before a man of about fifty, with drawn, humorless features, who gave her a look of surprise before exclaiming, "She's but a child, nephew! If her's tried for thieving, it'll be the gallows. We can't send no child to the gallows."

"We can!" retorted Matthew Claggett viciously.

"I'll tell 'ee what, nephew. I'll have her run out of the village, sent back where her come from," he offered.

Rachel flinched, but they took no notice.

"If her don't hang, her'll be back, causing trouble, Walter Riddaway." The young man gripped his uncle's arm urgently. "Yellaton was promised me. What could this chit do with it, and where will I be if I lose it? I'm to wed Amy Bartle in June and I cannot go back to living in at Wey Barton after that."

They spoke as though she was not there in front of them, but Rachel, looking from one to the other, could have read the whole argument from their expressions without hearing a word.

The leader of the parish hunched his head between his shoulders like a withdrawing tortoise and frowned. His nephew shifted restlessly, obviously irritated by the slowness of the decision. There was a long pause. Then Walter Riddaway turned abruptly to leave the room and muttered, almost inaudibly, "Bring her along."

Frightened that they might search her and discover the documents, Rachel had kept silent, not even daring to steal a glance at the room, knowing that the destruction of Penuel Jedder's will would end her only chance of establishing right to the land and mean certain death. So now she went with them without struggle.

Outside, a thick hill fog had reduced the whole world to a few square yards around the house, enclosed in blurred hedges and smoking trees, beyond which it dropped as dull, gray curd. Although there was no hint of the sun, the girl sensed that the time was still very early morning.

The two men set off at a good pace without speaking further, one on either side, the younger with a broad hand on her left shoulder. They took a footpath she had not found the previous night. It ran round the far side of the hare's-leg field and turned sharply downhill toward a small wood, which apparently belonged to the homestead too.

Despite the danger she was in, Rachel Jedder could not help looking about and straining her eyes to see the land, but it was impossible to penetrate the mist. All she could discover was that one field had been plowed, and its earth stuck to her boots in a way the sandy soil of

57

Norfolk would not have done. She wanted to bend and touch it, instead of being hurried away, and the weight of it clinging to her feet dragged at her self-control. Deep inside herself, she began to weep with terrible disappointment. It should all have been so different, bare fields and an empty cottage, a clean-swept fireplace to fill with kindling, time to rub her hands over the rough walls and peer into every corner and pace the boundaries and learn every tree and bush and warren and set, to find out the pockets in the pastures and where the ditches lay and how the ground lifted and fell, to be alone and solitary at Yellaton. To know that it was all her own.

Beech and hazel and ash and oak grew in the wood, picked almost clean beneath by the hogs her grandfather must have run there in summer. It was an eerie place, full of spectral figures and shapes distorted by the clouded air. The path, slimy with winter-rotted leaves, descended gradually, and once, when she slipped, Matthew Claggett gave a spiteful push to keep her a pace ahead.

Rachel knew the fog was to her advantage, and that if she were to escape, it must be before they reached the village, but he did not relax his hold for an instant and Walter Riddaway stayed close as a lover.

They began to cross the moor, the girl following a narrow trail and the men tramping through the heather alongside, moving without words through the restricted circle of their vision, totally enclosed now by the barrier of cloud which muffled all sound and destroyed all sense of direction and raised chimeras of marsh demons, tentacled and horned, and wandering spirits of the moor, which charmed travelers on days like this with their dizzying lights to drown in the bogs, or dance to death in magical caverns beneath the ground.

The first inhuman wail sounded remote and spine-chilling. They all heard it, and the easy stride of the men changed to a nervous scuttle. It skirled again, clamant and close this time, and suddenly, through the swirling mist ahead a monster appeared and sprang howling toward them with glowing eyes and long, pointed teeth and wild gray locks. Rachel's keepers screeched in terror and bolted in opposite directions as the beast leaped upon her, knocking her to the ground.

"By God! You come just in time, Sam," she gasped.

Scrambling to her feet, she stumbled after him, holding onto his tail for safety through the murk. Equipped with a nose which could sniff out a single tadpole in a pond, the gray dog was unhindered by the poor visibility and steadily led the way off the heath and down through a longer stretch of trees, which crowded at last into a valley divided by a fast stream.

By then Rachel could feel the sun through the last veils of the evaporating mist, and the dog turned as she let go his tail and gave him a quick, rare hug.

The brook, with little winding, bubbled into a lake enclosed on three sides by trees, its farthest open shore bordering an expanse of parkland in which a herd of red cattle grazed. A well-used path cut between the shrubs at the water's edge. Now that the air had finally cleared, the sky was revealed blue behind small bundles of white cloud, and Rachel came upon a sheltered, sunny clearing by an inlet. Her boots, which were worn thin and holed in places, had been chafing and her heels were blistered, so, sitting on pale tendrils of early ferns and the tangle of ground ivy, she pulled them off and slid her feet thankfully into the freezing water. It felt good against the broken skin and she squidged mud between her toes as numb bands formed round her ankles.

Matthew Claggett and Walter Riddaway, believing her the victim of a hellhound, would not come searching. They were probably congratulating themselves on their good fortune at being so easily rid of her, she thought to herself, inhaling sharply under a gut-jolting blow of hatred. The lake shimmered like an illusion, its sliding specula of bronze and tarn green mirrored in her eyes, which glared in rage as she longed to ensnare the two in curses of agony and torture and destruction. Her fist closed on a stone and hurled it into the water, which leaped in a cone of white to mark the vow of her revenge.

Sam licked her hand and she stroked his huge head and the soft flaps of his ears absently, growing calmer through the contact until she was able to direct her attention deliberately back to resolving her predicament. If she returned to South Molton, the lawyers there would probably demand money before helping her, or, worse, they might even know Walter Riddaway and produce other documents giving Yellaton and its land to Matthew Claggett after all. Her stomach rumbled loudly, reminding her she had not eaten since the previous afternoon. She had no idea where she was and could not risk going through High Chilham again. She gazed at the sunny park.

A horseman was cantering across it, his big bay rocking like a mettlesome toy, its mane and tail streaming freely and its head high and alert. Rachel recognized the animal before she recognized its master, Squire Waddon of Beara. Straight-backed and dressed in a wine-dark cutaway coat and doeskin breeches, he sat well and looked handsome on the horse, and she smiled as he deliberately scattered the red steers by veering to gallop through them toward the path leading to the mere.

All at once, the way to regain her land was as clear in her mind as if she had been planning it for hours.

She stood up eagerly and then stared with dismay at her clothes. The brown gown, so soft and respectable only a few weeks before, was now ragged and stuck with pieces of straw beneath the old cloak, and the chemise was greasy and certainly full of fleas.

"Yellaton. Yellaton," the voice in her head urged in a tribal chant, and she fumbled with stiff fingers at the buttons.

He had reached the far end of the lake and checked his mount to the

59

long fluent walk of a thoroughbred. The buttons were tiny and they held as though sewn in their holes, and Rachel swore under her breath and wrenched at the dress, so that they flew off like shot. The grace-note beat of hooves vibrated like a drum. Her cloak and dress were on the ground and she was struggling out of her shift. It was much colder than she had realized and her skin pricked and her nipples turned into little pink berries on her unformed chest, at which she frowned crossly. The rider's outline floated between gaps in the bushes. A few strides more and he would be past. She hissed the gray dog away and charged, splashing loudly into the water.

It was like running into fire, ripples of flames licking her body, searing her flesh until she wanted to flee from them screaming. Half turning, she saw the horseman come into the clearing, and an image of the sturdy house on the moor filled her mind. Clenching her fists and screwing up her face, she plunged, letting the furnace of the spring mere close over her head. Its molten metal knocked the air from her lungs and filled the molds of her ears with pain and set fast around her, tighter and tighter, until she was forced upward in a spin, as though squeezed violently from a tube. The squire was standing at the water's edge, staring over.

"Are you drowning?" he asked, with apparent interest.

"Oh, no, sir. I be taking the waters." Rachel gave a ghastly smile. " 'Tis a fashion at the sea, for the health, and 'tis most diverting."

"It is?" He looked doubtful, but his eyes were fixed upon her bare shoulders as, heroically, she kept her flat chest concealed below the surface and tried to look merry.

"Come out, wench," he said. "There are better games, I can promise you."

Rachel sent up a spray of sleet-hard droplets and moved nearer the shallows.

"You'll needs turn your back, your honor, if I'm to come out, 'cos I ain't clothed none," she said, praying he would hurry and not notice how her teeth were chattering.

Instead, he took three long strides into the lake, picked her up in his arms and carried her ashore, laughing as he laid her on the ground and dropped down beside her. Chilled, she clung to him mechanically, as his mouth scorched her blue lips. Afterwards she remembered thinking it was like kissing a baked apple fresh from the oven. Her body was white as a corpse, the nerve endings so deadened with cold that the twigs and pebbles on the ground beneath impressed into her back without hurting, and although his hands moved where they would, she might have been wearing several thicknesses of clothing for all the feeling they aroused. He opened his coat and she fused to him like a poitrel of ice, gripping him in glacial embrace, and he looked down at her pale face and the green weeds tangled in her long black hair, and grinned.

"Damme, 'tis like bedding a mermaiden."

The squire wasted no more time. He was an enthusiastic lover, tilting at her boldly, accurately and with speed, as though setting his horse at a five-bar gate. Rachel closed her eyes tightly and hung onto his shirt and for a few minutes was very roughly and uncomfortably jolted, and then it was over and he flopped across her, his shoulder sealing off her nose and mouth, making it difficult to breath.

She remembered the graceful, sensuous loving of Jack Greenslade, sensitive and tender and full of delight, and how easily they had spiraled to such fine-toned pleasure that even in her dreams it could not be repeated. A pair of tears unexpectedly welled onto her damp cheeks.

She rubbbed them away hurriedly as the man, still panting, rolled off her, hitched up his breeches and winked.

"That were more sport than taking a cold bath, were it not, mermaiden?" he swaggered, throwing her clothes over to her. "But you'd best dress yourself quick, before you catch a less agreeable fever."

He had intelligent, if dissipated, features, and was no more than twenty-five years old, carrot-haired and with the ruddy complexion of a devoted hunter of foxes. He sat on the ground watching her amiably as she pulled on her buttonless gown, then he put his own coat around her and drew her against his side in the sun.

"Now, mermaiden, how much money do you expect for this?"

"Money, your honor?" Rachel was genuinely surprised.

"Well, was it not for money you waylaid me?" he asked, chuckling.

"Oh, no, your worship. I swear it was not," Rachel answered vehemently.

He raised his eyebrows and waited. She felt full of shame and blushed, shaking her head as she reached for the cloth bundle containing the parchments, which was lying in the undergrowth close by.

" 'Tis true that I hoped you would stop, your honor, for I am greatly in need of aid," she whispered, avoiding his amused blue eyes and pushing the roll into his hand. "Please, I beg you to read these papers."

"A mermaiden with a mystery!" he teased, withdrawing his arm from round her and playfully tweaking her small nose before unrolling the documents and glancing over them.

"So you're old Jedder's granddaughter, come to take over Yellaton," he said, handing them back to her. "Well, these papers seem to be in order, so why half-drown in my lake, Rachel Jedder?"

In a flat, unemotional voice, she told him how the news had arrived at Wame's farm three months late and how the journey to Devon had taken a further three months, and then she described the man she had found living on her grandfather's holding and the events of that same morning. No unnecessary details were included and the long pilgrimage to Yellaton was made to sound almost commonplace, but Squire Waddon listened without interrupting and, when the story was finished, regarded her with admiration.

"You say you crossed the breadth of England alone and on foot, mermaiden? Why, few *men* would have dared it." He sat back from her in a movement of subconscious respect. "Upon my oath, Yellaton will be yours. I'll see young Matthew Claggett off the land this day."

Rachel seized his hand and caressed it against her face in a transport of gratitude. He tipped back her head and kissed her deeply and then held her away from him and laughed. Suddenly he seemed as natural and likeable as a young hound, and Rachel laughed back.

"Seems I should have waited till you warmed up, mermaiden." He tugged a lock of her wet hair ruefully. "Stap me, but it was an odd coupling, with you colder than the north wind! Not unpleasing, to be sure, but not to be indulged in often."

As he helped her to her feet, he brought a coin from the pocket of his coat and put it into her hand.

"Leave Penuel Jedder's will with me and I shall see Walter Riddaway this afternoon. Return to Yellaton at dusk. You will find no one there and no one will dispute that the property is yours from that hour on."

He vaulted onto the big bay, turning it neatly on its hocks and raising his hand in salute.

"All good fortune to you, Rachel Jedder," he said, smiling, and cantered away.

Rachel opened her fist and her eyes widened at the sight of the bright gold coin. Squire Waddon had given her a fortune, enough to live on for months and months, a whole guinea.

She sat down slowly and hugged her knees to her chest. She was almost warm again and there was money in her hand. She knew she had made a good friend in him and that Yellaton would finally be hers within only a few hours, and yet she felt melancholy, almost sick at the way it had happened. The young man was well-intentioned and he had thought it all a great romp; so should she, and yet she did not. She stared into the water, only half-understanding the sensation of dull pain. It was as though, for that brief hour, she had been forced to return to pauper servitude to pay for the miracle of her land.

She straightened her back and moved her head to shake off the mood, remembering the resolution made after refusing the fat gentleman at Thetford Forest inn, to make use of all experience, however unpleasant. Brooding was a luxury which only wasted time, and there was no place for it in her life. She had always been exploited, but now she was free and the owner of a house and holding. Nothing else mattered.

Flounces of water swept along the shores and the willows opposite hung their slender branches, verdant with opening leaves, into the shallows, like a row of girls washing their hair. A light haze of insects, brought out by the sunlight, quivered above the surface, and every now and again unwinding springs of ripples betrayed risen trout. An orange-tip butterfly, strayed from the open park, fluttered curiously round

Rachel's head before settling on the fluted leaf of a wild lily, and the strong scent of cinnamon rose as she turned to watch it, bruising a patch of sweet sedge with her hand. Sam came lurching through the mud like a foundering rowing-boat, clambered out, shook himself and padded up, licking his chops. Moorhen and duck bustled about the lake and there were a few small feathers caught in his coat. Rachel glowered at him accusingly, and his breath, stinking of stagnant water and fish, blew over her and confirmed her suspicions.

"Pigbelly!" she pushed him away. "Why didn't you bring it here, with me that empty I could eat horse fodder? Greedy guts! What were it then? A duck, I'll wager. Well, I hope Squire catches you next time."

Despite her intense hunger, she decided to spend the rest of the day there in Great Wood rather than risk meeting up again with the parish warden of High Chilham and his nephew, or with any other hostile person.

It was queer to realize that she had actually spent a night in her own house on her own land without seeing much of either. All her thoughts fixed upon the hour when they would be revealed at last, as though lifted out of a box and laid before her. Yet, although she was so eager, her life of adversity had taught her patience and she was able to make herself comfortable in the quiet clearing and even to spend an hour or two in suspension between sleep and wakefulness as the sun slowly crossed the sky and the shadows wheeled round their objects and the play of light and water enameled the lake with ganoid scales; until bird voices began to crescendo to evensong, and the basking flowers quivered and curled and closed. The half-moon appeared like a shell on the deepening blue, and a fox slipped between the trees like a trailing, rust-brown scarf, and it was cockshut.

The girl and the gray dog walked steadily up the hill and across the moor, deliberately refusing to hurry, delaying the moment the better to enjoy it. As they neared the homestead side of Yellaton wood, they heard voices and cautiously left the path to work their way to where they could see without being seen.

The Squire and one of his servants were watching Matthew Claggett and his uncle sullenly load a pair of pack ponies. Occasionally the Squire would query an object and order them to return it to the house, and once Walter Riddaway appeared in the doorway with a wooden crate full of hens, only to be forced to leave it on the ground.

"But I've worked this place for six month, your honor," Matthew Claggett protested loudly. "I got a right to summat."

"A right to the gibbet for abducting Penuel Jedder's granddaughter," snapped the Squire.

"Pardon the boy, your worship." Riddaway hastily pushed in front of his nephew and bent his head. "He be that maized, he don't know what he'm saying."

"Get on with it, man!" Squire Waddon was obviously becoming dangerously bored with the whole business, and his horse mouthed its metal bits and stamped restlessly. Then, as the two villagers tied the last rope round their loads, he wheeled and galloped off down the path. His servant waited behind until the packhorses were led away before following his master and disappearing into the trees.

Rachel did not move until the last echo of their presence had died and the moor was completely silent. Then she and the dog stepped into the open and walked toward the house of Yellaton.

The sky was washed pink, and to the west, rivers of red gushed from the falling sun between deltas stained sulphur and mulberry, and the linings of the clouds glowed like hot coals, and streaks of harsh color fired at the moon in the cyclic war against the soft gray smothering sand of night. Beneath, the olive swell of the moor rolled smoothly to the horizon, ageless and timeless, its interlocking slopes formed eons before over forests turned to stone, secretive and voluptuous and treacherous, offering little, but frequently vandalizing lives and progress, crops and hope, through storm and rigor and witchery. Yet, to Rachel Jedder on that first night, Beara looked as gentle and peaceful as a sleeping cat under the lurid sky, and she was filled with love for it.

Dusk began to settle over its haunches, changing it into a vanishing landscape of vapors and shadow, a place of the imagination, unreal and full of mystery. The wounded sun died, leaving only a trickle of blood, and Rachel, grown aware of the fading light, turned at last to the house.

Yellaton was built of cob, an ancient mixture of clay, gravel, straw and horsehair, with a roof of thatch. Its walls were several feet thick, rendered and lime-washed. The casements were small, glazed and deeply embedded for protection from the weather. It looked as if it had stood exposed on the brow of that hill for hundreds of years, strong and defiant, as though it had grown out of the very moor, its timbers the last of the petrified forest beneath. The house had a presence which recognized and accepted the girl as belonging there, and its breath was warm and reassuring as she entered.

Behind the stone porch, the front door opened straight into the long room off which she had been held prisoner the night before. Blackened oak beams supported the low ceiling and a high-backed oak settle stood to one side of the ingle opposite a plain elm chair. There was a window seat and shutters to close against the winter gales and a rugged table. Rachel went from one to the next of the furnishings, fingering each with awe and gazing about at the rough plastered walls, quite unable to absorb that they all belonged to her. She felt tense and daring, as though trespassing. Her small familiar cloth bundle lay on the floor and she picked it up to hold it tightly, almost for defense, and was surprised to realize that she was even slightly afraid.

During her travels the land had constituted all her prospects. She had pictured the house, of course, but always from the outside, seeing it only in relation to the fields and heath, while its interior had remained a vague, safe cave. Now, after the simplicity of owning no more than a cooking pot and a tinderbox and sleeping wherever her tired limbs folded, it seemed too large and too full of objects. She approached the settle warily, never having sat on such a piece before, and perched primly on its edge, with ankles crossed and knees together and her hands folded in her lap like a lady.

Sam ambled through the open door and padded around, his long tail banging against the walls as he inspected each corner. Then he walked to the table, lifted his leg, urinated casually against it and strolled out.

Rachel leaped up with a yawp of horror and ran a few steps. The liquid was trickling down to form a puddle on the flag floor and she stopped to gape at it, transfixed. Then her whole body began to shake as a wave of hysteria rose and broke in wild, rollicking shouts, and she laughed until her eyes puffed with tears and her face and stomach ached and she was sprawled weakly in the wooden chair, and every time the gulping hiccups began to ease, the recollection of the gray dog's sublime unconcern set off a new spasm, until she was rolling about completely helpless, all the apprehension gone. And the sobbing laughter became gurgles of chuckles and then little spurts of giggles and finally a wide and happy grin.

Last light was dimming fast and she lit the candle, no longer nervous, but joyful. The room drew into the gentle glow, and, for the first time since her birth, Rachel felt absolute security enfold her with its metal petals into a center impregnable against the brutal elements and rootlessness and despots of her past. This was the meaning of home, she knew suddenly, and for as long as she held on to the house of Yellaton, Yellaton would hold on to her. She looked about her with a new and profound contentment.

A door in the corner led to a narrow flight of wooden stairs and she climbed them eagerly, cupping the flame in her hand. They led to a passage which ran the length of the house, with a dipping ceiling and uneven walls in which were four doors.

Rachel opened the first and walked into a smell of apples and onions as thick as a curtain and, seconds later, was hit smartly on the forehead by something hanging near the door. Raising the candle, she saw strings of onions suspended from the white-limed beams, and a floor covered a foot deep with dead leaves. Feeling around in this crackling carpet, her fingers soon found the first apple and she bit into it hungrily. Its sharp sweetness filled her mouth like wine, and her eyes closed as her nostrils flared to catch its spicy scent. Laying the candle holder in the doorway and munching greedily, she rummaged in the leaves again with beating heart and pulled out another two coarse-skinned fruits, still surprisingly

65

firm after the long winter, and there were obviously many more lying safely stored. She leaned against the wall savoring every mouthful, ecstatic at the realization that she was surrounded by food in plenty and that Yellaton would never let her starve again. She saved the cores carefully, picked out two more apples and closed the door behind her.

The next room smelled musty and was empty except for a truckle bed and chair, both of oak and obviously homemade. There was a damp patch shaped like a grotesque face on the ceiling and spiders' webs formed sticky black traps in the corners and over the small window. It seemed a sad and neglected place, which made Rachel shiver and turn away.

The third door opened into what must have been her grandparents' bed chamber. It contained a chest of drawers and a big four-poster bed, in which Matthew Claggett had apparently been sleeping for the cover was dirty and tangled, just as he had left it that morning. Rachel pulled it off with instinctive distaste, to discover a bulging, big mattress beneath, a real feather bed. She dived in and sank so deeply she could not imagine the cover ever being necessary. The mattress billowed up around her like cotton wool, so light and snug it would have seduced her to sleep in minutes had the gray dog not begun barking below and an alarmed clucking reminded her that the crate of hens was still lying at his mercy outside the front door.

The last door in the corridor was ajar and showed a second flight of stairs leading down. Rachel hurried as fast as her long skirts and the flickering candle would permit and, at the bottom, found herself in the kitchen.

Shouting the dog's name angrily, she raced through to the long room in time to see him pawing violently at the fragile timber of the crate, while the hens scrabbled over each other, cackling in terror. Rachel smacked him hard on the snout, which made him blink and sit down in bewilderment, so that she immediately felt guilty.

"Well, you got to learn, Sam. These isn't fowl for thieving. These is *our* birds and you're to leave them be," she tried to explain, not meeting his eyes, and then turned away to drag the crate into the kitchen.

There, opening it cautiously, she caught the nearest hen, and turning it upside down, she felt the gap two fingers wide between its pelvic bones and smiled to herself. It was in lay and there would be eggs to eat. The next bird was less satisfactory, the space between the bones being almost closed. Rachel took its feet in one hand and its head in the other and jerked, breaking its neck expertly. The reflex of its nerves thrashed its wings for a minute, and when it went limp, she plucked it before it had time to grow cold. The rest of the released birds flew in ruffled confusion to their perches for the night.

Kicking the ashes aside in the hearth, Rachel laid and lit kindling from a heap on the floor, blowing hard with a pair of bellows to speed the

66

flames and then propping a tent of split logs over them. Soon the walls were running with hectic reflections and the room was alive with cracking wood and the savory smoke of burning ash.

She put the plucked hen in a rusty iron cauldron, half filled with water from a bucket left by Matthew Claggett, and hung it over the fire on the iron chimney crane.

As it boiled, she began to sort through the clutter of discarded junk littering the room, examining each item and making individual mounds by the back door to take outside in the morning—tools, harness, logs and debris. She worked fast in a bustle of excited activity, sweeping dazed hens off the table, stacking the dirty platters and pots in a corner and yelling happily at Sam every time he gave in again to the temptation of a roosting bird.

There was an egg in a wooden measure and another in a large dough trough, which her grandmother must have used to make bread. Rachel thought about her as she dropped them into the bubbling water beside the chicken. What had been her name? Where had she come from? When had she died?

She tipped a chair forward, sending its load of rubbish skidding to the floor and, moments later, sat down to peel her boiled egg, putting the other down on the straw for Sam, who swallowed it, scalding and complete with shell, in a gulp. She would find out about them all, Penuel Jedder and his wife, their brothers and sisters and nephews and nieces, her uncles and aunts, who must have died in infancy, even such as Matthew Claggett, who, she realized for the first time, was related to her, too. All her family.

It took over two hours to clear the kitchen and Rachel finished feeling as lively as when she began. By then the fowl was cooked, and she planned to work all night on the rest of the house as soon as she had eaten.

She lifted it onto a circular wooden trencher and its appetizing smell exploded, causing the gray dog to dribble and Rachel to burn her fingers and then her lips while tearing off the first leg and biting into it ravenously. The meat came away from the bone easily in thick slivers, firm and succulent. She held the joint with both hands, leaned her elbows on the table and buried her mouth and chin in the fuming thigh, gnawing and champing, the juices smearing her face and running down her neck, her eyes closed tight in an ecstasy of feeding, the rich steam condensing in her hair and clothes and blotting out all other senses except the glutting of her hunger.

She threw the stripped bones to the floor and dug her nails in above the wishbone, ripping away the soft, white flesh of the breast and stuffing it between her teeth until her cheeks bulged and her jaws ached. The dog crunched the bones and laid his huge head on her knee and moaned. Rachel paused from gobbling the second leg to peel off the skin of the bird, like a fat-caked cloth, to give to him, along with both wings and the parson's nose.

When her own stomach felt packed to discomfort at last, she moved over to the seat in the inglenook to rest for a few minutes before starting work again. There, in the funnel of heat, her eyes became dazzled by the lights of the capering blaze and closed, not to open until morning.

CHAPTER FIVE

The farm buildings were set behind the house in a square, enclosing a cobblestoned courtyard, in the center of which was the well. Rachel Jedder, newly wakened, was about to fetch water when a muffled groan carried through the kitchen wall and drew her attention to a door, so shadowed that it had remained unnoticed the night before.

In the shippen beyond, two garnet-red cows were tethered. They had short, blunt horns and sturdy hind- and forequarters, and bellies swelled, like risen dough, with ripening calves. She stared at them in disbelief and then with a rapture which made her skin crawl, and they returned her gaze through dark eyes stretched with watchfulness.

It had seemed almost certain that all her grandfather's stock had been sold after his death, except perhaps for a few near-wild sheep out on the moor, and so the appearance of these two milk-full, fruitful, sweet-breathed beasts suddenly touched the future with gold. Rachel Jedder knew that their milk would make cream and butter and cheese to market and food for herself, the dog, the poultry, a pig, and for their own two calves, which in turn would provide heifer followers to build up the herd of her ambition, or bull beef for salting and selling. Their dung would rot down into compost to enrich the land, increasing the harvest, making succulent the grass. And at the end of the great cycle of their lives, after their leather had been turned into heavy boots or jerkins or thornproof mittens for hedging and pads for the thatcher's moleskin trousers, and their hollowed horns had been carved into handle and spoon, drenching cup and ointment holder, even their dried blood and crumbled bones would be returned to feed the soil which had sustained them. They were the foundation of survival and the promise of prosperity, and Yellaton would grow upon their backs.

Rachel felt awestruck by her own luck. It was like having a wish granted before it had been made, and she walked around the two animals in simple joy, stroking their warm backs as their ears flicked to track her movements, and noticing how summer coats already lay silken on their heads and necks, although the jacket of winter fur still wrapped them from shoulder to hip. They looked alert and, although a little thin, in unusually good condition after the long winter. Matthew Claggett had cared for them well.

The temptation to run out and see the rest of the holding immediately was almost irresistible, but Rachel guessed that the exploration would take several hours, and meanwhile both she and the red cows were hungry. She pitched hay to them from a heap in the corner and then, not knowing where the dairy was, fetched a terra-cotta jug from the kitchen and, crouching down beside the nearest, directed darts of thin milk into it. Although they were obviously near the end of their lactation, the combined yield was more than enough for her needs. She drank a draught straight from the pitcher and then ladled out a bowlful for the dog and another for the hens, which she chased, shrieking and casting feathers, from the house.

Off the kitchen, a cold, north-facing pantry lined with slate shelves contained one almost-empty barrel of salted-down pork, two hard farm cheeses and a flitch of fat bacon, from which she cut her breakfast to eat on the way.

On the other side of the back door was a utility room and beyond that a storeroom with crocks of flour and flax bags of seed and potatoes, and two casks of cider and one of beer; an end door led to the dairy, where all the work surfaces and shelves were also of slate. Upon them stood earthenware and tin setting dishes and fleeters for cream, a pair of sycamore beaters, scotch hands and a coopered plunger churn for butter making.

A dairy yoke hung on the wall. It was made of willow, skin-smooth and neat as a high collar, and a fine patina glazed the grain, the polish of long use. It might have been carved by the same hand which had made the elm chair and oak table in the house with such skill. Certainly it was a much better yoke than the crudely chiseled one at Wame's farm, and it showed, Rachel thought as she tried it on, how much Penuel Jedder must have cared for her grandmother. It lay light and comfortable across her narrow shoulders and was so well balanced that when she attached a pair of scrubbed wooden buckets to its hooks she hardly felt their extra weight.

Unexpectedly Rachel realized that her own mother, Grace, must have used the yoke, too, to carry the milk years before, and all at once she felt lonely. It would have been so good to share all this with friends. How she and Sarah Hallet and Thomasin Tripp and Harry Stuckley's wife would have run from room to room of the house, pointing out each amazing object and screeching together, and poor young Sam from Wame's farm would have clung to her, stuttering over the little room full of apples, and Jack Greenslade would have turned somersaults and hugged her tight as they happened on each find together.

She slowly put the yoke back in its place and looked around the dairy again, and its cleanliness and order confronted her moment of depression like an accusation. Yellaton was giving her gifts beyond even the secret hopes of most men, gifts Matthew Claggett would have murdered for. Every essential was being provided: shelter and food, fertility and tools, space in which to keep the harvests and the stock, a real home in which to marry and grow sons and prosper. Only her own effort and faith were being asked in return. Contrite, she pressed her fingertips against the limewashed wall and then stepped out into the courtyard.

Every essential was being provided. Suddenly Rachel knew what waited opposite in the long, low reflection of the house. She knew as though it were visible through the dense cob. With clenched hands, she ran to the wide door and through into the darkness, stumbling as her eyesight adjusted to the change, umbras gradually hardening into big, solid objects as she pushed past, hurrying the length of the building to where it was waiting, part of the last, vast shadow. She flung open the other door in the wall behind and a wedge-shaped block of sunlight slid forward. Penuel Jedder's horse looked down at her with gentle interest.

Rachel burst into tears without knowing why. Tears as large as glass beads dropped over the curve of her cheeks, past her open, smiling, crying mouth and down her neck and the bony expanse beyond, to be absorbed damply by the facing of her frock. Her happiness was as keen as pain.

The mare bent her neck and blew through her nostrils, standing quite still as her new owner approached. Although she was only of medium height, her withers not much higher than the girl's head, she looked strong, with muscular flanks and shoulders and straight, clean legs. Rachel wiped her eyes briskly and put a hand on the lowered head. The mare did not jerk back, but allowed her to scratch behind her ears and rub her long, white-blazed nose and finally hold her whiskered muzzle with both hands and open her mouth. The marks of the front teeth had disappeared and dental star was present, and there was a hook on the back edge of the corner incisors in the upper jaw. She was no more than seven years old, with many years of working and breeding life ahead.

The girl tried to recall everything she had noticed in and around the stables at Wame's farm. The handling of working horses was a mastery strictly reserved for the teamsmen, the horsemen, most valued of all farm workers, and so she would have only her few remembered observations for tuition. She found a corn box and tipped a scoopful into the manger before topping up the rack with hay. The horse dropped her mouth into the feed, exhaling noisily with pleasure, and forgot her new owner.

· · ·

Heat raked the outside of the stable like dragons' breath and stopped Rachel Jedder with unnerving force as she emerged so that she gasped audibly. It was like stepping into what seemed to be a cool, shallow pool and feeling boiling waters close over her head.

While she had been finding her way around the house and buildings, the sun had rolled closer to the world, and now the air rippled like fluid, lifting haystack and trees and shed, earthbound giants, to quiver in its currents, and the barn on the left rocked and bulged against the shock of this freak foretaste of summer.

As she raised her face to the hot fingers of light, they pressed her eyelids closed and electrified her skin and pushed her back against the wall, and then something mystical happened. The sun swooped nearer, a rushing lava with rays like spears, blaze upon blaze, melting her hair into a helmet of tar, stopping her nose and mouth with burning wire wool, dissolving her muscles, cauterizing her bones; the smell of iron-branded hooves, ashes to ashes, heat beyond endurance, until it seemed she was transnatured into the ancient structure of Yellaton itself, and the spirit of the land concentrated into a sublime white flame about her and consumed her very soul.

Distantly, she understood that she was no longer an isolated and rootless creature, but joined irrevocably with the place, and possessed. It was as though she had traveled out of time and beyond materiality to absorb the essence of all those who had gone before, right back two thousand years to the old Celt who had first gouged the hare's-leg field out of the Great Wood.

She returned, disoriented, imagining herself lying on embers and then surprised, upon opening her eyes, to find herself still leaning against the wall, her body wet with sweat, staring ahead at a footpath which led across the clearing in front of the barn to a small orchard. She walked unsteadily to it, pulled off the torn and rancid wool dress and sat down on the grass in her shift. The heat clanged around the parasol of branches like a cage.

Rachel did not seek explanations for the strange experience, because visions and miracles and supernatural phenomena were not uncommon, and each step she had taken since her arrival had led there. The gathering of the first handful of soil had brought awareness that this windswept hill on the rim of the moor was much more than a piece of good fortune, more than a mere acquisition, and so it was easy to accept the confirmation of that belief.

The stained glass of the new leaves turned the glare of the sun into church light, mote-filled and soft, and the lichen-covered bark felt refreshing against her bare arm. Most of the trees were gnarled and cankerous with age, but a few had been planted in recent years as replacements, and she observed with satisfaction that between them they would provide plenty of apples for making cider, a drink to which she

had quickly adapted since reaching the West Country, and even preferred to ale.

Knots of pink-veined buds overhead began to loosen in the warmth, a
few petals opening to release a wisp scent of apple blossom lighter than
dew, and a fleet of seven straw skeps moored below fired bees noisily into
the flowers. Ants herded their aphids underground for milking. An
alarmed earwig, exposed by an upturned stone, gathered her pale babies
under her abdomen and hid them, like an old hen. The orchard, which
might have seemed passive to a hurrying man, was frantic with activity
to Rachel's hungry eye. The herbage swayed and shivered and stirred
and twitched and the ground vibrated under the microscopic feet of
thousands.

A tiny fly flew into the navel of a web near her resting face and tugged
at the skeins, as though ringing a bell to bring the spider crabbing over to
inject the drop of poison with a bite. The victim's struggles lessened, then
ceased against the creeping paralysis. The spider returned to the outer
cord of its web and the bloodbank of the fly hung alive and immobilized.

All belonged to her. She was excited by the thought. The fruit grove
and grasses, the dark earth, the inexorable insects were hers; even the
beech opposite the barn, so mighty a tree that a cross section of its bole
would have made a table large enough to seat all King Arthur's knights,
and its lowest boughs were as thick as the trunks of more common trees.

Centuries before, in its youth, the winds pushing toward Exmoor had
continually elbowed it aside so that folds had developed in its smooth
gray hide and the crown of massed twigs had been swept off-center. Yet
the branches had gone on stretching and spreading until now it stood,
like a prehistoric, many-tentacled sea anemone, groping at the ocean of
the sky and reducing the house and stables and cowshed and barn and
orchard beneath to pebbles. Rachel could see through its skirt of young
leaves to the bare reaches high above, higher even than the spire of
Norwich Cathedral.

"Mine," she said aloud to convince herself. "Mine." And then was embarrassed by the blasphemy.

Her thoughts floated away and nearly an hour passed before she eased
to her feet again to walk on between the trees. There was a small mucky
enclosure beyond the barn, the emptiness of which was explained by the
fat bacon, hams and salt pork in the house, and the girl pondered over
how to raise money for a piglet. At seven shillings sixpence, it would be
an expensive though necessary investment to ensure next winter's meat,
but if the cows gave quality milk after calving, it might be possible to sell
or barter butter enough—maybe even to buy a second small pig to breed
from later.

In Norfolk the mistress had sold butter for one shilling twopence per
pound weight at Shaltam. Rachel picked up a stick and made several
rows of scratches in the dusty ground and then scored through each in

turn. It took some minutes to calculate that, if the price were the same here, she would need to sell thirteen pounds of butter for the two hogs. She grinned suddenly at the picture of herself working out how to make and spend more than a half-sovereign—she who had never held so much as a farthing in her hand until three months ago.

The three fields of Yellaton met at a corner by the pigsty, the little hare's leg bearing to the left; the plowed land she had crossed the day before with her captors, and which she later discovered was known as Yonder Plat, bordered by the apple trees behind and the wood, to the far right; and Brindley, at five acres the largest, lying between the other two.

Brindley was evidently the field reserved for the hay cut. Summer and autumn grazing by sheep the previous year had close-cropped the turf, preventing coarse Yorkshire fog and bent and creeping couch from suppressing the fine-bladed Timothy and meadow fescues, which now grew long and glossy, breeze-brushed into silky feathering on the wing of the rise and tinted with sorrel plants. Thistles spiked through here and there and Rachel noted them with mixed sentiments as she walked round the edge, for although each would have to be rooted out, their presence was a sign of rich and fertile soil.

George, the cowman at Wame's farm, had once told her the funny story of a blind farmer and his son who went to inspect a farm up for sale. Upon arrival, the old man had ordered his son to tie the horses to the nearest large thistle, and when the boy replied that there were no thistles the farmer had turned right around and gone home.

Over the surrounding hedge she could see her own small woodland tacked onto the horn of the moor like a horseshoe, its last trees straggling into Great Wood itself, which when spread down the hillside, blocked the long valley and finally climbed again to fringe High Chilham village, picked out clear and vivid on top of the opposite knap.

Rachel inhaled slowly as her eyes scanned the view. Beyond the white houses and square-towered church, the land slanted past the Squire's distant mansion and park, down to where two rivers crossed the lowlands, curving to east and west like a moat around the fortress of Beara, and from there the countryside lifted in harmonious domes across a comforting band of small farms and villages to where Exmoor reared at last to form the entire northern horizon with a sweep of color, plum-brown paint strokes on charcoal slopes; greens, verdant and muted and raw and fading in swatches and patches along its heights. Thirty miles from hidden Combe Martin to Monksilver. Across all England there had been nowhere comparable.

On impulse, she grasped two handfuls of the long, lush grass and pulled them from the sward, bruising them in her fists to free the sweet tang of their juices before sitting on the ground and flinging them into the air to land all over her hair and face and breasts.

Work would start tomorrow and there might never again be another such day in which to discover and dream, rest and eat, stroll and marvel, luxuriously unrestricted by time or duty.

The flint years in the workhouse and at Wame's farm had left Rachel Jedder emotionally stunted. Apart from affection for little Sam, the apprentice, she had experienced only feelings of fear and hatred, and the journey to Devon had been too hazardous to permit more than the slightest relaxation of her habitual guard. She had learned to appreciate beauty with surprise, through exquisite scenery unexpectedly revealed and through having the time to look. Jack Greenslade had touched her for a moment and then frightened her off, so, although she would not have admitted even to this, only the gray dog had managed to fawn his way close.

But Yellaton made love persistently and potently to all her senses through the rich smells of its earth and blossoms and the salad taste of fresh beech leaves; honeysuckle and convolvulus caught at her fingers with their tendrils; and its birds, in the passion of their spring pairing, sang all their songs for her. In every direction the landscape was of such piercing beauty that it gave almost physical shock. Yellaton offered the sanctuary of its thick walls and thorny hedgerows, promised faith for her faith and would not be denied.

Rachel rolled over to lie like a hare in the grass, bright-eyed and content, with the sun on her back, swinging and crossing her bare legs and breathing in the summer spice of her own cantle of the world, amazed and thankful and full of love at last.

The rustle in the hedge sounded like the gray dog returning from his own explorations and she pretended to sleep, waiting for him to paw at her shoulder and push her head with his nose. When nothing happened, she looked up again to see the whiskered face of an elderly man staring through a gap in the shrubs. His eyes widened and watered at the sight of the girl in her chemise, and then the head withdrew.

"Good morning," she called after him mischievously. "I am Rachel Jedder."

There was quite a long pause before a gruff voice answered, "Daniel Lutterell." And his footsteps sounded in stumping retreat across the adjoining pasture.

Well, at least she did not have Walter Riddaway for a neighbor, she thought to herself, smiling over the image of the affronted old face. Standing up, she could see that his bordering field sloped to others, which were stopped by the spinney where the charcoal burners had their clearing, but the fact that there was no farmhouse in sight established that his holding stretched farther than that.

Rachel climbed the embankment, watched his diminishing figure and then dropped down into Yonder Plat. This had been divided into two sections to give an acre of winter wheat, planted last year and already well grown, and an acre and a half plowed and recently tilled, most probably with barley. Weeding would be one of the first chores, she realized wryly.

Her rambling tour took her back through the woods to where an iron-flavored spring dribbled into a moss-clogged trickle, and on through her grandfather's vegetable garden, overgrown and rank with rotting cabbage stumps. She sniffed and rubbed at the heavy chocolate loam with fascination and drew more water from the well, finding a fern-covered cold shelf cut into its wall near the top and admiring the plunge of its sheer rock shaft, thirty feet to the liquid black eye.

In early afternoon she turned the mare into the small pasture and watched her roll with clumsy enjoyment, hooves scrabbling in the air, heavy body thumping from side to side, neck straining with the effort, looking as though she would never manage to rise again, and then, astonishingly, scrambling to her feet with a doglike shake before settling down to graze with matronly dignity. She looked to be in foal, and Rachel crossed her fingers, wishing it not to arrive for another month, for May-born horses were known to be unreliable.

From around the hare's leg, she picked the last of the primroses and counted the number of different hardwood shrubs in its hedge. The other fields had hedges made only of beech and thorn, but this one also had hazel, rowan, oak, elder, ash and holly. Rachel did not know that this signified its great age, one hundred years for each specimen. The old Celt himself had probably trodden out the path by which she, too, had first arrived.

And the sun shone all that cloudless day, highlighting golden hairs in the mare's black back and the steel needles on the nettle leaves, catching in the red rooster's iridescent tail, flashing in the windows of the old house, warming earth and blood, quickening life and illuminating all the marvelous spectacle that was Devon.

By the ancient boundary hedge, Rachel listened to the steady champing of her horse and the blackbird in the thicket, and saw Beara roll south to become a forest, and then the blue-gray aloofness of Dartmoor and, finally, the faintest of shadows, like islands low in the sky, Roughtor and Brown Willie of Bodmin Moor. It was as though the whole of the west was flaunting itself in the light and the heat and the sun just for her, pouring love potions into her and binding her with a heartbreaking spell from which there would be no escape.

It was difficult to know where to start. The barley needed hoeing and the sheep, if there were any, should be found on the moor and the horse should be worked. The neglected garden needed clearing and planting with vegetables for herself and potatoes to feed the pigs. There was no bread baked, and dozens of small jobs had been exposed by her tour.

Rachel Jedder, rising before dawn, thought to try a few hours at each task, to achieve something of everything.

It was a dank morning and the fire took a long time to light. The cows were sulking, refusing to let down their milk to her strange touch, the one in the far stall kicking so determinedly that she had to be clouted—which made matters worse—and then hobbled. The gray dog found and ate two new-laid eggs before she could stop him, and by the time the first long furrow for the seed potatoes was trenched, what remained of the brown dress had disintegrated, she was soaked through with drizzle and perspiration, and her tough-skinned hands were torn and full of thorns from the brambles. Back in the kitchen, the fire was nearly out and had failed to heat the cloam oven in the wall.

It was while she was chewing morosely on a piece of cheese that she realized all the laborious hand digging was completely unnecessary. She tutted over her own stupidity. There was a small one-horse plow alongside the tools in the shed, and she had often watched young Sam and the teamsman at Wame's harness up, and seen the big plow there slice easily through the soil, its mould board inverting all the weeds. It would be easy.

The mare tolerated her inexperienced fumblings with good nature and forgave her for not knowing to lay the plow on its side for sliding over the ground before urging her on; and they managed to reach the garden in under an hour. Rachel set her at a tangled stretch of land and she threw herself willingly into the collar. The plowshare bit was dragged forward a few feet, and stopped as the coulter became caught in a large root. When the girl went to inspect it, the mare veered to the right and the whole contraption capsized, causing the animal to kick over her draught chains in fright. Rachel calmed and freed her, manhandled the plow upright and rehitched her, and by then the ground was churned to mud.

They tried again on an expanse clear of undergrowth. The mare strained, the implement dug in, moiled very slowly forward and stopped, leaving the girl to puzzle out how to adjust the coulter and wheels and bear down on the handles to make a more shallow cut before the next attempt. Then muck built up on the wooden board like pastry and had to be scraped off with a stone before the furrow turned and they could move on—to stick once more; and the wet earth turned into a thick soup around her ankles as they tried again and again, and then again, the girl pulling and heaving pointlessly, the share clogged in the sod, the wheels encrusted. The mud spat all over them and sucked the plow, gurgling and helpless, into its gummy bog, and, in trying to haul it out, the mare sweated and groaned, her legs buckling, until Rachel, sobbing with frustration, became afraid that the foal might be lost if they continued. Besides, it was dusk. The day had gone.

Disconsolately she left the plow overturned in the rain and led the horse to the stable, washed her down, tied a matting of straw over her steaming back and fed her. It was dark now and Rachel herself was shivering too much to be bothered trying to find food in the cold kitchen before crawling upstairs to bed.

Daylight showed that her dress and shift were beyond repair. Wrapping their remnants over her quaking shoulders, she peered around the room and saw a small closet set in the wall. Inside lay a bundle of old clothes, and, pulling them out, she realized they had belonged to her grandfather—three smocks, two shirts, stockings, breeches and a waistcoat. There was no sight of anything which might have been worn by a woman. Her grandmother's garments must have been given away after her death, as was the custom.

Apparently her grandfather had not been a big man, although the clothes were still far too large for Rachel. She giggled over the breeches, with their front flap; but there was a pair of strong greased boots, which would fit when stuffed with strips of her torn clothes, and the smocks would cover her to the ground. They were made of coarse dowlas and so voluminous she could wear layers of rags beneath for warmth. Best of all, there was a coat, tough and durable, to give protection from the rain. It, too, reached the floor when she put it on, and the sleeves flopped over her hands like hoods. She rejected the temptation to cut them to size with a knife. If the coat were to serve a long time, it would have to be properly stitched and well treated.

She picked up the breeches again. These were made of stout cotton fustian with leather patches at the knees. Wind threw rain against the window. The linen smock would soon be saturated, but not these. With a self-conscious snigger, she pulled them on, buttoned the bottoms, nearer her ankles than her knees, and padded off to the kitchen to find a piece of straw string to tie around the waist.

It was too late to waste time lighting the kitchen fire, so she milked and fed the bad-tempered cows, looked after the poultry and the horse, and set off optimistically for the garden with a spade over her shoulder and Sam at her heels.

For days the rain fell and waterlogged the soil, which grew heavier and heavier to dig. It was far too cold and wet to think of tilling the vegetable seeds in the storeroom, which would have washed away or rotted. The yeast, saved from the last brewing of beer, was going sour, and so the bread she baked came out hard and flat. One cow went dry and the kitchen was as filthy as it had been when Matthew Claggett had lived there.

Twice Rachel Jedder went out on the moor to search for the sheep, following a narrow, deerlike trail which scratched through the heather to the south of the house and crossed another, wider track within half a mile. She was afraid to stray from these in case she lost her way, because

Yellaton clouded over behind her and quickly disappeared. The gale bullied and jostled, making her ears ache and her nose run, and raindrops bit her cheeks like swarming mosquitoes. The rutted, matted moorland was alien, without cottage or beast and, when she called out occasionally, in the hope that the sheep, or even some other person, might hear, the wind simply absorbed the cry, as though it had never been.

Then, during her second search, bells sounded fairylike a long way off, and Rachel closed her eyes gratefully for a second. She had found them.

Hurrying to the top of the next rise, she searched the out-of-focus terrain ahead and saw, moving like a cloud along the floor of the combe, a great flock, several hundred strong, being herded by a man and a pair of bustling dogs. She had turned away, disappointed, before realizing that the shepherd might well have seen her grandfather's sheep and would certainly know how to recognize them.

She ran swiftly down the hill, bounding over the clumps of ling and past the spur-heeled whin, shouting. The man stopped and inspected her through small, stupid eyes. He was short and square in his smock, and his nose and mouth sloped forward like a muzzle from his forehead, giving him the look of one of his own ewes. Rachel smiled, but he did not smile back.

"Pardon, master, but have you seen the sheep belonging to Penuel Jedder?" she asked politely.

He stared for so long she thought he was not going to reply.

"Penuel Jedder was my grandfather." She felt she should explain.

There was another lengthy pause before he said slowly, as though unaccustomed to speech, "I bain't no maister."

"Your pardon," she apologized, quickly. "But do you know where his sheep are?"

"I be John Thorne's shepherd, maid." The man shook his head at her mournfully. "Ben Squance I be called."

Rachel sighed inwardly and repeatedly slowly, "I am looking for Penuel Jedder's sheep. He was my grandfather. Do you know them?"

Suddenly the man swung his hazelwood crook, which hissed as though alive and fastened round the hind leg of one of the flock, making Rachel jump nervously at the speed of it; but the shepherd paid no heed. With a twist of his wrist, he turned the overfleeced animal onto its back and pointed to the letter *T* branded on its nose. Then he released it and drew a triangle in the soil with the tip of the crook.

"*That* be the mark of Jedder sheep," he said, pointing down at it.

He stood gazing blankly as she climbed the hill once more and turned for home. She waved, but he did not wave back. After that, she decided to wait for finer days before going out to search again.

For the next weeks Rachel Jedder floundered desperately about, rushing from one intractable task to the next, unable to find what she needed, rarely knowing how to do anything properly, trying to tackle skills which men spent years learning. Too lightweight to move heavy obstacles or uproot deeply embedded brushwood, she did not even succeed in planting five rows of potatoes.

The same rain woke her again and, feeling exhausted, she slumped further into the bed and let the feather mattress puff warmly round her. It was so good to lie safely there, listening to the storm beating on the old house, and she admitted to herself that even in the worst of it Yellaton and Beara were always movingly beautiful: rain, shutting out the entire landscape like a dusty window; or flying in from the southwest, fleet as a great black swan, blotting out Dartmoor and then the forest, chasing and mounting and finally subduing the light; or gliding like a veiled bride over the moors, trailing elegant long-fingered hands through the heather and followed, far off, by pearly streaks of fair weather forerunning another shower.

It could be done, she thought, remembering the widow who had kept a cow and geese and a pig without much trouble on a few acres in Sauton. She had owned less land than Rachel but had also been very, very old. Rachel knew it could be done and searched in her mind to discover where she was going wrong. The answers filtered slowly through her drowsiness.

On many days she had gone without food altogether and on the others her only nutrition had been small pieces of cheese, bacon and an apple. Her last real meal had been the chicken killed on the night she had taken possession. Surrounded by plenty, there had been no time since then to eat properly. In the mornings she had been in too much of a hurry, and too tired at night, when the house itself had been cold, unlit and unwelcoming. It occurred to her, in the healing coziness of the feather bed, that although she had always been accustomed to extreme hardship, hot meals and one warm place to sit were not luxuries but necessities for anyone working to the limit of strength outside in all weathers.

Then she considered the design of the past weeks—how, on the way to start cutting back a hedge, she would sharpen a rusty billhook and see that the scythe and the sickle needed attention, too, and then remember that the cream pans in the dairy had not been washed, and notice that a latch had come off a door and that rain was flooding into the stable from an overflowing water barrel. These and a few more minor matters could use up the time until mid-afternoon, allowing only a few hours for work on the hedge, and in the following days a whole series of new crises would prevent her from returning to finish it.

Perhaps it required as much tenacity to put aside the less important chores as it did to force herself to attack seeming impossibilities, such as the clearing of the choked ditch down the moor side of Yonder Plat. Rachel understood at last that it would take more than willingness to labor and good intentions to make a success of Yellaton. Strict organization was needed.

From now on, after the basic daily care of the animals, she must take on only one specific job at a time and refuse to be diverted by other than emergencies until it was completed. In this way, slow and steady progress could be made. She would also stop and be idle for a short time in the middle of each day, and eat cooked food at night, and on Sundays she would try to do only essential milking and stock feeding in order to spend the rest of the day less strenuously, sewing and tidying the house and planning out the coming week.

Heartened, she dressed without haste and went downstairs, and it was not long before she was sitting on the settle beside a log fire in the parlor, dipping the hard bread into a bowl of hot, fresh milk, with the dog stretched like a long, shaggy mat under her feet. It was Sunday.

As though her wishes had been overheard, the weather lifted at last to gusty, drying days with turgid gray cumulus drawn in convoy across the sky and shafts of sun directed over the land like searchlights. First the air and then the soil warmed, and Rachel raked the ridge over the last line of potatoes, spaced the peas and beans out in their trenches, like beads for threading, and seasoned rows and rows of shallow drills with sprinklings of pepper-fine seed. It was a late planting, but she guessed that most of the seed would still develop and fill out through the summer. Nature always ruled for growth.

In her circuit around the holding each afternoon, her eyes grew wiser to the promptings of each field. The barley leaf was as long as her middle finger, and the grass to be mown for hay was already taller than the winter wheat and making almost visible growth. She could see minute nodes of emerging flowers roughening its stems. One more week and it would be ripe. She stared to the light, bright south and hoped.

Apart from scandalizing old Lutterell and the brief meeting with Ben Squance, the shepherd, Rachel Jedder had seen no one since reaching Yellaton, and she had been too tired and busy to want company. It was only when the sound of hooves clopped along the path and a man's voice shouted that she felt suddenly eager, and ran, laughing, to open the door to Squire Waddon.

A peddler leading a packhorse stood in the courtyard and sniggered as her face fell. "Mornin', mistress. I heerd tell as 'ee be living to here."

Rachel's smile was startled into reappearance by the word "mistress," and, as his glance took in her grandfather's smock, she felt thankful that it was not the Squire after all and that the mild weather had made her discard the breeches.

"You'll be needin' a length of cloth." The peddler was already opening a pannier and lifting out a roll of taffeta knowingly.

"No," Rachel, firmly refusing to look at the delicious green cataract of material.

He shrugged philosophically. "Leather stays, then."

"No!" She was insulted. Only old women wore those. "I'll take needles, some thread and a pair of scissors."

They were in her hands almost before she had finished speaking, and as she turned to fetch the two coins, he slid into the house and stood with head bent, looking at her slyly from under his brows.

"I be mighty thirsty, mistress," his voice wheedled. He was not a young man, and Rachel perceived that although his packs were full of fine fabrics, his own clothes were old and torn, and his quick movements did not disguise his fatigue. She waved him to wait in the kitchen while she brought some cider.

The leather mug emptied as though smoothly poured over a limp, dry plant which instantly straightened up and lifted its head in relief, and she filled it again.

"You ain't been seen at church," said the peddler. "And there's all High Chilham awaiting to set eyes on 'ee. Better watch out for the parson, 'cos young Squire can't guard you agin him."

It was no surprise that he was so informed about her. No stranger could walk through a single village in all England without every inhabitant knowing who he was and where his destination.

" 'Twere a proper smart trick you played on Matthew Claggett," the man went on approvingly. "But it ain't made you no friends."

Rachel, who had been about to eat her midday dinner of bread and cheese when he arrived, cut some for him and passed it over.

"They ain't going to help you none come haysel and harvest," he added dolefully.

" 'Tis no matter," she replied, pleased to have someone, however pessimistic, at her table. "I'll manage."

He ate only the soft center of the bread, leaving the crust, and then took her knife and with its handle crushed the slice of cheese before putting the crumbs into his mouth.

"No teeth, mistress," he explained to her curious glance. "Now, lookee, Rachel Jedder, in return for your kindness, I'll give 'ee a length of taffety for a gown for church and you can settle with I at Michaelmas."

The girl thought of the way the lustrous pale-green material had draped in stylish folds from the pony's back, and she could envisage herself, with all eyes upon her, walking regally through the arched stone doorway to the parish church, the dress rustling luxuriously—the envy of every woman there.

She shook her head regretfully. A weaner pig would cost less than such a garment.

"Cotton, then. Fine lawn," he pressed. "Or wool, softer than a mother's kiss."

"No. One of these will pass," she answered, holding out the man's smock she was wearing. "I shall cut it and restitch it and dye it with weld."

81

The peddler, who had been looking extremely doubtful, beamed, stood up and hurried outside, returning moments later with a twist of paper.

"Indigo powder. To you, one farthing," he said triumphantly. "And no trouble a-hunting for weld flower, or making up tints."

Rachel handed over the coppers and walked with him to his pony.

"Have a care, mistress," he said. "And may God increase your fortune afore I be by come Michaelmas."

Rachel knew that his warning was correct. Although allowances were made for the seasonal pressures of farming life, and the thought of facing the hostile village crouched so threateningly before her, it was true that if she did not attend church soon, the parson could bring her before the ecclesiastical court. This could force her to make public admission of her crime before the entire assembled congregation of High Chilham church and to promise never to offend again. It would be a most shameful way to begin local life, and disobeying such a ruling might even mean imprisonment.

That evening, by rushlight and the kitchen fire, she began cutting and redesigning the best of her grandfather's smocks.

The grass was ready, its flowers making furred rods and balls and pendulous ears on the tips of its stems, and dense masses of white clover spreading beneath. Rachel, carrying the scythe and a sandstone rub in a leather pouch, and accompanied by her dog, reached Brindley field with the sun. Grasping both handles of the scythe, she swung it in a ground-hugging arc through the crop, as she had seen the men do at Wame's farm, and, much to her surprise, a swathe of grass fell neatly outward. She swung again and the same happened, and her mood gladdened. It was not going to be as hard as imagined.

Her efforts initially were uncoordinated, her steps not synchronizing with the sway of her body, and the whole movement lacking the rhythm essential to an even advance. Gradually, however, the jerkiness was mastered and finally reduced to a practiced rocking which propelled her tidally forward. She found it was better to stop frequently to hone the scythe to a reed-edged sharpness than to try to continue after it began to blunt, when the grass would be mauled and split instead of cut cleanly through.

After two hours, it was intensely satisfying to look back at the broad spun ribbon of green hay leading to the gate, and she lay on the bank for a few minutes before unwrapping the fat bacon and bread from their cloth and drawing the oak bottle of beer from its shelter of cool, broad leaves.

Rachel Jedder felt fulfilled as never before. At last she could look over the lovely land and see her own marks upon it in the fragile emergence of the cotyledons of the seeds planted in the garden, the raked and weed-free soil ready for the next tilling, the clean stable and shippen, and now the ripe grass falling by her hand. Her mind visualized its turning and stacking, and winter, when the June scent of it would fill the old buildings as she filled the racks of her beasts.

Finishing her breakfast, she jumped up quickly to begin work again, for the sun must not be wasted. By midday she had cut two field lengths, she had a stitch in her side, and when she lifted the mug of cider to her mouth, her hand was shaking. Before returning to the field, she stripped off all the rags she wore as undergarments and was left clothed in the gritty linen smock.

By the end of the day the pace of her scything had slowed to a stumble and her hair clung to her head, wet as though washed, one shoulder seemed wrenched, and the stitch in her side made it difficult to breathe. Her head and all her limbs ached and the smell of the newly mown grass was as stifling as a sweet dust.

She supped without tasting at a broth made the night before from onions, potatoes, wild garlic, thyme, basil and a chicken carcass, and slept with a hand over her red eyes; but only the twinge in her side was left the next morning.

Her body, as she ran her hands over it, was as firm as a bud, starkly without fat, and even hard in places, thighs and calves, flat, taut stomach, compact buttocks like small farmhouse cheeses—all tempered since infancy by unrelenting physical work and by her pilgrimage from Norfolk to Devon. An unwomanly body, she admitted, but planed and useful, a machine for carrying out Yellaton's demands and withstanding abnormal punishment. It had staying power and recovered fast. In an age when men and women of her class had to be callused and strong just to cheat death, Rachel Jedder, lightly built as a dragonfly, was exceptionally tough.

At work once more, she turned over the grass cut the day before, fluffing it up with the pitchfork to dry in the balmy air, and after breakfast she began to scythe again. The shorn mane fell in tresses and the sun dried its virescence to a dull blue-green. Its juices made a humid steam behind her as the temperature of the day rose and suspended the sky over the moor like a hot Wedgwood disc. The ache under Rachel's ribs throbbed and grew to pain again, slim and lancinating, thrusting deeper with every swing of the blade, until the afternoon became a conflict between its assault and her determination to keep going, and this time it did not fade but lay like a cone of metal in her flesh all night.

Two long days' toil, twenty hours, and only a quarter of Brindley field mown. The girl tossed yesterday's swift-baking cut, altering her breathing and her movements to try to accommodate the pain, each step taking her nearer to the scythe and its echoing blade, until she took it into her hands and bitterly turned to face the rippling virgin spread once more. The automaton of her fit body reacted with braced back and ready arms; her legs paced the lea with ease; but the pain, the torturer, had life of its own, boring like an augur through her vitals, pinching closed her lungs with its claws and forcing out her breath in groans, vomiting back the food she tried to eat, blinding and deafening, and reaching at last the exclusive confrontation between itself and her own implacable will. She no longer knew what time of day it was or felt the sweat tears from her forehead sting her eyes. She only knew that she would scythe and stack her hay, and that every acupoint of her being was in anguish.

"Maid! Maid! Come here!"

"Maid!"

"Maid! Come!"

His voice took a little time to penetrate the barrier induced by the secret clash within her, and then she barely looked up. Rachel had been half-conscious of his presence on the other side of the boundary several times, but he had not spoken. Now there were only two hours of daylight left, and a stop for a few pleasantries would bring the work to a halt because she knew she would be too debilitated to start up again.

"Maid! The scythe, maid. 'Tis set bad."

Rachel stood still and turned her weary eyes toward his voice, seeing only a flesh-pink blur in the misty hedge.

"Fetch 'un here, maid!" Old Lutterell directed, and she walked slowly over. He reached through and took the tool, putting its heel into his armpit and stretching his arm and hand down its shaft. " 'Tis this way. The first handle goes so as 'ee can just touch 'un with your finger."

He passed it back and she carried out the instruction before he continued, "Now then, put yer elbow against the handle and fix the second handle where your fingers reach agin."

"There! Give 'un here!" He took it again and measured from where the grass nail went through from the point of the blade to the heel, formed an arc to the handle and adjusted the point so that it made an equilateral triangle to the heel again. Then he propped the scythe on his forefinger by its lower handle from where it swung, perfectly balanced.

"See!" His head gave a pleased jerk as he handed it back to her. " 'Twill be easier after this."

"Thank you," mumbled Rachel, who had tried to concentrate in order not to forget the setting, but was swaying, at the limit of endurance.

"You'd better way be going in, maid," he said. "That hay will needs pooking at first light, for 'twill rain by afternoon. Leave it be now and bide a bit."

She nodded bleakly, having no alternative but to take his advice, for with the lowering of her guard of rage, the pain had cast its hooked lines through every artery and reeled in all her force. The scythe slipped unnoticed from her numb hands into the grass it would reap, and she stumbled unaware along the uneven way back to the house. The smell of the red cows was so faint it was almost a memory as she buried her head in the pillow of a flank and milked by reflex. She ate to obey her own rule and climbed the stairs to lie awake and mortgaged to the wildcat.

And then it was another breathtaking dawn, fresh and gilded, the sun rising like a yellow balloon and the countryside glistening as though seen through water. So clear a dawn that far-off farmhouses and villages were buffed into bleached white stepping-stones from Beara to Exmoor and the silver and enameled rivers twined up the arms of the dales like bracelets. The cottages of High Chilham village, three miles away, were so sharply defined she could see every window and door and even the bells in the church tower, and the trees between reared like lizards armored in green scales.

Rachel wept as she raked and heaped the hay as old Lutterell had instructed. He had said it would rain, and in the night, with her own mind appalled by the sinfulness of it, she had found herself praying for that rain, for the release, for the remission, just for a day. But there were obviously going to be twelve more perfect hours for haymaking, and only her exhaustion persuaded her to follow her neighbor's advice, because it made an excuse to carry out a less demanding task.

Each haycock was as high as her chest, and she built them slowly, smoothing their sides with care so that the hay in the center would remain dry in any weather, moving reluctantly farther and farther down the field, and closer and closer to the fallen scythe. When the last mound was completed, she sat on the turf to eat, looked tearfully toward Bodmin and saw that its outlined heights had vanished behind a cloud, plum-dark and swollen like a wineskin with rain. A genie of a breeze was conjured up, and it bounced the cloud gently over the forest and the heathland, and then, just before reaching Yellaton, burst it. There was a quick downpour, followed by a light but steady mizzle, and Rachel, delivered, went indoors.

There was plenty to do, but she did nothing except sit hunched over bowls of soup by the fire, or lie like a fetus in the womb of the feather bed, thankful for the sound of the raindrops, like mice in the walls. She had never felt really ill before and was shocked. Yellaton, and therefore her own future, depended on the harvesting of the hay to maintain the cows, the mare and even the sheep (if they could be traced) throughout the next winter, that they in turn might maintain her. If the rain fell for too long, the crop would spoil. The urgency was desperate and she knew she should be railing against the weather and trying to strike bargains with the Almighty and the Devil for it to end. Yet, lying cupped over the pain, like a hand over a candle flame, she passively accepted her helplessness and the sovereignty of fate, and the problems seemed so distant as to be almost irrelevant.

Against the barrier of her stillness, the pain began to retract, inch by inch, withdrawing its thorns one by one, striking again without mercy only when she moved, but slowly, surely, diminishing, retreating to the point of its birth in her side, where her fingers massaged instinctively, like an animal licking a wound. It shrank so that at last she slept, and by the time the sky brightened it had become merely the hint of a hurt, to be ignored.

She lifted the scythe again and swung it nervously, but after a few strokes accepted that Daniel Lutterell had been right. The job was still a hard one, but now the newly set implement worked *with* her muscles instead of against them, and the pain did not return. The weather held. The grass fell in ripples across the whole width of Brindley field, was tossed, and dried to a tawny green.

There were no wheeled vehicles on the holding, to the girl's confusion, as she wondered how her grandfather had brought his hay from the field to the clearing by the barn where the remains of last year's ricks stood. Eventually she decided that the only way would be to load it onto a curious sledgelike object kept in the shed and obviously intended to be horse-drawn. It was ideally designed. She raked the hay into rolls, lifted them onto the sledge and led the mare round the orchard to the yard, where, recalling as much as possible of haysel at Wame's farm, she began to construct her first stack by making a deep base of crossed sticks and then pitching the hay on top to form a circle and building on that, shaping it as it grew. As it rose higher, she had to pitch up several forkloads at once and then climb a ladder to put them in place, and not for the first time she wished for the hands of some useful companions.

She gathered hazel sticks from the hedgerows, split them into quarters, twisted each in the middle and bent it to form a giant hairpin to fix the straw thatch which would protect the top of each rick. She made long thatching ropes of straw by hooking the first coil over a gatepost and twisting to incorporate more and more strands until the required length was reached. Then she tied bundles of straw, positioned them carefully and stapled them to the hay, and finally plaited a "cap" to seal.

Rachel stood back and gazed at her first haystack. It was ragged and clumsy, but to her it looked like the best rick in the whole of England, better than any champion exhibit, because it was her own.

Still the sun shone and the rest of the haycut made up another rick, squat and stubby, but more expertly finished than the one before. Finally she tied in the last strand and jumped to the ground to survey the completed little group with jubilation. It had taken three weeks, more than two hundred hours of labor, but she had done it. Alone. The hay was safely, securely, beautifully gathered in.

That evening she fed the mare extra corn and ate ham hock and beaten eggs, picnicking outside, where she could keep admiring her own handi-work until the light faded.

Contentment softened her features and made her playful, and she danced with the gray dog, who looked down at her philosophically when his front paws were placed on her shoulders. Next Sunday she would brave the village in church, she promised herself—proudly, because they would all know how she had harvested her hay without their aid. Then, to celebrate, she drank her grandfather's cider until it felt as though she were swimming through the sherbet night to the music of her own singing, old songs of maids and swains, and ladies and lovers, and the sorcery of England.

Rachel Jedder was undeniably drunk by the time she went to bed, followed by the dog, who sensed intelligently that she was in no condition to put him out of the house as usual. As her head dropped, the room turned upside down and went through a series of fairground spins, in the middle of which she lost consciousness.

Later, when the dog started burrowing into her back with blunt claws and barking insistently, she squeezed her eyes more tightly closed and crooked away from him. Her head felt several times its normal size with aches, which rammed each other in the noise until she lost her temper, sat up and yelled at him. But the animal refused to quiet.

A faint odor crept up through the floorboards like the announcement of a roasting meal and made her mouth water before her brain translated it. Suddenly she was wide-awake and pulling on her clothes and descending the stairs three at a time, flinging open the back door to the rust-red night, across the courtyard, through the stable, fumbling with the latch in the dark, terrified and knowing.

The raging wall of light blasted her face as she erupted into the clearing. It dazzled so that the whole moor and all the farm buildings seemed to be burning and roaring and crashing around her. Then, gradually the blaze divided into two separate fountains of flames, playing in wreaths of orange smoke and showering each other with starry sparks, and she saw that both hayricks were on fire.

CHAPTER SIX

Rachel Jedder felt her heart petrify. For a moment she was unable to move as she watched the cremation of all her hopes. Only her mind tumbled on to the terrible consequences, to the selling up of her beasts, followed by her own slow starvation and ultimate destitution, and the final return to the workhouse.

A high wail of anguish unlocked the paralysis and she rushed to the water butt, plunge-filled a wooden bucket and flung its contents at the nearest stack. A black circle appeared hissing in the center of the globe of gold and wisps of hay escaped into the air, pursued by flames, to flare for an instant and scatter as ash; and even as she refilled the bucket, the hole in the fire closed as though it had not been.

"Oh, God! Oh, God! Let them not burn! Bring rain! Let them not burn!" It was more incantation than prayer as she threw bucket after bucket at the holocaust, which exploded salvoes of fireworks in return and defended its territory with an unbearable sirocco.

The fires altered like mirages, appearing as red-hot boulders, then melting to metal, and spurting upward as viscous fluid shot with multicolors, and changing yet again into scarlet silk. They reached for each other with deadly passion, swirling, swaying, revolving in unison to appear from great distances as two dancing goddesses. But Rachel saw only the destruction.

"Faster! Move faster!" she ordered herself, aloud. "Soak one side! Save some of it! It's *got* to be saved! You fool! You fool!"

She tripped, spilling water, and the blaze teased, drawing back in clouds of steam from the accuracy of her aim, then changing direction in the wind and creeping over the charred earth in red tendrils to the base of the shed to climb, like a plant, up the wooden sides. She screamed and hurled more water, but the fire vine only grew more profuse and blossomed, tapping the solidity from the beams and the strength from the joists until the flimsy frame disintegrated clumsily onto the store of tools within. The heat from it frizzled her hair and scorched her lashes. The butt was nearly empty and there was no speedy way of drawing water from the well.

"Help me! Help me!" It was a real prayer now, her soul in despair searching for the Savior. "Please, Jesus!"

And then she saw them, in the reeking shadows behind the soaring beacons. Figures moving. People coming. Three men.

Rachel was filled with exquisite thankfulness. "Hurry! Hurry! There's still time," she shouted, starting toward them. They glided like specters, divided, rose and floated and, in the smoke, seemed to be fading. "Be quick! There's sacking. We can beat it out!"

Brushing the water from her raw eyes, she raced through the brilliance and into the darkness beyond, blinded and with arms outstretched. "Where are you?" She peered, straining, into the fumes and could see no one. "Where are you?"

Then, in the cool moorland night she could just make them out, running away down the hill. And a man laughed.

Rachel Jedder understood. Fury surged in her stomach like bile and mixed with the incense of the burning hay to choke her as she wheeled back between the bonfires to grasp the bucket again and dart to the well, to haul up more and more water, driven by rage, although she knew it was futile.

The fires burned lower and lower, turning each into humps of glowing embers to be doused, in the end, by rays from the white-ribboned east, which widened into morning over the black and dusty circles. Rachel Jedder sat numbly in between them, unseeing.

Swollen-faced and smeared with soot, she was beyond definable feeling. The anger had burned itself out, like the flames, and had left her as empty as the cast shell of an insect. Sitting there, she would have liked to cry, or sleep, or hide, or crawl into some deep, dark corner like a beast to die, but she had not even the strength to close her eyes. Her brain slowed to a fitful pulse, erasing the memories of the acrobat's loving, and the miracle of reaching Yellaton, and the promise in the drawn arrow of each seed. She could not even remember the lighthearted celebration of the evening before. It was as though she had reached the end of a lifetime of unrelieved oppression, with all the fight slammed out of her, and even the details of the struggle forgotten. She felt very, very old.

The sense of total defeat lasted. Her realization that the loss of the shed and the hay were not the total catastrophe she had first imagined made no difference. The Squire's guinea was still intact, a cow could be sold, and some more hay and basic tools bought in. It might even be possible to take a second haycut in August. She knew. But she also knew her enemies in High Chilham would return, and so there seemed to be no point in working, or even in considering any new project.

Sometimes she would go out and look at the two black circles in the clearing as though hoping the sight of them would rekindle her emotions, but she felt nothing, blank. Only the demands of the animals forced her from bed each day.

The cheerful sound of whistling did not arouse her curiosity, nor did the sight of the stranger riding toward Yellaton from the south, where there was no near settlement. When he called her name, she turned away and did not look up when he dismounted and walked over to her side to stare down at the scorched earth.

"Did you know that the sea lies no more than five mile from here, beyond yon ridge?" He pointed west. "And the road from Bideford to Exeter runs behind that rise, only a half mile away?"

His accent told her he was not a local man, but, fenced in by despondency, she felt no interest and did not answer.

"I could help you, Rachel Jedder." He smelled of tobacco and horses and leather and salt, and she drew back. "My friends and I would pay gold for your own sound sleep through nights when the wind clatters like passing travelers, and for the use of a corner of your outbuildings."

Only his voice moved in closer. "Gold enough to build better, of cob, which will not burn down, and to buy brand-new tools and more hay than your beasts could eat in two year, and still leave some."

Rachel felt her inquisitiveness being dragged unwillingly forward, and held her position, refusing to face him. For the first time since the fire, her mind began to stir, but barbed and rejecting, insisting that the man go away.

"Think on it, maid, and I'll be back for your answer."

He had read her thoughts and she heard the saddle creak and the chink of the bit as he mounted, and the hooves, soft and unhurried on the peat-based heath. Then, when he was some way off, he began to whistle again, and she twisted round at last to watch him ride toward the hidden road.

Her throat had tightened and her mouth was dry and she felt baited, as though a game was being played, with herself as victim. She went to the vegetable garden, where buttercups and shepherd's purse were already threatening the young plants, and halfheartedly prodded at the soil with a tapering piece of wood, which did not manage to replace the hoe and soon broke against a small stone.

Days had passed since she had inspected the holding and now, restlessly, she did so, and was invaded by its signs of neglect. How fast the season turned! The barley was six inches tall and should have been hoed a month back, and the surrounding old heather and gorse burned down to bring new edible shoots for the cows. The thistles and nettles were almost waist-high, the hedges grown ragged.

The man was a free trader. It was obvious. There had been so much smuggling of brandy and tea in Norfolk that every village idiot had known of it. Thinking about him irritated her, as though he had had no right to break up her depressive trance and entice her toward the gallows with such ideas. Yet, an extension of cob built onto the stables would look fine, and how could the corn be cut without a new sickle? It was the whistling which had been infuriating, indicating his certainty of her agreement.

That evening, unable to settle, she moved around the house, pretending to tidy or sit down to stitch or begin to cook—and all the time wondering how much gold, and when he would return. By morning, it was all spent on buildings and stock and shiny new implements.

Following the direction he had taken, she crossed the heather to the top of the next rise and saw the track below, just as he had described. It was a mucky, narrow trail, no more than two packhorses wide, but well used, and Rachel was surprised she had not discovered it before. Descending to its edge, she looked back. Yellaton, in turn, was now obscured by the mound. It was ideally placed to be the warehouse for contraband on the first stage of its journey inland and the girl resolved to bargain hard.

For the rest of the day she stayed within earshot of the house, and then, some time in late afternoon, the hill began to echo with the flat, tinny sound of bells, muffled at first, but growing louder in bursts, as though attached to the legs of a troupe of morris dancers, and, hurrying to a window, she saw the stranger herding a small flock of sheep toward the holding. The deep-voiced, masculine grumble of their bleating and the tintinnabulation crescendoed until the air reverberated like the drunken end to a saint's day.

Rachel was crestfallen. It seemed she had been mistaken about the proposition and that all the man wanted was to rent her buildings for stock, or to store grain; although that did not make much sense. She opened the front door to a jostle of wool, which he parted by riding through it, touching his forehead in bantering deference.

Rachel had not looked into his face until that moment. He had brilliant dark eyes, alive and full of humor, and a smile which displayed clean, even teeth, unusual at a time when most adults had gaps in sets rotten and broken with decay. The wind had tousled his hair, which was thick and black, and he dismounted so close to her that their hands were almost touching, yet she did not step back.

He said nothing for a full ten seconds, while the amusement died in his eyes, which grew swart and unreadable, and she felt a twist of disappointment at the reaction she recognized so well. Then he waved casually toward the flock.

"I hear you've been looking for these."

Rachel spun round to stare at the animals and bit her lower lip with delight.

"You mean . . . my sheep? These are *my own* sheep?" she asked, her voice rising to a yelp, so that they retreated with alarm on their long, unfriendly faces.

"All thirty-five of them," he confirmed. "Though you may have lost a few, the lambs will make up for it. There's near thirty of they."

The girl, skirting round, saw that despite the lack of attention, the group looked fit and, although many of the ewes were limping, only one or two crumpled and unhealthy beasts would have to be culled.

"Their feet need cutting back and I'll help you with that tomorrow," the man offered.

"Where did you find them? How?" she wanted to know, jigging from foot to foot excitedly and looking at him with naive admiration.

"I know the moor and I asked a few folk," he replied simply, starting to lead his horse around the end of the house. "Now, drive them after me and we'll put them up in the hare's leg for tonight."

Rachel swung her arms and shrieked a series of staccato whoops and the sheep bundled forward, their lambs giving doll-like cries of high-pitched panic. Merged into one amorphous creature with many hooves, they tattooed over the burned circles and through the orchard to the field, to rush past the stranger, who was holding open the gate.

His coat flicked accidentally against the tips of Rachel Jedder's fingers and the shock sped up her arm and neck to inflame her cheeks, and as she looked away, hiding behind instantly hooded eyes, she knew with

91

apocalyptic clarity that she wanted him. She wanted him more than she would want any other man as long as she lived.

"I do not know your name," she observed, her head lifting defensively.

"Will. Will Tresider."

"Will Tresider," she repeated, almost to herself. She needed to curl her hand in his, to be drawn against him and touched by him. Almost submerged by this unforeseen fever, common sense operated at last.

"How much will you pay for the use of my buildings?" she asked, quite coldly.

Will Tresider gave his irresistible smile, reached out unexpectedly and lifted her onto his horse.

"We'll talk of that in your kitchen, mistress," he said, and led her, speechless, back to the house.

His silhouette in the doorway was thickset and rugged, and, still trembling slightly from being returned with delicacy to the ground by his broad hands, she moved so that the table stood between them, and determinedly compressed her lips. If he guessed her feelings, he might treat her as a fool and give her no moneys at all.

The dim light of the room turned her skin luminously pale and enlarged her strange, glowing eyes, so that she appeared to be imaginary, as though if he merely brushed against her, she would disperse as fragments of mist. But he did not underestimate her. The story of her journey and struggle had leaked all over Beara and Gammation and crossed the river as far as Appledore, and he knew if even half were true, she must be made of iron.

"Do you want gold or kind, Rachel Jedder?" he asked, knowing the response.

"Gold."

"Wise maid." He tossed a compact metal casket of tea onto the table and laid a silver-topped flask beside it. "We'll drink to that in kind."

"How much?" she insisted, meeting his eyes stubbornly.

" 'Twill depend upon each cargo." He sounded grave, but was secretly entertained. "We're generous, wench. Don't doubt you'll do well out of it."

She fought to remain expressionless and managed to give a brisk nod before leaning to swing the warm kettle over the center of the fire and take mugs from the dresser. Will Tresider went outside.

Rachel was bewildered. How could she have fallen in love with a man whose name she had not even known? And so quickly? Only that very morning he had seemed irritating and bumptious. She wondered what had changed, but there was no answer, only amazement that she had considered him annoying in the first place. However, she was still sufficiently in control to realize that betraying these extraordinary feelings would not be in her real interests, and she resolved to maintain an icy distance.

The kettle began to steam, forcing her to attend to the tea. As there was no teapot, she spooned some of the expensive leaves into a jug, poured boiling water over and stirred, then strained the dingy brown liquid through a rag. By the time he returned, she was sipping absently, her mind so dislocated it failed to register her dislike of the drink, which was manifested by her wrinkled nose.

He pushed the flask to her and, as she took a more pleasurable swig of the harsh spirit, put an oblong parcel on the table.

"To seal our agreement, mistress."

He noticed her hands shaking a little as she unrolled it and wondered if she was afraid of him. All the tales about her did not mean she was without fear—such a slip of a chit living all alone on the moor. The glare from her blazing hay had been seen from Exmoor, and afterward, the people of the villages had muttered at the wickedness of it. Will Tresider had a startling desire to take violent revenge on Matthew Claggett and his companions for the terror they must have caused.

She was drawing a folded cloth from the parcel and loosening it out. A shimmer of green swished to the floor before her incredulous gaze. It was the taffeta the peddler had tried to sell. Moved to tears, she shook her head mutely at him, all her resolution gone.

Will Tresider came round the table to hold the fabric up and it was like dressing her in a flow of green sea. Her long hair spilled in strands, shining as though wet, and he saw himself reflected in the jade pools of her eyes, and he understood. Her mouth opened, full and childlike, and he took it, elated as its curves yielded to his own and then began to respond softly, searching and pleading, the taste of the brandy mixing with her own special sweetness to make a dazing intoxicant.

He felt her stand on tiptoe to stretch her arms round his shoulders and lean her straight body against his, so slight and light that each knew he could have crushed all life from her with one unyielding clench, and as his hold tightened, she pressed the closer, dizzily inciting his power and the risk of her own destruction. It was like holding a wild young falcon, and suddenly he was completely unnerved by tenderness. For minutes he stroked her head and kissed her closed eyelids, gently, protectively, before the warning clanged in his brain.

At twenty-eight, Will Tresider was both ambitious and daring. Several years before, grown tired of near starvation on ten shillings a week as a casual laborer and fisherman of Kent, he had decided to use his knowledge of the ocean to better advantage. There were riches to be made, with the aristocracy and the gentry and even the parsons happy to pay well and no questions asked for their brandy, tobacco, tea and silks, and even playing cards. Already he could buy a blood horse and sport a velvet coat, if he chose, and his plans for the future included no clutter of dependents. Much as he enjoyed a lusty woman, this was a dangerous young maid, and it was not at all his intention to become involved, especially when he had to do business with her.

Reluctantly his hand withdrew from her grass-scented hair as he extricated himself, mentally furious at his own stupidity.

"Be ready to do the sheep at midday tomorrow," he said brusquely, avoiding her startled glance and leaving in some haste.

Rachel burned for Will Tresider all that night. She lay with the length of taffeta spread over a pillow and her lips and hands against its cool, smooth surface, as though it was his skin. She talked to herself, murmuring what he would say and whispering what she would answer. She felt his muscles harden around her and his kiss repeated over and over again.

Months had passed since the human friendliness of the traveling fair, and the loneliness which had been underlying her recent life was now exposed in the ardency of her need for him. It was not simply the compulsion to make love, but to talk, to have his companionship, the guardianship he had unintentionally offered, and to be within his smile. Unable to translate or explain them, such were Rachel's emotions as she waited dreamily for him; and, when he rode into the courtyard at last, she ran to hold the reins, all her commitment trustingly displayed in the radiance of her upturned face.

He gave no greeting, just looked through her, dismounted and tramped off toward the field. He might as well have slapped her. At first she could only blink with disbelief. Although he had drawn back from her so abruptly the day before, it had been too late to disguise his own feelings. Now she knew he was pretending, cheating, and, as she led the horse to the stable, Rachel became arrogantly hostile.

She joined him in the hare's leg without speaking and he caught the first sheep, rolled it off balance and showed her how to hold it quiet with its hindquarters on the ground and forelegs in the air, while he pared back the horn from its cloven hooves with a sharp, curved knife. The overgrowth was so extensive that mud and dung had been trapped beneath it, setting up infection, and the animal's feet were distorted. As it was cut away, the stench of rotted flesh escaped like a putrid bubble and he applied a caustic paste from a horn container to the black and bloody mess beneath.

Rachel pinched her nostrils together and tried to snatch breaths from downwind, but already the air all around had become clotted with the smell, which was to increase to a gut-dissolving gall as the afternoon progressed.

Tresider finished with the first sheep, hooked in the next with the shepherd's crook he had brought and grasped a leg.

"I'll do that now," declared Rachel purposefully, and he took control of the animal from her and handed over the knife. The sheep struggled feebly and managed to twitch its foot each time she began the narrow angle of the cut, so that she had to start again.

"Come on, maid, or it'll take all week." He was impatient after a few minutes.

"Jack Lobcock!" she thought coarsely, gripped the animal tighter and sliced, glaring at him, slit-eyed, as the rind fell from the end of the blade.

It was very hard labor, performed at an awkward angle, and her back soon ached. The animals groused and wriggled and her hair kept blowing in her eyes and the knife handle began to rub a blister on her forefinger, but she refused to show stress in front of Will Tresider. Instead, she silently worked out how the task could be done next time by herself alone, with a system of roping each sheep down long enough for her to treat it while sitting on it. Rachel Jedder had long ignored humiliation by biting on mental puzzles, and her power of concentration was so intense that it could annihilate most external pressure and discomfort, although not the consciousness of this man's presence.

Every hoof of every ewe, even of those which were not lame, had to be cut back, and Will Tresider watched as she crouched over each, her small, obstinate face guarded and closed. The fetor was nauseating, the sore on her finger began to bleed, and he remembered the cramp which had seized his own back and shoulders when he had helped shepherds in the past. With a mixture of admiration and guilt, he knew she would not give up or complain until the job was done.

Releasing the twentieth sheep, he announced, " 'Tis time for a seat and a drink of cider." And slid his hand under her elbow to help her up, giving her no time to protest.

It would have been easy to condescend and smile at the rigid, short figure walking ahead of him had he not seen the visible signs of her increasingly successful effort to run the holding alone and been reminded that she had survived all the dangers and rigors of a three-hundred-mile march across England, unaccompanied. There must have been men. She was not a virgin, he thought, instantly jealous, and wondered if she had been raped. The idea enraged him, and it was then that he realized his rebuff had been a crass mistake.

Impulsively he stretched out a hand, but let it fall without reaching her. She would not be won so simply this time. She was so proud and stubborn that she might not be won at all. He felt sick, as though he had unthinkingly let a pearl fall from its oyster shell back into the sea.

"Have you been long at Yellaton, Rachel Jedder?" He thought to begin trying to attract her again through conversation.

"Near four month."

It was disconcerting to have him sitting in her kitchen. He had rolled up his sleeves and his bare, muscular forearms resting on the table were deep brown. Arteries, enlarged by the heat outside, ran under the fine hair which covered them, and, remembering how they had tightened round her the day before, Rachel accidentally spilled some liquid from the full tankard.

"Winter wheat's come on well," he persisted.

It was daunting, the way those unearthly green-and-brown eyes had

95

changed with her withdrawal, almost as though she could no longer see through them, as though they were blind. Yesterday they had been so vital, glinting and sparking in the ivory setting of her face, and disturbing then, too, but magical—mossy and umber, malachite and topaz, sea jewels fringed by curling thick black lashes, which he wished now he had touched with his fingers. There had been no answer to his last comment, and he was determined to make her talk.

"What will you do at harvest? You'll need help then," he needled.

"I'll manage," she replied, turned on her heel, and left the kitchen to return to the field.

There they argued.

"You hold the last few beasts and I'll do their feet," he offered.

"No. I cut as good as you now," she pointed out with some conceit. "And 'tis my job."

"And my turn, Rachel Jedder. Now, hold this 'un steady," he insisted, grasping an animal by its greasy fleece.

"They be my sheep and it's *I* should treat them." She held out her hand for the knife.

Had his own hands not been full, he did not know whether he would have kissed or spanked her, or both. As it was, he growled threateningly, "Hold 'un, woman! Or I'll let 'un go!"

After a burning cinder of a stare, she gave way ungracefully, almost flouncing as she grabbed the sheep from him.

From then on they worked in silence, growing weary in the closeness of the late afternoon and developing headaches under the weight of the odor.

At the far end of the field, one of the red cows bellowed. The man stuck the knife into the earth to clean it and then pushed it into its leather case as she set the last ewe free to scamper to its mewling lamb.

Red-faced, stinking and shiny with perspiration, Will and Rachel looked up, accidentally catching each other's eyes, and he grinned, a heartstopping spread of fun, impossible to shun. She felt the corners of her own mouth twitch and slewed around as the cow bawled again.

There was an unnaturalness about the big animal's stance by the hedge which set her running and realizing simultaneously that this sound had been reaching them, unnoticed, through the noise of the flock, for most of the day.

The cow was standing with her back arched, eyes wide with fright and breathing heavily. A dark patch of sweat stained the hide over her flanks and a pair of tiny milk-white hooves could just be seen emerging from her vulva.

"She's calving," Rachel shouted, looking hard at the hooves and wondering why she could not place what was wrong with them.

Will Tresider strode across the pasture and stopped to examine them. "They're upside down, Rachel Jedder. These is back hooves. She's trying to get a big calf out back'ards and needs a hand, so you'd best get some rope."

Rachel had not run so fast since escaping from the fat gentleman's bed at the inn by Thetford Forest. Her fatigue and the cramps in her muscles were obliterated by the imminent birth of this first calf. A heifer would be the beginning of the herd. A bull would bring in money and keep her in beef for a year.

By the time she returned, the cow was lying down, oblivious of her surroundings and straining every two or three minutes.

"Tie the ropes round the calf's legs, Rachel," instructed Will Tresider. "No! Not round the hooves, or you'll pull them off. Higher. Above the fetlocks."

The hooves felt rubbery to the touch and the legs brittle, as though they would snap under traction, and Rachel began to feel afraid.

"Will it die?" she mumbled, as though the mention might hasten such a calamity.

"Might do, Rachel Jedder," he said honestly. "But we'll try and see as he don't."

After checking the knots she had tied, he held the two lengths of rope as though about to take over. She fidgeted warningly, and he offered them with slightly exaggerated courtesy and that smile, which made her flush.

"Don't pull except when she'm pushing, and then use all your might," he directed. "And stop when she stops."

The cow raised her tail and humped her back and tensed her muscles and moaned. The girl dug her heels into the soft ground, hung on to the ropes and jerked back with all her strength. The calf did not move an inch. Seconds later they tried again, and again, and, after nearly fifteen minutes, Rachel knew she was going to have to ask Will Tresider for help. She tossed her head and, at the next contraction, heaved again, her feet curling to keep from slipping, her hands cut by the tightened rope, arms wrenched to the limits of their joints and her face puffy with the exertion; but it was useless.

"You're not heavy enough, Rachel Jedder." He put a kind hand over hers. "Sometimes it takes several men to bring out a calf like this."

Stupidly she felt her eyes fill with tears and she ducked her head so he should not see. Imagining she was still vexed, he was placating.

"I won't have near enough weight myself near the end, and then we'll have to pull together."

He kicked a deep groove in the ground, drew the ropes round his back and braced himself hard against them as the cow strained. After a couple of vigorous contractions, the calf's thin legs slid forward a few inches and then some more, and finally, with a little rush, its hocks suddenly appeared. The red cow struggled to her feet and stood docilely staring into space.

"The calf can't breathe. It'll die." Rachel was frantic at the delay.

"Patience, maid. Let the beast rest," said the man. "Her's more important to you than the calf and she'll need all her strength soon enough."

After a few minutes, the animal lay down on her other side and with a series of massive efforts managed to expel the entire hind end of the calf.

"Now, Rachel Jedder! Now!" shouted Tresider, and the girl scrambled between the ropes in front of him to pull as though not just the calf's life, but her own, depended on it. The blood rushed to her head, her eyes bulged in their sockets and her tired spine cracked. Reluctant as a terrier from a fox earth, the body of the calf was dragged backward.

"Pull harder!" yelled Will, "or you'll lose 'un." As she began to feel herself blacking out under the pressure, the calf, damp and living and still half-encased in the silky remnants of the protective water bag, slid onto the grass.

The cow clambered to her feet and turned to gaze at her baby through eyes liquid with maternal love. She sniffed delicately at it and then began to lick, her big tongue rasping over the fragile, bony frame, cleaning away the remains of the birth, coercing the blood to circulate and the muscles to harden, while the calf lay steaming, with that look of tranquil incomprehension on its snub face which marks all newborn mammals. Rachel wanted to pick it up and cuddle it to her. She touched its round black nose, and the cow tilted her horns and glowered with such unmistakable menace that she drew back.

In less than a quarter of an hour, the calf began struggling to stand, rump up first, staggering as its forelegs unfolded and splayed out before it. For a few seconds it swayed groggily, and then crumpled without change of expression into a heap of legs. Rachel laughed infectiously, and Will Tresider felt a band as hard as metal constrict his chest.

There was mud in her long hair and blood and dirt up to her elbows and all over her face. Her grandfather's old coat had been discarded earlier and the cut-down linen smock hung like a shroud. From a distance, or even near to, she looked like a grubby ragamuffin, and yet, with all the cares and obduracy gone, the transparency of her delight was illumed.

The hardships of the day came back to him, and images of her frail form pitting its pathetic strength against cumbersome, boisterous beasts and being hopelessly outweighed were projected on his mind—and yet what power she had. It was tangible around her, the air charged with her determination and single-mindedness and a magnetism compelling Fate itself to bend a little. He wondered if she knew she was different from other women, and extraordinary.

The calf bumped into its mother, searching her rib cage for the teats. Rachel laughed again, looking around naturally to share with him, so rapturously happy, lifted off the ground like a cloud in the billowing smock, grass and leaves and summer seeded in the green of her eyes.

Changeling, alchemized from a quick-silver being into a butter-soft maid.

He wanted to tell her, but knew this was not the time. Instead, he asked, "Don't you want to know what you got there?"

"It don't matter," she said. Heifer or bull, she did not care. "Leave them be. They look that pretty."

"They do," he agreed.

At last the calf blundered against the warm, full udder, curled its dark tongue round a teat and lost it, butted the bag with imperious infantile claim, opening its mouth like a human child wanting a comforter, found the teat again and attached itself. Its tail quivered and waggled, and its stomach grew round and tight as the rich yellow beastings were gulped down, carrying more precious immunities than man would ever devise.

The cow cudded contentedly, as though she had spent the whole day grazing. There was no sign of the prolonged and punishing drama of her afternoon. But Rachel had gone very white, the color drained from her lips and her eyes hollowed in dark shadows. In the opaline light, she diminished and drooped, her own luster quenched.

" 'Tis evening and time I was gone." Will Tresider was careful not to challenge her exhaustion and relieved when she followed him unprotesting. He wondered how many times she had trailed back to the house, cold, wet, toilworn and alone.

In the stables he saddled up with practiced speed and led his horse into the courtyard, while she stood quietly by, and he knew if he took her hand he would not leave.

"Sleep well this coming Thursday, Rachel Jedder," he advised, then, giving a look of certain feeling, rode away.

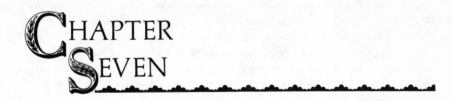

CHAPTER SEVEN

Although there was a southwesterly blowing and the packhorses jogged silently over the dense heather, the gray dog heard them while they were still a quarter of a mile away, and he scratched, growling, at the door. Rachel had kept him indoors, in case he should attack them, and perhaps for self-protection, too. Now she left the feather bed to look out on the night.

They came without lanterns, a biblical caravan of pilgrims across the dusky moor, and passed under her window, lumpy with wide panniers and heavy, oval containers, each as big as a pregnant ewe—two strings led by four soundless human shadows. The end of the house hid them from sight as they bunched past the outbuildings and crossed the barren black circles of ash to the barn.

Maybe Will Tresider had looked up and seen her, naked behind the glass in the metallic light of the new moon. Rachel smiled to herself and put on a crisp, clean smock. It smelled of lavender with vervain and speedwell and myrtle and mercury, love herbs which she had also bruised and rubbed into her hair and skin that evening.

Shutting Sam up, she went quickly downstairs and through the passage, already so familiar that every knot in the woodwork and hollow in the flagstones were identified.

In the courtyard, she stood by the well, where the air was still and mild, completely sheltered from the wind by the solid cob rectangle. The stars in torches and splashes and specks and glims on beyond mortal sight sprayed from the plunging moon in myriads across the navy sky. More brilliant here than in Norfolk, they made her feel both exhilarated and unimportant, less than an ant. The vicar in Sauton had once described stars as pinpoints of light proving heaven, but Rachel only believed that heaven, by day or night, in any season and all weather, was Yellaton on Beara Moor, and by their immaculate perfection overhead they confirmed that.

Low voices and the stealthy sounds of objects being bumped and dragged across the floor of the echoing barn tempted her inquisitiveness. Despite Tresider's orders to the contrary, she had made up her mind right at the beginning to watch, and later find out who the free traders were, out of interest—and also as an insurance.

The stables were sweetly moist with the mare's breath, and movements in the stall told that the animal was wide-awake, too, ears pricked and nostrils flared to catch the smell of the foreign horses outside. Rachel, tiptoeing past, shivered in spite of all daring and felt her skin roughen with gooseflesh. The smugglers could react dangerously if they saw her, and it might have been more sensible to have brought the gray dog after all. She would stand well back in the dark building, but whatever happened, she had to see the man again.

The wraith of his presence had continually insinuated fragments into her thoughts and interrupted her labor so that in the middle of a chore she would find herself staring into space, her fingers tracing her own lips or pressed against the place he had held on her arm. His mouth, his hands, the way his hair curled at the nape of his neck, the spread of his back, all obsessed her and she had constantly pictured him again in the hare's-leg field. There was an aloofness about a man concentrating exclusively on his work which was seductive, and she had always felt similarly aroused by the sight of Jack Greenslade practicing his acrobatics, oblivious of her presence.

Rachel Jedder was not introspective. She accepted who she was and her own emotions without question and, although initially startled by the suddenness of this passion, she did not try to analyze it, but instead went over and over every look and gesture and word and circumstance of their two meetings with a potent mixture of longing and apprehension, which had become combustible during the waiting days.

The arrival of Tresider had brought about the recovery of her sheep and the birth of the calf, and she saw these momentous events as omens signifying that he was destined for herself and Yellaton. Her own feeling of injured dignity had not withstood the last look he had given before riding away.

Slowly, carefully, she opened the far door and slid a wedge beneath to hold it ajar. The wind gusted into the stables like royalty, making her take a bowing step back, just as a stranger stumbled past, bent under a redolent cloth-wrapped bundle.

"Ain't you finished with them tubs yet?" his voice grumbled. "They be blocking the way."

"Why don't you put yer shoulder to a few and see how you fares, Ben Cooke." It was a boy's irritated reply.

"Less cheek and more elbow grease, young Tom. There's no time for such argiefying with sunrise in less than two hour."

Wood rumbled over the cobblestones and Rachel edged forward to see Will Tresider helping a gangling lad roll kegs into the barn, while the man who had passed with the tobacco-scented bale stood irritably by. The nags waited with lowered heads in two patient groups, those already unloaded sagging gratefully and nosing about for grass, the others still foursquare under their weights, like carvings. There was no sign of the fourth man, who, she imagined, must be inside stacking and camouflaging the contraband.

With the casks of spirits out of the way, they were able to work faster, almost running with the boxes and cases and rolls, while Rachel, picturing the extraordinary harvest being stashed on her property, squeezed herself with excitement and longed to rush forward to help. Only the vow she had forced upon herself not to make the first move toward Will Tresider restrained her.

The owl called like an old friend from the great beech and a deer barked far away. The three men were breathing heavily under the strain of the weights and the need for speed, and when they spoke at all it was in monosyllables.

"Shift 'un, lad!"

"No! That 'un there!"

"Six more and we're done, Will."

The horses shuffled about, easing their stiff limbs, and although there was still no sign of dawn, the sky lightened to a royal blue and the moon, so overblown when they had arrived, diminished to a compact lamp.

"Last one," grunted Ben Cooke, and the thin boy flopped against the wall, his long arms and legs dangling, like a rag doll. There was a final thump within the barn and the last man appeared, burly and bearded, in the clearing.

"Appledore tomorrow, Dan," Tresider said.

The fourth man nodded and made for his horse, pushing a pack train into line on the way.

"At the Rising Sun?" Ben Cooke asked.

"Same as usual," confirmed Will.

A few minutes of confusion and muttered oaths and they were gone, leaving not even the vibration of a hoofbeat on the air.

He walked through the open stable door to where she was standing pressed back against the wood in the darkness. He did not touch her, and when she looked into his serious face, all the flirting fantasies and little games she had been inventing for this moment became nothing. She turned and walked before him, through the house and up the stairs, wordlessly. In the bedroom, she faced him and he undressed her slowly, and neither spoke.

They became lovers in agony, Rachel Jedder and Will Tresider, meeting like blades in a silver war, in blood and snow, with parched and wounding hands, driven together by the broken petals of the past, like birds with spurs for wings; the tearing of their skin rasped the enclosed air of the room, fusing the song to the thorn, bone to bone. And her love was loosed painfully from suffocating deprivation, finally released by its own true and terrible reflection in his eyes, and his worldliness was cut down by the voluptuous purity of her submission.

When it was over, they lay without moving, hardly breathing, close-locked and becoming inseparable, without alternative or plan, because there was no longer any choice.

Later, much later, they talked hesitantly, without sense, as lovers do.

"Did you know?"

"Yes."

Their fingers began to cross the deserts and groves of each other's bodies, peacefully.

"And think of me?"

"Mmmm." She smelled of hothouse flowers.

"At night, before you slept?"

"All the time, my heart."

And then it became easy, Rachel spiraling round him, provoking with her small pointed tongue and sorceress's eyes, surprising him with mischievous inventiveness, enticing and tantalizing, agile as an ermine, joyful as a stream.

102

"Rachel Jedder. How beautiful you are."

Amazed, she raised her head and whispered self-consciously, "I'm but a plain maid, Will."

"Beautiful," he repeated, enveloping her in his arms and laying her back in the down-filled bed. Her cheeks and lips and breasts were rosy from love and the pellucid resin of the sunrise dripped down to set her in its amber, and she abandoned all self and surrendered to him.

And far into the day, when they rested at last, her head fitted into the hollow of his shoulder and her arm relaxed over the curve of his chest and he eased her belly against his hip and let his hand remain comfortably on her waist, for they had found that position in which to grow old together, and they slept.

It was not easy to leave him lying. Asleep, he looked younger and vulnerable, his disheveled hair curling over his forehead and his finely shaped mouth softened to boyishness. The severe lines of vigilance and even the laughter creases were no longer there, and the still lashes and strong black eyebrows emphasized the opaqueness of his closed eyelids with their filigree of fine blue veins. He was such a handsome man, and she wanted to laze over him with kisses, inspiring his sensuality even before he awoke. But Yellaton was always waiting.

It became Rachel's custom to rise first because he rarely returned before dawn, and then so secretly he was often stretched beside her and drawing her close while she still dreamed. Sometimes he would place two, or even three, cold gold coins in the line between her breasts, and on such mornings there would be gentleman's clothes piled on the bedroom stool, a white silk shirt with lace jabot and ruffled sleeves and a gold-embroidered overcoat with gilt buttons, and she would find the barn empty. At other times, his boots might be wet and sandy, with shreds of seaweed stuck to their soles, and the barn would be jammed with barrels and bales behind a screen of logs.

Their days became shaped, the regular jobs of feeding and milking, making butter and bread and cream and cheese, preparing food for the evening, and gardening being completed while he slept. Then, after midday, they worked together with the new tools he brought back. They sheared the sheep and cut the hedges and cleared thistles and nettles and ditches. Will cut some of the coppice on the border of her wood and felled an ash to provide fuel for the next winter and taught her how to make hurdles from withies.

Yellaton became neat and clean-edged, its crops pushing powerfully upward, broadening their healthy leaves to procure and exploit the sunlight, its livestock growing sleek under gleaming coats and feathers. Summer with its lingering days mellowed the brashness of spring into a bower and the sharp scents of new life to a more ravishing perfume. The meadows bloomed with wild orchids, their mouths seductively open, and poppies like hearts, and in the damp woodland, sundews and teasels gave siren smiles to tiny flies and ate them. Sweetbriar and honeysuckle held the hedgerows in pleasurable bondage, and giant, furry bees staggered from foxglove to foxglove, bewitched by gold dust and drunk on nectar.

Rachel wondered how it had all happened, and compared her past with her present, humbly. The years of pauperdom always haunted, and she would look at her land, glorious under the limpid sky, and at this dark man who prized her, and feel superstitiously afraid, as though no more than a wrong thought or an unlucky sign might conjure the whole into a chimera. Often she awoke expecting to be in the rat-infested corner at Wame's farm, but there he would be, with his arm possessively around her, lover, father, brother and child.

After so many arid years, it was hard to restrain herself from continually demonstrating love by caressing and rubbing against him like a cat. Sexually she could not have enough of him. As they sat drinking cider in a break from their work, he would notice her hands pulling at the grass with subconscious eroticism, or see her blush for no apparent reason; he would sense lust in her restlessness, or in a smile, or in that fathomless, inerrant look, and at his knowing grin she would laugh and come to him without inhibition. They made love in the fields and on the moor and in the chair by the kitchen fire, and once against the wall of the well, when he bent her back so far that she saw the water far below and shrieked for mercy; most of all they made love in her grandfather's feather bed. In countless artless ways she beguiled him and he adored her for it.

On her own in the evenings, she struggled with fine materials to make gowns. Mistress Wame had taught her very basic stitching and cutting, but only on the roughest fustian, and Rachel was uneasy about the rich brocades and velvets Will kept bringing. She knew that even if she managed the dressmaking successfully, she would never be able to wear the gowns because they would be far too ostentatious for a country maid, and, in any case, she felt far more comfortable in the old smocks. So, not a garment had been finished when one day he spoke, unexpectedly, of her life.

"I know how you are about the folk in High Chilham, Rachel, and rightly so, but you got to go out from here."

"Why? You bring everything I need," she pointed out defensively.

"If you're not seen soon, they'll make real trouble and you know it. You need friends."

"Squire won't let them do nothing." It was a thoughtless remark, which she regretted immediately.

Will Tresider looked stony. "That's why Matthew Claggett can set the place alight whenever he pleases, I suppose," he said sarcastically.

She flushed and kicked at a log in the hearth, her hands twisting together, and guessing how apprehensive the idea made her, he unbent and teased, " 'Tis not like you to be feared of a herd of old hogs."

"If you'll come with me?" She knew it was an impossible request, and he shook his head.

"Set a day in your mind, Rachel Jedder. Finish your dress and go," he advised firmly.

The gown refined her. It changed her walk and carriage and emphasized her oyster-pale complexion and high cheekbones and slim arms. The unfamiliarity of it made her shy, so that she moved stiffly and seemed haughty. She had pinned her hair up under a lace-trimmed cap and matching lace frilled round the bodice and ruffled the sleeve of her chemise, where it emerged from the green taffeta just below the elbow. She might have been the daughter of a nobleman, and Will Tresider's eyes widened.

He had grown accustomed to the waif smudged with soil, her hair matted with burs, and it had been an effort not to laugh early that morning at the sight of her shivering as she scrubbed and sluiced herself by the well and actually immersed her whole head in a bucket of icy water to wash her hair! But now she was unrecognizable as the Rachel Jedder he knew.

For the first time it occurred to him that they could go very far together. There was nothing they could not achieve, fine house and horses, carriages and hirelings. Only her rough hands gave away her mean background. He kissed her little pink marzipan feet and helped her on with new shoes, and she was ready.

She looked at him, eyes huge with alarm, as the eight bells of High Chilham began to ring far off.

"I've brought you a gift." He handed her a charming painted wooden fan, obtained from a French captain only the night before, and lifted her slightly off the ground to meet his height. "You look like a princess, little one."

She closed her eyes, her lips asking for his in a most unregal way, which made it an exercise in willpower to put her down again. "After church," he promised.

The weather had been fine for some time and Rachel managed to reach High Chilham without too much mud splashing onto her long skirt. There was no looking glass at Yellaton and so she had been unable to see herself, but the expression on Will Tresider's face had given her confidence and she kept looking down with pleasure at the rustling material and the decorated leather shoes as though they were being worn by another woman.

A path led off the track to the back of the church and she considered taking it in order to arrive discreetly, then changed her mind, marched boldly into the village square and through the lych gate to the cemetery, just as the last stragglers were entering through the studded oak door. She paused, straightened her back, held tightly to her new fan and walked in.

The entire congregation turned to gape. She did not know where to sit and every pew seemed full. For a long minute she stood and stared back at them, until a very old man came forward and indicated a central seat.

"That be Penuel Jedder's place," he mumbled and shuffled off.

The children did not take their eyes off her, rolling blank orbs of astonishment at the sight of a face they did not know. Strangers never passed through their remote hilltop village, because it was not en route to anywhere. The women peeped furtively, the flick of their eyelids betraying scrutiny of the green gown, and although the older men assumed demeanors of disapproval, their sons nudged and jiggled their eyebrows to attract her attention, thinking to themselves that although she were a skinny kind of a maid, wi' her little parcel o' land up Yellaton a man could do a lot worse. Rachel ignored them all.

The service quavered to a start with the pitch pipe, an unmusical scrape of bass viol, violin and flute, and the congregation's tuneless chant, which the rector's very secular tones led with bored assurance. She could just see the squire in his boxed pew talking quite openly throughout, as though at home in his own drawing room, and there was some delay as one of the gentlemen in his party was reminded to come forward to read the first lesson. The second lesson was read by Walter Riddaway, as senior churchwarden, who met her bold glare for an instant before looking down at the great Bible, his pained features lengthening even further.

When he had finished, instead of proceeding with the usual order, the parson pointed to the door of the church, which was opened by the old verger. To Rachel's surprise, a girl of about her own age walked in very slowly. She was bareheaded and wore a white sheet about her shoulders and was without shoes. Carrying a white rod and weeping, she faltered down the aisle to kneel before the pulpit, while the villagers said the Nicene Creed, at the end of which her lips moved in a whisper.

"Raise your voice and be heard!" ordered the parson.

The girl's head bent sideways into the shelter of her hunched shoulder and her voice was as shy and high as that of a rebuked child.

"I, Jane Clarke, do confess and acknowledge that I have been delivered of a female bastard child unlawfully begotten on my body by—" She broke off to weep loudly.

"Continue!" roared the parson, like a redcoat officer.

"—by Stephen Pincombe of Kingford," she gulped.

A gratifyingly scandalized twitter united the congregation, which twisted as one to gawk at a blushing man, standing in acute discomfort next to his obviously vengeful wife.

"Be silent!" the rector shouted and leaned forward to browbeat the girl below. "Complete this confession before all, Jane Clarke!"

"And I also entreat the congregation to pray unto God for my forgiveness and better life," she sobbed. "And that this my punishment may be an example and terror to others that they may never deserve the like. Amen."

106

Rachel felt full of pity, and full of anger at the gloating faces of her neighbors in the pew and the parson's indifferent bullying. She tried to imagine what it would be like to have to live the rest of one's life in the middle of this village, with its tight, unchanging community, after such a public humiliation, and was thankful for the isolation of Yellaton.

For the remainder of the service she stood and knelt and sat and stood at the appropriate times, blocking out the unpleasant little scene and the people around her by fixing her eyes on the exquisite oak screen which crossed the church beneath the chancel arch and separated the nave from the choir. Its tracery was finely enhanced by carved leaves and cherubs, and slender stems branched into the tabernacle work of the rood loft above. The beauty of its detail obscured the dullness of the sermon, which concerned the divinely ordained structure of society and which she had heard many times before; and then the parson's voice was racing impersonally through the benediction and the service was over.

He stopped her at the door to ask why she had not attended before. She had been without decent clothing, she explained, and at that moment young Squire Waddon, about to climb into his carriage, gave her a flourishing bow and the parson let her go.

After that first exposure to High Chilham, it was easy to return, and Rachel Jedder began to go regularly to the weekly market, which was held in a field on the village outskirts. Folk rode and walked, carrying their produce and driving their stock to it from a radius of about five miles, and there she bought hay to replace that lost in the fire and a pair of weaner piglets and more implements and a breeding set of a gander and two geese, just as planned.

The faces became familiar and a natural inquisitiveness prevailed over the reserve of some of the younger women, who began to speak to her, some even muttering behind their hands against the arson at Yellaton. Rachel, with the caution bred from experience, was always polite, but revealed nothing. Gossip of more work being completed at Yellaton than a maid could possibly do alone must have been common, but no one hinted at Will Tresider's presence and she knew they were waiting to see whether she wed or fell, or whether she might yet accept a local land-hungry lad as husband. She was not aware that her love affair with Will had given her a bloom of happiness, and it was not unflattering for a girl who thought herself unfeminine and almost ugly to see the young men begin to swagger and show off, with false wrestling matches and boisterous banter, when she appeared. Only the ubiquity of Matthew Claggett, with his unswerving scowl of hatred in the background, prevented her enjoyment of the market.

Passion and gold and social release peaked each day and night, and Rachel Jedder's spirit fanned open in the new atmosphere. Suddenly, at seventeen, abundance and prospects were hers and traits previously restrained by the miserable conditions of her childhood were liberated. She discovered herself to be a natural extrovert with a cheeky and acid wit and a penchant for clowning.

Will Tresider taught her to dance, which she did with uninhibited pleasure, raising her skirts indecently and acting out the roles of imaginary great ladies and bawds to the whistled tunes. With his encouragement she became daring and a little wild, openly wearing the luxurious gowns she had originally thought so unsuitable. He was entranced and, despite protests from his companions, began to ride with her to the Rising Sun inn at Appledore and to other taverns where business was done.

There in the smoke-marled lamplight, as cider idled through her veins, she sang old Norfolk songs and showed off her fresh confidence in sauciness and exaggeration and listened, thrilled, to tales of shipwrecks and storms and the ritual war of cunning between the preventive men and the smugglers, until, sometimes after a full working day and the colorful battery of crowded, raucous places, with fumes of ale pricking her eyes and a mind packed with amazing information, she would fall asleep like a blissful infant.

Then Will Tresider would carry her into the pine-sharp night and set her before him on his horse and ride home to Yellaton. She would be only half-conscious of the steeply angled climb after Bideford bridge to the overhanging black surf of the woods, and later, the gauze-fine draught like a damp kerchief on her hot face and the taste of heather told her of the moor where, although ground-nesting birds burst screeching from under the hooves and the wind from the wings of night hunters ruffled her hair and apparitions like stupendous faces in the fire flickered to the sky, none mattered, because she lay against his chest like a mouse and was safe.

Throughout all that love-drugged summer, if she thought of the future at all, it was only in certainty that the present could never end.

By late August there were over one hundred guineas in her metal box, and Will Tresider had expanded his team by several more men and the area of his trade as far as Bristol. Often he was gone for days at a time, but when he returned, they would talk eagerly of schemes to increase the land and stock.

Sometimes the sweep of his ideas left her stunned. They would replace the old house one day with a mansion as big as the squire's, he promised, and she had no cause to disbelieve him. But when the winter wheat was ripe, with the barley soon to follow, and he was too busy to help with the harvest, his advice shocked her even more.

"Hire labor," he said casually.

"What, Will? Have a man working here? For me?" She felt her flesh creep at the thought.

"Why not, maid? There's gold enough," he reasoned.

"No! I could not!" she demurred timidly.

"Well, 'tis either that or cut the corn yourself, Rachel Jedder." He was blunt. "You know I got to be Porlock way and then go on up the Severn."

"I'd not know what to do with him, Will," she said helplessly.

"You'd best not do nothing with 'ee, my lovely, or you'll have me to answer to," he teased, then added seriously, "Just tell 'im what to do, Rachel. Pay one shilling sixpence a day and as much as he can drink."

"Don't I help him none?" she asked.

"You'll have enough of picking and pressing apples, if you want cider for next year, and besides that's lighter, better work for a woman than scything corn."

Rachel remembered the pain of the hay harvest with a shudder and agreed.

Nathaniel Babb was an elderly man, but the only one available from High Chilham at a time when all hands were turned to the harvest. He had a lagging gait, a melancholy face, and sighed deeply and often, and there were a few sniggers at market when she hired him. Rachel soon discovered why. He did not have the expected failing of taking time off behind her back, nor was he drunk by midday. He was just excruciatingly slow, pausing to consider each stroke before making it and meandering up and down Yonder Plat in anything but straight lines, so that the swathes of corn fell across each other in all directions and some were trampled.

During his first morning break, as she walked down the other side of the hedge, she heard him groaning at regular intervals, as though from long habit, like an old dog, and by dinner time, the sight of the mess he was making at half speed was more than she could tolerate.

"You ain't moving straight, Nathaniel Babb," she pointed out, her nervousness overcome by annoyance.

"Them allus says that," he nodded, amiably doleful.

"And I wanted this wheat ready for stookin' by tomorrow evening, but you won't be finished in time."

"No," he agreed sadly.

"Can't you go any faster?" She was exasperated.

" 'Tis the problem with the world today, mistress, all this haste." He sighed like a bellows.

Rachel lost her temper. "Well, if'n you can't do better, you won't get no mutton when the job's done."

"That's right, mistress." He confirmed she was taking correct action.

"And precious little cider."

"True enough." He picked up the scythe as though hauling a full bucket up from the depths of the well and shook his head. "Now, if 'ee goes crackin' on, mistress, us'll never get harvest in."

Nathaniel Babb was unbeatable. Over the next two weeks, she threatened and bullied and cajoled to no avail. She marked his line across the field with sticks, but he simply scythed through them and zigzagged away. She even did some mowing herself and left him to come behind tying sheaves, but that caused even more chaos, if such were possible. The sheaves disintegrated at a touch and collapsed on each other, and it seemed half the corn was left on the ground. The waste was dreadful to see. Only the blessing of sustained good weather stopped Rachel from going mad, and in the evenings, long after he had gone, she would work on, gleaning and tidying the muddle he had left. Had she been alone, it could not have taken more time, she realized furiously, and when Will Tresider upon his return expressed surprise at the day's work still outstanding, she exploded with a tirade against old Nathaniel which did not cease until he covered her mouth with his and kissed her until she was incapable of another word.

There was only the final short stretch of stooks to load and bring into the barn. The mare was harnessed to the sledge. Surely, even Nathaniel Babb could not sabotage that. Rachel left him in the middle of the day and tiptoed upstairs to wake Will. As she leaned over his slumbering form, he suddenly grabbed her and pulled her down, yelping with laughter, into the bed.

"You ain't got no shame, Will Tresider," she giggled.

"Right enough, mistress." It was a flippantly accurate impression of Nathaniel Babb. Then, as he drew her close, he added, "And I ain't got much time either."

Rachel tensed with disappointment. "But I thought you'd be home a while now."

"There's a ship making a run to Mouth Mill tonight with the biggest consignment of geneva and brandy we've ever handled," he explained. "There's a buyer for the lot in Bristol and I can't take no chances with it."

She buried her face in his shoulder.

"I'll bring you something pretty," he promised. "You can have anything you ask for, my lover."

"Anything?" she asked at once.

"Yes."

"Let me come with you, Will," she said impetuously.

He laughed and tugged her hair gently. "And who would milk the cows tomorrow?"

"I'd just come to Mouth Mill tonight, to see the ship and be with you. Oh, it would be that exciting, Will Tresider. 'Tis what I've wanted since you first come here."

"It ain't possible, Rachel," he said, frowning. "We're going straight to Bristol, so how would you get home?"

"Well, I got here from Norfolk without knowing the way, didn't I?" she argued the undeniable point. "And I've rode so often to the coast now that I could find my way back blind drunk."

As he looked extremely doubtful, she moved provocatively against him, biting the lobe of his ear, then eeling just out of his reach, until he pinned her arms firmly to her side and relented. "All right, all right, hoyden, you can come, though, by gar, I don't know what the others will have to say."

"You are good to me, Will." She slid over him like honeysuckle.

"I am that," he agreed wryly.

There was a timid tapping on the door and the old laborer's glum voice was heard asking, "Be 'ee in there, mistress?"

Rachel gave Will an alarmed look before answering, "What do you want, Nathaniel Babb?"

"The old sledge has broke, mistress," he replied.

The girl closed her eyes to keep her patience and called back, "You wait in the yard and I'll be down in a minute."

He scuffed audibly away, although they had been unaware of his arrival, and she murmured to Will, "Do you think he heard?"

"Voices, but not what we spoke," Will answered lazily. "The door's solid enough."

He reached from the bed to fondle her leg as she pulled on her shift and petticoat.

Day stayed long at that time of year, and it was almost eleven o'clock before the dark was thick enough to cloak their departure that night. Rachel Jedder, perched on her mare's broad back like a sparrow on an ox, felt a frisson of anticipation as they set out. There was no moon, which Will Tresider said was well. The less light the better for such a venture; and their ride was through an hour of cat-black, coiled masses, flexed to spring.

They had reached the rock on the track leading to Brownsham Wood when he stopped, cupped his hands to his mouth and made the powerful, churring call of a nightjar, low and penetrating, to be answered from a copse on the right, and they veered from the way and cantered into the trees to meet two faceless horsemen.

As Rachel reined in, these jerked their heads and spoke with low urgency to her man, whose reply was short.

"A woman's bad fortune, 'ee knows well, Will Tresider," she heard one mutter.

"You ain't forced to be party here, if it's more to your liking to stay home and poor, Alan Pope." Will was cool. "Now, if you're with us, stand watch on the road."

The man shrugged and rode off sullenly. The other dismounted with Tresider and Rachel and tied their horses to stout branches before descending the long valley to the beach where they hid in the narrow opening to a small cave.

It was a night as deep as fur, as claustral as a cell, with a flat sea like a length of widow's weeds, its ripples in their meeting with the shingle no

111

louder than a man smacking his lips. Only the even rhythm of his breathing told Rachel that Will was close, and the intensity of her fixed gaze on the water created hallucinations of black-sailed sloops and rowing boats, like shoals of whales. It was a cramping wait, yet she was too exhilarated to find it tedious, and when a flask was passed between them, the brandy instantly fired her face and made her fast heart drum. The packhorses were hidden in a larger cave round the point of the cove with the rest of the smugglers, and the signaler was somewhere above them on the cliff.

She prayed for at least a breeze that the ship might not be delayed, and then, simultaneously, they all saw the blue light on the ocean which told of its coming. After nerve-stretching minutes, during which Rachel could picture the signaler struggling frantically with flint and steel to light his tallow candle, the will o' the wisp of his horn-sided spout lantern began to hop and swing just below the sky.

The horses, their hooves gloved by wet sand, crabbed across the beach under the shells of their wooden saddles and the oarsmen's plash drew in like rising fish. Then all the shadows imploded into action and Will was gone from her side.

Sailors jumped into the water waist-deep to haul the boat ashore and unload its illegal cargo: tubcarriers heaved and roped the casks onto the tolerant beasts. The sounds of their activity were magnified in the numb air and became echoes of the landing of some ancient invading force, splashing out of the Atlantic, distorted by massive weights on their shoulders, moving with the minimum of communication and the determined dispatch of experience.

A second rowing boat lurched in as the first was pushed back to sea, and a string of horses clattered up the stony floor of the valley, while another batch filed from the cave. The pace slowed slightly and there were grunted oaths as the men tired. Out in the bay, the ship strained at her anchor, poised for escape. The last barrel was rolled onto the sand.

The blast of the carbine repeated over and over as it ricocheted off the rock walls. It was followed by a moment of total silence as every living thing froze with shock.

Then a voice shouted, "Stand, in the name of the King!"

And the bight erupted into savagery. A group of preventive officers charged out of the murk straight at the smugglers, and vicious hand-to-hand brawling broke out. The horses, tied together, galloped off in serpentine panic, like a disappearing Chinese dragon, and another shot exploded. A sailor in the rowing boat slumped over his oars. All over the beach men kicked and battered each other, thumbs gouging into eyes, knees thumping into groins, a pistol butt detonating a brain-filled skull. Roars of pain and rage.

The preventive force was outnumbered and the free traders were dirty fighters, using knives and rocks and metal barbarously, and Rachel, from her place in the cave, witnessed one hold his opponent's head under water for far longer than the deepest breath could last. Then, to her terror, one of the officers began running straight toward her.

"Will! Will Tresider!" she screamed, and a second figure baled out of the melee.

The two men pelted up the beach and Tresider flung himself on the other's back as he reached the cave. The struggle was short and bloody and then the customs man was pinned against the cliff and Rachel saw his face. It was Walter Riddaway.

Suddenly Will was beating the face against the shale and it corrupted before her eyes into a wet black pulp, and when he released it, the body slithered to the ground and did not move again.

Rachel recoiled, a moan crammed behind her fist, which was pressed against her mouth. She stared, sickened, at Will Tresider's hands, which had caressed her with such tenderness, appalled that they could have battered a man to death before her eyes, and he read her thoughts.

"You'd have hung else, Rachel Jedder, and me, too," he said tersely, and then, gripping her wrist, began to pull her after him to the path. At the opening to the valley they looked up and saw, waiting beyond the mill, two mounted dragoons, blacker than the night itself, aggressively blocking the route. Wheeling round, he dragged her back along the beach, through piled seaweed, which popped and slurped as they slithered over the rocks and turned the foot of the promontory.

His men and the sailors left the defeated preventive men, like heaps of discarded clothes, on the sand, and followed into the narrow cave where the second string of horses was huddled, blowing nervously, and on through a series of smaller caverns, holding to each other's jerkins and feeling their way without light along the wet and slimy walls, slowed to a stumble until they emerged at last onto an unexpected finger of sand much farther down the coast and from there managed to scramble to the cliff top.

"Dick Trosse, take three and deal with those dragoons. You two tars wait here, in case they come up this way. Then get back to the ship, if you can."

"Ship's gone, master," replied one of the sailors, and when they looked out to sea, its surface was as blank as glass.

"Join us, then," said Will, looking round the group. "Where's Dan Salter and John Revell?"

"Done for, Will," replied one of the last to arrive. "I seen John Revell go down and passed Dan's corpse on the way here."

Tresider nodded briefly and continued with his orders. "The rest of you wait till the militia's been taken care of, make sure there's no more of the buggers skulkin' about and find the packhorses what was brought up here ready. Then load the others and we'll carry on as planned."

"What about you then, Will Tresider? Where be thee going to?" a heavily built man asked, suspiciously.

113

"I'll meet up with you at Porlock," he answered.

"You're goin' wi' that woman, her as brought all this on," the other accused, and the men bunched together, murmuring angrily.

"If you want to stay alive and make any gold out of this night, you'd best get that cargo on the road quick," Will warned and, unperturbed by their resentment, turned his back, pushing Rachel on ahead.

As they hurried away, she glanced over her shoulder and saw Dick Trosse and three others set off along the cliff edge and the rest of the gang begin to split into two parties, just as directed.

They ran for about half a mile in a semicircle to reach the wood where the horses were tethered, slowing to a painstaking furtiveness for the last few hundred yards, but seeing no one; the horses were as they had left them.

"We'll walk quiet as far as Clovelly Dykes, Rachel. Then go hard as you can for Yellaton. No matter what, you keep riding, understand?" he instructed.

"What about you?" she asked anxiously. "Where will you be?"

"Right behind you, my lover, so ride on," he said, and bent to kiss her lightly, and then with quick urgency, before lifting her into the saddle.

They reached the crossroads, touched hands briefly, and her mount jerked forward as he slapped its hindquarters to send it on its way.

Then the wind whipped off the hood of her cloak and pulled loose her hair as the mare pounded through the dark over the rough ground. Rachel, crouching forward, tried to shelter behind the wire-drawn mane and pick out the obscured landmarks through streaming eyes. She rode over Horns Cross and passed the almshouses with an instinctive shudder, cross country, avoiding Moorhead posthouse, on as far as the lime kilns to ford the River Torridge at Weare Giffard. News of the night would be traveling as fast, borne by running informers and half-asleep messengers and perhaps soldiers who had escaped.

And, as she rode, truth confronted her with its merciless stare, told her that her insistence on joining Will Tresider had indeed caused the trap to be set and the death of so many men that night; for old Nathaniel Babb must have listened into their conversation and informed to Walter Riddaway.

The night caught her into its dying, and she dreaded the flashing, powered horizon ahead, but the heartbeats of the horses' hooves pumped them both into the moment when nothing could be concealed and the price had to be paid.

"You know that I have to leave Devon now, Rachel, and never come back."

They had dismounted at Yellaton at last, exhausted, torpid with the pitilessness of it, and he was standing with her beside the ancient hedgerow.

"Too many people know. Everyone knows about us—that I must have

114

been the man Nathaniel Babb overheard. I daresn't stay here longer."

She could not speak, could only look at him in trust and pain, like an animal, and hold to a soft-leaved stem to steady herself.

"Come with me! Back to Kent, where we can be wed." He cupped her face in his hands and smiled his soul-rending smile, and falling rain confused with her tears. "We've money in plenty, my little lover, enough to buy a place there as good as this—better. Wed me, Rachel Jedder!"

The rain fell on the land and released its smell, earthy and potent, recounting of blood back through time and the line to come, her line, here at Yellaton where it had always been, and how each year it would give back grain for sinew, growth for seed, new life for age. To her.

Will Tresider knew and pulled her against him, forcing her head fiercely to his body. "There are other farms and you *love* me. You love *me*." Intruding with male rage between her and this rival.

His hair was fine in her fingers. Until they met, she had always imagined grown men had coarse hair. She searched, eyes closed, for the hollow of his neck and the pulse of the great vein against her cheek, but Yellaton, in mists and heat, with its brutalities and bribery, its despotic demands and the sonorous gong of its seasons, could not lose.

His embrace slackened until his hands were drawing down her arms, and he gazed over her head into the distance.

"None of my men comes from High Chilham and I'll pay them well that they won't talk." He began making his withdrawal behind the screen of practicality. "You'll be safe, Rachel Jedder, never fear."

But still he could not let her go, could only lean back from the balance of their hands as daylight advanced, silver-armored over the brow of the east.

"They'll be here prying and hunting soon enough," he said impotently. "Word will be out over the county by now."

Inside herself, she was clamoring her need for him, that she wanted him, to go with him, that life alone, without him, was inconceivable, that she would die. Her nails dug into his palms and a blackberry strand from the boundary hedge hooked its thorns into her hair. He made a rueful face and untangled it.

"I understand." It was a whispered murmur before he came to her mouth, as though kissing a sacred book. "I know, Rachel."

He mounted the big horse which had brought him to Yellaton and looked down at her for an unendurable, immeasurable time.

Rachel watched Will Tresider gallop swiftly away over the sloping moor ahead of the dawn, until the bright chestnut of his horse became indiscernible and the serration of their motion was filed to level flight by the distance and he became less than a soaring lark and then sped beyond sight, taking her with him, and leaving only a husk on Jedder's land.

CHAPTER EIGHT

Grief. Grief pervaded all; time, the space in which she breathed and the breath, every particle of everything around her, each cell of her own body. All Yellaton was encapsulated in grief.

For a while, Rachel lost her sanity over the loss of Will Tresider and ran about the place howling and pulling at her own hair and smashing things she had come to treasure and clawing at her own flesh and deliberately colliding against damaging objects, wanting the self-inflicted pain, until some shred of the instinct for survival returned in a germ of fear of her own violence. This, together with almost physical collapse, restrained her.

But her brain still raved, searching dementedly for ways to bring him back, in disguise, or to live hidden and emerging only after dark, or to face his accusers and win. Then she thought only to see him again, of taking the horse to go after him, although days had passed; of leaving everything and going to Kent to find him. Alternating between talking out impossible plans to herself and sobbing over the realization of their impossibility, the real heartbreak was the inevitable acceptance of the fact that there was no way in which she could ever contact him again, because he could never return and she did not know where he was, and neither of them could read or write.

The soldiers had come early in her distraction and found a ragged, incomprehensible girl, who had alarmed them with her abnormal, parti-colored eyes and mumblings. There had been no sign of contraband or of the man they hunted, and they had been relieved to hasten away. Rachel was completely unaware of their visit.

The passion burned itself out at last, leaving her unnaturally quiet, in a near trance, the agony replaced by a sensation of being disembodied, so that she looked down upon herself from a height, trailing mindlessly around the holding.

Will had been so much more than a lover. Through him she had found herself, discovered who she was and learned to be self-appreciative. The security of his love had freed her and given her expression. He had taught her to dance and to sit in the sun and to luxuriate in the sensation of fine materials against her skin and to care about herself, and she had gazed at her face in the looking glass he had given and realized that it was not ugly, as she had always believed, but unusual, even attractive.

His admiration had encouraged fun and frivolity, near-sinful hedonism to a parish pauper child who had known only killingly hard labor and exhausted sleep and who had had to strive for every mite of existence. He had changed her entire outlook so that never again would life consist only of actuality. Through his eyes, she would see it as challenge and spoils.

It was this understanding of what their relationship had meant and of his gifts to her which could never be taken away, which helped to bring about a slow recovery to a state of sad acquiescence. She began to force herself to participate again, for his sake at first, and then for herself, that the creativeness of their love might not be wasted.

The very young cannot remain in mourning for long, and Yellaton, with its neglected animals, persuaded her gradually away from the lost past and lonely future into the present once more. There had been changes during her period of withdrawal, changes in herself. Love had matured her, rounded her hips, and, to her surprise, she noticed breasts developing at last.

In spite of her overall melancholy, Rachel Jedder was now aware enough to be proud of these new breasts and often looked at the almost indiscernible mounds they made in the line of her dress. Before going to market or church, she would push them upward under her tight bodice, so that a hardly visible shadow formed between them, and it was only after several more weeks had passed and her waist had thickened inexplicably that she realized she was pregnant.

Will's child. Walking through the autumn woods, she stopped under the tree where they had often kissed and leaned against its rough trunk again and closed her eyes, imagining. If she had prayed, she could have asked for little more than to be given a part of him, to have a son like him. Her hands spread over her stomach and for the first time since the night of the smugglers she felt very close to happiness.

A few days later she remembered Jane Clarke stumbling bareheaded and without shoes up the aisle of High Chilham church; and the weeping words repeated in her memory.

"I do confess and acknowledge that I have been delivered of a bastard child. . . ."

Rachel Jedder went cold. How they would relish her humiliation and the stigma upon *her* child: this foreigner, the woman who had usurped the rights of one of their own and caused the death of another, brought to public shame at last. As he grew, Will's son would be taunted by village boys about how his mother had crawled before them all. It would never be forgotten.

Mutinously Rachel vowed it would not happen. Even excommunica-

117

tion, with its following risk of imprisonment by the civil courts, could not force her to perform such a penance. She did not know how long she had been pregnant or how much time was left, and she wished she had more information on the business of human childbirth, but she knew more about farm animals than about herself. Wild thoughts of bringing up the child secretly ran through her head. Working quietly on Yellaton, she pondered over what to do, and then, one early morning, as the distant village rode like a ship on the low September mist, the solution presented itself.

That Sunday she dressed with great care in a yellow silk open robe with laced bodice and pannier skirt over an embroidered underskirt, and matching embroidered bows secured the cream lace ruffles at her elbows. Before putting on her tulle cap, she took the rags from her hair and bunched its curls on either side of her face, and, drawing on her shoes, she knew she had made herself look as fetching as possible.

The church bells began to ring as she started out, but she did not hurry. Purple heather and brightly rusted bracken colored the hills and hollows of the moor and spiced its air with autumn, and ahead the squire's woodland was a palette of fiery tints. Already the warm, moist wind, with wafts and sudden flurries, was in rehearsal for its winter storms and the sky was as littered with a debris of leaves and birds as a city street with rubbish.

Rachel, wishing Will Tresider had known of her pregnancy, agonized over where he was. Everywhere she went and everything she did repeated what they had done together and kept the pain of their parting sharp, and there was no way of knowing how he would have judged what she had to do.

The bells stopped and stragglers were half-running to the church, but still she made no haste. If anything, she walked more slowly and arrived after the oak door had been closed. As she pushed it open, the verger bustled forward crossly and gestured her into the last pew instead of to her usual seat. From there she could see every member of the congregation. All was going according to plan.

Rachel Jedder mouthed automatic participation in the service but heard none of it—her eyes were too busy scanning and her mind comparing, as though she was at market studying stock.

Their faces were all so familiar that she did not need to see them. A number regularly greeted her visits to the village with undisguised enthusiasm, and although only Will Tresider's bold, dark looks captivated her, she supposed some of them were handsome enough, but good looks did not lift bushels.

The men of High Chilham chanted the responses and sang the psalms that Sunday unaware that most of them were being rejected: too thin, too short, too fat, too old, and one, too simple. Then, on the far left, four pews down, she found what she was searching for—powerful muscled shoulders and arms outlined firmly under the sleeves of his jacket and a wide bull neck rising firmly from a strong, straight spine. The solid, broad back of the man who would work for her and Yellaton and Will Tresider's son. Robert Wolcot's back.

He had not been among those who flirted with her at market, but she had noticed him there, buying and selling with his older brothers and his father, who owned a farm on the other side of the village, and she recalled his face as being weather-beaten and rather serious behind a sandy beard. The family were comfortably-off yeomen, and had she been a pauper still, she could not have aspired to such a man, but it was very different now.

Matins ended at last, and as the congregation filed out, she fumbled in the pocket of her gown and dropped the little fan Will had given her, stooping into the aisle to pick it up just as Robert Wolcot was about to pass. They almost collided, and she glanced up, blushing a little at her own impudence, into a pair of very honest gray eyes, which did not waver upon meeting hers. Rachel had to force herself not to lower her own gaze modestly, and as they looked at each other, an entirely unexpected expression, which she could not quite read, crossed his face. It might have been relief.

He walked directly to her on the market field that week and spoke without guile.

"I would pay my respects, Rachel Jedder, if 'ee be agreeable to it."

Rachel felt her worries lift and float away, and she gave him a brilliant smile of assent.

He was older than Will Tresider, over thirty, and had been born and bred in the village. Had she been tempted to think him stupid for having been so easily ensnared, she would have been wrong, because he was shrewd and knowledgeable about country matters and not without insight into human nature, as she quickly discovered.

Their courtship had progressed respectably, with early-evening walks and conversation, which centered mainly on farming and revealed little of each other, for about three weeks. They had just been watching the charcoal burners at work in the wood below Yellaton when he led her away from the clearing to sit on a fallen tree.

"Us needs be wed soon, Rachel Jedder, afore folks talk." He looked at her steadily.

Startled, she turned away and muttered guiltily, "Does it show?"

"No," he said.

"How did you know then?" she asked.

He had not touched her before, but now he took her chin in his hand and made her face him. "I know everything about you, Rachel. Always have," he said. "I seen you the first day you come through High Chilham, all wet and worn out, and I loved you then, maid."

Stunned, Rachel stared at him and then stammered, disbelieving, "Why? How could you have wanted the dirty waif I was?"

"Oh, 'twere like an early lamb come in from the winter moor, half dead and starved." He smiled down tenderly. " 'Twas easy to mind for 'ee, wench."

She felt ashamed and could not meet his eyes. "You never come and spoke, like the others at market."

"Weren't no point," he replied. "You, being with Will Tresider, wouldn't have looked at I."

Rachel felt tears rise and dipped her head, but he held onto her arm and continued talking.

"I know you'm with child, Rachel Jedder, but you be a good maid and hardworking and will make a proper wife. 'Tis enough for me, if you'll have me as husband."

She nodded mutely and he let her go, briskly leading the discussion to the matters of the wedding and his move to Yellaton.

Within a fortnight, Rachel and Robert Wolcot were married simply, and the night of their wedding showed she had chosen well. He was a considerate and caring man, and although memories of Will Tresider ran uncontrolled behind her closed eyelids, she was unexpectedly grateful for the warm, secure presence of this new husband in her bed.

He followed the habits of his lifetime without a break to celebrate. The only holidays were the holy days, when fairs and revels were held. So, daily, he rose just before dawn and went to the fields.

Few of the important jobs of the season had been carried out in the weeks since Will Tresider's departure and now it was necessary to work hard and fast to beat the coming frosts. But soon the potatoes were harvested and clamped in straw under a hard mud casing, and Brindley field was plowed and half of Yonder Plat fenced off for the pigs to root in. Removing and burning the stubble from the other half was the most slavish work of the year, for the breast plow was a clumsy, spade-shaped tool attached to a long, curved shaft and pushed forward inch by jarring inch by the hips and thighs. It took Robert Wolcot a whole day to skim off the root-bound top layer from a quarter of an acre of land this way, and each evening he returned to the kitchen, unstrapped the protective leather pads and slumped over the hot meal Rachel brought, dumb with exhaustion.

He worked so wholeheartedly and gave such ungrudging affection that she could not have failed to respond. The clean, warm house and well-cooked food were her way of expressing thanks and, becoming genuinely fond of him, she tried to anticipate his wishes and put his comfort first.

The fetus grew, and because she was so slightly built her belly swelled rapidly. Once he looked at her wistfully and asked, "Why did 'ee wed me, and not one of the others, Rachel?"

"I wed you for your gurt strong back, Bob Wolcot," she answered, grinning.

He smiled, too, thinking it was a joke, and did not ask again.

The village, with its sharp eyes, knew the truth but made no audible

120

comment. Through her husband, Rachel was now related to half its population and they were careful to include her in their greetings and activities. It was not wise to risk ill feeling in such a cut-off and static society, where a quarrel might involve an entire family and last for generations. So the people had developed a particular behavior toward each other, designed to avoid confrontation.

Matters were rarely approached directly but reached instead via tortuous routes of courtesies and oblique reference. Arguments were so hedged about with pacifying safeguards as to be unrecognizable, and refusals, almost unheard of, were only incurred if the petitioner were witless enough to make a tactful change of subject impossible. Market bargaining alone was conducted bluntly, in the oddly high, slightly lisping voices of the locality, which had amused Rachel in the beginning, but which disguised an unparalleled tenacity in holding onto farthings.

Then it was winter, and from morning till night the rhythmic thwack of the flail sounded from the barn, where Robert Wolcot threshed the corn. On the increase of the moon they killed a pig, and Rachel, with the help of one of his sisters, managed to use every part of it except its grunt, making brawn from the head and sausages with the blood and gut, hanging the sides in the great kitchen chimney to smoke for bacon and curing the fat hams with juniper berries and sugar and brine.

Her larder was full of pickles and preserves, fruit jellies and maturing cheeses with a taste as sharp as a bitten tongue. Cat's Head and Redstreak and Bitter Scale, the last of the cider apples, were crushed in the small stone mill pulled around by the horse and sandwiched in long straw to be pressed several times in the ancient oak cider press. The juice was poured into casks and the rosy smell of it clung to her hair and clothes and wafted through the house past Christmas.

In an attempt to stifle disturbing retrospection about Will Tresider, Rachel crammed all her time between waking and sleep with work, running the dairy and feeding the beasts, preparing chickens and rabbits and rooks for the table, washing and scrubbing and mending, spinning and making rush lights each evening, but he lingered just behind her consciousness all the same.

Yet, the pregnancy brought tranquillity. She did not visualize the coming baby, but rather felt pleasure that her vast girth and tender breasts had been caused by him, the discomfort proving that, wherever he was, he was bound inescapably to her. Because of this, when she looked into the future, as most people do at New Year, it was not difficult to persuade herself that she was content with the unchanging prospect ahead— that Yellaton's fifteen acres would be her home and Robert Wolcot her husband for the rest of her life. She would have his children, too, and merge with his family until eventually the adventures of the great journey, and perhaps even the wildness of her love, were forgotten.

In January, Robert's father, old Thomas Wolcot, died. He had disliked

121

Rachel Jedder and disapproved of the marriage, and although she was concerned for Robert in his filial distress, the event did not seem of direct importance to her. The farm went to the two eldest brothers, but there was a little money, which was added to her own cache in the Cornish tin box under the bed when they returned home from the burial in High Chilham churchyard.

She held her husband's head until he slept and then, in that twilight pause, released her imagination to roam again over Yellaton with Will, through the orchard, full-leaved as it had been, to the hare's leg, where newly shorn ewes gambolled in astonishment at their unanticipated weightlessness, on to the border of Brindley, and then they took an unexpected route, through an unknown gate in the boundary bank and round the edge of Daniel Lutterell's nearest fields until they came to a stretch of rough land, apparently cultivated once, but long since left to return to the moor. It was so clear, so real, that when she bent to pick a flower, a thorn hidden in the grass scratched. Will gave her a quick push forward and her eyes were suddenly wide open and staring into the darkness of the bedroom. The tip of her finger felt sticky and, putting it to her mouth, she tasted blood.

"Robert! Robert!" She sat up and shook the sleeping man hysterically. "Wake up! Wake up quick!"

He turned over in alarm and caught her hand. "What is it? What's wrong with 'ee?"

"Down by Lutterell's, is there a piece of old ground, Robert?" she asked, gripping him in her anxiety.

"What's this? Be 'ee maized, woman, rousing me at this time of night with fool questions?" He flopped back into the mattress.

But Rachel shook him again, insistently. "Tell me, Robert! I've had a dream. Is there a bit of land there? Is there?"

He groaned and drowsily rolled against her. "I believe as there is, Rachel. Yes. Now, will you let me be?"

"Robert! We got to buy that land. It was in the dream and there's gold enough for it. Robert!" she gabbled.

"Fath, Rachel!" He sat up angrily. "Stop this maundering. What's got into you? Now you give over chountin' and git to sleep."

But she threw her arms around him, almost weeping in desperation. "I must have that bit of ground, Robert. I never seen it, but 'twas in the dream. There was a gate in the bank that led to it and the gorse tore my finger and I know we got to buy that land—for Yellaton."

There was a long silence and then she felt him relax beside her and stroke her hair with his rough hand.

"Don't fret, maid. If it matters so to 'ee, you can have the land, though 'tis a coarse piece; but I'll look into it in the morning."

Rachel hugged him fiercely, unable to thank him in words, or to explain that somehow her life had been changed that night. Its purpose had been revealed and an ambition born which would not let her accept the straightforward outlook of wifeliness and motherhood again.

As he lay down once more, her husband patted her head in a bemused way.

"Womenfolk with child be expected to want raw onions and strawberries and such," he murmured. "But I never did hear of none craving a bit of land."

The spread of Rachel's vision was poor indeed. It lay at the foot of a slope, where all the bitterness of the moor drained into marsh, and must have been spongy underfoot even in the dryest summer. Telltale irises and arrowgrass and tussocks of rushes and reeds grew in profusion and Robert Wolcot carried out his inspection without enthusiasm.

"What could 'ee do with it, Rachel? 'Tis too wet for sheep, and no good for tilling, even steers wouldn't make on it," he pointed out glumly. "And 'tis north-facing and cold."

But Rachel saw only the expanse, that it spread right along the edge of Moses Bottom wood and, from there, as far as the corner of Great Wood.

"There must be ten—fifteen—acre here, husband," she said, her eyes hugely avid. "Why, 'tis as big as the whole of Yellaton."

"If 'twere big as Squire's park, 'twould still be of no use, maid," he protested. "Daniel Lutterell would have put 'un under the plow hisself else."

"Oh, he's an old man, with a good farm but no sons. What would he need wi' it?" she argued. "And there ain't no one else near enough to want it, so he'll be well pleased to sell off cheap to us."

"Give 'un away, more like," grumbled Robert Wolcot.

She took his hand and looked up into his face persuasively. "We could keep on both the heifer calves and the foal, and next year's calves, too, with this land. Ditches would drain it fine."

He stared at it morosely, visualizing the labor involved in cutting channels across such an area.

"We could soon get it done together," she said encouragingly.

"That's not women's work." He grinned down at her big stomach.

"Weren't no man here when I come first, so I don't know nothing about what's *women's* work," she reminded him with asperity. "Just as soon as the babe's born, I'll be out here with you, husband, till the job's done."

A passion of cupidity took hold of Rachel Jedder when Moses Bottom was secured for Yellaton. She snatched the document of ownership from Robert Wolcot's hand, crushing it in her greed, and was unable to leave it behind, even while dragging him down the hill to take traditional possession by pacing the length and breadth of the new ground.

Pinched by the north wind, it stretched inhospitably before them, defying the hand of any man to coax it to fertility, but in Rachel's mind it was already lush with fine grasses, and ten red cows were sheltering under the trees, swishing away the summer flies with their tails. Laughing with glee, she waddled, with remarkable agility for her condition, into the very center, to splash ankle-deep in the bog like a fat and happy duck.

Robert Wolcot forgot his disgruntlement and roared with laughter, striding over the clumps of bulrushes to pull her out and bundle her back to the house. As he rubbed her dry before the fire, she kissed him with tenderness and love, with true meaning for the first time since their wedding.

Later, when he had gone, Rachel, shawled in a warm cover before the blaze and alone, visualized the whole of Jedder's land, now curled around Lutterell's farm like a hand, and planned the years ahead.

Rooks nested in a knot of elms near the house for the first time, a lucky sign, for they would only build where there was money. They flapped around like windblown rags, stealing each other's nesting materials and squabbling all day, and spring returned, its air hung with hawks. Kestrels and buzzards and sparrow hawks hunted leverets and unguarded eggs and were chased across the moor by aggressive pairs of crows. Wild geranium and violets beaded the grass under the bud-blistered hedges and constellations of stitchwort starred the corners of the meadows. The swallows streaked over the house like a shower of arrows, as the old woman who acted as midwife for the whole district arrived from the village.

Rachel, orphaned in early childhood and raised with little female contact, had thought the first contractions were a gastric upset, but when Robert Wolcot hustled her to bed, she waited calmly. She had seen the foal's birth dive from the silent mare, and the ewes' instant scramble to their feet after the soapy emergence of their lambs, and was not afraid of the brief and natural discomfort to come.

The widow looked at her and raised her eyes heavenward, and by nightfall Rachel was being slowly and messily and bloodily gutted.

" 'Tis a pullet laying a goose egg and all that hollerin' don't help none, Mistress Wolcot," the old woman scolded unsympathetically. "What with 'ee no wider than a clay pipe, 'twill be a miracle if 'ee lives to see morning."

The curtains around the box bed panted and the canopy descended in a suffocating vermilion haze of pain. Consciousness slipped and returned and time was lost, and the mouthing midwife seemed a long way off as Rachel was trawled down from the back of her throat by huge seine nets of pressure. Lower, lower, dragged inside out by scalding hands, until a she-devil shouted terrible blasphemies and Will's child tore open her narrow body and reamed his way out.

The old woman held up a fat and shining silver salmon by its tail and then Rachel heard the sound of it splashing in the bowl of warm water and was too fatigued to care, or even to question that it cried like a baby, and then the midwife was back and laying a red-faced bawling infant in her arms.

"A boy, mistress."

He had a mat of black fluff on his head and she sought, yearning, for Will Tresider's eyes.

"Blue eyes," she murmured, disappointed.

"They all got blue eyes first and some changes later." The widow showed contempt at her ignorance. "Now give him the titty."

She held the baby's head to a breast and he gripped the nipple with unsuspected strength and the milk oozed achingly, and Rachel, resting back on the pillows, suddenly engulfed by affection and well-being, gathered him close to her, discovering his delicate ears and fingers and feet, and the way his head fitted into the palm of her hand, and that he was not only Will's child. He was hers.

"Jedder." She looked down and named him. "Jedder William Wolcot."

By the time she was fit enough to leave the house again, Robert Wolcot had hacked a wide gap through the boundary bank and hung a wooden gate across it; the first hollow drain had been cut and filled with stones and brushwood, and he had started work on an angled ditch to channel water from the center to the edge of the new land. Within weeks, the rushes began to die back, to be replaced by a down of grass filaments, and, by summer, the cows, their yearling followers and two fresh calves were grazing there.

Three haystacks, each the size of a cottage, grew stubbornly from the ashes of the previous year's ricks, and the long, dry season led to a good harvest which filled the new granary with grain. The acquisition of Moses Bottom also brought extended grazing rights on Beara and so the flock was increased, and Rachel's insistence on sowing a field of turnips, as had been done in Norfolk, ensured that their stock came through the severe frosts of the following winter in good condition, while those of others, kept by more traditional methods, starved.

Very slowly, the gaping, meaty wounds caused by her separation from her lover were healed by the unwavering confirmation of her belief in Jedder's land and by the sight of his son growing within its protection.

The teamwork demanded by their continual labors and the achievement of such impressive improvements to Yellaton drew her closer to her husband. Never again would she feel the blood-speeding rapture stirred by Will Tresider, but, watching Robert play with the dark-eyed infant as naturally and fondly as if he were his own boy, or pacing back and forth for miles across the plowed earth, broadcasting seed with unfaltering accuracy, or dragging in loads of peat cut from the moor, gradually kindled a deep and respectful love for him.

Physically it was easy to be acquiescent and comforting to a man who offered such unselfish care, and the discovery in the new year that she

125

was pregnant again was pleasing. Her condition seemed to be a kind of personal offering to his goodness, although, strangely, in the following months she hardly thought of the coming child at all.

The baby, another boy, was born with only slightly less brute force than her first, but the great wave of maternalism she had experienced at that birth was not repeated when he was given to her. Had he not been as chubby and likable as a fat, blond puppy, John Wolcot might well have been rejected. However, he was perfectly content to eat and sleep through his early months, requiring remarkably little attention—unlike his half-brother, who, between rare smiles which reminded her more of Will each day, continued to besiege her with screaming demands and remained her unreasonable delight.

To Robert Wolcot the arrival of his firstborn was an unexpected miracle. As he lifted the baby from its cradle, he was overwhelmed. A sensible, traditional man, he had thought children to be the exclusive concern of women, and it had not occurred to him until that moment that fatherhood would mean more than the acceptance of a natural responsibility in his life. Now, as he looked at the clenched fists and strongly kicking legs and at the little pointed penis, he suddenly understood the enormity of his own creation—that he and Rachel had made another human being—his son, a man.

John Wolcot gave a reflex grin and Rachel, lying damply exhausted in the feather bed, was surprised to see tears shine behind her husband's eyelashes.

Then he laid the infant beside her, looked at them both for a long minute, shook his head and went out. Late that evening he returned to the bedroom with a huge bunch of wild pinks and candytuft and broom and honeysuckle and buttercups and poppies for Rachel.

"I ain't done much today," he confessed sheepishly. " 'Cos I thought as these might please you and I bin working on summat for our John."

He handed her a tiny spoon, perfectly fashioned from walnut and sanded to a marble-smooth finish, with a lamb's curly head carved into the handle.

Such was his love of his new child that in the early days Rachel was afraid he might overlook Jedder, but she underestimated her husband. Soon both boys were with them all day in the fields, where Robert Wolcot spent as much time with the older as with the younger, carrying them on his back, rolling with them on the ground and talking to them as though they were already grown, explaining each task, pointing out the coming changes in the weather and the condition of the stock and the signs of each season.

It was a year of torrential and continuous rain, with the price of wheat higher than it had been in living memory. In the towns there were food riots, and in the country, first the hay and then the corn harvest were virtually ruined, but Robert and Rachel worked side by side

126

with the inbred peasant philosophy that their losses would be balanced in the end, as indeed they were.

Mutton sold well, offsetting the slump in the market for wool caused by the war in America, with its subsequent loss of colonial trade. The sows' litters thrived and the mare gave birth to another filly foal. By autumn, the two milking cows and two heifers were all in calf and there were three young heifer followers and a yearling steer. Hams and sides of bacon hung in the kitchen chimney, and there was enough stored grain to grind for winter flour, and a gaggle of fattening geese hissed around the outside of the house: in all, more than ample food to feed the family through the next twelvemonth, and to provide small baskets for Jane Clarke, the village girl so shamed in church, in whom Robert and Rachel took a special interest. Rachel, obsessive from her hungry past, would check and double-check the supplies and continually add to them, alternately feeling an illogical fear that there was insufficient, despite the contradictory evidence of her own eyes, and a guilty greed at the spectacle of such plenty.

In reality, she had finally attained an almost impregnable position, adored by her hardworking young husband, and with her children growing healthily and quickly, as though out of Yellaton itself, which became richer and more exotically sensual every day.

Its stunning discs of color revolved around time, brass August and October copper, iron-black December and silver March. Ice-bound ripples on the white, calm landscapes of winter broke into the crashing, luscious rollers of summer hedges. It spiraled in the ceaseless wind through speeding clouds and humid mists and sun and storms and rain, which slipped off its sides in incessant mercury streams—taking from each, rejecting nothing. It tasted of salt and fruit. It smelled elemental of the loam and air and flame and waters of surety, of immortality. It endorsed that Rachel's position was armored and ascendant, at last.

Spring came again and she was past her twenty-first birthday when she realized she was expecting a third child and accepted the knowledge with resigned stoicism. It was the way of nature that a married woman should conceive almost annually, but pregnancy slowed life down so, and morning sickness was inaptly named when it continued through most afternoons and lasted from the second to the sixth month—by which time her narrow body was already cumbersome and her activities restricted.

Then she could not carry out work she had planned and was frustrated by the distance to the village, while ahead, like a gory red cave, loured the prospect of the birth struggle itself, which the midwife told her with relish would never grow easier, on account of her stunted size, and would probably kill her in the end.

As the time drew closer, Rachel became moody, irritated by the two infants and impatient to the point of indulging in tantrums with her big,

127

uncomplaining husband, who vacillated helplessly, trying to do the right thing but only succeeding in annoying her further.

"If you'd wait till I come, I'd have lifted 'un for 'ee," he said anxiously, after she had pulled the heavy kitchen table to one side in order to scrub beneath it. "And such work isn't no good just now. 'Twill injure 'ee."

In the day or two before her time, always possessed by the animal instinct to nest, she cleaned the house with ferocious energy.

"Any injury will have bin caused by you, Robert Wolcot," she replied viciously. "It wasn't I as put this in here." She put an angry hand on her bulging belly.

His face became colorless and stiff as he turned away, and Rachel burst into tears, so that he returned and put his arms round her, looking guilty and out of place, as men do in such situations.

"There won't be no more chillern, Rachel," he swore. "I'll see as 'ee don't have another after this."

"And how will you do that, you gurt fool?" She smiled up, tearfully. "By sleeping in the shippen?"

"If needs be," he vowed earnestly.

Lights glinted in her witch-banded eyes and she pulled his head down, meeting his mouth with her full lips in such a sensual denial of her condition that he was surprised into responding and involuntarily drew her against him.

"I don't think so, Bob Wolcot," she giggled. "I can't see as I'd care for straw, after being bedded for so long on duck down."

Sarah Wolcot actually caused less pain than had been envisaged, because she was so small. Minute and perfect, she lay in the wooden cot like a briar rose. Her skin was as delicate and whisper-pink as petals and her large, unseeing eyes were almost violet in their darkness. Her mother touched a wispy pale-gold curl tentatively, bemused by having borne such a child, who, from her sweetly shaped mouth to her little arched feet, was flawlessly beautiful.

Robert Wolcot was instantly enraptured by his daughter, cupping her in his horny hands as though she were breakable and calling her loving names, his lark, his pet lamb, his dear lill' soul, his pretty. If she awoke and cried in the night, he was first to her side, lifting her tenderly and walking the room, rocking her in his arms until she slept again. The two boys were taught that it was their duty, above all, to protect her, and she was paraded round the village to be admired by every member of his extensive family.

In September, it was he who insisted that she be taken to the Barnstaple Fair instead of being left in the care of Jane Clarke, although she was less than twelve months old. She sat in a pannier basket with him on his horse, with John clinging on behind and Jedder with Rachel on her mare, and they set out at first light down the steeply wooded slopes to Langleys Ford and by the long, winding, secret lane, which came out below Chapelton, where the main road, already alive with country folk, led through Bishops Tawton to the town.

The fair spread from North Walk to the Strand and into the Square, and Rachel wondered nostalgically if Jack Greenslade were there. She had not kept her promise to meet him that first year and imagined he must have wed and had young ones of his own since then. In her mind, she could see him somersaulting and tumbling again like a dancing harlequin, and her eyes eagerly searched for him.

It was strange being among fair people again. Suddenly, the years between were eliminated and that special feeling of camaraderie and friendship and inimitable closeness returned with a rush that made her blink and swallow hard. For although she was now established as a respectable wife and mother, Rachel Jedder knew that the only people who had ever truly accepted her had been the motley itinerants and performers of the traveling fair. Throughout the rest of her life she had always been viewed as an outsider, first as a despised pauper, and still, because she had not been born in the locality of High Chilham, where she would remain a foreigner until she died.

So, despite these showmen around her at Barnstaple Fair being total strangers, she gazed at them with real affection, feeling happy and at home, as though they were known and familiar.

The booths were crammed together, a monkey walking a tightrope over the wares of the cheese vendor, the puppeteer's box adjoining a pie and pasty seller, and all decorated with painted placards and flags and carved shutters and embroidered hangings.

A large stuffed glove, symbolizing openhanded welcome, was exhibited in the northwest window of the Quay Hall, and every now and again the excited, pushing mob in front of the building was scattered by a cantering flock of sheep or a runaway horse or a man discovering that his pocket had been picked; and bells and beating drums, roaring bullocks and shouting showmen made a mad music, which veered noisily about in the air like a swarm.

At midday, the mayor of Barnstaple, preceded by a gaggle of portly mace bearers and beadles, paced slowly through the center of the proceedings to the High Cross to proclaim the fair.

"Oyez! Oyez! Oyez! The Mayor of this Borough doth hereby give notice that there is a Free Fair within this Borough for all manner of persons to Buy and Sell within the same, which Fair begins on this day, Wednesday, and shall continue until twelve o'clock on the night of the sixth day . . ."

Bob Wolcot bought fairings of ribbons and a little china cup for Rachel and Sarah and nuts for the boys and they all followed the procession to the South Gate, where the fair was proclaimed again.

". . . during which time the Mayor chargeth and commandeth on His Majesty's behalf all manner of persons repairing to this Town and Fair

129

do keep the King's Peace. And that all Buyers and Sellers do deal justly and truly and do use true Weights and Measures and that they duly pay their Toll, Stallage and other Duties upon pain that shall befall thereon. . . ."

The dignitaries marched on, with diminishing enthusiasm and perspiring red faces, to the bottom of Cross Street, where the mayoral tones, so forceful an hour before, repeated the proclamation for the third and last time in a hoarse growl, which had weakened to a whisper by the last paragraph.

". . . And if any Offences, Injury or Wrong shall be committed or done by or to any person or persons within this Town Fair and Liberty the same shall be redressed according to Justice and the Laws of this Realm. God Save The King!"

There were loud cheers, the mayor wiped his forehead and nodded rather brusquely and all scattered to enjoy themselves.

Bob Wolcot played skittles and brought gin for Rachel and ale for himself and the children, and they watched youths shying stones at tethered hens, and dogs baiting a fine red bull which had had the tips of its horns, ears and tail cut off. Her sons and husband thought these great sport, but Rachel said it was a waste of poultry and a good beast, and little Sarah cried, until they gave her a gingerbread man from the tray of a hot and flushed girl in charge of a group of squabbling, crying younger brothers and sisters.

It was near the end of the day when they found the small tent set up a little apart from the main row of exhibits. A gaudily colored painting of a brown-skinned woman wearing a headdress hung with gold coins was nailed over the opening, which was red-curtained, and the swarthy man guarding it looked hard at Rachel.

"A penny to have your fortune told, mistress," he invited.

" 'Tis not for God-fearing folk," said Robert Wolcot, taking her arm, but Rachel stood still and looked back at the gypsy.

"Hear what the future holds," he wheedled.

"Wouldn't do no harm, Bob." She smiled persuasively at her husband, who was looking stubborn. "And I shouldn't be in there long."

"Needs courage to learn what tomorrow brings," the gypsy challenged.

Rachel freed her arm decisively, handed over the coin, parted the curtains and walked through. Inside, it was so dark that a small lantern was needed to provide just enough light to reveal an outlandishly garbed woman sitting before a draped table on which lay a clear round glass ball.

She beckoned the girl to sit down and asked, "Cards or crystal?"

The beryl glowed pale green and seemed to contain movement, fleeting as vapors, and Rachel, hypnotized, pointed. The fortune-teller stared into it, the expression in her eyes becoming remote and her pupils expanding blackly over her irises as the globe shimmered with indefinable mysteries.

130

"Yours is a rare, uneasy route, mistress, for death leads the way," said the gypsy woman unemotionally, her face blank. "Poverty through death and Riches through death and Sorrow brought by death and Freedom given by death."

"That was the past," Rachel pointed out quickly. "The deaths of my mother and grandfather."

"Death strikes very close and death strikes often and death strikes soon." The woman continued as though she had not spoken.

"Who? Who will die?" whispered Rachel, feeling blood drain from her heart. "Is it Will Tresider? Jedder, my son?"

"A golden carpet and a white mansion, just as revealed in the ring of stones." Again her interruption was ignored as the gypsy woman pronounced her fate. "Your mark is over a high hill and a long valley and will spread further when you see your own reflection on the other side of a life."

"I don't understand," Rachel pleaded.

"What you love will be lost. What you want will be gained."

"I need to know more. Tell me more."

"There is no more, mistress. Death is the price."

The crystal was empty and clear. The gypsy woman's eyes had closed. Rachel stared for a long moment and then ran out.

Robert Wolcot took one look at her face, seized her wrist and strode between the sellers of sweetmeats down to the stable behind the Three Tuns Inn, where the horses had been left. The two little boys had to run to keep up, but Rachel was still trembling when they reached the yard.

Her husband looked at her furiously and without sympathy. "What did I tell 'ee?"

She started to sob out the fortune-teller's words, but he shouted, "I don't want to hear none of 'un. They are evil folk, they gypsies, and speak wicked lies and I won't have no more of it."

He shook her hard, actually hurting her, before picking her up and dumping her unceremoniously into the saddle. He placed the children, mounted himself and rode ahead, leaving her to follow him home, miserably; far more depressed, finally, by this, his first display of real ill humor, than by the fortune-teller's riddles, which, upon reflection, had been mainly incomprehensible.

She reached out automatically and her husband arose at the same time. In the dark, her hand blundered into the baby's face and felt it burning wetly against her palm. Soft, shallow gasps galloped into her hearing and terrorized her awake. Then he was there, catching up the child while she fumbled to light a candle.

The flame seeded and burgeoned in the airless room and Robert Wolcot stared down at his infant daughter and aged twenty years. Her cheeks and lips were raw with fever and she shook convulsively, her arms and legs twitching, a dark rash and shiny skin of sweat covering her

131

whole body. He let out a great groan and hugged her to him, until Rachel unlocked his rigid hold and laid her back in her crib, binding her tightly in a woolen wrap, whereupon he slumped onto his knees and wept noisily.

Rachel moved with exaggerated control to conceal her own horror, which was as much at her husband's disintegration as at the child's sickness—along to the room where the apples were stored and where bunches of herbs hung and their roots dried out; down to the kitchen to make up a decoction of lovage to draw the heat; returning to the bedroom as the sun's first rays slanted through the east window to land in a square of light on the sickbed and frame in brightness the fine rash covering the whole of the child's body.

Instant memory of that hideous last summer in the workhouse when one infant after another had caught a cold with a hard, dry cough, and then fever had risen and broken out in angry spots, just like this. The measles, they had called the disease, and two thirds of the pauper children had died.

The baby whimpered as the herbal medicine was administered on the little wooden spoon and her mother noticed her bloodshot, watery eyes with dread.

"What's to do?" Robert Wolcot was tugging at her sleeve abjectly. An hour of mortal panic had drained all his natural confidence and left him impotently dependent.

" 'Tis a sickness I had in the poorhouse and I lived through it," she lied, trying to sound unconcerned and give him heart. "If this potion don't drive the flush off, juice of tormentil will do it, never fret. You take care of her, while I make some up."

She hurried away, unable to bear looking at them, and, for the whole day, cooked tidbits of chicken breast and calf's-foot broth and egg custard and made up drinks of herbs and honey and mixed a poultice of boiled sage and lupin with barley meal and rough suet to spread on a cloth and place hot on the baby's chest, working as though sheer industry might cure. But the food was refused and the liquids dribbled out and the poultice made the child scream so much that Robert tore it off, and as he strode the room that night, the fever continued to devour and Sarah began vomiting in his arms.

The nearest doctor lived in Bideford, and he was a rogue who would have delayed days before calling and then arrived drunk, so the people of High Chilham preferred the advice and drenches of Isaac Cottle's son, who could read and owned a book on the treatment of medical matters, and cured horses and cattle as well. Robert Wolcot fetched him before dawn.

The healer took the sick child out onto the early morning moor, stripped off all her clothes, then, kicking a resting sheep up from the ground, laid her, face down, in the form left by the animal in the turf.

132

Rachel ran forward, protesting, "No! Pick her up! It's wet and cold here. Stop him, Robert! This can't do her no good."

"Leave her be, mistress. Her mun breathe in the vapors left there by the sheep till the earth goes cold, for 'twill stop all the coughing and cool the blood."

He held Rachel back as she struggled to reach the baby, shouting again, "Robert! Robert!"

But her husband only shook his head dumbly, and after about five minutes Amos Cottle released her to snatch the infant into a cloak and rush her back to the house.

Sarah Wolcot died two days later. She had been a matchless child, so beautiful and good, always blithe, an angel child. Rachel stared at her still, small body and was clamped by a tempered and terrible band which allowed no tears, and from which she knew she would never be released. For the rest of her life, the image of that dewy, sweet face would flicker around the edge of her thoughts and dreams, losing the sharpness of its focus with time, gradually melting into a lacy impression, perhaps no more than the mist of a remembrance, but forever haunting and forever pain.

After his daughter's death, Robert Wolcot sat in the inglenook seat in the kitchen and rarely moved or spoke. He would not eat or drink, and it was Rachel who tended the stock, milked the cows, looked after the boys; and who stood in the churchyard and saw the baby buried. Her husband was not at her side, and because her bereavement was borne in such isolation, and unshared, the sorrow hardened into a glittering black jewel which was to outlast even the precise recollection of the lost child herself.

In the week that followed, she would go to her husband sometimes and put her arms around him and force his hand against her breast, trying to imbue him with her own strength, pleading silently with him to return from the locked world of his grief. In late afternoon, she would push little John to him, to look into his face and tug his hand and prattle of the day's events, but Robert would only pat the child's head listlessly and look through him with unseeing eyes.

Then the man, too, became ill, and Rachel nursed him as his body scorched and his mind raved, but although she whispered love, and cried and raged and taunted him to stay alive, he would not. The drunken doctor from Bideford bled him, but the fever stayed high and his breath became thin, and he would not fight back. They said he died of pneumonia, but in truth he had lost the will to live.

The fortune-teller's words had come true. Death had struck close and often and soon. Death had led the way. Rachel Jedder, lying alone once again in the great feather bed, recalled them with quiet fatalism.

She carried out her tasks automatically now, rising early, as always, and working hard on Yellaton. The villagers thought her soulless because she went to market and continued her business as before, not showing a suitably open distress, which would have been respectable. The Wolcots had actually made her apparent refusal to mourn their excuse for excluding her; because, of course, they had not wanted her in the family in the first place.

None knew she sorrowed for him in an inexpressible way, too private for words or public lament, missing, with almost physical pain, his quiet and steady presence, his big, comfortable body, his devotion. His passing had taken the ease from the old house and left only a chilled vacuum in which she had to continue.

Winter came with a huelessness that seemed fitting, short, wet days following one after another to become weeks and then months of mild and depressing anemia. Even the great skyscapes were unrelieved by any variation of tone or light, but stretched to Cornwall like dirty gray wool, and the attacking ruddiness and gilt of the autumn moor were pulped to soft and soporific shades, dun brown and mouse gray, veiled olive slopes and fumid rises, which echoed Rachel's long mood of numb submission.

Her sons were too young to be company, or much comfort, and the feeling of lonely isolation returned and was familiar. It went back to her beginnings and held more reality than the short span of contented domestic security provided by Robert Wolcot. This quickly reduced to a stamp-sized picture somewhere behind, and ever outshone by, the brilliance of Will Tresider's time, in the far distance of her mind.

She worked quietly and patiently and methodically, saying and reacting little, and accepting, finally and without defiance, the bitter lesson of her experience—that all human relationships were transient and only Jedder's land endured.

CHAPTER NINE

Snow fell lightly in February, just feathering the back of Beara Moor, while avoiding the combes. It flurried in a fine spray onto Rachel's face as she inspected her flock in the night, and its keen cold was solace. The thick animal smell of the ewes was emphasized by its freshness, and they dropped their lambs in steamy bubbles of such heat that falling flakes melted in the air and a patch of bare, dry heather was left around each beast. Jedder, who was now five years old, and John already knew how to check their condition by day, and so a twenty-four hour watch was maintained and, between periods of fitful sleep, Rachel managed to oversee all the lambing with very few losses.

Then two heifers, having been taken to the Wolcot farm bull the previous year, calved for the first time, uncomprehending and bellowing at the contractions and unexpected pain, yet instinctively completing each stage of the deliveries without panic. They shifted from side to side and occasionally kicked at their bellies, breathing faster and arching their spines, and lying down at last in intense concentration on the business of giving birth. Rachel's soothing voice no longer mattered as they finally discovered with amazed and gentle fulfillment their living, staggering, nuzzling offspring.

Each hour was full and there was no time to brood over the past, and the days became weeks of little speech. Although spring came late in a swirl of cold winds which delayed planting, the close and fruitful contact with the year's new stock eventually did bring peace again to Rachel Wolcot.

It was April before she hung the full basket of grain from her shoulders and began tilling barley in Yonder Plat. Robert Wolcot had shown her how to broadcast the seed without wasting too much, and although she was so short in stature, she managed to coordinate her pace and the spreading of each handful into a clockwork accuracy.

Followed by her two small sons, who were set to scare off the gangs of hungry and persistent birds, she marched back and forth like a wound-up toy and found herself satisfied by the precision of it and the pleasurable ache in her swinging arms and the hope that, if the year went well, each acre would yield forty bushels of grain at harvest, as well as straw for bedding and feeding steers.

The first swallows returned, wrens sang with operatic might in the hedges, the ducks sat, at last, on clutches of eggs laid a month later than usual. The earth in the kitchen garden was rich and weed-free and friable and easy to trench, because her dead husband had prepared it so well the previous year. Handling it brought him close again and made her tearful in remembrance for a while as she covered the rows of chitted potatoes and showed the boys how to drop peas into the holes made by the dibber.

They hoed the winter wheat together, as crushed leaves appeared, fluttering palely on the beech trees like fragments of rags, and green stippled the hedges once more. Then the dandelions flowered, massed suns in the lane verges, to be picked on sunny afternoons for Rachel to stir and rack and cork up in stone bottles, time bombs of honey-clear wine to be exploded twelve months on.

" 'Tis my turn to feed the hogs."

"You'm too little, brother. You'm only fit for pickin' popples."

135

"I's big's you."

"You'll fall in and old sow'll crush 'ee and gobble 'ee up, 'cos you'm a runt."

"I's not a runt! I's not!"

The boys squabbled as they struggled to the sties with the bucket of swill and rested it perilously while Jedder climbed the low wall. The giant sow ran through the muddle of squealing piglets with unexpected speed, opening her mouth to bare short, lethal tusks as he grasped the wooden handle and staggered. She began to lower her head, pinpoint eyes glinting with greed and bad temper, until, with a desperate heave, the child managed to tip the bucket, and its hot, stinking contents sploshed into the trough below. The pig dropped her snout into it gluttonously. Rachel, watching from the orchard, sighed and shook her head at the risk, then went on balancing on the top rung of the dangerously rickety ladder and sawing through the canker-rotted branch.

"Come and lead old Bess over the hare's leg, John," she called.

"What about I then?" demanded Jedder jealously.

"You muck spread with me," she said.

"Awww!" he whined with disappointment. "John always gets Bess. 'Tain't fair."

"Her goes best with him," Rachel pointed out.

It was true. The mare followed her youngest son like a pet dog, as did all the beasts on the holding. He could walk up to the most excitable steer or right into the shelter of a farrowing sow and remain unharmed. They reacted only with gentleness and pleasure at his presence. It was a gift. High Chilham folk, hearing of it, recalled Rachel's great-grandfather, a horseman renowned for his way with animals, who "could break a wild colt off the moor in a week without a whip," they said.

Jedder, on the other hand, was the opposite, making the cows roll their eyes nervously and the ewes scatter as he rushed noisily among them, waving a stick impatiently and succeeding only in sending them all in the wrong direction, which made him shout the more.

Like all country children, the boys were expected to work for almost as many hours as their mother. They scared birds from the young corn by rattling wooden clappers, or picked stones from the turned earth for mornings at a time, or weeded, or watched sheep, or cleaned harness, or dragged in wood. In a society which regarded children more as miniature adults than as beings with different and special needs, anything that came within the limits of their strength was regarded as acceptable and normal employment, and already the aggregate of these contributions eased the burdens of Rachel Wolcot's own long labors considerably.

The years on Yellaton had given her many skills and developed her slight body to enable it to cope to the maximum of its weight with the daily need to lift and maneuver sacks and animals and iron tools. Now, although her duties filled sixteen hours of each day, for seven days of every week, the work was balanced, and she never reached the extremes of endurance and suffering incurred during her first summer.

She went to market only when necessary and her isolation ceased to seem lonely, becoming instead a restorative solitude. It was good to walk alone through the underwater light of her damp woods, with the warm rain refreshing her skin as she brushed past wetly polished shrubs, and sometimes she and the children would take time to play, unzipping handfuls of seeds from their stalks to fling at each other and at the joyful gray dog, or rolling in the long grass until coated with the scent of its bruised stems, or paddling in the rill which had cut its course across the foot of Moses Bottom after the draining of the marsh.

On the pretext of tracing the flock, they would walk over Beara and she would point out far-off landmarks, and where the Bideford-to-Exeter road lay and the directions of Mouth Mill and Appledore and the sea, and she would talk compulsively of Will Tresider (with the excuse to herself that Jedder should know about his father), until they reached beyond Huntshaw Cross to where they could see the ocean and Lundy Island lying in the haze of distance to the west.

The summer was cool, but despite the chilled, wet start to the year and the belated sowing there was a good harvest, and at the end of September she hired the same two lads who had brought in the hay to cut the corn. They were the only outsiders to have come onto her land since her husband's burial, yet she did not miss the company of others and no longer noticed the attempts of the younger village men to attract her attention at church. Instead, she deliberately sought and found gratification in the fertility and beauty and prosperity of Yellaton, and especially in the sturdy growth of her children. Remembering the stick-thin limbs of the workhouse children and the warped frame of little Sam at Wame's farm, she would look at their strong legs and straight bodies with thankful joy and know that the land in its bounteousness had created them so.

Her thoughts were not permitted to dwell for long on sadnesses, and by nightfall, too tired to feel restless, she slept the reachless and total sleep of a person wholly consumed.

Then, after an unusually warm November, it was winter again and, for two hours each afternoon, she forced herself to thresh the corn with the eelskin-linked flail, gripping the hickory shaft and beating rhythmically down on the sheaves with its hollywood truncheon to knock the barley out of the ears, choking in the chaff-fogged air of the barn and wincing as splinters of straw fired into her eyes; grateful that the brief, dim days forced early retreat into prolonged, sheltered evenings by the great fire in the kitchen.

The garden had been superficially dug over and was now a chocolate slab by the house. Most of the ditches were clear, and the pigs and poultry, released onto Brindley field, had already rooted and scratched well down into the soil and broken up the stubble, saving her the impossibly hard task of paring it off to burn. By Christmas she could look around the holding with some smugness, knowing that all the vital work of the year had been completed, that her larders and corn bins were full, the root crops clamped and the tools cleaned and stored.

Laurel and ivy and bright-red berries dressed the chimneypieces and shelves, and the kissing bough of evergreens and candles hung from the ceiling as a crown over a bunch of mistletoe. Roast goose and carrots, spiced ham and turnips, and rich plum pudding and mince pies. The cider was ready. Clouded and spiky, it went down like drinking nails. The bells rang out, their peals crossing the valley and rising to the old house like a formation of plangent, jeweled birds.

Then Rachel Wolcot heard singing, as bold and cheerful as a lighted tavern in the mole-dark eve, and opened her door to the carol singers, farmhands and their wives, visiting the outlying farms and settlements. They grinned their quick-eyed, gap-toothed smiles, waiting for her reaction after the year of exclusion. She laughed without malice, gave them a penny and poured out the ale mulled with nutmeg and sugar and egg yolks and cloves, with baked apples dropped in, sizzling, and felt herself grow happy and light-spirited once more.

After Robert Wolcot's death, Rachel had put away her colorful clothes and dressed only in plain wool and fustian. These had seemed proper wear and suited her feelings at the time, but the festivity of that Christmas revived the longing to dance again, to be noticed and recognized and, although she would not have admitted it, to be courted once more.

She lifted the lid of the ancient carved chest in the bedroom and gazed down wistfully at the folded garments. One by one, she lifted them out and spread them on the bed, the sea green of the peddler's taffeta, the yellow silk worn to catch a husband, the crimson-and-gold brocade in which she had danced for Will Tresider in Appledore, the velvet-hooded cloak, pine green to blend with the night, in which she had fled with him from Mouth Mill. Fashions might have changed in the cities and spas since they were made, but in the villages and even in Barnstaple such dresses would turn heads for many more years.

She pulled off the dull gray of the day, bundled it up and stepped into the most luxurious of all, a gown of apricot bombazine extravagantly trimmed with ribbons and gold thread, flounces and bows and lace.

The looking glass Will had brought her stood on the old chest of drawers. Angling it carefully, she gazed into its soft, silver light to see a young face, creamy-skinned, with full, erotic lips and sad, pagan eyes, a proud and stubborn and interestingly clever face. Rachel Wolcot winked cheekily at the image, tossed her black hair and watched her own reflected eyes gleam with an almost forgotten sense of fun. Will had taught that life was infinitely richer than mere industry and survival. Suddenly she knew that it was time to answer its shout once again.

Cold cut the next morning in a sharp-edged and hoary block out of the night and Rachel realized that, while still preoccupied, she had already fed and watered and cleaned out all the stock, completed the milking and scrubbed the dairy utensils. The fires were lit and the boys drooping sleepily over their hot milk, bread and fat bacon at the kitchen table. Outside, the ground was granite-hard with frost, and the prospect of another day threshing corn or painting protective tar on the stable timbers or cutting frozen flatballs for cattle feed was not appealing.

She changed from her heavy working clothes back into the apricot gown, although market at High Chilham was days off. Bideford and Barnstaple were rejected because of old associations and Exeter was a day's ride away and too foreign. Indecisively she tidied the dresser and buffed the two brass lamps and folded clothes, which had been airing near the heat, experiencing for the first time the claustrophobia of her enclosed existence on Beara Moor. She wanted people about her, needed to hear their voices, longed to be in the middle of a milling crowd. Then she remembered it was Tuesday—market day at South Molton.

Saddling the mare and calling out a few last-minute instructions to Jedder, she wheeled away from Yellaton and cantered down the valley path, through the woods and then the village, with a curt wave or two to known faces, impatient when it was necessary to rest the horse by walking, on past the Black Mantle, where she had first seen Squire Waddon, to arrive in the town less than two hours later.

Yeomen down from Exmoor turned as Rachel Wolcot strolled round the pens looking over the cattle and sheep. There was a vibrancy about her which drew attention. The change of mood had given her presence an air of spirited arrogance and her movement fluidity, so that when she walked, her petticoats swished provocatively. She looked mettlesome enough to be a challenge and ripe enough to be picked, and the old farmers, who knew a showy filly when they saw one, sighed with nostalgia.

The auctioneer babbled and concluded unintelligible negotiations. Dealers slapped hands with satisfied customers. Ewes lamented and bullocks bawled and live hens, their legs bound together, lay on the bare earth with their beaks open and silent with fear. She made her way through the pannier market, fingering some dairy muslin and a pair of pattens and the newfangled barrel churn for making butter, and buying two sheep bells before emerging into the square at the other end of the building.

The Exeter mail coach was unloading, its horses sweat-damp and hollow-flanked, their heads dropped to the ground. Rachel watched the passengers clamber out with casual curiosity. Then, suddenly, there was an explosion inside her head and for a moment she was stricken sightless and then the square tilted and she found herself holding onto a column in front of the Guildhall while Will Tresider stepped from the coach, caught the bag flung down to him by the whip and began walking away.

Rachel Wolcot picked up her skirts and ran into the road. A pony drawing an overloaded cart reared and its driver swore, but she sped on without noticing, pushing between two men talking outside the Unicorn Inn and causing a woman to drop a basket of eggs. He had reached the livery stables by the time she caught up and grasped his arm, tugging him to a stop and burying her head in his shoulder.

"Will . . . Will . . ."

"What's this?" The voice sounded startled.

Full of apprehension, Rachel slowly raised her head, and looked into the eyes of a complete stranger.

"This Will of yours is fortunate indeed to inspire such attention from so charming a lady." He spoke courteously, looking at her with amused appreciation.

Rachel felt a blow of disappointment and then stared, fascinated. It was almost her lover's face, a different expression, but the same well-shaped mouth and strong nose; only the eyes were gray and more deeply set and the forehead smooth. And this was a gentleman.

"Your pardon, sir." Her blush spread down to her breasts. "A mistake. I thought you were another."

"A delightful mistake." The stranger bowed and smiled so nearly the same smile, then looked toward the stables, as though about to move on. His dark hair curled against his neck as Will's did, and his height and the set of his shoulders were so familiar that she could not let him leave.

"You have come far?" She heard herself gasp out.

"From Plymouth, ma'am," he replied, still focused beyond her, searching for the ostler.

"And have you much further to go?" Rachel pressed, recklessly.

"To the village of Umberleigh."

"Umberleigh!" Eagerness lit her tone. "Why, 'tis on my way home. I ride right through there on my way to Beara Moor."

The man turned his head toward her again, lazily taking in the diminutive figure, the expensive but unfashionable apricot bombazine gown, the rough hands and the extraordinary, compelling pool-green-and-umber-colored eyes.

"Then we must travel together," he said.

He hired the best horse in the stable, tossing money to the groom carelessly, and she felt ashamed of her shaggy old mount as he drew back to let her pass. As they left the town, she kept glancing at him secretly, spellbound by his likeness to Will Tresider and by the fact that she had never been accompanied by such a gentleman before.

He wore a calf-length greatcoat with two capes at the shoulder and the largest silver buttons she had ever seen, and once he consulted a heavy gold fob watch which was hung on a gold chain across his waistcoat. Despite the long, dusty journey from Plymouth, there was not a mark on his buckskin breeches and he rode with the bearing of an officer, eyes straight ahead.

He had returned from sea, he told her, finally come ashore to stay after ten years sailing between Africa and Cuba as captain of a slaver.

"A slaver!" Her eyes widened. "You seen black men then?"

"Hundreds of 'em, ma'am." He grinned.

"And they be real black?"

"Black as this nag here." He thwacked the rippling shoulder of the horse with his cane and the animal sprang forward, only to be jagged back by the reins.

"And the black don't rub off none?" Rachel persisted, now quite hypnotized by such glamour.

After the trollops and painted boys who hung around the ports, her rural naivete was diverting. His eyes narrowed and twinkled. "If you scrubbed 'em with chloride of lime, such as is used to clean ships' tubs, they'd just come up the blacker," he assured her.

Then she chattered of Yellaton, boasting of its acreage and of the quality of her stock, so that he should not imagine she was just some country wench with nothing but family good will.

"And I got plans to add to my land," she boasted. "I know where there's another piece of near twenty acre, and I'll have that when my boys are a bit older."

He listened with a politeness which eventually made her feel embarrassed, in case he thought her foolish. Perhaps his own family owned hundreds of acres and he was returning home to run the estate. Aged in the mid-thirties, he was far too young to retire, unless it was to live off a private fortune, and the description of her small homestead must seem laughable.

Rachel went quiet and for a mile or so they rode in silence until, from the brow of a hill, they saw the cottages of Umberleigh clustered on the bank of the River Taw in the valley below.

"May I know your name?" the gentleman asked.

"Rachel . . . Jedder." For the first time in six years she took up her own name again with impulsive decision.

He introduced himself in turn. "Harry Blackaller, ma'am." And, inclining his head slightly, he added, "My path lies west from here, but before taking leave, may I say that your company has done me honor, Mistress Jedder."

Rachel saw a narrow track branching to the left, and by the time she raised her hand in farewell, he was already cantering off along it. She continued on her way feeling unnerved by the encounter.

Memories of Will Tresider returned with tormenting intensity after Rachel's meeting with the stranger. It was as though they had been

141

parted for hours instead of years and as though her marriage to Robert Wolcot had never been. The cool order she had striven so hard to achieve in her life was destroyed by the tumultuous old feelings, so that for days she moithered distractedly about Yellaton and her nights were passed once more in tears of regret and lovesickness.

Then, gradually, the idea began to form that seeing the gentleman again would defuse the ferocity of this reactivated passion. But she had no reason or excuse for going to Umberleigh, and although he lived a mere ten miles away, such was the gap between their social circumstances that it was quite possible they might never come upon each other at all.

As Rachel rode to High Chilham market the following week she fretted over how to make contact and despaired. She sold two hams without bargaining and absently ordered a pair of sheep shears and a peat knife from the village smith before riding down to Seth Bartle's, the horse-breaker, to see whether his new stallion would suit her youngest mare in the coming spring.

The horse was a majestic specimen, ebony black, with four heavily feathered white legs as thick as church pillars, far heftier and more muscular than any horse she had ever seen.

Seth Bartle paraded it, snorting and sidling, before her with excessive pride, explaining how it was one of the first of what would become the greatest breed of draught animals, bred by a famous livestock expert called Bakewell and brought at great expense all the way from his farm at Dishley in Leicestershire. Rachel wondered if such a sire would throw too big a foal for her mare, but was assured all would go well. She gaped at the colossal creature with undisguised admiration and, despite the high fee, booked the service.

"Upon oath, that's the most magnificent horseflesh I've ever set eyes on."

Rachel knew the voice instantly and whirled round. The gentleman from the London coach was standing by the gate behind them.

He doffed his hat and stared directly into her eyes. "There's none to touch Seth, here, when it comes to knowing a good brute, Mistress Jedder."

He seemed pleased, though not at all surprised, to see her again and went on, without giving her time to greet him. "Now, Seth, have you found me a nag?"

"Can't say as I have, Master Blackaller." The horsebreaker sounded oddly surly.

"Well, why don't we take a look around?" The gentleman walked resolutely across the yard. "You'll accompany me, Mistress Jedder?"

He gave Rachel his arm and swept her toward the stables. Behind them, Seth Bartle muttered and led the stallion away.

A variety of horses and ponies ranging from hunters to cart horses

142

occupied the long row of stalls, and the weights on their tethered halters thumped against the mangers as they turned their heads and pricked their ears at the sound of human movement.

Rachel, her senses quickened by the gentleman's nearness in the gloom of the building, was acutely aware of the close, still air and the generous, earthy smell of the horses and the heat of his arm against her body. Sex had ceased to matter to her since her husband's death and she had neither missed nor even consciously thought of lovemaking during the past year. Now a wave of languid warmth rolled over her, and as she glanced up at him in the half-light, this man seemed, in fact, to be her adored Will, and her hand tightened involuntarily.

Although he must have noticed the touch, he gave no sign but instead pointed his cane at the curved and gleaming hindquarters of an elegant hack and said, "This would do me very well, do you not agree, Mistress Jedder?"

"That hoss bain't for sale, Harry Blackaller." The horsebreaker was truculent as he walked through the door. "Belongs to Squire Waddon."

"What's he doing here?" asked Blackaller.

" 'Ee be a young hoss as needs a bit o' training yet," Seth Bartle replied reluctantly.

"Well, tell Waddon I'll give a hundred guineas for him," the gentleman drawled.

"You tell 'un yourself, Maister Blackaller, *sir*." Seth Bartle laid sarcastic emphasis on the courtesy address.

Rachel was stiff with astonishment, first at the exorbitant price offered for an animal which had not even been viewed in action, and then at the horsebreaker's hostile response.

However, the gentleman was already leading her back into the sunlight, and before she had time for reflection, she found herself returned to the saddle in a practiced movement hauntingly reminiscent of the way Will had suddenly lifted her onto his horse at their first encounter. For a second, need and loneliness pinched her small face and curtained her eyes. Then, schooling herself, she straightened her back and lifted her head.

"Good day, sir," she said with a radiant smile to the stranger, and swinging the mare away, rode toward the village, relieved that she had managed to regain her dignity but crestfallen by such an unsatisfactory conclusion to their second meeting.

Often, in the days which followed, she reproached herself for not having been bold enough to make a display of her interest. Yet she had to admit that Harry Blackaller's behavior toward her had only been that of any well-bred man toward a respectable woman of short acquaintance and had not evinced any particular attention on his part. He had not held her gaze or her hand for a fraction of time longer than necessary. He had hardly spoken to her and then had said nothing which could be interpreted as more than amiable good manners. But every word and gesture replayed to her over and again, like the single tune in a musical box, and on the screen of her mind his features began to overlap and finally replace those of Will Tresider.

She toiled the harder at Yellaton to escape the mental anarchy caused by the two men, rising earlier than before, deliberately wearing out her body during daylight with physical work, and spinning wool late into the taper-lit night until she fell asleep over the wheel. Her face grew even paler than usual and dark-red smudges of fatigue and strain turned her eyes into round onyx stones.

An oak had fallen near the footpath, which wound through her woods and over the moor to the village, and the labor of sawing up its branches warmed her in the frore mornings and was repetitious enough to need little concentration. She attacked it daily with unnatural energy, loading the moss-coated logs onto the sledge, heedless of rain and mud, and of the ruin of her dress. It must have been midday when the shadow moved between her and the pallid sun and she looked up.

"Trying out me new nag, ma'am, and thought I'd pass this way," he said.

Rachel, instantly ashamed of her bedraggled and dirty appearance, hung her head and muttered a greeting.

"I would be mighty appreciative of some refreshment, Mistress Jedder." The gentleman spoke as though they had met in town and she were perfectly attired. "This brute is taking some breaking."

He brought his whip down on the lathered hindquarters and the horse squealed and shied. Rachel noticed its flaring nostrils and fearful eyes and the heavy iron bit making its mouth froth, and was relieved to find something to talk about.

"You managed to buy him off Squire, then," she observed, starting to lead the way to the house. "But I thought Seth Bartle had broke 'im."

"Couldn't break a donkey," sneered Blackaller and then, with an oath, dug in his spurs so that the animal plunged past, splattering her with even more mud.

She caught up with them at the front door and let the gentleman in, glad that the parlor fire was already set with dry kindling and bracken which only needed a flame to blaze. She gave him a mug of cider before racing to the courtyard to swill her face and arms with sleety water from the bucket by the well. She fought out of her torn clothes on the way up the kitchen stairs to the bedroom, pulled on the green taffeta robe, which had been Will's favorite, fixed a bonnet over her tangled hair and managed to join him in about ten minutes.

The gentleman gave absolutely no sign of noticing the transformation. He sipped the cider, accepted a second pouring, talked of the season, described the last meet, diverted her with a couple of stories of his days at sea and then took his leave.

Rachel stood by as he mounted, her emotions swiveling between the

144

obsessive need to know that he would return and fear of appearing brazen. He gathered the reins and on impulse she hooked her fingers round the noseband as the horse jerked his head nervously, almost lifting her off the ground.

Then, breathless with daring, she asked, "Will you be passing this way again, sir?"

He met her gaze with light eyes which knew everything and answered, "Without doubt, Rachel Jedder."

A month went by and Harry Blackaller did not come. Rachel relived every second of their meetings countless times. She analyzed every nuance of every glance and movement and phrase, searching for intent and meaning and finding only contradictions. Perhaps, in fact, he had simply been riding over Beara to exercise his horse. Maybe she had only imagined that he knew how she felt, or, worse, that he might well have seen her yearning and merely been amused. He had given no sign of finding her attractive. He had paid no compliments. There was a steely remoteness about him which filled her with unease and was addictive at the same time.

The village market drew her with weekly regularity, and she stretched out her visits to it until the last beast was sold. She went to other nearby markets, which had never been of interest before, and, once she journeyed all the way to South Molton and trailed around the town in order to have the excuse of passing twice through Umberleigh. All in the hope of seeing him again, by chance.

At Yellaton, she now did very little work and found that little an effort. She thought miserably of Will and the gentleman, and the gentleman and Will, and cried a lot.

It was obvious that she had just been crying when she opened the door to him at last, late one afternoon. Dartmoor was firing rain horizontally against the old house like buckshot, and the water was splashing off his hat and cloak and boots. A massive bolt of passion stabbed through Rachel Jedder and she put out two trembling hands and drew him inside.

"Was caught in this devilish storm on the way back from Bideford," he said, as she took the wet cloak and unwittingly hugged it to her.

Behind him, the young horse stood, dull-eyed in the downpour, its head low and flanks heaving.

"Shall I put him in the stable?" asked Rachel.

But Harry Blackaller, ignoring the question, slammed the door shut and strode to the fire.

"Some mulled beer would be the saving of me, Mistress Jedder," he announced, turning to stand with his back to the heat as Will Tresider had so often done.

Rachel sped to the kitchen and thrust an iron poker into the heart of the fire there. Jedder and John were helping Luke Morrish. For the first time, she and the gentleman were truly alone. By the time she had filled the jug of ale from the cask and spiced it, the poker was red-hot and ready to be plunged into the drink. Before the beer had stopped hissing and fizzing, she was rushing with it back along the passage, pinching her cheeks to make them pink and praying that her eyes were not too bloodshot.

When he said he was hungry, she ran for ham and cheese and bread and pickled onions and butter, which she had intended to sell, and she prattled inconsequentially, unable in her jittery excitement to avoid sounding birdbrained.

"What do slaves eat?" she questioned. "Do they eat like beasts or men? Corn or bread?"

"Like beasts, ma'am, they eat mainly plants, rice and red peppers and garlic, and for meat they eat goat and alligator."

"Goat!" she shuddered, and wondered what alligator was but did not like to ask.

Outside, the night began to yawn over the dark gray day and Harry Blackaller asked for his cloak, which had been put to dry in the kitchen. She watched as he adjusted his tricorne and picked up his whip as they neared the door.

"Do not . . ." Rachel murmured.

"Do not?" He looked slightly surprised.

"Do . . . not . . . go." She was beyond caution now. "Stay . . . please."

He gave a faint smile, stepped back into the room and said, "Of course."

But she did not hear, for she was already in his arms, pressed against him, reaching to find his mouth, unaware that his hold was very light and his lips did not respond as Will's had done.

He followed her upstairs and allowed her to kiss and sigh against his skin, and Rachel, lost in the human warmth and contact, deliriously bewitched by the closeness of the man so like her lover, abandoned herself to him, weeping, ignorant that all the loving came from her and that he took her perfunctorily.

"Oh, Will," she whispered, and the years of longing were assuaged.

And afterward, lying against his back as he slept, she was too emotionally overwhelmed even to notice the stealthy ash flavor of disappointment.

She awoke first and, raising her head to look at his still unconscious form, was startled to find that he resembled Will Tresider much less while asleep. His face was thinner and his mouth more compressed and turned down, and where his hair had fallen back she saw that two deep lines angled across his left temple from between his eyes, like scars. It was like finding a complete stranger in her bed and she was troubled about what he would think of her behavior when he, too, awoke.

At that moment he opened his eyes, sat up and stared ahead blankly.

Rachel waited for a few seconds before murmuring hesitantly, "Good morrow, Harry Blackaller."

146

He grunted, but did not look around.

Gently she put out her hand to hold his, but, to her humiliation, he twisted sharply away, jumped briskly from bed and began dressing.

Rachel froze. She had never before been so unmistakably rejected, and she felt both mortified and offended. Sitting with her knees drawn up to her chest, she thought dismally of how she had degraded herself, pursuing a man who had only used her for a night, and then only because he had had little option. She glowered at his back, noticing that it was really quite narrow and had spots on the shoulders, and gradually she recalled, with growing scorn, the previous night and his ineptitude as a lover. How could she ever have compared him with Will Tresider? Hatred for herself, and even more for him, choked her.

He finished straightening his neckcloth in the looking glass, deliberately ruffled his hair into boyish disorder and walked back to sit on the foot of her side of the bed. The dawn sunlight was so dazzling through the east window that he could not now be well seen through it and that cunning likeness returned with searing vehemence. Rachel tautened and waited, holding onto her anger as the last guard of her pride.

Harry Blackaller fixed his pale eyes on her for the first time since waking.

"Well, Rachel Jedder," he said, with a familiar and heartbreaking smile. "It would seem we had better be wed."

Rachel was so shocked that for several minutes she could find nothing to say, and then her temper exploded.

"How durst you sit there and bam me so?" she raged. "I'm a plain countrywoman and I admit to have acted foolish, very foolish indeed, with regard to yourself, but it don't give you no right to stay on in my house and make little of me now, sir. So I'll be obliged if you will take your leave and begone."

His grin grew wider as he listened, until she paused for breath and sat back against the pillow, flushed and shaking with indignation.

Then, lolling across the far end of the bed, he drawled, " 'Pon oath, Mistress Jedder, you are gravely mistook. I am asking you to tread the flagstones to the altar once more, to be my spouse, my bride, my lady, my wedded wife, my helpmeet, the matron of my bosom.

"Would you prefer me to kneel before you, though 'twould be none too easy in these boots? Or smother you with roses—which must mean delaying until the bushes flower in June? Or would you be won by the arrival, one a day for a week, of seven black boys, each bearing an embroidered letter on a kerchief, spelling out 'Marry me'? Do you await some token of faith perhaps? A curl of my hair in a gold locket, a sprig of the sacred thorn of Glastonbury to treasure? Or should I achieve some miraculous feat, such as discovering another continent the size of Australia, or persuading the dowager Lady Grenville to fart before all?"

Rachel, whose animosity had given way to bewilderment and then to disbelieving mirth as he rattled on, was giggling by the time he ended.

"Enough, Harry Blackaller." She raised her hands. "You are forgiven, and now you can be off, with no ill feeling between us."

"Do you still doubt?" His expression became serious and he moved through the sunbeam to stand over her, speaking very slowly. "In all solemnity, Mistress Rachel Jedder, I *am* asking for your hand in marriage.

It was not possible—a gentleman to espouse a workhouse girl. It was unthinkable, like the mating of a thoroughbred with an ass, or hacking down a marble wall to give access to a bullock cart, or a cross-pollinating of orchid with weed. It was outrageous, against all the laws of society. Sacrilegious. Why, even if the gentry could not prevent it, the church must forbid such a union.

However, the church ordered no such bar. Instead, three weeks later, it opened its doors and gave the incongruous couple its blessing.

Rachel Jedder, by now in a state of emotional confusion, heard herself take the vows again and watched incredulously as Harry Blackaller held her hand and slipped a gold ring onto her finger.

Outside, the entire village had found reason to have business in the square, its collective opinion carefully masked behind indecipherable faces, the men sphinxlike in their neutrality and the women sly as cats. But Rachel, walking from the church on the arm of her gentleman, was too dazed to notice any of them.

It was as though she were being led, almost against her will, into another dimension, where everything appeared to be the same and yet was unfamiliar and threatening. It was not simply the speed with which she had found herself remarried, but also the way it had come about, which was so perplexing.

From the time he had managed to persuade her of his serious intention, Harry Blackaller had visited her three times only: once to tell of the posting of the banns; once to present a length of magnolia satin for her gown; and once to go over the final arrangements for the day. Each time, he had kissed her fraternally on the cheek upon arrival and departure, made her laugh with a few stories about well-known local characters, and had left quickly, without a single gesture of love or desire.

Rachel had searched his eyes for response and recognized none. Only the publicly official preparations for the ceremony were evidence of his professed concern for her. She had wondered if this was the way of the nobility, a form of behavior designed to protect the honor of the chosen bride until the wedding night—although in her own case it was rather too late for that.

In the very last days her confidence had ebbed away, leaving her gripped by scared uncertainty, and now, as they emerged from the church into the blustery March morning, panic overtook her. She stopped and turned and stared in consternation at the stranger she had just married. Harry Blackaller smiled down tenderly and gave her hand a little squeeze.

A delicious transfusion flowed through her, honey-sweet and healing and lucid, anointing and curing all her anxieties in an instant. Letting her head fall back, she gazed up at him, her face made beautiful by a transport of adulation. Everything would be all right.

They returned to Yellaton on a broad gray horse, Rachel riding pillion, her arms around her husband's waist, her body happy in the warmth which filtered through his coat, her face resting between his shoulder blades, and when he helped her dismount at the house, she locked her arms around his neck, rejoicing at being in his hold.

Harry Blackaller disengaged himself and remounted calmly.

"Have no fear," he said. "I shall be back by nightfall." And, with a merry wave, he rode off.

Rachel stood in her satin wedding dress before the door of her house too stupefied to move. She stared unseeing across the blank miles of the moor and sensed the intolerable message of the pointlessness of her own existence and the futility of love.

Then stumbling indoors and up the stairs, she took off the gown in a slow, wet trance of tears and went to the glass, as she had done only a few weeks before. Now, an uncoordinated face looked out at her through ophidian eyes, the mouth puffy and blotched from crying, the nose bumpy, a face without symmetry, or the aquiline structure of fine breeding, or the rosy plumpness of youth, an ugly face, an ugly, ugly face and a skinny, scrawny body, which had borne three children and still looked prepubescent. How could Will Tresider have loved her? What had Robert Wolcot found in her? And why should a gentleman like Harry Blackaller have made her his wife? No matter how hard she tried, she could make no sense of it.

At last she trailed down to the kitchen, scraped some vegetables and jointed a fat hare which had hung three days in the pantry, and dropped them all in a pot of cider to hang over the fire. The boys were staying with Jane Clarke and it was dark before five o'clock. Six hours later, she was still waiting, motionless, in the erratic light of the flames, the candles having burnt out long before. An hour after that, at midnight, she went to bed, alone, and did not sleep.

Much later still, the uneven tattoo of a walking horse carried through the night silence like the sound of an irregular heartbeat, and died at Yellaton.

"Rachel!" she heard him roar as he staggered through the door below and knocked over the table. "Rachel Blackaller!"

She pulled a cloak over her naked body and hurried to him, though by the time she reached the room, he had crashed into more furniture and was irate.

149

"Rachel Blackaller! Why were you not here to greet me? Where is the light?" He was very drunk.

"It is late, husband, and I grew tired," she explained, steering him toward the stairs.

"A fine bride it is who is too lazy to stay awake for her master on her wedding night," he grumbled, stumbling and cursing as he fell.

She remained carefully impassive and made no reply.

"I am the master here now, you know," he mumbled. "Master of you and your precious Yellaton."

Rachel felt her skin prick and go cold. A small black leech of a thought hooked onto her mind and she physically shook her head to be rid of it.

She had seen with her own eyes how Harry Blackaller tossed gold lavishly to ostlers and innkeepers and bought fine clothes and horses. He had money in plenty, and, besides, he was a gentleman. Yellaton to a man like him must be no more than a peasant's allotment.

"Pull me demmed boots off, woman!"

He had collapsed onto the moonlit mattress and, as she tugged until the soft leather came away, the room filled with the smell of ale and sweat and gin and unwashed feet.

Then, tiptoeing round the end of the bed, she slid into her side and against him, but his back was turned, and when she leaned to kiss his arm, he was already snoring.

Harry Blackaller stayed in bed all the next day. Rachel fed her stock and did the necessary morning work on the holding, trying to keep her disappointment at bay and to invent excuses for him. Men often got drunk at their own weddings. There were probably many more nuptial nights passed as unsuccessfully as hers than anyone would admit.

In early afternoon, she collected Jedder and John from the village. " 'Tis easy seeing you ain't done much sleepin' in the past twenty-four hour, Mistress Blackaller." Jane nudged and simpered at her drawn face, and Rachel smiled wanly.

He was still asleep when she returned, and then, at dusk, he called for food, which he ate blearily in bed by rushlight. She took the empty platter, put it on the floor and waited uncertainly.

Suddenly he took her wrist and moved over to give her room beside him. In nervous eagerness, she reached to be held in his arms and caressed and loved at last, but he was already pulling up her skirts and pushing her legs open. Then he was lying on top and thrusting into her, and it hurt because she was so unprepared. Then it was finished, and, minutes later, he was asleep again.

Rachel bit on her lower lip and clenched her fists till the nails cut into the palms. After a while she gained enough control to straighten her clothes and creep away.

The milking was done, the beasts fed and her sons put to bed, and, when all the other evening tasks were completed, she seated herself on the elm chair in the parlor and tried to work out what had happened to her.

Again she examined everything which had taken place since she had first seen Harry Blackaller in South Molton. She picked, as though at a scab, at her own behavior and forced herself to accept, for the first time, that however great his likeness to her true lover, this man was not Will Tresider, and however much she desired him because of the similarity, he never would be. But he had usually seemed jovial and debonair, despite being undemonstrative in love; so she concluded, philosophically, that marriage to a generous gentleman would not be such a hard mistake to learn to live with. Though why Harry Blackaller should have wanted to wed her remained an enigma.

Eventually she made her way back to the bedroom for the night. His breathing was deep and even, and as she settled in, he did not stir. Tired out, she lost consciousness almost immediately.

In the dream, Farmer Wame and the innkeeper from Thetford Forest were both pawing her bony body and grouching about it and then they began to argue over her, each pulling her away from the other, and all at once her eyes were wide open to the black room and someone dragging at her arm.

"What? Will? Harry? What is it?" she muttered, trying to clear her head.

"Turn over, you stupid bitch."

He wrenched her over to lie face down and shoved the pillow under her stomach and then she felt him kneeling between her legs and probing with his fingers and then she was screaming and screaming with pain and shock and revulsion at what he was doing to her.

"You'll wake those brats," he hissed, clamping a hand over her mouth. "Now, lie still and get used to it, because this is what I like."

She was too agonized to struggle and, long, long after it was all over, remained paralyzed with terror and disgust, until dawn, when she leaned over the side of the bed and was violently sick on the floor.

Her new husband opened his eyes in an expressionless stare, swung to his feet, dressed and left. A short time later, Rachel heard the scuff of his horse's hooves pass beneath the window and canter off.

For the first time since birth, Rachel Jedder was completely imprisoned in fear. Previously she had had frights and often tasted dread; but this fear was different, a fungal growth which had spread imperceptibly over and through her and was always there. At last, she recognized it as the emotion which had whispered through her entire relationship with Harry Blackaller from the beginning.

Now, lying in the reeking room, trying not to think of the experience of the previous night, but repeatedly attacked by its images, she felt irrevocably soiled. It was as though even her blood had been changed to sludge and the flesh under her skin made gangrenous. Making for the door, she plunged downstairs and out into the courtyard to sluice herself with bucket after bucket of water and rub her body raw with salt.

When the two little boys came out curiously, she shrieked them away, and later, when she had dressed and was subdued to a numb detachment, she was cold and distant with them, antagonized by their maleness.

Her husband did not return that night or the next, or the one after that. Five days passed, and instead of being a relief, each hour of his absence stretched her nerves more tightly, until she flinched at every sound and started back from her own animals when they shifted unexpectedly. Knowing he would come back, but not knowing when, made each passing moment a torment.

Then, on an April day, so fresh and sunny that it had succeeded in superficially lifting her spirits with its charm, stones cracked away from striking metal horseshoes on the path again and she ran to hide in the dairy.

He did not stop at the front door as usual—she could hear the horse continue around the west end of the house and cross the cobblestone yard. There was a rapping on the back door and a voice called out, "Mistress! Mistress Blackaller!"

Rachel's pulse stopped and then raced at the reprieve. She closed her eyes, rubbed the back of her hand across her forehead, inhaled in a gasp and stepped out to meet her old friend the peddler.

He studied her from under shaggy gray eyebrows and began business immediately, selling her ribbon and muslin with an ease which was both unusual and somehow unsatisfactory. No evasion or persuasion, no studied disinterest to change into reluctant reappraisal. No bargaining. It did not seem right. He carried the goods into the kitchen and took her money with an air of reproach.

She ladled thick broth into a bowl, cut a hunk of bread and asked, "Cider or ale?" as she put them before him.

"Cider, mistress, thank 'ee."

He helped himself to a good spoonful of pickle and raised his mug to her. She poured for herself and they sat without speaking while he supped noisily, but with no haste.

By the time he had finished the second bowlful, she had drunk three tankards of her own scrumpy and simply waved at him to help himself from the jug.

He examined her again and scratched his chin and finally said, "Why did 'ee do it, Rachel Jedder? What possessed 'ee?"

"Do what?" she asked dully.

"Wed wi' that varmint Blackaller, o' course, maid," said the peddler, shaking his head in puzzlement. "I couldn't believe 'un when I heerd."

Rachel assumed a formal stance and said severely, "Master Blackaller is a gentleman."

"A gentleman!" The peddler spluttered over his mug and burst out laughing. "Well, if he be esquire, I be the Prince o' Wales. Gentleman, indeed! Why, his mother was a Barnstaple whore, what died o' the pox."

"You dirty old liar!" Rachel shouted. " 'Tis a lie. He was a ship's captain and has property at Umberleigh."

The peddler stood up and steadied himself against the table.

"I may be dirty and old, Rachel Jedder, but I bain't no liar; leastways not in matter such as this. Your ship's capt'n weren't niver more than a third mate what got run off in the end for cheatin' and thievin' and all manner of other wickednesses. I tell 'ee, there bain't a ship this side o' Portsmouth as would hire Harry Blackaller agin. And, as for property, his sister and near about ten chillern live in a hovel Umberleigh way and she'm no different from their mother."

"No! 'Tain't true! Can't be!" cried Rachel desperately. "He's rich. I seen it."

"Aye, he had a bit o' gold when he first come back," agreed the old man. "But I can tell 'ee for fact that he be owin' now. Harry Blackaller don't hold wi' gambling on winners somehow."

"Lies! Lies!" Rachel's voice had dropped to a whisper.

The old man could not look at her strained face.

"Someone should've warned 'ee," he muttered. "Didn't seem possible when I heerd it, not of you, mistress, nor of him either. See, Harry Blackaller was never known to show much fancy for women. Folk used to say 'twas why he went to sea."

Rachel gave a yowl of fury, picked up the terra-cotta jug and flung it. It missed him narrowly and smashed against the wall.

The peddler moved with alacrity to the door, putting its solid panels between them and then peering round the edge to deliver a few final words.

"Listen, mistress, I bin comin' here this past seven year and I seen 'ee make good in this place and I knows the sweat and tears it has cost 'ee, so heed my words and watch out for that husband o' yourn, Rachel Jedder. He don't mean no good by you."

His head disappeared quickly, in case she should use it as a target for another missile, but all the fight had gone out of her.

Long after he had gone on his way, she remained standing limply before the fire, knowing everything he had said was true, and understanding at last. Harry Blackaller was a penniless scoundrel, who had not married her for love, or even for lust. He had married her to become the owner of Yellaton.

CHAPTER TEN

"Look at yourself. Why, 'twould strike a dog blind. 'Tis no wonder I stay away from here, with you as misshapen as a toad and stinking of vomit."

Rachel was pregnant and Harry Blackaller never ceased to point out that the sight of her disgusted him.

"Damme! Give over the vittles and get thee gone!" He snatched the plate of food and studiedly seated himself with his back to her at the table.

"Little wonder a man is driven from his own house to other company, when the woman he weds turns herself into such a lump o' suet," he needled on. "Begone to the bedchamber and do not come out again until I depart!"

They had been married half a year, but it had taken only days to discover that everything the peddler had said of her husband was true. When she had confronted him with the accusation that he was neither a gentleman nor solvent, he had laughed.

"Whoever told you I was either, wife?" he had scoffed. "Not I."

" 'Tis your speech and dress and the gold I seen you spend," was her artless reply.

"A man can wear and say as he pleases, I believe, madam." He made it sound so reasonable. "And you were not to be noticed complaining of the sight of gold."

He had stayed for two days, bringing all her nightmares alive during the hours of darkness, and then riding off, not to be seen for a week.

The pattern of the relationship was formed, except that once she became visibly pregnant, he had ceased all physical contact and restricted himself to verbal abuse instead.

Rachel should have been grateful for that, had she not felt so ill and dejected. She toiled far harder than was wise in her condition and the little boys gave what help they could, but nothing would persuade Blackaller to labor, and, with no man to work the land, the holding was running down rapidly from neglect. It crushed her to see it.

She had managed to till the corn but not to keep it weed-free, and, in

May, too afraid to hire lads in case her husband should have questioned their payment, she had brought in some hay with the aid of her sons and her one friend, Jane Clarke, though this was not enough to keep the beasts in feed over the coming winter. Now, she had no idea how even the poor barley harvest of that year was to be gathered.

Soon after their first confrontation, Harry Blackaller had demanded money to settle a debt, and when she had denied having any, he had coldly and repeatedly slapped her until her face was cut. Then he had shaken and hit the children before her eyes, but still she had not revealed the existence of the Cornish tin box. They could all survive a beating, but poverty was a life sentence.

"Sell that bay you bought off Squire," she had shrilled at him. "He's worth a hundred pounds."

"The brute went to the shambles a month back. Dropped dead under me on a ride from Porlock," he had snarled back. "Why else, think you, would I ride such a cart horse as the gray? Seth Bartle has much to answer for, selling me such a weak-livered nag."

Two quick recollections of the mettlesome young horse, looking proudly from his stall and, later, standing disconsolate and overridden in the rain, flickered across her imagination, but by then the man was tearing Yellaton apart in his search for her money.

He had ripped open the feather mattress and tested the floorboards and turned out cupboards and drawers. The rooms had filled with feathers and dust, like snow scenes trapped in glass. The children had run to the stables and then to the orchard. The gray dog, which had removed upon his arrival to the security of the barn, took himself off to the moor, and Rachel just looked on listlessly, thinking of all the time and stitching it was going to take her to repair the damage.

Harry Blackaller emptied sacks of flour and feed and even prodded through the haystacks with a long, pointed pole. In the end, he had hurled himself onto the old horse and careened angrily away.

It was not until later that morning that she discovered the batch of cured sheepskins was missing. The brass hames from the mare's harness disappeared soon after, and then he sold the heifer calves she had intended to keep on as followers. John Pincombe collected the pig, which had been fattening for the family, saying he had already paid her husband for it, and allowing no argument by slaughtering it on the spot and carting off the carcass.

Now, sitting apathetically on the edge of the bed, Rachel stared into space, her hands clasped over the belly mound of the coming child. She was listening once again, as she had done countless times since her wedding day, for the sounds of his going, her mind compressed to a pinhead of intense concentration. At last the hoofbeats, from shaking the very ground, became faint echoes of themselves.

Her fingers felt under the pillow end of her side of the four-poster bed

155

and reached into the secret compartment Robert Wolcot had made to hold the tin box, with its coins padded in rags, so as not to clink. It was still there, safe, where he would never find it.

There were men's voices outside the house, their rumble fading and swelling over the contours of Rachel's labor. Then, as the muscles contracted to form that last merciless wall of expulsion, the cacophony of a whole flock of sheep seemed to fill the room, their bleating like a gale, their running feet like thunder.

"What is it?" she moaned, confused.

"Don't 'ee fret none," answered the midwife. " 'Tis nothing, mistress. Nothing at all."

Then the parturition took over and Emma was born, not flawless and exquisite like little dead Sarah, but red-faced and bald and undersized and puling. Harry Blackaller's child. Her mother looked at her and gave a weary sigh.

"Lucky for 'ee her be that puny, mistress," the old woman commented with her usual lack of tact. "You're not built for bearing chillern and I allus expects each time to see 'ee out."

Rachel managed a weak smile. The sounds of men and sheep had gone, hallucinations caused by the great strain, she thought. Similar fantasies had occurred before.

For two days she rested in bed with the new infant, relieved that her husband did not bother to visit her, or view his offspring. Sometimes she heard the movements of the household below. Jane Clarke brought her food; the boys, now aged six and five, looked after the animals. She breastfed on demand and dozed betweenwhiles.

On the third day, when she went downstairs, Jane fussed around her a little and the boys gave their new sister a cursory examination, and there was an indefinable air of awkwardness about them all.

Rachel looked from one to the next, noticing how their eyes would not meet hers.

"You had better tell me straight," she said.

"What, Mother?" Jedder asked innocently.

"What you done wrong while I been lyin-in," she replied firmly.

"Nothing!" both sons and Jane chorused.

Then Jane added, "The boys ain't done nothing amiss, Rachel."

"Well, something's amiss, Jane Clarke," Rachel responded with suspicion. " 'Tis writ all over your faces."

The three exchanged glances and then Jedder shrugged.

" 'Tis the sheep, Mother," he said.

"What about them? If they've gone off, 'tain't nothing to worry about. They'll be found soon enough," Rachel reassured calmly, and then with some anxiety, "There's no sickness, is there?"

They shook their heads and Jedder took a big breath.

156

"They bin sold, Mother," he burst out. "There wasn't nothing us could do. Harry Blackaller sold them."

Rachel dumped her new baby into Jane Clarke's arms, left the kitchen without another word and went to the stables, where she saddled the pony. Her friend called out, protesting, as she rode from the yard, but she was too deep in angry thought to hear.

Harry Blackaller had browbeaten them all for long enough, and she, Rachel Jedder, who had crossed the breadth of England alone and who owned land and a good house, had allowed herself to be intimidated. He had systematically stripped the holding of precious assets before her eyes and sold the food her children needed and she had been too cowardly to oppose.

Hatred, which had been smoldering beneath the repression of the past months, blazed at last as she galloped over the moor. She would find him and disgrace him into handing over the money for the sheep. She would prohibit him from returning to Yellaton again. Harry Blackaller would be stopped this day.

After tethering the mare, Rachel strode into the Star Inn, ignoring the few customers in the shabby parlor and going straight through to a back room, where she knew men played dice and cards. The room was empty.

She turned to the innkeeper, who had followed her, and demanded, "Where is my husband?"

He spread his hands. "He were here last night, but there's no saying where he's to now, mistress."

"Did he lose money here?" she asked aggressively.

The man's eyes refused to meet hers and he grimaced dismissively.

" 'Tis you and those like you, tempting men to spend more'n they got, as causes women and chillern to go hungry," Rachel spat at him, before storming out.

She rode through the woods to the horsebreaker's yard, called him over to the gate and said, "I needs know where Harry Blackaller might be to."

"I don't have no truck with that husband o' yours," Seth Bartle replied sternly.

"But you know where he is likely to go," Rachel persisted. "Places where there's games of chance and such."

He looked at her and relented. " 'Twould be better if you went home, mistress. Being newly delivered, you shouldn't be riding out in this bitter cold."

"I got to find him," she answered stubbornly. "Be there no race meeting today?"

"None as I've heard of." He rubbed his chin and shook his head. "But him and his company do go to the Golden Lion, and then there be the Globe at Kings Nympton, but 'tis a fair way off."

She thanked him and turned the horse to the stony track down to the bridle path, which crossed waterlogged meadows bordering the river, and soon the skirt of her dress was splashed wet by the cantering hooves and she was regretting not wearing more than a shawl against the east wind.

The Golden Lion was almost empty, too, and the landlord had not seen Blackaller in a month or more.

"Not since 'ee were caught pauming cards and I chucked him out."

So Rachel went on to Kings Nympton, arriving just as a group of young horsemen drew up and threw the alehouse keeper into such a pother that he only had time to wave agitated arms of negation at her query as he bustled about, taking their orders. But she could see Harry Blackaller was not there, and, indeed, that this tavern also was oddly deserted, with only a couple of whiskered old farmhands sitting at the end of the refectory table nearest the log fire. She wondered where to go next.

"Make haste, bluffer!" one of the gentlemen shouted to the potman. "The match began at two."

The match! The cockfights! Of course, *that* was where he would be, and that was why there were so few men in the taverns. Rachel returned quickly to her mount, rode the hundred yards to a small copse, where she waited until the young blades finished their brandies and began to move off in a rowdy bunch. After they had gone a little distance, she emerged to follow quietly.

The noise scrambled up from the far side of the brow of the hill and babbled down to meet her before the meeting came into sight, crammed into and around a great grange barn on the grounds of a ruined monastery.

A few children ran about on the grass between the groups of men surrounding each owner, or trainer, as he armed his contenders with long silver spurs attached by leather thongs.

The gamecocks were sleek, their tails, wings and hackles cropped to fighting trim, their plumage metallic red and black, purple, green and orange, iridescent in the hard December light, and their owners held them against their breasts and talked to them anxiously, while clamoring and shrieking gusted from within the barn.

"Six to four Nonpareil!"

"Royal Red five to one. Five to one Royal Red!"

"Bold Henry! Bold Henry!"

"Flying Champ!"

"Bold Henry! Bold Henry!"

"Done!" Hands slapped. "Done!"

To Rachel, accustomed to the unpeopled moor and little country markets, it was a multitude. There must have been one thousand people present. Gold and silver and copper clinked and rang, indifferently pitched on the ground or surreptitiously slipped from hand to hand in a reckless dance of chance. She had never seen such sums, such prodigality, and she stood transfixed as fortunes were exchanged by noblemen, and craftsmen risked their businesses. Poor men threw away six months' wages, women lost the last pittance lying between their children and famine, and rich men became beggars before her eyes. All for the sake of a fight between two birds. It made no sense at all.

Finding one man in such a surging throng seemed impossible, yet if she waited until it separated and scattered at the end of the day, Harry Blackaller might not be traced again for weeks. Rachel tied up her horse and walked uncertainly toward the wagon-wide doorway to the barn, reaching it as a cheer went up and everyone began pushing forward, and she found herself crushed in a solid, pungent casing of bodies, long since sewn into their underclothes for the winter months of the year.

Then, jammed against a post by the inside wall, she climbed hastily to avoid injury and unexpectedly secured for herself a clear view over all the heads to the arena of the cockpit, which had been constructed as a round, wooden platform fenced by a ring of planks, against which the spectators pressed so tightly that no combatant could flap to freedom.

Two cockers stood in the center and thrust their birds forward until the beaks made contact and the yellow eyes of each glittered with rage at the challenge of a rival. Then, at a signal from the Master of the Ring, the men backed to leave the arena from opposite sides, turned and released the fighters simultaneously.

The gamecocks circled each other with wary strut, their hackle feathers rising in aggressive ruffs, their combs like ruby coronets. Then, without warning, both leaped high, wings thrashing, talons splayed, to clash and explode in the air like a shattering prism of violent color. They landed, tearing and pecking at each other, the first blood pouring from the hole in Nonpareil's head where an eye had been. Breaking apart, they whirled instantly to face each other, parrying and weaving and dodging, but never wavering in the fixation of their hatred. Another combustible impact, made the more deadly by the absolute silence of the participants amid the demented baying of the crowd.

"Henry! Bold Henry!"

"Nonpareil!"

Fine, curled feathers floated gently upward with obscene grace. The birds bounced weightlessly off the wood, one now totally blind, the other one-eyed and trailing a broken wing, but still pecking viciously. The next attack left them both spent and staggering helplessly around the ring, their feathers clotted with blood, which had sprayed the patrons like the spots of a disease.

The owners climbed back into the arena to collect and set them to again, according to the Rules and Orders for Cocking, with the bill of the blinded bird touching the torn neck of its opponent. There was a brief and desperate flurry and Nonpareil managed to sink a spur into Bold Henry, who fell to the ground, blood spurting from his beak and, amid uproar from the onlookers, twitched once and died. The sightless champion, sensing victory, managed to raise his head and crow.

The entire fight had taken no more than eight minutes, and, as the money began its frantic passage from hand to hand once more, and the victims were removed, before Rachel's disgusted gaze two more men were already climbing into the ring, each with a bold and brilliant bird cradled lovingly in his arms.

It was then that she caught sight of Harry Blackaller on the far side of the barn, his head inclined solicitously over the blond curls of a young girl. She jumped down and plunged into the mob, elbowing stomachs and kicking ankles to make it give way to her. Indifferent to the oaths and the quick, sly hand which pinched her bottom in passing, she reached the place just as another frenzied roar announced the end of another match.

Blackaller let out a wild whoop, and as his companion turned, Rachel realized that the golden curls belonged to a beautiful boy and she saw her husband drop silver crown pieces into his open, full-lipped mouth.

Outraged, she hurled herself at the slim form, grabbing a handful of the soft hair and shaking the boy's head until the coins fell clattering to the earthen floor.

"That's my silver from my sheep, you scrub," she screeched. "An' you can have that filthy ram cat till your arse drops off, but you ain't having my silver, Miss Molly."

The boy squealed and put protective arms round his head as Rachel snatched the pieces from the ground and spun to swing at her husband, catching his face with her nails and scoring parallel scratches down his cheek.

"Now, you give over the rest of my money, Harry Blackaller, and don't you niver come back to Yellaton again."

His face was without expression as he stared down at her, only his pale eyes betraying an implacable and unforgiving menace.

People had moved back to form a circle of curiosity around them.

He took her wrist in his horny seaman's fist and squeezed, ignoring her struggle to break free, closing the grip to a bone-crushing vise. In slow motion, her fingers loosened and the coins dropped into his waiting palm.

Blackaller beckoned his companion close and deliberately posted them back into the grinning mouth. Then, hooking his thumb into Rachel's dress at the cleavage, he hauled her after him through the door of the barn and out into the open. A crowd, eager to see the end of the scene, came too.

There the man put a hand on her shoulder and gave a sudden, forcible tug, which ripped the bodice from the sleeves of the gown, leaving her nearly naked before all.

160

"Now, bucks and bloods!" he shouted. "The wench here wants gold. Which among you could put her to good use and oblige?"

A few drunks laughed. The rest went silent and began to look embarrassed. Rachel, overcome with shame, bent her head and tried to draw the torn material over her bare breasts.

Her husband plucked it from her and held both her arms behind her back, bellowing, "Come along now! 'Tis true she ain't too well covered, but I can guarantee her's in no way deficient in the essential points and can sing quite a fine song. What offers for some sport, gents?"

The watchers began to back away, murmuring disapproval among themselves, and then parting before a tall, determined figure.

"That's enough, man!" Squire Waddon spoke with anger. "Mantle your wife and take her home."

" 'Tis a private matter and none o' your concern," Blackaller retorted.

The squire stepped so close that their faces almost touched and he completely hid Rachel from public view.

"You are to escort your wife from this match and not return." He gave the order firmly.

"I know everything about you and this slattern, Waddon," her husband sneered. "So don't come throwing your weight around here. There ain't nothing you can force of me."

The squire answered with quiet threat, "You are a known felon and sharper, Blackaller, and there are at least half a dozen good reasons to have you arrested and sentenced to jail, and even to the gallows. If you wish to remain a free man, you will leave now. And you will be seen to treat this woman in a decent manner in the future."

The two men glared at each other over her shivering frame for a minute and then Harry Blackaller shrugged his shoulders and muttered a curse, turning away and dragging her behind him toward the tethered horses.

"One moment!" Squire Waddon called and came after them. Stopping at Rachel's side, he took off his greatcoat and put it over her shoulders. She gave him a fragile smile of gratitude and walked on.

Harry and Rachel Blackaller rode a short distance from the cockfights in silence, until they were out of sight, where he drew slightly ahead, leaned to catch her reins and yank both animals to a halt. His face was woodenly inscrutable, like a soldier's mask, his eyes so narrowed that they could hardly be seen looking over at her.

"Be sure I shall see to you later, madam." The level tone made the words more malevolent. "And you will rue this folly until your dying day."

Then he was cantering away, and she was left, huddled in the squire's coat, to face the long ride home alone, and never again to recall the torment of that afternoon without flinching and mentally burning with mortification.

. . .

161

It did not take the man long to lose the remainder of the money from the sheep. Then he returned to Yellaton. He arrived, sober and quite early one evening, walking into the kitchen and up to his wife without a word. The two boys backed against the wall, conditioned by the atmosphere of fear always generated by his presence.

Rachel, who had gone white, stood very straight, her chin up and lips tight.

"Upstairs," he said.

She did not move.

He laid a long, flexible rod of willow on the table before her and pointed out, almost amiably, "There is a matter to settle, wife, and it can be done here, before the brats, or in the bedchamber."

She climbed the stairs with nervous dignity, and then she was kneeling, bent over the old wooden chest and the willow whistled high above and whipped the first weal across her back, through the thin material of her gown.

Rachel Jedder clenched her teeth and vowed not to cry out and the slim wood sliced and the dress slit and her skin broke and the intense, edged cuts swelled into a hot, wild pressure, which built up inside her skull, threatening to rupture her eardrums and burst through her eyes, and then she lost consciousness.

When she came round, the new baby was crying below, its wails thin as vapor rising through the floorboards. Her husband was lying on the bed staring up at the roof, and he took no notice as she struggled to her feet, changed her clothes painfully and stumbled away.

He would go soon, she thought, releasing the tears at last as she suckled the child. He always left after a couple of days. But this time he stayed on and turned life into a prolonged misery of torment by day and abuse at night.

It was a violence far worse than the plain vandalism of uncontrolled rage, because it was the product of an intelligent and sadistic mind and effected with uncaring contempt, the same way, no doubt, as he had punished the captive slaves on the ships he had sailed.

The children were ignored, if they kept out of his sight, except when he wanted to use them to bait Rachel, whom he treated with special and deliberate cruelty, designed to quell all spirit and subdue her to cringing and abject obedience. It was as though her natural independence was a personal affront and had to be destroyed.

So, when a beating did not make her plead, he would shut her sons outside in the dark and cold for hours, until John began to whimper, or they crept off to huddle in a hollow of the straw. She remembered the blackness of the rat-ridden barn at Wame's farm and felt sick that now her own children were being subjected to the same terrors, despite all the efforts and travail of her past.

Sometimes he would make the whole family stay up through the night, refusing to allow them to sleep before dawn, or she would be forced to stand beside him all day, waiting for an order.

Once, when the baby began its mewl to be fed, he shut Rachel in the stair cupboard and left the infant outside. Emma Blackaller was a sickly child, colorless and feeble, whose piping cry would not have aroused a resting bird, but it dragged, strong as a hawser, on her mother's instincts, building up to an irresistible compulsion as the minutes moved over the hour, until Rachel was pounding on the door and clamoring to reach her.

The woman protested and raged and tried to reason, but her husband just smiled the smile she had once thought so like Will's and introduced some new refinement to the wretchedness of their existence.

Yet somehow she could not break down before him. Even though she sensed that to humble herself completely and crawl to him might end their suffering, she was unable to do it.

"Please . . ." she would begin. "Harry . . ." And could go no further.

About once every fortnight, he would go off and stay away for twenty-four or even forty-eight hours, returning drunk and smelling carnal, to sleep and eat and lazily brutalize his wife for the next few days. During that time some farmer or cottager from the district would appear and remove whatever property he had sold to pay for the excursion; a heifer, or the second of the two youngest horses, or a nearly new implement. Even the hay crop was sold before it was cut, and eventually the pigs, the young stock and even the stored seed necessary for their future food had all gone. Only the old mare and a dry cow and a few rusted tools were left.

Yellaton, which had withstood the negligence of the previous year, began to crumble from continued neglect. As Rachel became thin and hollow-cheeked, breaches began to appear in its unclipped hedgerows and its gates broke from loosened catches. As her eyes became lifeless and her hair began to fall out through ill health and stress, the doors and beams were rotting where rain seeped in through unrepaired holes. The farm buildings, left unpainted and without maintenance for a twelve-month, began to fall apart, hinges corroding from lack of grease, wood drying out and cracking, nails snapping, shutters swinging and breaking in the wind.

She had neither strength nor inclination to make the daily inspection and did not see how the weeds choked the ditches and smothered the once-productive vegetable garden, reclaiming the cultivated land for nature. With remarkable rapidity the homestead began to return to the moor, bracken sprouting in its fields, heather inching over the banks, gorse rooting in the plowed earth. With no sheep to keep the turf cropped, coarse mat grasses strangled the clover and fine-leaved fescues; thistles and dock and cow parsley and nettles and hogweed flourished and then freed their seeds in millions to the warm, drifting airs of late

163

summer. Alongside Rachel's degradation, Jedder's land was disintegrating, soon to disappear.

The two years since she had walked out of High Chilham church married to Harry Blackaller had seemed longer than the whole of the rest of her burdened life, and ahead lay only the bleak, monstrous inevitability of the future. Already Rachel felt senescent, and all that was left of the audacious, bonny girl who had danced for Will Tresider was a calcified padlock of determination to hold the last, minute trace of her own self and keep it intact.

The man was manifestly much more physically powerful than she and unrestrained by any morality. There was no option but to accept his domination and try to execute his impossible commands, but mental tricks could sometimes divorce her from her actions: picturing a secret recess of Yellaton with such concentration that she could will all but her shell there, or repeating a chosen word over and over in her head, could distance what was happening to her.

And she kept her hatred alive. It showed dull red at the bottom of her black pupils. In the privacy of her soul, she never gave in, and whatever he did to her, he knew it.

Then, in June, it was apparent that she was pregnant again. It would not have happened yet, had she been able to continue breastfeeding Emma for the usual eighteen months, she thought exhaustedly, but the milk had stopped months earlier. Drawing up the soil around the few potato plants, she wondered whether to feel relief. Her body was already thickening, which meant that Harry Blackaller would not touch her over the next months, and perhaps she would die in childbirth. Rachel found herself praying that this time the midwife would be proved right, for the probability of fifteen, or twenty, or even many more years with such a man was beyond endurance.

Although it was summer, when food should have been plentiful, there was little to eat because there had been hardly any seed to sow. She had successfully squirreled away small hoards here and there the previous autumn, but there had been no point in trying to grow more than would meet their minimum needs because her husband would simply have sold the surplus. There was no corn to grind for the coming winter and the last barrel of flour in the pantry was half empty. Only fruit cropped in superabundance during the hot, wet weather, and they were grateful for that.

The fetus developed far faster than the previous children. Her stomach seemed to expand visibly each day and to push up under her ribs until she could only take short, fast breaths. Climbing the stairs, bending to pull carrots, and dressing became extraordinarily difficult. Quite soon she was unable to milk the old cow, which had unexpectedly produced a calf that spring. And still the unborn infant grew. It was as though a great tureen, like the silver one at the Dean's house in Norwich, was strapped to her body. She could not sit or lie comfortably, and there were frightening times when her heart galloped in her chest and color flushed her face and sweat broke out in pricking droplets all over her skin.

Blackaller was revolted and, unable to tolerate being near her, stayed from the house for longer periods, which was the only charity in the cumbrous months of waiting.

By October, the food had almost run out. There was no meat. The poultry had been killed off. The cow had developed udder inflammation and suddenly gone dry. Only vegetables and fruit and nuts and bread were left to eat.

The children looked unhealthy and whined a lot, and Rachel fretted over what was to become of them. There was still money concealed in the cache, but if she went to the village to buy supplies, word would reach her husband and the consequences of that were unthinkable. Yet if she did not find a way to obtain stores, they would certainly starve when the snows came and sealed them in.

The money had been kept with the insane idea of being able to use it to start again one day, or to escape. At times she had been tempted to take it and run to Kent to find Will, and leave the man, the children and the holding behind forever. Now, each evening as she laid the platters of boiled potatoes before the spindly boys, knowledge of its existence and the comfort it could buy haunted her.

Her husband had not been about the place for over a week. Finally Rachel decided to try to ride to Bideford, buy as much as she could and hide it in corners of the outbuildings while he was away. It was the last chance before her condition made any action impossible and the elements closed the road.

She awoke earlier than usual and went into the passage to put her ear to the door of the children's room. There was no sound. Outside, the moor was silent under a customary seasonal fog. She moved back to the side of the bed and, with considerable awkwardness, went down on hands and knees and reached under for the tin box. The unborn child kicked angrily as its cell was compressed against the floor, and Rachel gasped with the effort. Then her fingers were gripping, and, with a squeal, the box slid from its slot and into her hand. Puffing, she sat back on her heels and opened it.

One by one she unwrapped the precious coins and laid them on the sheepskin rug. There was still a goodly sum there, enough to make her rich by comparison with laboring folk—easily enough to keep the family fed all winter and still buy in seed and a few young beasts in the spring, enough for her to ride straight through Bideford and on and never return. But she knew she would not. She picked up a gold piece.

The bedroom door cracked open. She swung around. In two strides, Harry Blackaller was standing over her.

165

"Seems I am come just in time, ma'am," he said, softly.

Rachel gave a moan and scrabbled for the treasure. He placed the toe of his boot against the small of her back and gave a gentle prod, just enough to topple her, and then, as she lay, panting and watching, he bent to collect the coins, one by one, picking up each with exaggerated care and dropping it with a clink into his other hand and counting aloud.

"One guinea . . . two guineas . . . three guineas . . . five guineas . . . five pounds and ten shillings. . . ."

"No! No!" shouted Rachel, heaving herself forward to lie over the spread of gold.

The man crouched, his hand darting forward to grip her neck, causing her head to snap back so that his breath exhaled full into her face and she was forced to look into his ash-gray eyes.

"You lied, bitch! Taking oath there was no money, while I had to live like a pauper and be the butt of every wiseacre and pass months incarcerated in this coop for lack of means."

" 'Twas you! Squandering all we had on races and matches and prizefighters and your whoring boys," she shrilled. "Taking what weren't yourn."

"But 'tis *all* mine, Rachel Blackaller, like I told you on our wedding night. This hovel and everything in it belongs to me, including you, drab." He took her face, digging his fingers into her cheeks and making her mouth pucker and twist. "And were I not a merciful man, why, I could have you charged with stealing this gold from your husband and you would dangle."

"There are no vittles and we are hungry," she cried desperately.

"Less idleness would have grown a fine harvest, wife. I believe wheat is fetching fifty-two shillings and eight pence a quarter."

He took her long, black hair and jerked her off the floor onto her knees.

"Now, pick up the rest!" he ordered. "And be done with this foolery."

"We need stores . . . for winter." She could feel the panic rising as she scraped the coins together and began to scoop them up.

"I fear you must be a thriftless housekeeper to require such a prodigious sum to keep yourself and a few brats," he jeered.

All the money was now clasped tightly in her hands. Rachel felt dizzy and heard her own voice, distantly.

"Do not take everything, husband. The chillern will starve."

"Then 'tis feckless to keep on producing them, madam," he said, holding out his right hand and waiting.

She clenched her fingers round the metal discs and held them to her in an unconscious attitude of supplication.

"Leave enough for us," she entreated. "There is plenty and you will not miss a guinea . . . a crown."

166

Blackaller's voice rose with impatience. "You will get nothing if I am delayed here longer."

It might almost have been an offer. Rachel slowly relinquished her hold, and the money, the sum of all her loves and labors at Yellaton, streamed into his grasp.

At last her resistance gave way, the mutinous months of self-control collapsing, and she groveled, clinging to his knees, sobbing and begging, beseeching pity for the children, for them all, promising anything, everything.

"You have been a railing and crabbed scold for a man to have as spouse, a clapper claw, in truth," he commented, and then, pointing at her belly with distaste, asked, "How long till you are rid of that?"

She gulped, startled a little, and replied. "Only two more months."

He held up a gold guinea and smiled boyishly, the corners of his mouth tilting upward.

"If I give you this now, what will you do for me then, wife?"

"What you will," Rachel promised brokenly. "Whatever you will."

He regarded her with mocking doubt. "Aye, but will you do it merrily?"

"I swear it."

"And ask sweetly for my favors, as a willing wife should?"

She nodded dumbly.

"Show me how you will ask. Smile. Smile!"

The coin glittered and in its light were the images of the past, the workhouse, Wame's farm, beggars dying on the roads across England, vagrants being harried out of the villages. She tried to smile.

"Now! How will you ask?"

"Please . . ."

"Go on!"

"Please . . . please . . . my husband . . . take me."

Harry Blackaller choked with laughter and slapped his thigh.

"Why, ma'am, I was unaware that you cared," he ridiculed. "But I fear I cannot wait for you to whelp yet again."

And he stepped past, shoving her aside so that she sprawled back to the floor as, still laughing, he left the room.

Rachel Jedder gave a prolonged, primitive cry of agony as the horse rang away and the sound of her husband's mirth at the greatest jest in the world brayed over Beara.

It did not matter any more. Nothing mattered. Rachel had ceased to care. She did not care about the children, or about herself, and, finally, she no longer cared even about the land. Now enormous and almost immobilized by the weight of the coming child, she had become a vacant lump of rolling flesh, a jellyfish passively bumping around the kitchen, an ungainly sea cow grunting on the stairs, a washed-up, bloated carcass beached on the bed. Without sorrow or humor, shame or affection, she automatically carried out the few duties she could and obeyed whoever gave instructions: Blackaller, Jane Clarke, even her eight-year-old son John.

"Leave that, Mother," he would say, as she tried vainly to bend to light the fire, and she would stop and merely stand and stare at the unlit logs.

"Lean against the wall to rest, if 'ee can't sit comfortable," Jane would advise, when she came to help, and Rachel would meekly stand against the rough plaster, although it hurt her jutting shoulder blades and she would rather have used the smoothly planed door.

She hardly spoke at all, and her pinched features had become lined and simian. It would have been impossible to tell her true age, that she was only twenty-six years old. She looked over forty.

Her husband was rarely seen, arriving only occasionally, flushed and keyed up, fresh from the tailor in richly embroidered waistcoat and overcoat, and knee breeches closed with silver buckles, on a new thoroughbred horse, to boast of winnings, sneer at his family, snore a night away and make off the next morning. Taunting a blown-out, blank-eyed woman who did not seem to hear the insults and did everything she was told was poor diversion.

Once, in a peculiar fit of generosity, he brought them a hindquarter of beef, won at a meeting. Rachel had to be stopped from cramming the raw meat into her mouth, and when it was spit-roasted, she and the children fell on it like jackals.

The winds turned. The low tangle of green growth, which had shaded the summer earth, withered, baring brown stems and the thick, dark soil to the sky once more. The very last leaves fluttered from the trees. Winter came down from the north. At a race meeting near Exeter, Harry Blackaller lost one hundred and fifty guineas, his blood horse and his watch.

A dashed good friend gave him a lift in his curricle to South Molton, from where he was forced to walk the thirteen miles home. The first ten gave time enough to form another plan and he stopped long enough in the Golden Lion at High Chilham to set it up.

Rachel was sleeping on her back when he arrived, baleful and frozen. Moonlight showed the hump of her outline under the cover and her gaunt, open-mouthed face. She smelled.

He thought of the fun of the past weeks, the horses soaring over the sticks, champagne and brandy with Fortescue, Bafset, Rowe and the rest. Cocks and dogs and men fighting for their amusement. Great sport. How they had all reined in around that young dell walking alone through Pyes Nest Woods and each taken a flyer at her to the whistling acclaim of the others, then chucked down a few coins to stop her infernal blubbing before riding off. She must have been about twelve and that was old enough. That night he had won a mint at dice, and they had all roared up to Bath, where there had been that juicy boy bought off Philip Marwood for the week.

Harry Blackaller stared morosely at his sleeping, misshapen wife and heartily wished rid of her. If fortune favored him, this coming whelping would kill her off, and then he could put the boys to work and that whining girl in the poorhouse and sell up the whole barren bog and be out of it.

Rachel stirred and groaned and he shook her viciously cursing under his breath.

"Arouse yourself, Mistress Blackaller! I have news," he announced. "Bloody end to me! But you are a slothful fussock. Wake now and hear the news!"

She opened her eyes and tried to drag herself upright without success, and he grew irritated and leaned over, so that she had to fall back and look up at him blearily.

"Come Saturday, you tidy yourself and the house up proper, 'cos there are folk coming from High Chilham for the sale," he said.

"Sale?" She blinked stupidly. "What sale?"

"The sale of Moses meadow and wood, of course, wife. 'Twas decided today to sell it off. Ain't no use to us and I need the gold."

He grinned at her sleepy consternation and left the room.

Moses meadow! The dream land. The land for which Will's spirit had returned and had guided her to secure, and which her first husband had slaved to drain and clear. Part of Yellaton. *Jedder's land.*

Those summers when the cows had swayed through its rich pasture and young colts had galloped to play in and out of its stream, and she and dear Robert Wolcot and their children had sat in the shade of its oaks at midday. The golden, heartbreaking past. Rachel lay helplessly on her back and huge tears brimmed from her eyes and gushed down the sides of her head into her hair.

Morning, with sun lighting the flat, bright stratus in the east, and, to the north, the sky coldly blue behind a dappled formation of small fleecy clouds. She lumbered from bed out of habit, her skin slack, her eyes empty, and thudded heavily down to the kitchen, where the boys were already organizing the necessity of heat and scorching a mess of cold potato brown on a dry griddle to give it more flavor. They took no notice of her, nor she of them, and when they had eaten they left.

By then, the blue had been blotted out and a fresh southwesterly was blowing. Long mares' tails were streaming under the gray ceiling, which gradually lowered until its strands were sweeping over the ground and dusting the distant woods. The air lisped and hissed and the light was alternately increased and dimmed by the driven cloud, which thinned just enough at times to reveal a white moon of a sun still riding above them.

The man slept and Rachel sat and gazed at nothing as the wind's

169

strength intensified, punching the bare trees aside with scatterings of branches, its cross-currents backfiring like some unimaginable racing contraption of the future.

Toward dusk, the boys returned and chewed on a large baked potato each and glowered at their mother. Outside, the sky had become sulphurous, and cumuli massed into phalanges on the horizon and advanced ponderously over Bodmin Moor and Dartmoor and the wide, inland plain between and over and beyond Beara, and it was night.

The cheeks of the gale bulged and the mists condensed into fine rain, into fat, melting drops, into the splashes of countless fish mouthing the surface of the earth, into brittle glass pellets shattering on impact with the ground. The invasion accelerated to hurricane speed, the drone and chanter discord of its refrain shrieking in off the Atlantic at seventy . . . eighty . . . at one hundred miles an hour, until the old house quaked and rocked, as though uprooted and bowled away on the ocean. Even the bed, in which Rachel and Harry Blackaller lay side by side in bitter awareness of each other, shuddered, and above them the roof timbers creaked as snake rattles of the storm whiplashed under the eaves to flick clothes and objects to the floor.

There was the slightest pause, as though the force was halted for a stroke, then a cataclysmic blast powered across the countryside, toppling trees and wrenching out bushes and shrubs and hurling standing oxen onto their backs. With a volley of booming, riving and cleaving wood and a sheet of rain slanting into the room, a section of the thatched roof was suddenly ripped off and blown away.

Grousing and swearing, the man roused the boys to help roll up the feather mattress before the downpour soaked it through, and Rachel moved wearily to spend the rest of the night in their small truckle bed.

By dawn the wind had lost ferocity but was still blowing hard, and the bedroom was littered with debris which had dropped in through the gap in the roof. Ballooning, livid clouds in the south forecast more severe weather soon.

"If the storm gets under that hole this nightfall, 'twill take the whole thatch off," she observed dully.

Never a man to make an effort, even Harry Blackaller realized she was right and that a temporary repair would have to be made. Grumbling, he collected some old planks and placed the ladder against the side of the house. Rachel stood at the foot and watched him climb to balance precariously at the top. The wind blustered and shook the ladder.

"Vengeance tear you!" he yelled down. "Hold it steady, you birdwitted bat!"

She moved forward, and as she did, the coughing air shifted the ladder. The man yelled again and flung out an arm. The ladder was jerked away from the cob. It stood upright for a moment and then crashed back with its human load to the ground.

He landed face down beside a moss-coated rock and lay quite still. Rachel, his wife, looked on his prone body and remembered everything.

A hand twitched. Someone would be blamed for the accident. She would be the one to pay. Rain had plastered his black hair into thin strings and revealed a round bald patch, unnoticed before, no bigger than the crown piece she had begged of him. Her eyes fixed on it, fascinated, and she heard again the chink of the coins from the Cornish tin box as he had toyed with them to tease her. In two days, Moses meadow would be sold. Jedder's land.

The man stirred. Soon he would arise and accuse her and surely thrash her this time, despite her pregnancy. Suddenly, the gale was roaring in her ears like water and the pulse in the pits of her eyes drummed and she saw the star of release at the end of a white-hot tunnel. The instinct for self-preservation engulfed all else, and, in the irrefutable grip of its impulse, she bent and seized the great lump of granite and lugged with all her being.

An acute pang, keen as a fleam, bit through her abdomen to her spine. The boulder jolted from its bed, and, with the transcendent strength of madness, she raised it up to her breast, took a crying, lung-splitting breath and smashed it down on her unconscious husband's head.

The winds stilled, the birds silenced, all growth stopped at the terrible instant of the sin, and when she looked up, the moor and the sky, the long, low house and the far forest were stained with red. Her lips drew back and her teeth bared in God-defying grimace. Rejecting the signs and the hideous echoes of the splintering skull, she pulled at a lifeless arm, refusing to acknowledge the lunging throes in her belly, hauling the body onto its side, until the mud-covered head rolled back and hemorrhaged over the stone.

Rachel Jedder staggered to the door of her house and collapsed. Her young sons found her there and helped her indoors to the parlor settle, frightened by her clay-white face.

"Tell Squire," she whispered, rocked by the spasms. "And fetch Mistress Squance, for my time is come early."

The brothers hurried to carry out the instructions, but not before Jedder went to stare at the body of his hated stepfather with undisguised loathing.

"I'd have done you in myself one day, you pox-ridden, bastard!" he shouted at it. "You be best off dead."

CHAPTER ELEVEN

People came. Squire Waddon and the churchwardens, other officials and a large group of curious villagers.

"Wasn't no love lost twixt they two," they murmured.

The screams of Rachel in her premature labor carried to them through the hole in the fatefully damaged roof.

"Talk sense, man!" the squire snapped, as the rumor was repeated to him. "Look at that boulder. You all know Mistress Blackaller's condition and the slightness of her build. How the devil could any woman have lifted that? Eh?"

They nodded their heads quickly, not wishing to offend or appear slow-witted.

" 'Twas an accident, quite obviously," the squire decided, with all the authority of his position as local Justice of the Peace. "That fool Black-aller did not secure his ladder and fell backward from it onto the rock. And good riddance to him, I say."

With a dismissive wave, he remounted his horse and rode off, effectively ending the matter. All agreed he must be right. 'Twas a proper gurt licker of a stone. Even Ephraim Thorne, the blacksmith, would have had a job to raise it, and anyways, that Harry Blackaller allus were a good-fer-naught. And they drifted off.

Upstairs, the old widow splashed icy water on Rachel's unconscious face to bring her round.

"You can't go fainting none, mistress," she shrilled. "Just keep 'ee pressin' down, for 'tis twins you got here."

A pack of ravenous beasts tore at her innards with claws and fangs and her flesh felt as pulpy and bloody as raw liver. She could not try any more, nor did she care what would become of her. All she wanted was to let go and tumble down into the black velvet void.

"Push! Push!" bullied the midwife, flinging more water.

Then Rachel heard her boast smugly to someone else in the room, "I said her'd die in childbirth and I bain't niver bin wrong yet. Her's done for this time."

Annoyance nagged through the red agony. "Stupid old crow! How

172

dare she!" Rachel let the anger fill her mind and tighten the muscles from the back of her neck to her feet and then she gave one final, mighty push, till the veins stood out like a blue net all over her body and her face turned puce. The slurping slide of the emerging second baby and the awareness that she was still alive were the last sensations she knew.

It was very quiet when she opened her eyes, and she was quite alone. Above, it was vaguely surprising to see new thatch. She remembered the storm and the events which had followed it with instant clarity and wondered how the thatcher had managed to complete the work so quickly, almost overnight.

Light was brightest in the south-facing window, so it must be around midday. She had slept much longer than usual. Lying without moving, she wondered where her two new babies were, whether they had lived, and whether her friend Jane Clarke had arrived, but she did not worry. Instead there was a feeling of complete peace.

She could not recall when she had last enjoyed such serenity, and then came the understanding that she was free. It was done. Blackaller was dead, and even if they arrested and hanged her, the land had not been sold and her last days on earth would be free. She relaxed into the safe, deep-bosomed feather bed of her ancestors and went back to sleep.

Low voices ebbed and flowed through her stupor and finally roused her again. Jane was leaning over anxiously, and gave a great sigh of relief as she looked up and smiled.

"We thought as you'd never come to, Rachel."

It was dark, and rush tapers lit the area around the bed. In the background, Jedder, John and Emma stood like small, flat cutouts.

"Have I slept all day?" Rachel asked, surprised.

"All day!" exclaimed Jane. "Near a week, more like!"

"A week! My gar! What about the little 'uns?" She began to sit up and found her limbs feeble and unmanageable.

"Don't 'ee move now! Squire sent a physician and he said as how you're to stay put," her friend said quickly. "And the babes is all right. You got two boys and I been putting them to you for feeding reg'lar."

"But what about you and the children?" The customary pressures of her life returned in tears of weakness. "There ain't no vittles and no gold."

"'Tis all right, me luvver. Parish give us ten shilling and rector's daughter brought groats and tea and bread."

"The parish!" muttered Rachel bitterly.

"Aye, the parish. And we be grateful for it. Us would have starved else," Jane pointed out firmly, then, seeing Rachel's eyes begin to droop, herded the children toward the door, although Jedder hung back.

"No more than a minute, then," she told him. "Your ma needs rest."

Rachel looked lovingly into his brown eyes as he approached. He was

173

growing fast, despite their hardships, and had all the handsome vitality of his father. He took her hand, turned it over and placed a silver crown piece and three coppers into it.

"These was in Harry Blackaller's pockets. 'Twas all he had," he said. "And ain't nobody knows but I, 'cos they'd have took them off us to pay summat."

"Come here, son," murmured Rachel, and kissed him when he bent to her. He blushed self-consciously, then gave a cocky wave as he left the room.

Rachel was fed on bread sops with salt, pepper and butter for three days, then water gruel, dry toast and weak tea. She was given no milk until she had progressed beyond veal broth to sago and tapioca puddings and a half-pint of stout a day, which was provided from charity funds.

The newborn twins, Richard and Joel Blackaller, were tiny but resolutely demanding and apparently determined to stay alive. And very slowly she, too, recovered strength, although it was several weeks before she was allowed to leave her bed.

There was plenty of time to think of the recent years, with all their sorrows and gruesome climax. At first, feelings of guilt and confusion and fear of God's punishment made her shrink and cry in secret. She tried to bar the final gory evocation of the dead man from her consciousness, but snatches of it would splatter onto her mind when least expected: that twitching hand, the open mouth, the trickles of blood from his nostrils, the unrecognizable foul mess exposed when the stone had rolled to the ground; and she would shudder and shut her eyes and cover her ears and bury her head in the pillow, as though fending off a physical presence.

There were other memories, too, stretched tight as curing hides, of the searing nights and ugly days of his tyranny. She tried to eliminate them but they invaded persistently, and her dreams were full of jumbled catastrophes, in which she lost her hair and teeth and was disemboweled, in which she fought eternally to clear a jungle where two plants grew for every one hacked down; nightmares of rape, of humiliation before laughing crowds, of the workhouse children rising from the grave and proving to be her own.

Then, gradually, all the mental maggots and imaginings began to group into a loose order and it became possible to reason once more, and Rachel Jedder realized that throughout this period of self-doubt and perturbation, in the honesty of her own heart she had never once, not for an instant, regretted the murder of Harry Blackaller. However great the sin, the saving of the land and the rescuing of her family and herself were its justification.

After that, with a vow never again to put their lives and security into the hands of another, she shut her mind, finally and irrevocably, to the haunting recurrence of her bloodstained memories, ignored the baiting images, and refused to consider the matter again.

174

Besides, there were the urgent problems of survival and, beyond that, the restoration of Yellaton to its former productiveness. The position was much worse than when she had first arrived on the holding so many years before. There was no stock and no seed, no stores, and it was midwinter, with herself and five children to maintain. The parish had made an exception in giving help to one who owned land, and certainly would not provide more. At least she was glad of that, for accepting their charity had sickened her.

It was while she was lying considering such things that word came from the Wolcots that Robert's brothers would take in John as a back-house boy on the farm. This was the only contact they had made since her first husband's death, and Rachel bit her lip, wishing she could throw the offer back in their faces but knowing she could not.

He was a shy lad and he sobbed as he left home with his few clothes in a bundle, but he was eight years old and many a boy started work before that.

Jedder, the oldest, was already contributing what he could through casual work for local farmers, trapping rats with a hazel stick and noose (for which he was paid by the tail), or rattling a wooden clapper to scare crows away from pulling straws out of the stacks. The latter was an especially cold and tedious job, worked at from the time the birds appeared at first light until they roosted at twilight.

He was an expert with a heavyheaded poacher's club, which he could throw to stun a starting hare while walking home at night, and he had learned the local way of catching rabbits with a long, strong blackberry runner. With all the thorns removed, except for those covering about four inches at the thin end, the bramble stem was fed down a rabbit hole and given a few twists when it would go no further. If it had come up against a rabbit, the twists tangled the prickles into the fur and the animal could then be pulled out of its burrow into the open.

He chopped wood for folk, swept chimneys with a bunch of holly tied to a long pole, caught pigeons, and occasionally, by mistake, of course, a long-tailed pigeon, which looked remarkably like a pheasant. Each skill took patience and time, but it brought home food or a little money, and money bought flour and flour made bread.

As soon as she was able, Rachel took the barren old cow and the five shillings and threepence and went to High Chilham. The weather promised badly and there were six more months to go before any kind of crop or vegetable could be gathered to feed them, even if she had seed to plant. During the weeks of her forced inactivity, the question of what to buy for the best had vexed her continually, and she was no nearer the answer; potatoes were filling and cheaper than flour, but there was more goodness in flour and more could be done with it, although potatoes would include a few tubers to set in the garden. In neither case could she afford enough to keep the family through until summer.

175

It was hardly worth holding the market, there were so few beasts and so little produce to offer at this time of year. At the height of July and August, the great field bustled with sheep and lambs and cattle, and farmer's daughters selling cream and butter and eggs and vegetables from their pannier baskets, and smallholders proffering breeding sets of geese and secondhand tools and garden produce and their own service as laborers. Now it was almost deserted.

George Beare had potatoes, cabbages and carrots laid out, and behind hurdles alongside the sheltering hedge at the far end, thin, barren ewes, a couple of aged horses and another bony old cow, like her own, waited miserably. The village gathered from habit because it was a traditional excuse to meet and exchange gossip and see who was prospering and who faring badly, and for each to try to pretend he was doing well.

"Her's only fit for kennel meat," the butcher said, offering Rachel a pittance for the cow.

"What about her hide then?" demanded Rachel, affronted.

" 'Tis a moth-eaten piece. Look 'ee here and here." He pointed out scars.

"We'd be better off eating her ourselves," she protested.

"Do 'ee that then, mistress," he agreed without rancor. "She'll be a tough old bite."

He began to walk away. Rachel gave in and stretched out her hand for the few coppers.

Seth Bartle was passing and asked, "Be 'ee selling the mare, Mistress Blackaller?"

"No," she replied. "She's needed for the spring work. No matter what hardship, we got to keep her on."

"Must be all of fifteen year now," observed Seth. "And as I recall, she weren't put in foal this year."

Rachel shrugged. He knew there had been no money to pay the service fee for the stallion.

"Send her over to us, mistress, and I'll see 'ee right," he continued, lowering his voice. "There'll be a foal afore next winter, but 'tis twixt thee and me, mind."

Rachel touched his arm in thanks and he nodded before moving off. It was a kind gesture. A good colt would sell well, or, if by some miracle their fortunes improved, he could be kept on and raised for work.

She wandered across the field, still indecisive about the best purchases, exchanging greetings here and there and answering inquiries about her health and the condition of the children.

Peter Luckbreast's wife, Patience, nursing her latest and shouting at the other four youngest of her eighteen children, sold her half a dozen hens at twopence each.

"Did 'ee hear about that farmer over Broad Rush Common?" she asked. " 'Tis said he be hundred and thirty-three year old and been wed to thirteen wives."

"Beggar I!" exclaimed Rachel, duly impressed.

"If that husband of mine took another, he wouldn't find me objectin' none," the other murmured outrageously. "For 'tis fact that he be a terrible hard man to content."

Rachel could well believe it and giggled with her.

A group of youths were laughing and nudging each other in the corner.

"Them eats anything," sniggered one.

"Even old women's stays," guffawed another.

"Did 'ee get her in for them cold nights, Sam Babb?" teased the most daring of the bunch. " 'Tis said unmarried men gets up to some fearsome tricks."

The boys collapsed, pushing and rolling over each other with mirth.

"Now, git 'ee going! There's nought wrong wi' her." The man they surrounded was on the defensive. "Her come off Ilfracombe way, and they speaks highly of such critturs up there."

"An' us knows what's told of they Exmoor folk," mocked the bold one, and the boys collided in another fit of laughter.

Rachel approached out of curiosity and saw one of Squire Waddon's workers, red-faced, holding a shaggy-haired, curly-horned goat.

The animal raised its head and looked at the woman through queer oblong yellow eyes and sniffed the air delicately.

Rachel grinned. "What's this then, Samuel Babb?"

The man looked embarrassed. "Bliddy beast were sent to Squire as a jest and now he wants rid o' it," he explained. "An' we have taken some stick here today, I can tell 'ee."

"Do she give milk?" asked Rachel, mildly interested.

" 'Bout three quart a day. Her's in kid, but 'tis said as they'll milk right through."

"How does it taste?"

"Fath, mistress! I ain't took a mouthful o' the stuff!" The man was indignant.

"What does she eat then?"

"Hay and bits o' hedge and such. We tethers her at the edge o' the pasture."

The idea took hold and Rachel wondered how much the Squire would take for the goat.

"Three shillin'," Babb answered, too quickly.

"One!" She knew he would pocket some.

"One shilling and sixpence."

"And threepence."

"Done!"

And she found herself the possessor of an outlandish creature which everyone scorned, and she wondered whether she had gone mad.

"She don't like the rain none, mistress," Sam Babb called after her, and the village sniggered.

Apart from the hens, she bought a bushel of barley flour, two hun-

177

dredweight of potatoes and a cheese. It was not nearly enough to keep the family until the farmers took on casual workers in the spring, and it was certain they would not eat meat other than the rare game poached by Jedder, for many months, if ever again. But all the money was spent.

Once home, she tied up the goat in the stable and crouched to reach for the udder under the rough coat. To her surprise, the two teats were smooth and soft, like a woman's, and not at all like the rubbery dugs of a cow. Milk streaked in ringing pencil strokes into the crock, which soon filled.

Rachel took an apprehensive sip, and then another. It tasted different, a little sweeter and stronger than the milk she was accustomed to, but it was pleasant, and had it not been for the waiting children, she would have drunk it all.

The animal had chewed rhythmically and philosophically throughout the routine, unperturbed by her new living quarters, and when her long, warm ears were rubbed, she met the strange eyes of her new owner with her own strange eyes, calmly. Rachel gave her an affectionate pat. She seemed a wise buy after all, and in the thin months ahead it was the goat's economical provision of a pint of milk a day for each which was, in fact, to save them from malnutrition.

It was a savage winter, encased in frost and thrashed by ice-laden east winds, and they all ate more because of it. Rachel made great quantities of kettle broth from cubes of bread flavored with salt and covered with half hot milk and half hot water, and potato-and-onion stews, and saw them wolfed down. In less than a month, the stores were decimated.

After taking stock in alarm one morning, she set out to look for work in Great Torrington. The town lay only a few miles to the south and was prosperous, with fine new houses and thriving woolen and cloth industries.

Halted hungrily by the delicious smell of food wafting from the Black Horse Inn, she paused to enjoy the sight of the people hurrying about their business and considered where to begin. Someone called her name and, turning, she saw the peddler on the opposite side of the square.

"Where be thee going?" he asked.

"I need work bad," she explained, then pointed to the sacks on his two packhorses. "What you go there, then?"

" 'Tis the day us axwaddles," he replied, showing that the bags were full of wood ash, collected to make lye for washing clothes. "Lookee here, mistress, how well do 'ee stitch?"

Rachel screwed up her face. She made her own and the children's clothes, as every woman did, but in comparison with the minute, regularly spaced stitching of experts, her needlework was a cauchy muddle.

" 'Tis my opinion as you stitches good as a nun." The peddler winked at her. "And we have heard how you made gloves better than a gloving school afore you were wed."

178

Rachel chuckled. "You're quite right. True as I'm a lady."

"Come with me," he said.

They walked to a cottage in a narrow side street and a fat, pasty-pale woman with bloodshot eyes answered the old man's knock. After exchanging a few words, she returned inside and the peddler winked again at Rachel before leading his horses off across the cobblestones.

Fumes from wood being burnt in an earthen pot escaped in a blast through the open door, and Rachel could see several young children bent over their work in the cramped, airless room. She knew they sewed from eight A. M. until dusk and that, by nine years old, with five years' experience already behind them, they were faster and more proficient than she would ever be. The woman reappeared with a pile of cut leather and a bag of sewing materials.

"Us pays two shilling a dozen pair, after the first dozen and after the tools is paid for. Any spoiled leather is taken off your money and the agent collects monthly," she said shortly. "If the first batch be to standard, kid and chamois pays two shilling and twopence a dozen."

That evening, Rachel drew her chair and table as close as possible to the flickering rush tapers and began. Although there was a special needle provided, the leather shapes kept sliding away from each other so that the stitches were irregular. Then, at the foot of the bag, she found a little brass vise for holding the pieces together, but the first glove was already ruined. Wincing at the knowledge that it would have to be paid for, she decided to use it to practice on. It took until late at night to learn how to fit in the thumb and master the method of sewing, when with sore back and stiff hands and watering eyes, she put the work aside at last.

On waking, she started again. The holes were tiny, and if the thread was pulled too fast it tore the soft leather; or sometimes the needle went in at the wrong angle and stuck; too tight and the material was cut, too loose and the joining did not hold. The morning became afternoon before the trial glove was finished, and Rachel took it outside to examine in daylight. The polished brown skins were blotched with sweat from her fingers and the back was wrinkled and the seams crooked. It was a botch.

She sighed despondently and stretched and rolled her neck and aching head to relieve the tension in her shoulders, flexed her fingers and looked at the glove again. The seams sewn last were certainly a great improvement on the earlier efforts, but at her present rate it would take two weeks to make a dozen pairs, and more than a month before she could earn any money.

By midnight of the following day, a pair of "best man's" gloves were completed, ready to be sent on to the pointer, who would work the three ornamental lines on the back. Rachel looked at them with a pride and satisfaction which compensated for the physical discomfort of her seized-up hands and exhausted sight. Her spirits rose. Speed would come with skill. Soon she would be making three pairs a day, she planned optimistically, and in chamois. That would mean an income of three shillings and ninepence a week. It was a good prospect to sleep on.

Snow began to fall. She saw the first flakes while setting up for work in the parlor and heard the wind as she bent over the leather. The room grew imperceptibly darker until, raising her head a couple of hours later, she was astonished to see that the window was almost covered and the level of the snow was rising even as she watched. Within minutes the glass was completely sealed over.

Running through the house, she opened the back door to an opaque blur. The blizzard filled the courtyard and a massive drift had already piled over the cowshed and as high as the roof, leaving only the narrowest space along the foot of the west wall by which to reach the stable.

The density of the fall suppressed the sound of the wind so that its power conjured up the soaring white mountains in utter silence. The moors and woods had gone, all creatures and buildings were buried and there was no horizon. Rachel had never known anything like it. In a few hours the familiar world had been totally consumed by this noiseless, isolating, entombing mass.

Suddenly, she realized that before long it would be impossible to reach the animals and poultry, and, calling Jedder from the kitchen, she rushed through the closing gap to the stable.

"Best fetch in hay first," she shouted and flung back the far door. A solid wall of snow filled its frame. The way to the barn, the sties and the fields was already blocked.

The boy grabbed a rusty spade and began to dig into the barrier, pitching the sugarspun loads onto the floor behind him, like a burrowing fox. As soon as there was enough room, Rachel joined him with an old shovel and a strait opened up, to be filled instantly with a thick, moving fog of flakes, fine as dust, which was inhaled into the lungs and choked them with each breath. The two worked quickly and without speech until the outline of the barn loomed and then consolidated into reality. Minutes more and they had cleared a semicircle wide enough to gain access.

The hens roosting in the dark interior were easily caught and carried, three in each hand, hanging upside down, back to the kitchen. Then armfuls of bracken were brought to bed the utility-room floor and hay was stacked in the empty pantry. Finally the bemused horse and the goat were led into the passage and Rachel thankfully slammed the back door. They would all hole up together in the old house and the weather could do its worst.

The storm ended and the skies cleared during that night, leaving Yellaton so encased that, by first light, they could only see out of the upstairs windows to the magical landscape left behind. Twenty-foot-high breakers, pale gold under the frail sun, curled over the invisible hedgerows, the spray of their crests frozen to crystalline foam, boiling over the buried woods and calming to shining furrows on the feminine contours of the heath. Clumps of dogwood fanned, startling orange and yellow, like fires without smoke, and the bare trees cast shadows of purple and blue, and charms of small birds zigzagged and veered in disoriented shock above the ice-capped and glaciered surface. Muted dove-gray hills far off enfolded ethereal valleys, misted like dreams. It was a change both beautiful and awesome, and it filled Rachel and her son with an uneasiness they would not have admitted to each other.

She sewed all day and evening, and the next, and for the whole of the month, during which the snows cut off the West Country from the rest of England and cloistered Beara and Yellaton impenetrably. She sewed until calluses formed over the sores rubbed on her fingers, until her eyes narrowed with the closeness of it, and it became difficult to stand erect after the restriction of the workbench. Little Emma and the twin babies, fed when necessary, were left to crawl and fall and squabble and howl and sleep on the kitchen floor, while their mother attempted to increase her production by singing folk reels and dance tunes, or tapping out a fast rhythm with her foot and trying to sew to tempo, but no matter how much she pushed herself, no more than two pairs of gloves a day were ever completed. At a time when a female farm worker earned seven and a half pence a day and a frugal maidservant could actually save money from her annual wages, Rachel Jedder's hundred hours of meticulous needlework each week were to pay only two shillings and eightpence, a mere fourpence halfpenny a day.

The muck from the animals trapped in the back of the house built up and seeped unhealthily under the kitchen door. The air was always stuffy and the children were always hungry. When at last the level of the white tide began to drop, as though a plug had been pulled out of the basin of the world, they were weak and tired, and the food Jedder struggled to the village to buy on credit arrived just in time.

Rachel did not know that years were to pass before the cast of her life was broken again. The coming of the gloving agent on his donkey rapidly became the focal point of every month, and meeting the work target confined her more surely than shackles. Because there was never enough money to maintain the children through the unhurried, certain circle of seed and growth and harvest and seed, the making of the gloves became even more important than work on the land. Stitching and stitching in the dim kitchen, she sewed through the spring, which followed the great blizzard, and the summer, which followed the spring, without noticing either. She might as well have remained snowed in for all the difference the changing seasons made.

Jedder did his best on the holding and managed to grow enough to provide a subsistence, despite being just a boy. In order that his mother should not be distracted from her work, he also made all the necessary trips to High Chilham and brought back news: that prices were down again; that Stephen Pincombe, father of Jane Clarke's bastard child, had had to sell his farm; that Luke Claggett, Matthew's younger brother, had been press-ganged into the navy while drunk in Barnstaple; and the youngest Fortescue had been sent to the debtor's prison. But there never seemed to be word of her second son.

"John 'aven't been seen, Mother," Jedder would answer. "Seems 'ee don't get to the village."

"What about your Uncle William?"

"Oh, I asked him and 'ee told as John be fine," he said, unconcerned.

"Them Wolcots is all hard workers as 'ee knows," Jane pointed out during a visit. "So your John be kept pretty busy, I 'spect."

But Rachel missed her quiet child and grew less easily appeased.

" 'T'ain't right, him not being given a day to come home in six month," she complained.

"Times is hard, Mother." Jedder was matter-of-fact. "And he be no worse off than a 'prentice."

She slammed down the brass glove vise and stood up.

"Well, I'm out of patience," she announced. "I'm going to see our John this day."

The Wolcot holding lay two miles beyond the village in the valley of the Taw, its meadows, grazing fat steers, running alongside the river. Rachel had only visited there two or three times, while married to Robert Wolcot, and then had been made to feel unwelcome.

The yard, as she rode in, was swept so free of dirt that not a straw was left caught between the cobblestones, and the open shippens and stables displayed the same spotlessness. The whole place was so clean it should have sparkled, and yet, beneath the warm sky and surrounded by lush-leaved trees, it looked grim. Dried fox skins were nailed flat to every farm-building door, where most farmers would have fixed lucky horseshoes. The rear windows of the house were barred with iron and the front door looked as though it had not been opened in fifty years. Rachel hammered on it loudly.

Footsteps crossed the stone floors from deep within and there was a suspicious pause before Alice Wolcot, her sister-in-law, opened the door a crack and peered out.

"I come to see our John," said Rachel.

"He bain't here," she replied, but not before Rachel had caught the quickly suppressed look of scared surprise. "William took him up High Chilham."

It was immediately recognizable as a lie and Rachel pushed her aside.

"I'll wait till he comes back, Alice Wolcot." She marched into the musty parlor and turned to face the woman. "And be sure I won't leave here till I see my son."

Her sister-in-law scuttled off and could be heard talking in low, rapid tones to someone in the kitchen. A few minutes later, William Wolcot himself came into the room.

"Alice was mistaken. John's down Abbots Marsh with the cattle and not due back afore cockshut." He looked sulky and stubborn and his eyes would not meet hers. "Too late for you to wait and still ride back to Yellaton tonight, Mistress Blackaller."

"I ain't shifting," Rachel declared adamantly. "So you'd best send for him now."

"That boy be no worker," the man growled, drawing himself up to increase his height over her. "Been nothing but a burden to us."

"You're not the man to put up with a lad what don't work, William Wolcot," she responded with asperity. "If there was a scrap of truth in what you're saying, you'd have packed him off home long afore now."

"Well, you can take 'un today, mistress," he blustered defensively. "He be no loss here, I can tell 'ee."

"I'll fetch him myself and gladly," she stormed. "Now, where is he?"

"Skulking round the woodshed most like," her brother-in-law snarled. "Come here under false pretenses, that boy. He never were no Wolcot, 'tis easy seen."

He stomped from the room, muttering, and Rachel, filled with foreboding, ran from the bleak house and across the cold, immaculate yard toward the shed, from where the erratic rap of wood being chopped limped into hearing.

"John," she called softly, her eyes blinded from the brightness outside. "John."

There was a faint scuffle and her sight cleared to see the little pile of new sticks beside the stack of logs, but the boy was not there.

"John?" she called again, walking in. " 'Tis your mother, John. Where be you to?"

A shadow moved and whimpered and she rushed to it. Limbs as thin and brittle as starlings' feet reached out, and when she lifted him, he weighed no more than a newborn infant. She ran into the light and looked down, and wept to see him, huge-eyed and sunken-faced. Her plump baby, who always smiled. He weighed no more than a basket of eggs. Under a few rags, his ribs and hips and elbows and knees dug into her body like twigs, covered only by skin, which sagged into folds once filled with flesh. He weighed no more than a cat.

"Bastards! Bastards!" Rachel Jedder screamed at the blank-windowed house, and immediately regretted it as the child clung in fright.

"Don't fret! Don't fret! We're going home, to Yellaton. 'Tis all right now, my pet, my lamb." She rocked him gently in her arms and her tears dropped onto his hidden face.

The story emerged hesitantly, incident by incident, over the next weeks, of having been set tasks impossible for a boy of his age, threshing tons of corn and hauling barrels of cider, being knocked over by big, clumsy bullocks and trying to clear out pigsties several feet deep in solid muck, too heavy for him to lift; and of being deprived of meals as punishment for failure.

Rachel fed him goat's milk and eggs and chicken meat and remembered little Sam all those years before and cursed herself harshly. Knowing what happened to indigent children put out to toil, she had still let John go. Now, full of remorse, she blamed herself for her stupidity, for not yet having learned the one vital lesson of all her experience—that the protection and strength of the family lay entirely on Jedder's land. By leaving the homestead, or bringing in outsiders, the fragile balance was always endangered, and they were left exposed to a world which was mainly brutal and without pity.

Jedder was now ten years old and John was eight. They would be able to cope with much of the outside work, and as soon as Emma was three, she could start spinning. Among them they would maintain each other and gradually restore the holding to full productiveness. None would ever be sent away again. From now on they would stay together on Yellaton, whatever happened.

In early autumn, they all went gleaning on the squire's land, settling the twins on the edge of the field and then moving quickly over the stubble, eyes straining to see every ear of wheat missed by the rakes, picking with one hand and collecting in the other, which rested in the small of the back. A wisp of straw bound each fistful, which was then added to the others beside the stone bottle of water and the food basket.

It was good to leave the endless sewing and cramped chair and come to work in the open air once more. The colors of the turning leaves and the smell of earth and cut corn, and the spaciousness of the land and the sky, and the sun on her shoulders made Rachel happy.

There were cabbages and turnips and Jerusalem artichokes in the garden, and potatoes and carrots clamped behind the barn. Seth Bartle had seen that their hay was cut and stacked, and the orchard was so heavy with apples that there would be enough to make cider, to store for eating, and plenty left over to sell.

Young John had filled out within weeks of being brought home and now looked rosy and fit once more. Jedder had a terrier dog and two ferrets for ratting during the winter, and chicks had hatched, increasing her flock of hens and soon to provide a few cockerels for the pot. The gleaning was good and might add as much as two bushels of flour to the little harvest they had reaped from a hand-dug patch on the hare's leg, although there had been no plowing done. Barely sufficient stores, but enough. Rachel straightened her aching back for a moment and glanced across at her industrious children searching the ground and felt she had been given another chance to start all over again.

A spindle was put into little Emma's hands on her birthday in December, and fleece gathered from the hedges and furze bushes on the moor was washed and loosened and carded with teasel heads before she was shown how to twist and draw it out as the spindle spun. From then on, the child never went anywhere without wool in her pinafore pocket and the spindle swinging beneath her working hands. It became second nature to her, and the spun wool grew into skeins, which the agent paid for and took to Torrington, along with the finished gloves. Rachel believed she had found the answer at last. Together, on their own land, they would endure.

But the deadly mark of true poverty is that it is unending: undramatically, monotonously, from year to year, its hold does not loosen and the longest, most consistent and grueling labor cannot break its cycle. Decent clothes become shabby, fray and finally disintegrate into tatters, decisively setting apart and demoting their wearers in the eyes of the properly clad community, and there is never enough money to buy new ones.

On the homestead, the woman and her children drudged every single day of every week of every month, and the months became a year, and another, and a third, and then two more, but they were still unable to halt the almost imperceptible but undeniably downward spiral of their fate. There were no spare minutes: they collected acorns to fatten other people's pork, and mushrooms to sell; they picked stones for back-breaking seasons, plucked fowls, pulled up twitch roots from plowed land, caught seed-raiding sparrows. Even the twins, as soon as they could toddle, were expected to do their share, hunting for eggs and scaring birds.

But lack of implements meant that the ditches could not be adequately cleared, nor the hedges cut, nor the edge of the woodland coppiced. Make-do-and-mend repairs to the buildings did not last long against the constantly attacking elements, and there was no way of affording good new materials.

As necessary objects wore out, they could not be replaced, and every achievement meant not a move forward, but only that they retained the same position. Thus, each year's colt was sold to pay for little more than the mare's next service and, although two windows in the house had been blocked up, the pig had to be sold to pay the taxes on the other windows. The glorious summer of '79 with its bumper harvest resulted only in a disastrous fall in the prices of all farm produce, wheat fetching a mere thirty-three shillings and eightpence a quarter, where five years earlier it had sold for nineteen shillings more. Then, the mare herself had to be sent to market.

On the other side of Roborough village, the barn, outbuildings and stored barley of the Barlington estate burned down one night, and everyone knew it had been done deliberately, for the insurance, because the agricultural depression had driven Sir Roger nearly bankrupt. If men as wealthy as he were being brought down, how could the poor climb?

On mornings when the weight of poverty seemed even heavier than usual, Rachel would pick up her gloving materials, fill a stone bottle with cider and cut a wedge of cheese and two doorsteps of bread and walk to the one-roomed hovel on the far edge of High Chilham, where Jane Clarke lived with her aged mother in far more abject circumstances than her own. The three women would hunch over their needles close to the peat fire, Jane stitching garments for local customers and her mother mumbling toothlessly over the trimmings of exquisite lace which lengthened with painful slowness in her arthritic hands.

Rachel and Jane had much in common. They were the same age and had both been only children, isolated to some extent from the community through lack of close family ties within it. They had always liked each other and, in the days of her prosperity with Robert Wolcot, Rachel's regular visits had been accompanied by baskets of "surplus" produce from Yellaton, just enough to be helpful without causing embarrassment. The friendship which had developed between them down the years was warm and sure, built on trust and the instinctive understanding that women have for each other's lives and circumstances.

Now they talked about their children and the affairs of the village and the price of flour. They told each other jokes and Rachel would find herself laughing freely at Jane's outrageous mimicry of local righteous widows and pillars of the church. In fine weather they would take their chairs outside and, at midday, they would lay down their work and stretch and blink into the bright sun and walk down the lane, picking a few wild flowers and looking inquisitively over the hedgerows to see how far on Jane's farming neighbors were with the season's tasks.

"I see he's tilled potatoes then."

"Finished last week."

" 'Tis too early. He'd better watch out frost don't get them."

"He do plant them same every year. Likes to be first in village. Oh, I near forgot to tell 'ee, Rachel—" Jane nudged her excitedly—"David Pope were seen creeping away from Becky Bowden's cottage only the other day and now farmer Hookway has put Stephen Bowden to work in Ashcombe field so's he can keep a watch on her."

Rachel giggled. "Well, he can't work there forever."

"That Becky's got no shame." The other grinned. "You know, once she even told him that she'd been with me all afternoon, being fitted for a new skirt, and he come running down here to see if 'twere true."

"What did you tell him?"

"Why, that it was a devilish pattern to cut right and I'd never known it take so long to make a skirt." Jane's face was full of mischief. "I knew she'd been down Squire's woods with that young apprentice o' Hooper's, and him only half her age! But Becky and me were little 'uns together and her always did like a bit o' fun."

186

These shared days were full of simple pleasure, and the hours sped by. The women cheered and comforted each other in the loneliness and worry of their struggle against hardship, and it was easier to face the future of endless deprivation knowing that another was facing a similar prospect with courage.

Rachel, in her parlor, sewing through winter into another spring, looked longingly out across the greening heath and remembered Will driving her flock of sheep home, and how she and the boys had lambed them night after night after Robert Wolcot had been taken, each birth bringing so much hope and the assurance of good fortune. Yet, after it all, here she was, the owner of a house and holding, imprisoned in a tight wooden cage of a chair, caught in a web of thread. Another five years hence, and her spine would be deformed and her eyesight lost through the bad working conditions, and the situation would be unchanged, except that the land would have deteriorated beyond recovery.

Deliverance would not come of its own accord, nor could she force the way to freedom. They had reached the stage where only a wild gamble might succeed. Rachel Jedder knew that Moses meadow and wood must be sold at last, even though it cut into her reason for living to do it, and meant the betrayal of her first husband's struggle and conceding a posthumous victory to Blackaller. The smallholder George Beare had recently shown an interest in that land, and the money from the sale would buy tools, a few sheep and a cow; enough, perhaps, to escape from the poverty trap and give the family a stake in the future again.

The risk of failure was great. Prices might fall, as they had three years before, and the precious investment be lost, but she knew she had to take the chance, or condemn herself and her children and the generations to come to a destiny of suffering.

Without warning, the front door swung silently open, pushed by the hand of a moorland breeze tantalizing with the scent of new growth; sweet blossoming thorn and hidden flowers, lusty pasture and honey-sharp heather. Rachel left her work rebelliously and let herself be drawn into the brilliant morning.

There are transcendent, heart-speeding days in every West Country spring, which insist on optimism and faith. The light has a unique luminosity after the relentless whiteness of February and the broken cloud of March. The surge of life jolts the senses into awareness through the touch of turf damp from the last shower and the smell of sap and fresh herbage, the trilling of thrushes and the butter-yellow bubbles of massed primroses. April tastes of mint.

Rachel and her faithful dog walked, unhurried, in the mild air and felt their bodies unknot from hunched defense against winter. Their lungs drew in deeper breaths and the gray dog, who was now very old and rarely went out, discovered a forgotten lightness in his gait, which carried him unexpectedly into a clumsy, happy gallop. Rachel, with shining eyes, ran alongside and played with him, past the herb patch, its edges already curly with parsley and thyme, through the orchard of branches tufted with pale green beginnings, to stop under the catkin-hung willow by Brindley.

There Sam lay down, gasping and grinning and wagging his tail, and she leaned on the gate, pleased to do nothing. Ground elder had already appeared on the bare soil under the tree, and forget-me-nots had overgrown the path to the woods, turning it sky blue. The brown coat of last year's leaves had finally dropped from the shoulders of the beech hedge, and the barberry spikes were camouflaged with flowers, and brushstrokes of wild cherry lit the thickets. The severe straightness of the poplar windbreak was in a peach cloud of opening buds.

When she moved on, it was slowly, for the sake of her old friend, past the patches of celandines, lying like dishes on the banks, and the thorned tangle of blackberry and dog rose strands tamed by young shoots, to where Moses Bottom stretched before them.

The memory of herself as an ecstatic young bride, taking ownership for the first time, bounced ahead, and she followed it to the pond at the foot of the meadow, where the water was full of frog tadpoles, laid three months before, and toads were spawning under the floating lilies. Cowslips spread outward from the spinney, scattered and became early buttercups and then single dandelions, vividly picked out against the grass. It was a lovely place, and she and Robert Wolcot had made it so.

Rachel took a last look, then climbed the slope again, almost turned back once, but resisted and walked on. The only possible decision had been made.

On the way to the house, she bent, without thinking, to nip out the tips of young nettles, lifting her skirt to form a pocket for collecting them to cook that evening into an iron-rich, savory spinach on which to serve poached eggs to be eaten for supper with crusty bread. It took about an hour of rambling from clump to clump before the skirt held enough, and she came up to Yellaton from the south side.

A large basket lying by the porch was visible from a hundred yards away. It was stuffed with some material, and full of curiosity, she hastened to it. The white cloth moved, and raising it warily, Rachel saw that it enfolded a child, a baby of no more than a day or two old.

Anger made her scowl as she stared down. Infants were often discarded by ashamed or impoverished mothers in this age, but how could anyone have been so stupid as to suppose that she, with all her problems, could feed another mouth? It would go straight to the poorhouse. She herself would take it there that very hour.

The baby, so suddenly exposed to the light and the fresh wind, began to cry, not very loud but with real tears filling its unseeing dark-blue eyes. The woman set her face.

"You cannot stay here. We have trouble enough to fill our own bellies as it is."

The baby stopped crying, lay quite still and very carefully smiled.

"I wager you never done that before," Rachel chuckled, and instinctively touched its hand. The small fingers gripped her index finger and the smile vanished, to be replaced by an expression of pathetic helplessness.

"Well, you can come in to warm up, but no more," said she, refusing to listen to her nagging conscience. "Because you'm going to the parish, no matter what."

She carried the basket into the parlor, determinedly expelling the images of the workhouse at Shaltam from her mind. Then, tucking the cover around the child, she felt the damp and sniffed at the familiar smell of ammonia. The baby whimpered.

"There's no pleasing you. I suppose you want drying off now," she grumbled and lifted it into her arms.

A cascade of money fell from the white shawl onto the floor. Rachel let out a shriek and dumped the child back into the basket, bending to snatch the coins, biting each and blinking with shock. Real gold guineas.

Golden guineas. She placed them on the table, one by one. Unable to count in the orthodox sense, she calculated on her fingers and, on reaching ten, she rubbed a stroke in the polished surface of the wood and felt slightly faint as the marks became a row, longer than the one she had made when working out how much money Moses Bottom would fetch; longer even than the row of scratches cut in the stick to calculate the contents of the Cornish tin box after Robert Wolcot's death.

She sat down with her hands clamped over her mouth and her stomach churning. A miracle had happened. The land need not be sold. Seed and stock and food and tools could be bought. It was spring, the start of the farming year, the time to sow, the season of miracles.

Rachel Jedder swung the child in the air and whirled with it around the room. It burst into noisy howls, and she joined in from joy. Eventually she calmed down and rested the squalling infant on her lap.

"Hush you, for 'tis different now. You can stay on, seeing as you be paying for your keep." She undid the swaddling clothes and revealed the baby as a girl. "And I expect you'd have stayed on anyway, so you'd best have a name." She thought for a moment. "Jane! After my good friend Jane Clarke. We'll call you Jane Jedder, though 'tis rum, being of different blood, that you are the only Jedder child I have."

Rachel and her five children celebrated with halloos and hugs, and the two oldest boys ran all the way to the village and back to bring home tea and a ham (which was cooked with a freshly killed hen), and finest white flour, butter, black treacle, spices and candied peel, with which

189

their mother made gingerbread to eat with cider after the great feast. The youngest, who had never tasted such goodies, were overawed to silence by the glut.

Next day, Rachel walked to the horsebreaker's yard in High Chilham.

"This here is for the use of the stallion on my mare four year past." She held out the fee. "And I want you to look out for a useful young work-horse quick."

"Get on with 'ee! I wants none of your gold for summat as cost me nothing, mistress." Seth Bartle pushed away her hand outstretched with the money and added with undisguised interest, "The good Lord has smiled upon thee then, Rachel Jedder?"

She beamed back at him, nodding, but said nothing.

When he realized that details of the mystery were not to be forthcoming, he grinned and said, "Well, I be real glad for 'ee, Mistress Jedder, and I got a smart mare here as will make 'ee a proper job."

A brand-new plow and harrows, sickle, scythe and pitchforks were ordered from the blacksmith, a cart from the wheelwright and four weaner pigs from Morrish's farm before she rode off on her new horse to South Molton. There she bought the prettiest down-calving heifer in the market and a sheep pen of couples, ewes and lambs, to be herded onto Beara Moor within seven days.

So, at the start of the new decade, Jedder's land was reborn. A man was hired from the village to plow and harrow and sow the wheat and swedes before May. The whole family dug up the overgrown garden and planted more than enough potatoes and vegetables to keep themselves and the hogs for a year. And, in May, the pretty cow gave birth to a red bull calf.

Jedder frowned over it with disappointment. "We would have done better with a heifer, but I suppose he'll make good enough beef."

The calf clambered to its feet and stood, glossy and straight-legged in the sun, and gave a loud, protesting bawl.

Rachel looked, too, at the first farm animal to be born on Yellaton for three long years.

"No," she said. He ain't going to be no man's meat. I shall grow him into the finest bull in all Devon.

CHAPTER TWELVE

The silken patina of emerging wheat appeared on the freshly turned soil within days of tilling; the waterlogged lea drained its acid into the reopened ditches, dried out and released sweet growth for hay; the new lambs grew stocky and strong on the moor, and each step in the rapid restoration of her property stimulated Rachel Jedder like a drug.

Like the land, she, too, was rejuvenated. Her skin bloomed and her hair lengthened and thickened and shone, the taut, lined expression of care relaxed, and age fell away. Challenged and excited once more, she resented having to sleep at night and awoke, explosive with energy, at the first streak of each dawn.

Both physically and mentally she was at her peak, her powers of perception honed and her wits acute after the long fight against penury. In the daily inspection of Yellaton her eyes missed nothing, from a few tares in the corn to an additional ounce of flesh on one of her pigs. She could sense coming sickness in a beast through her fingertips and knew the sound of her own flock half a mile off. The inability to read or write had developed her memory, which could store and compare prices and weights and detail to a phenomenal degree. Mature and emotionally undiverted from her goals, a formidable woman had emerged from the years of want.

Determined to exploit her good fortune, she became obsessed with the idea of creating a financial foundation solid enough to withstand all climatic and market fluctuations. Her previous farming tactics changed from a simple self-sufficiency to a constant striving for sizable surpluses which could be sold and the profits reinvested to increase the family security.

Instead of waiting two years for the lambs to become adult, she sold them at six months and replaced them immediately with ewes, which were put to the ram earlier in the year than was usual and consequently lambed before spring, so that their progeny fetched the highest prices. The pigs were fattened fast and sold, the place of each taken by four or five weaners. More poultry was brought in and more crops sown than she and the children would ever require. Where other farmers were sparing with feed, Rachel, aiming for a quick turnover, fed her stock generously and was justified by their fast and healthy development.

At the weekly markets she soon gained a reputation for hard bargaining. Her knowledge of conformation and her ability to spot the best animals and reject the faulty was acknowledged with respect, and before long, farm beasts raised on Yellaton were keenly sought.

Since Rachel Jedder's birth in 1750 the population of England had increased by a third, and this, together with several recent poor harvests and bad seasons for livestock in the rest of the country, now caused the demand for food to exceed supply and farm prices to rise steeply. Her gamble in putting all her funds back into building a surplus paid off. The original windfall brought in by the deserted infant doubled, and then trebled, and Yellaton's thirty acres began to feel tight, almost as though the family was outgrowing them.

Thinking on how to expand by next Lady Day, with only enough money either to rent some extra land or buy still more stock, but not both, Rachel returned to the house, her mind examining the alternatives. A September afternoon, and the ancient gray dog was stretched out in the sunniest corner of the courtyard. She bent to stroke his soft ears, as she had always done when abstracted.

"What shall we do, then, Sam?" she asked. "If I take on the twenty acre up by Arnwood, there won't be enough bullocks to use it and, if I leave that land and get more steers to put on Brindley and Moses Bottom, they'll graze the place bare and all go down wi' scours or summat."

His ears were velvet to the touch. Sometimes he would still accompany her in a sedate trot as far as the barn, but nowadays he liked best of all to sleep in the sun, and all the additional food she had given him since their circumstances had improved had not made him less skeletal. He looked like the familiar of mythical wizards and kings who had galloped with them to defend highborn virgins and into the legendary battles of old. He looked like a wonderful, prehistoric creature found, perfectly preserved, in the peat graveyard of some primeval forest. But to Rachel he just looked contented, lying in the last of the summer heat, and she patted him fondly.

"You be a good old dog and no mistake."

He did not stir. A little fear squeezed her, and when she lifted his head, it lay limply in her hands.

"Oh, Sam! Dear old Sam," she whispered. "You bin the best friend I ever had."

She remembered their first bitter night in Thetford Forest when he had saved her from dying of cold, and the hundreds and hundreds of miles he had run by her side, across England and over and over Jedder's land and the moors, and the silly games he had played, and all the secrets and hopes she had shared with him, and the countless times he had sensed her disappointment and distress and come to lay his head gently on her lap.

Knowing that age had made his death inevitable made it no easier to accept, and Rachel held his great body to her and sobbed.

They buried him at the edge of the orchard, and it was as though she were sealing off the first half of her life. The gray dog had been the last link with that eager young girl, so open to ventures and romance, who had naively believed that the whole future had been freed from calamity by the gift of Jedder's land. Rachel the woman pictured her again, and it was like seeing a complete stranger, who had no connection with Rachel, herself, at all.

She took a handful of the moist, dark loam and cupped it in her palms for a moment, savoring its fertility and texture before scattering it over the body of the dog. Another apple tree would be planted here and he would be cradled in its roots and, with the uberous, life-giving earth of Yellaton, would bring it to bud and leaf and flower and burning red fruit each year.

And in that moment she understood that there had been a moving beauty about the gray dog's life, in the simplicity and rightness of its completed course. That raw callowness had led to a lusty and exuberant prime, which not even hunger had been permitted to curb, and then, with a certain mischievous dignity, he had become old and comfortable, and finally he had died, at the proper time and in the proper way, in the sun: a vindication of nature's true intentions.

Of all the living things, both human and animal, in her experience, there was not one she would ever be able to recall with such uncomplicated pleasure. Generous and funny and naturally responsive, he had given only enjoyment. And at last, Rachel Jedder recognized that she and the girl of long ago were still the same person, molded in thought and deed and ambition by a unique plot of land on Beara Moor and all it held. She said goodbye and knew she had not changed much after all.

The choice, too, was made. If she could not buy extra land and own it, she would not rent. More steers were bought in, and although they exceeded the number permitted to graze there, were surreptitiously released onto the moor to ease the overcrowding in the pastures.

Soon after setting up the holding again with the infant's money, Rachel sent all her children twice a week to old Crispin Bowden, a retired pedagogue who still taught reading and writing and figures for the love of it and for the small fee of one shilling a quarter. She was deeply impressed by the incomprehensible hieroglyphics scratched on slate which they brought home. None of hers would ever be given a parchment they could not read, she promised herself.

But Jedder grew bored with the inactivity of the class and shortly refused to continue, and Emma sulked and whined because no other village girl attended, and Richard and Joel behaved so badly, fighting among themselves and bullying smaller children, that, after beatings had proved ineffective, Rachel was asked to remove them. Only John stayed and studied until he could write with a neat hand and cunningly count in his head.

The origins of Jane, the waif, remained mysterious. Although her adoptive mother asked discreetly around the area, no one knew her parentage, and at the time she was abandoned, no maid or matron had given signs of an unaccounted condition to the gimlet-eyed dames of the villages; besides, who, with so much gold, could have been forced to part with a child? A strange business, but as the busy years passed and she grew into a pleasant and bonny little girl, it was forgotten.

Rachel Jedder was not particularly intense about her children. They had come into her world and she had looked after and protected them as she would a litter of kittens. They amused and irritated her and she felt genuine affection for them, but the imperative maternalism, powerful above all other drives, had not seriously invaded her emotions. Even when snatching starving John from the Wolcot farm, her rage had been that of finding a helpless young animal the victim of a merciless cruelty. She enjoyed cuddling the babies and playing games when they were very small, and later, their developing intelligence and wit had often provided her with pleasurable companionship. But she had always thought of them as completely separate beings, and never as extensions of herself.

Only Jedder had truly managed to reach her heart and that because he was a reflection of Will Tresider. Perhaps her own deprived background had left her incapable of a mother's traditional feeling for her own. Certainly she had always felt closer to her dumb animals than to her offspring.

Watching the foals grow from brittle-legged, fluffy-tailed shyness to gangling, boisterous yearlings and then into long-maned, satin-skinned, sensible horses was the most satisfying progression she could imagine, and each year she was stirred by holding the first lamb and feeling its tightly wooled body and fast-beating heart in her arms. The spotted piglets with their inquisitive snouts and tails like love knots made her laugh as they scampered round the sties, and she still could not resist the girlish impulse to catch one and hear it squeal. In truth, human babies, with their uncoordinated movements and grimaces, had never seemed half so appealing.

So it was natural that the red calf was especially captivating. Even at a few weeks old, he was broad-chested and stocky, with all the signs of that impudent self-confidence which makes a good bull. He had developed rapidly, making height and bone, legs strengthening to carry the final body weight of one thousand pounds foursquare, then putting on muscle and power in interwoven layers, which rippled and bulged under a sleek summer coat.

With a gang of young steers, he had jostled and galloped on the moor, challenging every unusual object, indulging in mock battles and emerging as boss. And, finally, he was fully grown, pink-lined nostrils flaring to catch female currents and the smell of rivals on the wind, dark-tipped horns like polished wood, thick-stemmed whip of a tail, scrotum swinging like a ripe overgrown fruit between his hind legs. He was like a massive red stone sculpture, larger than life. The steers backed off in a bunch. The heifers, nervous and excited, rolled their big stupid eyes, and Rachel was rapturous.

She named him Sovereign, because it meant both king and gold. From his birth she had spoiled him, brushing his baby fur and petting him with the excuse that he should become accustomed to handling, and later teaching him to drink from a bucket by giving him her fingers to suck and lowering his head to the liquid. At first, he had snorted and sputtered and butted the bucket and skittered away as the milk deluged them both, but soon he came running at the sight of her, and it was easy to train him to answer her call, just as the horses did.

As he grew, she ran her hands admiringly over his wide back and long, level hindquarters and thick-fleshed thighs and marveled at his big-boned shanks and the symmetry and controlled resilience of his shoulders. She would talk to him as she had once done to the gray dog, and he would cock his ears and watch her through full, mild eyes, and long after he should have turned ferocious and been chained up in a dirty, dark shed, he was still nuzzling at the pocket in her apron where the handful of corn was hidden.

"You watch 'ee don't turn one day, Mother," Jedder warned, keeping his distance from the beast.

"Not he, son. Don't I say as animals give back what they be given, and that crittur's always been treated good," she answered with certainty. "There ain't no reason for he to turn vicious, when no one's never been vicious to he. Ain't that right, John?"

Her other son nodded and smiled and scratched the bull's broad muzzle familiarly. "He's done you proud and no mistake, Mother. There's not another to touch him 'twixt here and Somerset. Why, they was talkin' of him again in Barnstaple Market only last week."

Rachel had created a local sensation by taking Sovereign to the Easter fair in the first spring of his maturity, not to sell (although there were plenty of bidders), but just to show him off. And from then on, his fame had spread until now she had to take bookings and limit the number of cows sent to him for mating.

"Dan Cobbledick offered me ten pound just to let him run with his herd for three month, but I turned him down," she told them complacently. "So he's bringing his best cows all the way from Chulmleigh."

Born as their luck changed, Sovereign was far more to Rachel than a magnificent bull. All his dynamic and panache had grown out of Yellaton's racy marl. The spread of his seed stamped the mark of Jedder's land on the miles around and his impeccable progeny promised an endless and

195

fecund line. In the stunning combination of his virility and beauty she recognized the embodiment of her own aims and aspirations and saw him almost as her own blood. He was a personal triumph.

Her oldest sons had strength enough now to take on all the heavy work and there was no need to hire extra hands for haysel and harvest.

John, steady and wise beyond his age, was in constant demand with his collection of ferocious-looking surgical implements and sulphuric potions and salves with which he charmed and cured the sick animals of the district.

The ash of a shrew was rubbed into swollen joints. As sheep were not dipped, those with scab were dressed with an ointment of goose grease and fish oil. A nail dug out of a horse or cow hoof was kept stuck into some bacon until the wound healed, to prevent the foot from rotting. He had mouth cramps and gags for restraining and dosing the largest stock, and fleams for bleeding horses or cattle with staggers, inflamed feet, eyes or brain. He would drench a pig by pushing a toeless old boot into its mouth and pouring the mixture into the open top, so that the animal swallowed almost without realizing as it chewed. His reputation had long outstripped that of the bungler Amos Cottle.

Jedder, handsome and high-spirited, was already causing shy maids to moon and catching the coquettish glances of the others from South Molton to Bideford. Always unsettled, he did the work required of him without shirking, but then made off nightly on a chestnut horse, as though unleashed like a hawk from its jesses to a special freedom upon which he depended for life.

Often he did not return until morning, and reports of fights and wenching and drinking began to reach the family through outraged fathers and indignant mothers whose sons and daughters had been trounced or seduced, according to their sex. Rachel dutifully admonished him, but without conviction.

Each day he grew more like his own father, and she was unable to look on him without a piquant shiver. Already he had a man's breadth of back and carriage, and the years of physical labor had molded his arms and shoulders. The line of his spine curved classically to small, distracting buttocks above the kind of long, smooth, athletic legs to which no male had a right. From behind, he could easily have been the Will Tresider of long ago. But when he turned around, his face was surprising in its youth: the brown eyes eager and unseasoned by the watchfulness of experience, bright and vital under straight, black brows, the line of his cheek and jaw not yet hardened by resolution or disappointment; and the engraved shape of his mouth, so commanding and desirable to the little country girls, still held touching vulnerability to an older glance.

He gave her the box early one morning, waking her from a deep sleep and staring boldly as she opened it. On the velvet lining lay a rope of pearls, warm to the touch and lambent from resting around a wealthy woman's lanolin-soft neck, beads of the dawn, their magnolia luster alive with flesh tones. Rachel was appalled.

"My God, boy! What's this?"

"They'm for you." He grinned, half cocky and half unsure.

"Where'd they come from? Where'd you get them?" She had dropped the box, alarmed.

Her son looked askance, clearly feeling that she should know better than to ask such a question.

"Bought 'em off a market stall," he lied, slightly sulky. "They'm for you."

She shook her head in agitation. Even to her untrained inspection, the pearls were real. Their serene radiance could not have been faked. "These never come from no stall, Jedder. There's a fortune here. They be real as the crown jewels. Now, how did you come by them?"

He tightened his lips and turned away with a stubborn expression so familiar that it took her off guard.

"Son," she said, more gently, "how could I wear such things? Half the constables and runners in the land will be a-searching for them."

He wheeled back, smiling again. "I thought of that and 'tis no trouble. They're to be made up to a choker and bracelet and maybe earrings for you, and 'twill be impossible to tell how they were afore. 'Tis all arranged Mother. You're not to vex yourself."

It was her lover's expression, irrepressible and playful, and, as it had so often before, the electric charge of his appeal jolted her. There was no mistaking it. He looked good enough to eat. She smiled without guilt, accepting the innocence of seeing her son through the eyes of a sensual woman. How extraordinary it was that she herself had formed and fashioned such a masculine being out of her own tissue and produced him from her own body. He was a very fine bull calf indeed.

"But where could I wear such things? There's no occasion."

She tried to continue the argument, but he pounced on the lack of certainty in her voice.

"There will be occasion, Mother," he declared emphatically. "And more than one. Many more. I know it. You'll be in fine gowns again and decked out in so many baubles and trinkets that these will seem like milkmaid's wear one day."

"Would you hang for such fancies?" she asked, instantly fierce with fear. "For 'twill come to that, if you follow this path." She shook the necklace at him and it rattled stealthily in her fist like a dangerous white snake.

He sat down on the edge of the bed and took both her hands in his so that the pearls twined round their fingers and bound them together.

"Harken to me! I'm no farmer, nor never will be, but even if I was, what's to happen when the girls and the twins are fully grown? This place is not big enough to keep four men and three women. Some of us would have to hire out as laborers, wi' no place to call our own, and the girls be sent into service. Well, 'tisn't good enough, Mother, and I got a better plan."

He stood up abruptly and left the room; but Rachel Jedder knew he was right.

The black crepe kerchief and the pistol were concealed in a hollow, under a saddle tree, in the cob wall of the stable. She found them only a few days later and understood instantly where the pearls had come from. Her son Jedder was riding the highways and had become a robber.

"I shall not sleep till you return," she told him as he left that night. Nor did she, but with aching ears heard the twig-snapping shuffle of his mount from afar and crept to wait in the shadow of the stable door for his safe arrival.

The smell of hay was as thick as syrup and her own heart hammer-loud as the faceless horseman crossed her eyeline like a phantom. In a replay of the unforgotten nights of the past, he came with secret plunder, glinting metal discs, which clinked into her palms like weighted gold rain.

Excitement formed a lump in her throat, so that she was unable to speak, and in the dimness all he could see were her fairy eyes, fathomless, moorland pools aglow with the trapped reflections of the moon and ringed by bright-green moss.

"How my father must have loved you," he breathed, almost jealously.

"Oh, he did." She was lost in a circle of memories. "He surely did."

After that, it was as though the past had caught up with her again: the days bursting with Yellaton's abundance, which stuffed full the stores and attics, the barn and the pastures, and overflowed onto Beara; cornucopian nights of melodrama and tension and terror and treasure, and the Cornish tin box filling until she was able to buy those cheap, steep-sloping, thirty-five acres by Arnwood, just as she and Robert Wolcot had once bought Moses Bottom, to add to Jedder's land.

The whole family went to claim and to plan the management of the sunny but broom-and-tussock-punctuated drop, onto which they drove the sheep that very same day.

Caution thrown aside, she herself would have ridden masked with Jedder had she not been haunted by the terrible consequences of the night she had insisted on accompanying Will to Mouth Mill.

Instead, she was exhilarated to return alone to the new field and look west to the homestead, her lungs almost exploding with the achievement of it. She was fully alive once more, opened up after the long withdrawal and despair, senses and feelings stretched to their limits, inspiration, hope, faith reborn and, above all, love—for Jedder, her son, for the great red bull and for Yellaton. Scanning the vale, she knew this was only the beginning.

In the shelter of her shrewd care, the family had progressed un-hindered: John and Jedder to adulthood and Emma to a comely, if rather plaintive, maid, who had already caught the eye of David Morrish, sec-ond son of Luke Morrish, who owned a farm twice the size of Yellaton, just the other side of Lutterell's. There was always trouble from Dick and Joel Blackaller, who stole folks' eggs and poultry and pulled girls' hair and lied as a pastime and had once stoned a cat to death; but they kept to themselves at home and were young enough to improve. Jane, the waif, was eight years old.

It was during this child's birthday month that John brought home a letter, which had been left for his mother in High Chilham.

She turned it over and over in her hands, squinting impotently at the writing and turning it over again.

"Where does it say my name?" she demanded, angry with suspicion. "Show me!"

"There, Mother." He ran his finger under the three words. "Mistress Rachel Blackaller."

"I don't hold with being called Blackaller. Jedder is my name. I'll not open it." She seized on the excuse.

"Blackaller be your name in law, Mother," John pointed out. "And you got to open it."

"What does it say there?" She stabbed a finger at the paper.

"Beara, High Chilham."

"And there?"

"Yellaton Farm."

"Yellaton *Farm*, eh?" Pleased, she looked at the words. " 'Tis right enough. This be a proper farm now."

"Mother, will you open the bugger, afore us all goes gray." Jedder, sprawled in a kitchen chair, could stand the suspense no longer.

Her hands shook as she broke the seal and unfolded the paper and looked at the scribbled rows before helplessly handing it over to John.

"Why, 'tis from a firm of attorneys in Cross Street, Barnstaple, request-ing that you attend their offices at your . . . earliest . . . con–ve–nience. . . ."

"I will not! I'll not go nowhere near them." Rachel, instantly imagining unthinkable disasters, was panic-stricken. Perhaps, after all these years, they had discovered an error and Yellaton did not belong to her, after all.

John, immersed in the letter, ignored her. "And you are to take Jane with 'ee," he said, puzzled.

"Jane? Jane? What would they be wanting with Jane Clarke?" Rachel questioned, by now irascible.

"Not Jane Clarke, Mother. Our Jane."

"Our Jane!" She was amazed. "Lill' Jane here?"

The family stared at each other, dumfounded for a moment, and then

199

all spoke at once, after much speculation and argument coming to the conclusion that Jane's mother had been found and wanted her returned.

"I don't want no Ma. You'm my Ma." Jane burst into tears and clung to Rachel.

Next day she was lifted into the saddle behind the woman who had brought her up since birth, and both rode the thirteen miles to Barnstaple in bewilderment and apprehension.

"And this is the child, Jane Jedder, whom you found on your doorstep eight years ago?" The lawyer was a bored, middle-aged man, given to corpulence and an unfortunate habit of periodically waving a kerchief in front of his face as though his clients had an unpleasant smell.

"We be very attached to the lill' thing, sir," Rachel said humbly. "Us doesn't want to part with she."

"Of course not." His quill squeaked. "Now, if you will sign your name here, the matter will be settled." He stood up and tapped on a parchment, and Rachel backed away.

"What matter? I ain't putting no mark. I don't never give my mark."

"But you must, Mistress Blackaller, before I can release the legacy."

She clutched Jane and glared at him over the top of the child's head without understanding.

"You do know why you are here, do you not?" he asked.

She shook her head.

"Why, Mistress Blackaller, for the caring of this child, you have been left the sum of five hundred pounds."

Rachel Jedder fainted.

Word of innovations from the outside world took a long time to penetrate the inaccessible region between the two rivers, Taw and Torridge, and was inevitably received with suspicion and downright disbelief. Newfangled notions did not appeal to the men of Devon and they did not believe in change for the sake of it. The county which had produced such heroes as Drake, John Hawkins and Walter Raleigh had no need of advice from the foreigners of East Anglia or Leicestershire.

When Rachel Jedder first arrived, there had been no wheeled farm vehicles in the district. Wood, dung, lime, hay and corn were all carried on sledges drawn by oxen or by packhorses, and most farmers still kept to these methods.

The advent of Jethro Tull's seed drill, the breeding experiments of Bakewell, and Coke's rotation of crops had made little or no impact, although they had been commonplace on Wame's farm in Norfolk. And the turnip, as winter feed for cattle, had only been recognized within the past few years. Before this the number of local cattle had been annually culled to a minimum of breeding and young stock, which were then wintered on poor quality hay and straw, and only the fittest had survived.

Originally it had been regarded as a silly female nonsense of Rachel Jedder's to give over so much of her limited holding to the growing of turnips. However, within a few seasons, the news that the roots could be sold off the field at thirty shillings an acre proved very persuasive. Then Squire Waddon had set the example by seeding one-third of his prime land with the crop and doing so well that he increased the area to half of his entire cultivated acreage over the next years.

There was a wet spring, followed by a short, sharp frost in May and then long weeks of warm, humid weather, in which the turnip fly laid its eggs in millions, and the eggs hatched into larvae, which systematically ate what was left of the frost-damaged crop. In Devon, one hundred thousand pounds' worth of turnips were destroyed.

Rachel looked over the ravaged stalks in the hare's leg and blessed her own foresight in insisting on holding surplus stores. The bullocks would have to be rationed, but none need be wastefully slaughtered.

Squire Waddon saw his blighted fields and groaned. His manner of living had not changed since his father's death, the expenditure always exceeding his income. He had married a peer's docile daughter, who had brought an ample dowry, but his fondness for games of chance and hunting and thoroughbred horses, vintage port, brandy and prodigal company had soon eroded that fortune, and he had been reduced this year to depending upon the three hundred pounds from the turnip crop. Its loss brought him to financial embarrassment, which not even the money left by his sister six months before could avert.

A sensible man would have restrained his habits and waited until the invaluable asset of his own productive lands reversed his ill fortune, but the Squire was known for his genial and lavish personality, not for his good sense. So he gave a hunt ball and, upon recovering from the barrel fever incurred by that, formally invited Rachel Jedder to take tea with himself and his wife, Lady Ann, at the manor.

She spent a week cutting and stitching and unpicking her gown, until Jane Clarke, who was a dressmaker by trade, took pity and completed the task. The length of ivory satin had come all the way from Exeter, bought and paid for, Jedder assured his mother, and with it a matching cap decorated with ribbons and feathers, and the very latest low-heeled satin shoes. Jane's completed design had a frill collar and half-length sleeves with three layers of lace flounces, and lace ruffles which frothed over the bodice, rippled across the exposed underskirt and tumbled in exuberant cataracts down the panels of the dress from waist to floor. It appeared to have been made of spun glass, delicate enough to pulverize at a touch, wispy as web, and Rachel, standing with her arms in the air as it was dropped over her head for the final fitting, wondered how she would dare sit down for fear a piece of the confection might break off.

Jane snipped away a tacking thread, twitched at the skirt and stood back.

"Needs summat else," she said with critical speculation. "The shoes is right and the cap."

Rachel picked up her painted wooden fan.

201

"Oh, no! You cannot take that!" Her friend was disapproving. " 'Tisn't near fine enough."

"This fan has always brought me luck. It come from France and 'tis staying in my hand."

Jane sniffed and shook her head. Rachel could be very set in her ways sometimes, and there was still something missing from the outfit.

"Gloves," she realized at once. "You're lacking gloves."

"But I ain't got none." Rachel looked momentarily dismayed, then caught the other's eye and, both struck with the same thought, they burst out laughing that, despite making so many thousands of gloves, she should never have owned or even worn a pair herself.

John was sent galloping to Torrington for silk, and that night his mother took out the brass vise to make one very last pair of gloves—for herself—and the next day, when she was ready to leave and had pulled them over her rough hands, none could have told she had not been born a gentlewoman.

Jedder clasped the choker of pearls around her neck and the bracelet over her left arm.

"Did not I tell you there would come a time," he whispered, and pressed his forefinger against her lips before she could speak.

In the impressive paneled entrance hall to Braddon Manor, a footman took her cloak and showed her into the drawing room, where she stood rigidly in the doorway for a moment. Squire Waddon saw a poppet-sized figure who looked like a young girl, pale-skinned and gauche. Her black hair was drawn back from her face in shining coils and the light streaming between the dark-green drapes round the tall windows emphasized the vert bands in her particolored irises. Without more ado, his experienced glance lecherously stripped away the mass of lace and revealed her to himself, naked, as she had been long ago by the lake.

"You have not changed at all, Rachel Jedder." He did not bother to lower his voice while bending over her hand, and she had the grace to blush.

Lady Ann was, in fact, younger than she by ten years and gently disposed. She asked kindly after her guest's family, mentioning each of the children, including Jane, by name, and watched with open admiration as her big husband stuffed large slices of fruit cake into his mouth and noisily washed them down with gulp after gulp of tea.

"Can't be doing with this stuff," he announced eventually, waving the little porcelain bowl in the air and belching with energy. "Beggars me why we cannot have stout quenching tankards of cider instead."

"I would have rung for some, Charles, if you had so wished," she replied peaceably.

" 'Course you would, my dear." He patted her on the head vigorously, as though she were a favorite hound, and gave a benevolent guffaw, then turned to Rachel.

"Now, Mistress Jedder. There are far too many of your cattle on the moor again, and folk are complaining, so what are you going to do about it?"

Completely taken by surprise, Rachel muttered about forthcoming markets and reducing stock.

"Aye, but this is become a regular problem," he pointed out, "and within a few months will be brought to my attention again, when your stock is built up once more. Will it not?"

She could not deny it, but spoke of her crop-rotation program and the reductions it had made on the pasture at Yellaton.

"I recall the time when you thought twelve acres and a bit of woodland were a royal estate, Rachel Jedder," he teased. "And how much land have you know?"

"Sixty-five acre, Squire." She looked abashed, then mustered her defenses. "But the young steers are such fit beasts, 'twould be a shame to have to sell them as stores and not fatted. 'Tis a proper quandary."

Lady Ann stood up and tactfully excused herself, leaving the room in a rustle of taffeta.

"Well, I have the answer to your poser," he assured her. "You come into some money a few months ago, did you not?"

Rachel stiffened, glared at him and asked suspiciously, "How d'you know that, Squire Waddon?"

"Several hundred pound, I believe," he said with a grin. "For adopting and raising young Jane."

"That is between me and the lawyer in Barnstaple, Squire." She spoke with asperity. "And 'tisn't right that you should have learned anything of it."

"My sister died six months ago, Rachel," he said quietly.

She gaped at him, not daring, for a second, to grasp what he was telling her and then she stuttered, "Your s-s-sister . . ." And met his steady gaze. ". . . lill' Jane . . ."

"We will speak no more of it, neither now nor in the future," he pronounced firmly. "And, to return to the matter of your cattle. I believe I have the solution. What think you of the mead which lies below Arnwood?"

"I don't want no tenancy, Squire," she stressed at once. " 'Tain't my way to rent land."

"And I would not have you as a tenant, ma'am, for fear of disturbing my peace of mind," he replied, his eyes merry. "However, as those meadows run so close to Arnwood, on the other side of which your own farm begins, I am proposing that you buy them."

"You be selling? Part of Braddon?" She stared, disbelieving.

"Only to you," he smiled. "Twenty-five acres of the best meadow for three hundred fifty pounds. 'Tis a bargain you will not meet with again."

"Maybe, Squire, but that land is still divided from Yellaton by a five-acre stretch and your wood."

203

Her quick mind had been cutting to the core of the idea while he spoke. It had always seemed that the squire, in his park-surrounded mansion, must be so rich that even his fine style could not shake his position. Down the years, from the time he had ridden so handsomely into her life, he had seemed the epitome of glamour. Yet, here he was selling part of the estate, selling land, first-class land. It was incredible, but Rachel Jedder did not intend to be overwhelmed by the notion.

"You shall have right of way over both," he promised.

"No, sir. Rights of way can be closed," she declared.

"You would not doubt my honor, Rachel?" He looked taken aback and slightly hurt.

" 'Course not, Squire. I won't never forget all you done for me and I know as you'd not see me wrong." She placed her hand fondly over his. " 'Tis just that, when we're gone, others will be in our places and I have to look to the future for the sake o' my chillern. Them that comes after may not be as good as you."

He took his timepiece from his fob pocket. It was half past five already and Sir Roger Barlington and Fortescue and the Grenvilles would be arriving at seven for dinner and an evening of cards.

"Damme, but you hide a stony heart in that dainty breast, Mistress Jedder." He grinned at her easily. "And it seems there is to be no appeal, so what say you to Arnwood and the five acre as part of the same lot?"

Rachel's stony heart jumped, but her expression remained impassive.

"Same price?" she asked. "Three hundred fifty pound?"

"You win," he agreed ruefully. "Same price."

She let out a squeal and flung her arms around him, kissing him full on the mouth, without inhibition.

"Your kisses are grown mighty expensive," he grumbled, in mock protest. "There was a time . . ."

She kissed him again. "I am real grateful to you, Charles Waddon," she whispered. "And I'll look to young Jane's rights, see her provided for proper and well married."

He held her close, crushing the cream lace and smelling her flowery hair. "I know it, my little friend."

It was still as radiant as noon when she left, the end of one of those lazily sensual summer afternoons when lovers lie in the long grass, too idle to do more than murmur of love, and the animals gather under the trees, nose to tail for communal protection from the flies; when the air is blurred with the sighs of the heated soil, and rivers and streams evaporate into steamy reflections of themselves across the sky.

She rode through the park, the way marked by great oaks planted by the squire's forefathers after Queen Elizabeth I had bestowed the land on them for valiant deeds, and for even more valiant diplomacy in surviving the reigns of her father and half-sister, and still finding her favor; over Arn brook, which fed the lake, and left through a vaporous copse, showy with purple loosestrife and flicked by the wings of August-silent birds and then, unexpectedly, out into the sloping-sided valley, on the brow of which Arnwood was angled like a cheeky green beret.

The small fields were divided from each other by flourishing hedges and filled with broad-leaved, vigorous vegetation. Rachel Jedder scanned the stretch through eyes too hypnotized to blink. This was no moorland open to the Atlantic blasts, ill-drained and sour. This was real farmland and cherished as such for hundreds of years, limed and dressed with manure until the loam was as rich as plum pudding, deep and black and easily worked to grow record corn harvests, the best and most nutritious turf, or the heaviest vegetable crops. She did not need to take it in her hands to know this earth. She could smell it, nitrogenous, meaty and vintage.

She tied the horse to a gatepost and climbed over in her satin shoes and fragile dress and breathed pure happiness. A piece of the Braddon estate had become Jedder's land, because she, the workhouse pauper, had bought it. She wondered whether her grandfather had ever coveted these meadows and what he would have thought. Perhaps in the beginning they had belonged to her own ancestors and now were justly returned. She knew instinctively that the Jedders had been on Beara and around High Chilham for far longer than the Waddon gentry. Her family had *always* been there.

A cloud of winged ants on their marriage flight danced in the air. Ladybirds and lacewings, bumblebees and butterflies glided in slow motion from seed to fruit, laying their eggs, drowsily, and the heat combed the short grass with light strokes, melting the blades into liquid and smoothing the leaves on the hedges into laminae as reflecting as mirrors. The young cuckoos were preparing to follow, with miraculous accuracy, the trail of their unknown parents gone on a month before, and a flock of swifts returned on the south breeze, after the first false start of their migration, and dipped to skim down the valley, like fish.

There was no one Rachel would have shared this moment with, not her son Jedder, not even Will Tresider. She began her walk around each field and up through the woods and, for an hour, took triumphant possession of the Waddon land, alone.

"Mercy on us, Mother! Are you hurt? Did you fall?" John rushed from the house, and for the first time she became aware of her appearance, muddied and scratched, with her hair full of twigs, and the pretty cap with its feathers and ribbons torn off and lost.

"What happened? Let me help." Her second son lifted her from the saddle and set her down, his face full of concern. The rest of the family crowded round, all asking anxious questions at once.

"I been down Arn valley, beyond the wood," she disclosed, taunting their curiosity, though unable to keep the excitement out of her voice.

"But your beautiful new gown is ruined," he said, baffled.

She looked down at the torn lace over the smeared satin and waved an impatient hand. "No matter. No matter."

The children gawked and she could contain the secret no longer. "I bought land! Land off the squire. Thirty acre. All Arnwood. Braddon land—for us!"

Dave Bartle was the first man Rachel Jedder employed to work full time on Yellaton. No one else would take him on, although he was the horsebreaker's cousin, because he had been born with a twisted spine and had fits. However, with Jedder spending more nights away from home and John called upon so often to treat sick beasts on other farms and the twins being basically unreliable and troublesome, another pair of hands was needed to do the regular maintenance jobs and move the herd and flock when necessary; and he had worked steadily enough alongside the family through harvest.

No one knew how old he was, except that calling out names and poking fun at him had been part of everyone's childhood. He had been adult when Jack Thorne was a boy, and, at fifty, Jack was now one of the older men in the village.

Rachel's sons partitioned off part of the loft above the stables to make a room, and he moved in, twitching his lopsided grin and jerking his head with pleasure. From that day, he brought his mistress posies and wild fruit and stone bottles of his own golden sparkling elderflower wine and pheasant chicks and plovers' eggs as daily offerings of gratitude and worship.

Rachel, carried away by such devotion, and by her own elevation to employer and purchaser of Braddon land, became plumped up with self-satisfaction and not a little arrogant, adopting mannerisms which thoroughly irritated the other women of the parish, such as wearing gloves to market, which meant having to point out her requirements instead of picking them up herself. She also carried a reticule to church (" 'ridicules' some called 'em, right enough") and made great play of extracting her coin from it for the Sunday collection. She wore fine clothes again and flirted outrageously with their husbands, some of whom were foolish enough to think she meant it.

The wives clicked their tongues and pursed their lips and reminded each other that "old man Jedder had been so mean that when he lit a fire you had to strike a flint to see it, and her, for all her airs and graces, had come from nothing."

Rachel knew that as well as they and, in fact, was reminded of it every time she rode over her farm, finishing up so pleased with herself and her remarkable accomplishment that she was quite unable to resist showing off. At last she had reached the ideal, unassailable plateau: the children long grown past the dangerous ages of infancy, the farm solid and shielding and large enough to support them all until they wed, and then to take in her oldest sons' wives and their children, too. They were beyond subsistence forever, well able to produce more than enough to cushion the worst of hard times: insured by what she had made of Yellaton, and invulnerable.

Sitting on the hillside below Arnwood, she looked down on Sovereign and his herd of Devon rubies below. He had been grazing alongside a young heifer, his head next to her head, and now dropped back a little to crop by her forelegs. He took no notice when she suddenly turned and reared onto another cow nearby, but as she lowered her head to the grass once more, he returned alongside, running his nose along her back. Then he was behind and mounting her. Startled, she moved forward quickly under his weight and then stopped, and he released her. The next time he went up, she stood quite still.

"Slyboots," Rachel called out, chuckling, and walked down to talk to him.

Before she reached him, he lay down, blowing noisily.

"You overdoing it, old redcoat?" she asked, rubbing his poll and wiping away a dribble from one of his nostrils with a handful of grass.

He looked at her blearily and grunted.

"Perhaps you do need a few days' rest," she agreed. "I'll have them fetch you up home tomorrow."

Dave Bartle was sent for him the following morning and took a long time returning.

"What kept you, man?" she demanded as he came sweating into the kitchen.

"Ee'd best come see the bull, mistress," he replied, his head convulsive with agitation.

Sovereign was standing, swaying and slobbering, in his shed, a stinking discharge running from his nose, and his eyes red with fever.

"God's mercy! Run for John, quick!" she shouted when she saw him, and felt the spasm of foreboding shake her body; and then she prayed incoherently, a rising hysteria garbling the words in which she had no faith.

"Our Father, Which art in Heaven,
Hallowed be Thy Name,
Thy Kingdom come. Thy will be . . ."

She hugged him to her, hands clasped around his neck. His healthy, gleaming hide was already dulled, the emphatic, carved muscles weakened to flab and his flanks sunken. He passed a stream of foul diarrhea.

"I believe in God the Father . . ."

Sovereign groaned.

". . . Oh, God! You done this to him!" Rachel Jedder cried up to the raftered roof, exchanging invocation for frantic accusation. "Like you done everything else!"

207

John's figure darkened the doorway, and without a word he approached the big animal, opening its mouth, pulling back its eyelids and feeling its ears.

"What is it?" Rachel hardly dared to ask.

He put a bucket on the floor and opened his leather bag to extract a fleam and the bloodstick, which was a small club turned from boxwood and loaded with lead. Then, tying a cord around the bull's right foreleg, he raised a vein, placed the razor-sharp triangular blade against it and hit that smartly with the bloodstick. Blood gushed into the bucket. Sovereign did not move. He did not even seem to notice, and, when the bucket was half full, John drew the wound together with a needle and a horse's hair sewn in a figure of eight.

"What's wrong with him?" Rachel questioned again.

"I think 'tis what they call rinderpest, though I ain't never seen a case afore."

"What be that then?" she wanted to know.

He gathered his instruments without looking up.

"Cattle plague," he said tersely.

Her fists clenched and she felt herself go cold.

"Then there's no hope?" she pleaded in a whisper.

"We'll do what we can. In the meantime, best check the herd."

Two of the cows looked tucked up and listless and were bled, too, and all that day he tried out every remedy he had ever heard of and many ideas of his own invention to save them and protect the rest.

By nightfall the bull was down, his legs unnaturally straight and his breathing labored. Rachel washed out his inflamed nose and mouth and covered him with sacking and talked to him, comforting, scolding and cajoling through the long hours. Sometimes he managed a sick, sorry look, but mostly his eyes were unseeing, and she knew he wanted it to end.

By the next day the two cows had died and the rest were obviously infected.

"Six of they be Dan Cobbledick's best heifers. What the devil will he say to this?"

She sent Jedder galloping to the Chulmleigh farmer and the village with the news.

"And stop by the rectory," John called out. "For holy water."

"Holy water!" His mother glared at him.

"'Tis the last chance," he said earnestly, reading her skeptical thoughts. "I can't do no more and folks say as the holy water sometimes cures."

When they returned to the shed, the great bull was dead.

CHAPTER THIRTEEN

Jedder's warning race was unnecessary. All over the district, cows which had had contact with Sovereign were already showing symptoms of this most virulent of infections.

At least ten years had passed since the last outbreak, but all remembered the devastation it had caused then and for many years previously. Now, once more, the farmers had to stand by and watch their stock slaughtered in accordance with the law passed in 1746 to contain the disease. Many saw their entire herds destroyed and received only minimal compensation, not nearly enough to replace their losses.

With bitterness, they looked over the moor to Yellaton and cursed Rachel Jedder; and the bitterness became hatred, aggravated by the sight of empty pens on market day and word of each other's plight, and by the news that some of her own yearlings, grazed downwind on the far side of Beara, had escaped and were perfectly healthy.

The people in their wrath remembered her penniless arrival at the scrubby smallholding and the way Matthew Claggett had been evicted and the death of Walter Riddaway and how she had buried two husbands, and they considered her expanded farm and prosperity and seethed with suspicion and accusation.

The women noted and whispered to their men that although she must be at least forty, she had barely aged. Her hair was as black, her body as abnormally slim, her white neck as unwrinkled as when they had first known her, and the few lines around her eyes might as well have been caused by the wind as by the weathering of years. And what of those eyes, with their unnatural, changeable colors, sometimes green and sometimes gold, so empty of expression? When she used them, folk were bewitched, cast into trances, just as had happened to poor Robert Wolcot.

Reports were heard from those who confessed to having seen her fly the moor and cross the full moon in the shape of a great bird, and the ghost of that unearthly gray dog was well known to haunt remote farms and cottages, hunting for unbaptized infants.

The rumors and tales increased, each slanderer adding detail and spice until there was no doubt left that Rachel Jedder was indeed a witch, who

209

had achieved her ends by spells and black magic and curses, and who had now blighted the whole area with her evil.

The people of High Chilham turned their backs on her or hissed at her from behind their doors. They refused to talk to her and kept their eyelids firmly lowered if she came near. When she went to market, her four sons had to go, too, not only to deal but to give protection, for at the height of the crisis it was certain she would have been attacked. As it was, more than one stone was hurled in their direction. Although they managed to obtain essential stores, their own produce had to be sent as far as Barnstaple to find buyers.

Only the lofty ruling of Parson and Squire permitted her continued attendance at church each Sunday, although none would share a pew with her. Even Jane Clarke was threatened by their friendship and for a time was unable to visit.

At first, Rachel tried to make amends. She called on Dan Cobbledick to sympathize and apologize, but he spat on her, a gob of thick, yellow phlegm which clung to her cloak. She offered milk to two families whose house cows had been butchered, only to be run off their land with a torrent of fanatical invective. Finally she sent her neighbor, Daniel Lutterell, a heifer calf. The year before, most of his sheep had died from foot rot. Now, he had lost all his steers and was too old and disillusioned to start again.

Dick and Joel returned with the calf the same afternoon, and in her distress Rachel turned on them.

" 'Tis typical that you two should be the bringers of ill tidings," she shouted.

Her feelings for the twins had always been ambivalent because they were inevitably associated in her mind with the nightmare memories of Harry Blackaller. The influence of his bad blood had been automatically read into all their childish misdemeanors, and there was no denying that they had always seemed to lie and steal without compunction. Every hour's labor had had to be forced out of them, and they had baited and tormented the animals to such an extent that finally they were forbidden all contact with the livestock. Even now, the young calf was staggering and sweating from having been hounded all the way back to the farm at a gallop.

Joel complained, "He called us devil's spawn."

"Aye, well, he'll live to regret that, brother," vowed Richard malevolently.

Their mother wanted to weep with frustration but could only snap at them instead. "You be useless good-for-nothings, the pair of you."

" 'Tisn't all bad, Mother," Dick said with a leer and, opening his saddle bag, hauled out a pair of large, white, dead geese. "He didn't get away with insulting we."

Rachel let out all her pent-up anger in a screech. "You slip-gibbeting, flyblown blackguards, with your thieving hands and bad shadow! God

210

strike me! But you be just like Blackaller. Ain't we got enough trouble?"

Richard stepped across the courtyard and stared down at her.

"Think you I can't do as good as the others, Mother? Jedder bringing gold and John near a saint wi' his soft ways. You always had more time for they. Well, I knows how to make Yellaton twice as big, which is more'n them's ever done. You're always calling us good-fer-naughts. Well, wait you and see."

His voice was cold and his eyes blank as he stood over her, looking so like his vile father that she actually shrank back, and then he turned and walked away. His twin slouched sheepishly behind.

Richard Blackaller had always loved his mother, wanting, even as an infant, to make her smile. So he had caught and brought her day-old chicks, squeezed lifeless by his impetuous fist; tried to carry in heavy buckets of milk, and spilled them; pulled up rows of young vegetables instead of weeds. He had pushed his way through the others to be nearest her, always ending up in the way in the crowded kitchen. Later he had shown off to attract her attention, pitting his strength against the muscular colts and stirks without understanding, and thrashing them into submission; winning fights with other boys by unacceptable margins, so that his opponents were left beaten up; and telling falsehoods to say what would please her, rather than the truth.

Whatever he did, his twin Joel did, too, and it seemed they were always wrong. Rachel smacked and swore at them, their older brothers browbeat them, the old fool of a schoolmaster had refused to teach them and boys of their own age were afraid of them and either avoided them or groveled before them.

They were a good-looking pair, above average height, dark-haired and light-eyed, with a certain swagger and an offhand attitude which appealed to the adolescent village girls, and were made the more intriguing by the disapprobation of parents.

At seventeen, Richard encouraged these silly adorations and relished devising tests to see what the maids would endure for his company. So, little Faith Pincombe tramped behind him all day across bogs and gorse-thorned stretches of the moor and returned home drenched and shivering, without even the reward of a kiss. Lucy Squance was put on a horse too lively for her to handle and bounced back into the saddle each time she fell off until it was a wonder she was not killed; and Ann Morrish often cooked and gave him potted mushrooms, or Shrewsbury cakes, or gingerbread, which he ate without thanks, but with enough belittling to send her away dejected.

Yet, the girls dallied by the Golden Lion Inn, or found reason to walk on Beara in the hope of meeting him, or lingered in the crowded church aisle after matins to be able to brush against him. If he winked, few were immune, and making them twitter and blush was so easy that he regarded them all with contempt.

The idea had been germinating for several months, ever since Mary

211

Lutterell had met his eye one day with such startling indifference that at first he had been convinced he was mistaken. He had made a point of singling her out to talk to, but her answers had been brief and she had kept looking beyond him to other friends, and when he had asked her to walk with him, she had made an excuse and refused.

His surprise at her lack of reaction had given way to pique and, when her father had shouted that he and Joel were devil's spawn, the churlishness had become vindictive and calamitously fused with fixed sibling rivalry—the desire to defeat his older brothers by some extraordinary accomplishment, which neither could hope to emulate, and which would give him lifelong status within the family. These conflicts had tempered into the plan.

On the afternoon of the village annual festival in August, there was a cricket match in which the squire led the village team against the men of Roborough for a set of ribbons presented by the landlord of the Ebberly Arms Tavern. The game had changed from being played with a curved bat before two stumps to the newer, faster sport using straight bats and a wicket of three stumps, and the whole parish was keyed up with patriotism. The green had been cut and raked as smooth as a carpet, and Ephraim Thorne, the blacksmith, whose reputation as a cricketer was unparalleled, was encouraged with copious draughts of ale the night before to unleash the whiplash of his bowling upon the challengers.

It was a magnificent match, High Chilham fielders catching and hooking and snatching the ball from the air, Ephraim bowling with uncanny reflex and relentless accuracy until the Roborough braggarts were all out for fifty-five. In the hot sun, the village, from urchin to octogenarian, cheered, grew mellow and well filled on cider and bread and cheese, and cheered again, until their side scored fifty-six for two, winning the game by eight wickets amid scenes of delirious glee.

Then there was a feast of beef and fowls and hares, tarts and cakes and puddings with apples, eggs, cream and breadcrumbs soaked in brandy, and a renowned fiddler came all the way from Barnstaple to help with the Wake celebrations.

Jedder was there, in velvet frock jacket and well-fitted breeches, dancing a merry jig with two maidens on his arms, while glancing explicitly at Mistress Thorne, the blacksmith's pretty, buxom wife, who primped and tossed her ringlets. John was courteously escorting Urith Luckbreast, whom he had been courting since spring, and the twins were part of a ribald, drunken gang, red-complexioned and thick-lipped from harvest scrumpy, making bets and roaring oaths at the back of the tithe barn.

"Come you on later," Dick Blackaller said to his twin. "I got summat to do on my own."

A group of girls, pink-cheeked and giggling, were gathered at the door preparing to leave. He pushed past them to his horse and set off at a gallop for Great Wood above Yellaton.

The path was quite wide from regular use and the summer had dried

212

its mud to a corrugated surface on which the horse's hooves knocked. Once within the boscage, he slowed to a walk and finally halted and heard the voices in the distance, followed shortly by the echo of another lone traveler.

In the diaphanous drifting light of the full moon, she was soon visible, trotting home, humming happily, her head still full of the singing violin and the dazzling lanterns and the hot faces of the lads she had danced with.

He urged his horse forward from the shadows to block the path and she squeaked with shock, then recognized him and exclaimed crossly, "You give me a right start, Dick Blackaller. What you doing here?"

"Waiting for you, Mary," he replied, leaning over to take her reins. " 'Tain't right that a maid like you should ride home alone after a ball."

"I be accustomed to it," she said, but drew herself up in the saddle, flattered by such attention.

He towed her pony alongside and then, turning his own mount, steered them both quickly off the path and into the trees.

"What you doing? Where's us going?" Mary cried, startled.

"I want to talk to you."

"Father be waiting. I promised as I'd be back afore midnight." She became nervous.

"Won't take long," he said steadily.

They reached a small opening where the moon's rays were concentrated and wild thyme and sage and fennel released their sharp scents into the night air.

He could see her face clearly now, worried, hyacinth-blue eyes and a baby's mouth, pouting irresistibly. The breeze had lifted her cloak back off her shoulders and the apple cushions of her breasts filled the muslin bodice of the dance frock and her arms showed round and dimpled at the elbows, with little milkmaid's hands clutching the pony's mane.

"Let me home this minute, Dick Blackaller!" she commanded in a high, childish voice. "Or I'll tell Father."

"I've a mind to marry you," he declared, watching the dolly mouth form an O of surprise.

Then she blurted uncertainly, "That be silly talk, for I have no mind to marry 'ee."

"Don't you like me then, Mary Lutterell?" he teased.

" 'Tisn't that exactly." She was too polite to admit it. "But I bain't ready to wed and Father'd never permit it."

"No matter." He dismounted and lifted her to the ground as well. "You seem plenty ready to me."

Before she had time to struggle, he had tugged her into his clamping arms and fixed onto the round strawberry of her mouth, biting and sucking at the tender, infantile lips until the salt taste of blood reached his tongue and he tumbled her to the ground.

As he broke off the kiss, she screamed and he grasped a handful of the

213

blond hair and wrenched, warning hoarsely, "Not so much noise, my beauty, or Richard will have to hit 'ee and 'ee don't want that, do 'ee?"

She shook her head and whimpered as her skirts were pulled up. She was like a fubsy pink piglet, plump-thighed and plump-bellied, and he played with her for a while, gloating over the way she wriggled under him and letting her believe she might escape. She was so soft and cushiony and chubby with her cherub's mouth and hands and foolish struggles and mewling. He nipped and pinched here and there, hurting just enough to make her gasp with fright.

Suddenly the game palled. Engorged, he rubbed against her and she froze at the contact. Then he broke in. No longer hearing her sobs, he raped her ferociously. Bloated with the white-hot ache and still holding back the better to lunge and pound at her with increasing brutality, inflamed by the luxury of inflicting pain, ecstatic as she shivered and cringed and moaned beneath him until, totally defeated by his attack, she went limp at last. She became a lump of flesh molded solely for his carnality, and finally he could abandon himself with a heaving shudder and a harsh croak of relief.

Afterward, he brushed down her dress and made her wash her tearful face in the stream and tidy her hair under its ribboned mobcap. He shook out her cloak and pinned it on again. Then he drew her against him once more.

"Now, 'tis time to tell your father just what you let me do to you," he taunted, grinning. "You been a bad maid."

"No! No! I beg you, Richard Blackaller. He must not know. He must never know." She began to wail again.

"But he's your father and ought to be told about such things," he argued reasonably.

"No! Please." She clung to him in a gratifying way and he pretended to ponder the problem, while she caught beseechingly at his hand.

"Well, I'll think on it this night and, if you be waiting here at sundown tomorrow, I'll tell you what's decided," he pronounced, with seeming reluctance.

She was there, of course, trembling behind a shrub, afraid someone else would come by and question, until she saw him striding across the clearing, tall and lean, his face the more threatening for being obscure against the sunset.

"I have thought on the matter," he was saying over her. "And I do not see how we can avoid telling your father what you done. So's we can be wed."

Speechless, she shook her head and plucked at his sleeve desperately. Daniel Lutterell was old and a devout Methodist. Mary, his only child, had been born after many years of marriage, and his beloved wife had died giving birth to her. The girl had been brought up with love, but very strictly and almost in seclusion. Only the recent intervention of her aunt had persuaded him to allow her to attend any village functions, and she knew, if he learned of her shame, he would never forgive her or recover from the disgrace.

"Do not tell him," she begged again. "For even if he finds out, he will not let me marry a son of Rachel Jedder, not after what happened to the cattle and with what folks say."

"We shall see." He spoke calmly and put his arm around her with authority, so that her face was pressed against a deerhorn button on his jacket, and she heard him continue, " 'Tis possible he need not know, if you be a good maid and do obey and please me." And his fingers began to undo the fastenings of her dress.

She grasped at the material and he stopped and stepped back.

"Take it off, Mary Lutterell, for 'tis time I saw you proper."

She flinched and he went on briskly, "If I have to tear it off, how will you explain the rents?"

Slowly she undressed and then stood, naked and blushing all over, as he walked around her, caressing her buttocks and squeezing her breasts before ordering her to lie down. He stood, leering, as he unbuttoned his breeches, taking his time as she waited, exposed and in terror. Then he was grinding into her again, boring into the fresh wound until she hung onto him to try to counter the agonizing jolts.

"That's better," he grunted, moving faster and climaxing in a series of massive, angry collisions.

"Be here tomorrow," he commanded, walking off before she had finished dressing.

After that, Richard Blackaller met and took Mary Lutterell daily in Great Wood and increased his control over her through a variety of imaginative punishments and intimidations until she was so cowed and sensitive that she became like a small whipped bitch, fawning and quivering to anticipate his wishes.

Several weeks passed before he commented casually, "You ain't had no woman's courses as I've noticed."

She bit her lip and turned away, agitated that a man should talk of a subject which women only mentioned in whispers.

"How long has it been?" he persisted.

"Not since the night . . ." she mumbled, ". . . not since before the Wake frolic."

His long eyes glinted and his teeth showed in an inexplicable smile. He pushed her onto his horse and vaulted up behind and set off recklessly through the trees, ducking to avoid the lowest branches before thundering into the open and down the hill.

"What is it?" Mary called, affrighted, but he only cackled, and as they clattered into the cobblestoned yard of her father's farm, she burst into tears.

Daniel Lutterell came to the door of the stables and glowered at the

215

scandalous sight of his own daughter perched like a hoyden in the Yellaton boy's arms.

"Get 'ee into the house, girl!" he growled. "And you, boy, get off my land!"

She moved to dismount, but Richard Blackaller tightened his hold.

"Sit still!" he insisted. Then, inclining his head in a mocking bow to the old man, he declared, "Maister Lutterell, I come to ask for Mary's hand in wedlock."

Daniel Lutterell's skin became livid and his eyes bloodshot, and, raising his cattle stick in a shaking hand, he rushed forward.

"You impudent scoundrel! Release her this instant! You're not fit to share same air as a maid like her!"

"Now, that be no way to greet your future son-in-law, Maister Lutterell," Dick jeered. "And 'tis certain I'm to be that, because her and me has shared more than air."

"What mean you?" the farmer shouted.

"Why, that I have got your pure maid here with child, of course," he laughed, as though at a huge joke. "So you had best give us your blessing quick, for no one else will have her now."

"What, Dick! 'Tisn't true! How could you say such a thing?" The girl rounded on him, her innocent blue eyes flaring with shock.

Richard Blackaller sneered. "You ignorant wench! Why think 'ee you've had no flow?"

"But that cannot be . . . it don't mean . . ." she began, flushed with embarrassment. "Father! . . . tell him it be not so."

Old Daniel Lutterell let out a heartrending groan of desolation, the groan of a man who had lost more than his life's worth, whose soul had been laid waste by anguish.

Still derisive, the boy lowered his darling daughter to the ground, swung the horse about and set off at a speed for Yellaton, where he burst into the kitchen full of the news.

"Did I not tell you as I'd more than double the size of Jedder's land, Mother?" he brayed, catching her round the waist and lifting her off the ground. "Well, I done it! I got us one hundred and fifty acre more."

"Put me down, you young rascal!" Rachel twinkled at his high spirits. "Now, what's this you be going on about?"

"Lutterell's farm. 'Tis ours! 'Tis ours!" he roared. "I'm to marry Mary Lutterell."

Rachel gaped at him. Then an expression of dismissal crossed her face and she clicked her tongue at his stupidity.

"That be one prospect you can forget, son, for no matter what you may want, or she may want, Daniel Lutterell will never permit it."

"You be wrong there, Mother," he corrected, with a smirk of satisfaction. "For he had no objection when I asked him not a half hour ago."

Rachel caught her breath and sat down on the nearest chair, unable to speak for several minutes.

Eventually she gave him a penetrating look and said, "You would not josh me on this, Dick?"

"No, Mother. 'Pon my honor, 'tis true."

Her mind dismissed the image, which had nagged for years, of the hand of her own land cupped impotently around Lutterell's farm, and replaced it with the glorious vision of owning the entire sweep to the north, from the house of Yellaton to the parish boundary of Tiddy Water. Richard Blackaller was laughing again, jubilant at the sight of her awed face.

"We'll have one of the biggest farms in High Chilham," she gulped and leaped up to hug him with joy. "Mary Lutterell! Who'd have thought it! You've made some match and no mistake."

Running to the pantry, she fetched a bottle of elderflower wine, poured its sparkling contents into two tankards, gave one to him and raised the other with unsteady fingers.

"I am real proud of you, my son," she toasted him, close to tears. "This day you have made our family great."

The following morning, Daniel Lutterell was found hanging from the central beam in his own barn.

When little Mary was brought weeping to Yellaton, Dick made no attempt to comfort her. Indeed, he virtually ignored her, and she would not look in his direction. Even allowing for the sudden death of her father, it was curious behavior in a newly engaged couple and Rachel Jedder was puzzled. She did her best to soothe the distress and could not understand the glances of sullen loathing she received in return. It was as though the child blamed her in some way for the old man's suicide.

"I know it is not easy to believe, but the sorrow will pass," she explained gently. "And, as soon as is decent, you can be wed. Then, before long, you'll find your life full and happy again, 'tis true."

The girl evaded her gesture of condolence, burst into another paroxysm of emotion and turned to leave the room. Opening the door, she blundered straight into Dick Blackaller and recoiled as though he had struck her.

At once, Rachel saw repeated in the guileless eyes the same revulsion and terror she herself had felt for Harry Blackaller all those years before, and in that moment she knew exactly what had happened.

"My God!" she breathed, overcome by a wave of nausea as Mary stumbled away from them.

"What be the matter?" He came and put a hand on her shoulder.

It was the touch of a specter and Rachel blenched.

"That girl hates you," she whispered. "You done some terrible evil to her."

217

"Weren't no more'n had to be done." He shrugged. "And she'll get over it."

"Blast your eyes!" she shrieked, distraught. "You be just like him. Wicked through and through."

" 'Twere you I done it for, Mother," he protested.

Rachel hit him a blow which left four white streaks across his skin.

"There won't be no marriage," she declared fiercely. "I will make sure of that, Richard Blackaller."

Her son looked at her with the same slatelike impassivity as his dead father and rubbed his cheek. "I do not think Mary Lutterell will want to bear an infant out of wedlock. Do you?"

"With one hundred and fifty acre to her name, she won't need to worry about that, you pea-brained fool," she rasped at him contemptuously. "They'll be queueing to church her."

Suddenly, the room felt stifling. Palpitations sent blood pumping to her head and she was overcome by claustrophobia, as though hot hands were covering her nose and mouth, and fingers pressed against her windpipe, and before her glaze sight an older face slipped, like a film, over her son's face and they become one.

Stopping only long enough to bridle the mare, she slid off the mounting block astride onto the broad bare back and clattered from the courtyard. Through the orchard and down the hare's leg, without even closing the gates behind her; across Brindley to the opening made by her first husband for access to Moses Bottom. From there she could look down on the neighboring farm in its protective cape of trees.

Lutterell's land began on the other side of the hedge, entry to it being at the farthest end. Almost expecting the old man to appear and halt her trespass, she started down the rarely used path. The overgrown rankness reared up and obstructed the way, menacing the mare's head with its antennae, snatching at her fetlocks and hooking into her chest as the woman kicked her on. Blackberry-warted branches whiplashed and crushed their blisters into purple stains on Rachel's skirt and tangled belladonna plants pressed their poisonous berries to her lips, and once a tapering ash rod recoiled across her eyes. A sparrow hawk took languid flight ahead and followed the line of the hedge in search of its cowering meal.

The descent grew steeper and, unable to see the ground, the horse slithered and stumbled over the stones and tilted her rider precariously forward. Gradually the sky, so vast over Yellaton, was reduced by the circle of woodland and moor to a small, tidy coif, and the majesty of Exmoor became a thin, undulating blue line. Trapped in the ring, the afternoon was close and hot.

Trickles of moisture ran down the woman's breastbone and her legs stuck damply to the mare's steamy rib cage. Berries, red, clustered on the holly and dangled orange from the rowan, and redwings attacked the scarlet hips, and the leaves were alight, crimson on the guelder rose, purple the spindle, long, bloody pendants from the cherry, the silver maple become candle yellow. Red admiral and tortoiseshell butterflies flitted with the October flame from plant to plant, like smoking torches, until it seemed as though the decaying year were being burnt out on the hillside. For it was almost the end of the party, the time of stale sweat and charred logs and spent drive and the lingering, slow-motion dance.

The seeds had fallen from the ears, been abducted by breezes, spat out by birds and shaken from the pepperpot of the poppy. The broom pods had split and bracken rusted, and the black grapes of the elder had dried out, had wizened and dropped. Beetles and bees and dying wasps crowded the ivy for its last, cloying flowers, and Rachel, emerging from the raveled track at last, saw the dusty marquetry of Lutterell's farm lying before her and was ravished by a lechery which blew a raw note and kissed with a dark-brown tongue.

Within its horny skin this land was fleshy with sheltered sward and fallow padding the kernel of its stone-built farmhouse. Hornbeam and sweet chestnut and oak, which would have been warped on the wind-twisted heights of Beara, grew to venerable magnitude here. Villavins Acres, Stoneycrows, Coltscorner, Eagle Down, the name of each enclosure held its history. What ancestral conflict had been settled on Battle Field, where flint arrowheads were still to be found in the soil?

Rachel looked up to the line of trees which separated the two properties.

"I shall cut those down," she thought to herself, and knew she was committed. It did not matter how it had been obtained, or to whom it had belonged. It would all be Jedder's land soon.

"How old are you, Mary Lutterell?" she asked the girl on her return.

"Twenty."

"So you're a bit older than Richard. When be your birth date?"

"Tenth November."

"Next month. You will be of age then."

The girl nodded pettishly, and Rachel went to stand close to her by the kitchen dresser.

"Listen, maid, I know what he done to you and 'tis my wish to help."

"Why should you, Mistress Blackaller?" She was almost crying again. "You being his mother."

"Do you want to see him own your father's farm?" Rachel goaded.

"No! That I do not!" The tears came in a rush.

" 'Tis a disgrace to have to admit it of my blood, but Dick would squander such a heritage." The woman shook her head and frowned. "He will leave you a pauper, as I was, girl. And your father's farm should be passed on to your own child."

"I know! I know!" Mary twisted her hands. "But what's to do? All that is mine becomes your son's when we are wed."

"Before you goes before parson, come with me on your birth date to Barnstaple, to the lawyer." Rachel spoke urgently. "For I have a plan and you must put your trust in me."

"You would aid me against your own son?" The girl was incredulous. "Why?"

"We are both women, Mary Lutterell," she answered simply.

Mary looked down at her feet.

"There is no one else but me," Rachel pointed out.

"What would you have me do?"

She answered coolly, as though stating the obvious, "You must give the farm to me."

"Never!" Mary's face suffused with color and she swung away angrily. "No!"

"It is between Dick Blackaller and Rachel Jedder—and your child will be my grandchild, Mary Lutterell." The woman turned the unwilling girl back to face her and repeated, "*My* grandchild. The farm will become his or hers upon my death. My testament will ensure it."

"No! 'Tis not possible! Father would never allow it! 'Twould shame his memory."

"Your father is dead and if Richard gain his land, I shall not work it. It will be let go the rack and ruin." The threat was quietly emphatic.

Mary gazed at her, tongue-tied.

"Look at my acres. Are they not well tilled and husbanded?" Rachel Jedder became persuasive. "Think you I could neglect such a fine farm as yours? You know I could not."

The girl shook her head in confusion and rubbed the back of her hand across tearful eyes.

"Mary Lutterell, if you give over the farm to me, I swear upon Christ's blood, I will pass it on to your child, my grandchild. The testament will be drawn up, signed and witnessed before your eyes by the attorney. It is my oath."

There was a long silence and then the girl whispered, so quietly that Rachel could barely hear, "But what of Dick Blackaller? What will he do when he finds out?"

Rachel Jedder put her arm around the hunched shoulders.

"Richard will do nothing, my lamb. Trust me. He will never inherit. I shall protect you and yours and justice will be done."

But she did not mention that the girl had no need to marry into the Jedder family at all.

For the sake of propriety, meanwhile, Mary Lutterell was sent to live with her maiden aunt, although other than Rachel and her son Richard no one knew the secret of the coming baby. The Lutterell aunt was mystified and incensed by the forthcoming wedding, but could do nothing to dissuade her niece from going through with it.

The clerk's quill seemed to scratch on for a long time, and yet, the document was disappointingly brief for one of such importance. The attorney perused it over his fluttering kerchief and Rachel noticed the damp creases in the fat folds of his neck and had the inconsequential idea that it was his own body smell, and not that of his clients, he was trying to ward off so obsessively.

". . . all lands belonging to me shall . . . before my marriage with Richard Blackaller, become the property of . . . to my issue . . ." he was murmuring. "Well, that is perfectly straightforward, Mistress Blackaller."

As he placed the paper on the table in front of Mary Lutterell, he looked straight at the older woman, sensing her authority.

Mary, awed, openmouthed and silent, marked a cross against her name where directed, and Rachel had to keep her hands locked together in her lap to prevent their trembling and betraying her excitement as the parchment was witnessed, sealed, rolled up, sealed again, and finally locked in a cupboard behind a heavy oak door in the corner of the dusty office.

"Is my will relating to this land complete?" Rachel asked.

The clerk handed over a second document and this, too, was solemnly witnessed and locked away.

"There now, 'tis done." She patted the girl's hand kindly as they walked back through Barnstaple. "And you're quite safe. Say not a word of this to our Dick until you be churched, and then you will live under my protection at Yellaton and I will see as he never does no hurt to you again, my chick."

"But where shall we all rest, mistress?" asked Mary, still tremulous.

"Jedder and John and young Joel shall go to live down your father's old place, and Jane Clarke will no doubt be more than happy to keep house for them."

"But what will you do with Father's land?" The girl was bewildered.

"Why, I shall farm it of course, alongside Yellaton." Rachel ruffled her hair and laughed. " 'Twill be in the best of hands, silly goose, never fear."

By the time Richard Blackaller discovered the truth of the conspiracy, he was inescapably married to the wench. The untrained girlish body he had so enjoyed had already been replaced by a girth of matronly proportions and she was hiding behind the unassailable barrier of his mother. He hung around the house for a week or two in brooding disgust, and then moved out to join his twin at Lutterell's, just as Rachel had known he would.

There was a dowry, not a fortune, but the comfortable amount accrued by a careful man throughout his lifetime, and Rachel and Jedder rode northwest to beyond Dulverton to buy and bring in good, clean cattle, while John journeyed south to Okehampton and drove back a healthy, hardy flock of sheep. Lutterell's farm and the additional grazing which came with it on Beara were restocked. In all she now owned fifty fine red Devon cows and three hundred in-lamb ewes.

A long new cowshed was built at Yellaton and a door was knocked through from the house to the old shippen bordering the courtyard, which was turned into two rooms, over which an extra floor was added with a passage and two further rooms. A full-time shepherd was hired and two little apprentices, a boy and a girl, aged ten and twelve, were accepted from the parish and given work no heavier than Rachel's own children had been expected to do at their ages.

Because times were still hard in the village and the surrounding district, the people realized that the Jedder woman could no longer be ostracized. Yellaton and Lutterell farms combined offered too much badly needed employment of casual labor. However suspect her rise from pauperdom to affluence, they could not afford to reject work, which others would quickly accept, especially as the traditional support from the squire's estate had mysteriously dwindled to almost token level. In turn, the family simply ignored the hostility they knew underlay all their local dealings, and carried on as before.

Jedder continued to cross between mundane rural daylight hours and the darker interests of his nights; although, wisely, he had moved farther afield, and late travelers between Barnstaple and Crediton now fared in considerably greater security than before. At twenty-six years old, he still showed no signs of wishing to settle but continued being diverted by the company of pneumatic married blondes of frolicsome and generous nature, with husbands conveniently away at sea, or in jail, or merely on the coach to London or Plymouth for trading trips.

John, the only one to retain goodwill in the neighborhood, because of his striking gift of healing and the patient soberness of his mien, became engaged to Urith Luckbreast. Respectable but poor and unable to add any material assets to the family, she would not have been Rachel's choice of daughter-in-law, but John, so seemingly mild, had a core of immovable determination when it came to decisions, and his mother knew better than to argue.

Besides, she was already preoccupied with fostering another and entirely unexpected possibility, as Peter Spurway from Torrington began paying unmistakable attention to Emma. The disadvantage in Jedder eyes that the Spurways were not farmers was virtually offset by the fact that he was the eldest son of the leading wool merchant in the district, whose interests extended to leather, meat, weaving and gloving as well.

Rachel, with her expanded flock of sheep and the memories of her years as an underpaid glover, could see the intriguing trading prospects and the poetic fulfillment in such a coupling and played the match with skill.

To pretty, birdbrained Emma she was disparaging about Peter Spurway because he had no prospects of inheriting land. To the young man himself she displayed only the face of stern disapproval and sensed that his own family was also exhibiting genuine opposition at home. At the same time, she constantly created apparently accidental situations in which the two found themselves together sympathizing with each other about the lack of understanding in their parents. As neither was over-endowed with intelligence, Rachel trusted that the stubbornness of natural stupidity would achieve the rest. She was not disappointed.

The young man did battle with his father and galloped out to Yellaton, red and sweating with nerves and triumph, to ask—almost demand—to marry the girl. For the sake of formality Rachel refused her permission at least twice and relented, in the end, with great and obvious reluctance and with the imposition of a year's wait before the nuptials could take place. Such unexpected opposition persuaded the Spurways that their son must be making quite a good alliance after all, and from then on, there was absolutely no possibility of the forthcoming marriage being called off. And the bypassing of the market middlemen for Jedder wool, leather and mutton began immediately.

Richard and Joel Blackaller became more uncontrolled and disreputable than ever, driven by the former's humiliation and savagery over the way the trap he had set had been sprung on himself. But they, too, took themselves farther off, to the taverns and gambling dens and quayside women of Barnstaple and Bideford. There Joel, convinced that his twin's marriage had made them all rich, wagered recklessly, and Richard gained such a barbarous reputation for perversion that only the oldest, poorest and most hardened whores could be persuaded to entertain him.

Rachel, totally absorbed in the running of the farms, had no time to listen to the rumors of their squalid behavior, and even when Squire Waddon took her aside after church one Sunday to warn of Joel's growing obsession, she paid no attention, except for feeling slightly irritated by the conversation. The twins had always been trouble. Now they were grown men and no longer her responsibility.

The moor met the woods and disclosed the view of Yellaton and Lutterell, gushing like a green waterfall down its side, and her pulse jumped, as it always did at the sight, and she forgot the squire's words and urged her horse home.

Charles Waddon himself was in a quicksand of debt. He saw the two Blackallers regularly at the same fights and gaming rooms he frequented to risk more and more money in frantic and futile efforts to recoup his losses.

Family silver and jewelry and objets d'art collected by his ancestors had already been sold and servants dismissed, and his promissory notes were held by friends and moneylenders alike. His sheltered wife, Lady Ann, unable to cope with such insecurity, had taken their children and returned to her father's house. In his struggle to recover position and fortune he was hardly aware of her leaving, but only saw luck, dangling like a rope of gold, just out of reach.

Foreclosure was inevitable. His creditors met and joined to press their claims. The manor and Braddon estate were put up for sale and auctioned one afternoon. They went to a north country industrialist, whose wealth had come from a water-powered frame which had put thousands of cottage spinners out of work because it required the setting up of factories and the employment of townspeople in mills instead.

It all happened so quickly and was over before the news reached Rachel Jedder. Of course, she had realized from the day he had sold her Arn valley that Squire Waddon was in difficulties, and then the staff reductions and his wife's departure were common knowledge, but it had never occurred to her that he would actually have to sell up.

As soon as she heard, she hurried to Braddon, not knowing what to say, but anxious that he should be assured of her loyalty and friendship.

Three massive wagons, each drawn by a team of six draught horses, were lined up before the house and a lot of strangers were unloading furniture from them. Rachel rode up to the man who appeared to be in charge and asked for the squire.

"Squire Were does not arrive until next week," he replied, in an unfamiliar accent.

"I don't know of no Squire Were," Rachel responded with asperity. " 'Tis Squire Waddon I be after."

The man gave her a look of contempt.

"Waddon left this morning."

"Where did he go?" she demanded.

"I neither know nor care, woman," the steward answered rudely. "Though, by all accounts, he should be in Newgate."

Sadness took Rachel and she turned away without another word, and on the slow walk home found herself deeply depressed. If she had paid more attention to the gossip which had crossed the moor, she might have been in time to wish him well. Such a good friend and protector should not have been lost without the chance to say goodbye.

Jelinger Were moved into Braddon Manor and within weeks had bought up Heanton, Boode, West Mill and Broadgate farms as well, enlarging the estate by five hundred acres.

He was a heavily set man in his fifties with a steel-gray cap of thick hair and exaggerated jutting eyebrows which cast shadows over his eyes and met in the middle to run parallel to a moustache like a metal bar. His face was fleshy but lacked color, its lines seeming engrained with grime from a lifetime spent working in enclosed and dusty conditions.

As soon as he took up his position as local Justice of the Peace, the people knew that the lackadaisical times of Charles Waddon were over. This new squire was a merciless man.

For stealing potatoes, he sentenced Nell Beare to be whipped through the streets of South Molton at the end of a cart. A cousin of the Cottles was transported to Australia for fourteen years after smuggled goods were discovered in a shed behind his cottage. For receiving the haunch of a poached deer, Amy Babb was sentenced to one year's hard labor; and twelve-year-old Gilbert Claggett was put in the stocks, although his feet could not reach the ground, to be spat on and covered in refuse for taking bread from his mistress's pantry.

Still dissatisfied with the size of his estate, Squire Were sought to acquire even more land, on his own terms, and mysterious accidents began to plague those who refused to sell. The corn-filled barn at Hooper's burned to the ground one night, and Seth Bartle had to have his best horse put down after the tendons in its forelegs were found cut through. Respectable people were discovered to have infringed obscure bylaws and fined beyond their means, and the rough-voiced outsiders who had come from the north in Were's employ took to jostling and frightening the unaccompanied wives and daughters of recalcitrant farmers in the lanes while their men were working the fields.

The manor quickly took over even cottages and smallholdings. Freeholders became leaseholders, yeomen became landless, independent homesteaders became hirelings and some became paupers. From being a neatly boundaried park with a demesnial farm and a couple of tenancies, Braddon spread to, and finally swallowed, the whole of High Chilham.

Rachel Jedder was at the bottom of the hare's-leg field, standing by the gate she had first entered upon her arrival at Yellaton so many years before, when the new squire and two of his men rode up.

It was a bleak December day and her skirts were soaked with mud from being trailed through the mire made by the steers. Her hair had come undone and she brushed its tangle back with a dirty hand, which smeared her face, as Were said her name.

"Mistress Blackaller, you have been using Arn valley and Arnwood and a further thirty-five acres on this side without proper title." He came to the point of his visit without preliminaries.

Rachel straightened and stared at him. " 'Tis my land, bought and paid for off Squire Waddon," she rejoined. "And the deeds is lodged proper with a lawyer."

"Unfortunately, Waddon was not entitled to sell that land, and therefore it still belongs to the Braddon estate," the newcomer replied. "But, as a courtesy, I shall pay you the sum of fifty pounds to compensate for the inconvenience of having to relinquish it."

There was no doubt he was bluffing and she took a deliberate stride to stand at the head of his big bay hunter before speaking again with icy authority.

"Jelinger Were. That land be Jedder's land—my land—and I don't never give up my land for nobody."

The animal was kicked forward into the gateway and Rachel, without moving back or releasing its rider from her metallic glare, pointed to its hooves.

"And you are on my land now. Trespassing, squire or no. So get you off and be on your way."

The whip in Squire Were's fist twitched and he glowered lividly at the undersized, filthy hag who had dared to insult him in front of his own servants.

"You have one week in which to accept my offer and return the deeds, Mistress Blackaller," he snarled, and jerking his mount, galloped off.

Rachel shut the gate and returned angrily to the house to be met by Mary running from the kitchen, incoherent with fright. It took minutes before she was composed enough to explain that Jelinger Were had called there first and ordered her, with threats, to tell her husband to sell up Lutterell's farm.

Rachel sat her in the big chair and made them both tea and patted her hand, trying unsuccessfully to disguise her own exasperation, in order to assure the girl she would come to no harm.

"He said as the land weren't never Father's at all. What could he have meant by it, Rachel?" Mary was babbling. "He said as how we'd be sent to prison. What shall we do?"

"He cannot gaol you, Mary. 'Tis all a lie to dismay you." Rachel tried to soothe her.

"But supposing as he can? I couldn't abide being put in such a place. I couldn't, with the baby coming and all." The crying became noisier. "You'll have to sell to he."

"I will do no such thing. Now, calm yourself at once, Mary Blackaller." The woman lost patience. "Jelinger Were won't get away with this and you are to stop talking nonsense. Sell, indeed!"

A few days later, when the girl, now five months pregnant, was walking slowly through the woods to the village, four of the Braddon estate's new henchmen appeared and ran their horses at her, reaching down to snatch off her bonnet and push her from one to the other. By a fateful coincidence, they harried her to the very place where Richard Blackaller had repeatedly raped her and she became so terror-stricken that she fell down screaming and began to miscarry. Alarmed by the results of their bullying and her obviously serious condition, the hired men fled, and it was several hours before anyone at Yellaton realized she was missing.

It was too dark to see beyond a lantern circle and, although the brothers shouted her name and searched all the wet night, she was not found before daybreak. By then the child had been stillborn and the girl herself was unconscious, and although they wrapped her in rugs and forced brandy down her throat and John bled her, pathetic little Mary Blackaller died before noon from exposure and shock.

As the old crone who dealt with village death laid out the body, Rachel

Jedder stood by, sick at the waste of it. The bonny, rosy color of the girl had been replaced by a watery paleness, but the skin was still downy and unscarred by time, the limbs still had a childish fullness, the breasts an unsuckled poignancy. Rachel thought of the way the protected young world had been so suddenly and totally destroyed, in only a few months, and she reviled herself with shame at having been the unwitting cause.

The door of the bedroom opened and Richard Blackaller cast a casual and uncaring glance at his dead wife before meeting his mother's look.

"She lies there because of you, boy," she accused.

But he merely shrugged.

There was an outcry over the death of Mary Blackaller. Coming in addition to the ferocious judgments and bullying rapacity of the new squire, the people of North Devon did not hide their animosity or the fact that they held him responsible, after his men had been overheard discussing the incident among themselves in the taverns. Jelinger Were had his carriage stoned when he went out and his servants were attacked, two of them so badly that they were never able to work again. For a while the atmosphere was so belligerent that he was forced to remain within the confines of the original Waddon property.

The story inevitably reached the ears of the old landed families of the area, who had not been impressed by the man's industrial antecedents in the first place and were now glad of an excuse to close their great houses firmly against him, offering no social courtesies and rejecting all his overtures.

Even after the situation became less heated, it was some time before he was able to openly pursue his aim to own all the land between Atherington and Roborough. Believing naively that the sheer size of his extended estate could eventually force county society to accept him, the longer he had to wait, the more he blamed Rachel Jedder for the delay and for the undisguised hostility of all.

The two hundred and fifty acres and moorland rights she now owned outright made up an indispensable piece in the jigsaw of his plan. Had it not been for the blunder by his men and the death of the peasant slut, his schemes to seize it would have been put into operation and would have succeeded. The Jedder woman would have found cattle let loose in her corn and laborers frightened off from working for her and unaccountable damage done to her buildings and crops and her stock unsold in all the markets. She would soon have had to capitulate.

As it was, he was forced to resort to more expensive and subtle tactics, and paid informants were set to work furtively in the towns of Bideford and Barnstaple, where special nights of entertainment were arranged with plenty of liquor and wenches and gaming, and invitations extended to carefully chosen parties. Then there were whispered meetings on which papers were exchanged for gold, and one by one the conspirators

227

and spies met up with the Braddon steward at the White Hart Inn and handed over their dossiers.

Then, just two months after Mary was buried, Joel Blackaller was arrested for debt. He owed the sum of three hundred pounds and all his marked pledges were held by Jelinger Were.

CHAPTER FOURTEEN

The power of a Justice of the Peace was almost without limit. Officially appointed by the Lord Lieutenant of England, the unpaid position was usually given automatically to the local squire. As magistrate, he could, at the Quarter or Petty Sessions, condemn men, women and children to prison, to hard labor, to be branded, put in the stocks, publicly whipped, fined, evicted or put to death. It was not necessary for him to have any experience of the law, and it was not unknown for him to invent laws to match his own prejudices.

Frequently he heard cases and pronounced sentence in the privacy of his own home, which was where Jelinger Were chose to have Joel Blackaller brought before him.

That his judgment was bound to be influenced by the fact that the entire debt was owed to himself did not hinder the process. This was, in the new squire's view, a positive advantage and the sole reason he had taken the trouble to organize credit for the youth and then buy up all his promissory notes. For no mother could stand by and allow one of her sons to be condemned to the unspeakable conditions of a debtor's prison if she had any means on earth by which to save him. Rachel Jedder would be forced to sell her land in order to raise the money to obtain the boy's release.

At Yellaton, after the first reaction of stupefied disbelief at the news, Rachel instinctively attacked Richard.

"Why did *you* not stop him?" She pinned him with a look of accusation. "*You* were always with him. *You* must have known what were going on."

"Weren't none of my business," he replied sullenly.

"None of your business! Vengeance take 'ee! Your own twin gambling and betting his way to gaol and it weren't your business! What can you mean by it? You always were useless, wi' less brains than a hen. What thought you would happen? What was to be the end of it? Thought you he would win it all back? Three hundred pounds! Damn and blast you for a fool!"

Exclamations and curses and questions and insults burst out in a geyser of astounded frenzy.

"And how could he have borrowed such sums? What sort of men would game with a penniless lad? I know sporting gentlemen, but I don't know of none as plays with boys with no funds." She rocked to and fro, her arms clasped over her breasts. "Three hundred pounds! Three hundred pounds!"

Then she stopped and caught her breath and stared at him as she discovered the answer.

" 'Twere you, Richard Blackaller! You done it!" Her voice broke hoarsely.

"I done nothing," he growled back. "Weren't naught to do with me."

"Joel believed Lutterell's farm were yours, did he not? And you never told him you did not own one stick of it," she went on. "You let him and others suppose as you were rich. That be how he were given credit. And that were why he went on with his games of chance and wagers. He were ever the weak and stupid one and he went where you pointed, Richard Blackaller."

She stepped forward, her tone risen to such a screech that her burly son backed away from her fists, like a big hound retreating from a lapdog.

Jedder put out an arm to restrain her, and John, who had brought the news, intervened in his low, sensible way.

" 'Tisn't no use going for Dick, Mother. We got to decide what's to be done for young Joel."

"Done? What can we do for him?" She whirled round. "He owes three hundred pound and not even Jedder here can lay his hands on that kind of money."

"There be only one way to make sure he don't finish in prison," said John. "Lutterell's will have to be sold. And Arn valley, too."

There was a very long silence while Rachel looked from one to the other of her children in turn and found them all in agreement. Expressions of surprise and incredulity and wrath and a final, unyielding obstinacy followed each other across her features.

"No!" she stated, arbitrarily. "The land will not be sold. Not one acre of it."

"You *knows* what them gaols is like, full o' vermin and sickness, men crammed in filth without air or light and them wi' no gold beaten and left to starve," John exclaimed urgently, standing in front of her where she could not avoid meeting his direct gray eyes. "The boy cannot spend the years of his manhood there."

229

"Them places is worse by far than any workhouse," Jedder put in.

"He be my brother," Dick Blackaller protested, stung to Joel's defense at last. "He be your *son*."

"Pity you did not think of that before," Rachel retorted. She had walked to stand with her back to the open fireplace in order to see them better as she spoke.

"You don't none of you know what you're talking of. There be six of us, besides Joel, in this family, and how are we to live off fifteen acre? Because fifteen acre is all that will be left if Lutterell and Arnwood go. And we'll be lucky to keep that."

"I can make a living at healing and Jedder does well for hisself," John pointed out. "And Richard and Joel could stay on and work the place. And Emma will wed."

"Not to Peter Spurway, she won't. Spurways won't have their son marrying into no poor smallholder's family," Rachel corrected immediately. "And what's to happen to old Dave Bartle and to shepherd and the two 'prentices? Are they all to be thrown out? The children sent back to the poorhouse because your dolt of a brother chose to throw away all our welfare?"

Emma had burst into noisy sobs at the idea of losing her precious Peter Spurway and the sons looked at each other in silence, unable to think of arguments.

"And lill' Jane, what'll become of her? Who'll want a pauper girl?" Rachel pressed on furiously. "Have you all forgot so quick the years when we had nothing, the bad times without enough to eat and all of us working like dogs and getting nowhere? Well, I have not forgot, nor never will. And not one of you, nor all of you together, is going to send me back to such a life, for 'twere worse than anything Joel be going to. And I ain't going to die in want and poverty in a rathole of some workhouse for any young pup."

Her chin thrust forward and her eyes frosted and her loose black hair seemed alive against the background of spitting, flaming logs. In some eerie way, she seemed to have grown so that she towered above them, and they were all overcast by her mighty shadow.

"Let me tell you straight and mind it well, my sons, not an inch of Jedder's land will be sold while I live, and I will not die until I know the land can *all* be left to one who feels as I do. And, after this day's exhibition, that won't be to none of you."

The three men stayed silent, heads down, avoiding her intimidating glare, and then, one by one, they left the room. The woman turned her back and stared into the fire, and behind her the sound of her daughter's sniveling stopped as Emma also slunk away.

In her mind, Rachel went to each of the vantage points from which she was accustomed to looking over her land: the edge of Arnwood, with the oval valley nestled beneath its wing, like a beautiful green egg; the footpath from where the unexpected oasis of the original homestead, with its rectangle of low-roofed cob buildings, its little orchard, three small fields and copse could be seen set alone in the measureless, rolling wastes of Beara Moor; the hillock beyond Brindley, beneath which the whole of Lutterell lay as though set out on a market stall, with each of its wares exhibited in an individual tray, chocolate-colored spinneys sprinkled with the first pale sprays of opening leaves, the dark-green ponds of old pastures, new leas and wheat fields glittering and glassy as emeralds, the deep-piled fallow, and streams, like adders lazy in the sun, sliding their slow ways to Tiddy Water and then on to the River Torridge.

Absolute, eonian land, where threadlike tendrils had tentatively sprouted from fallen seed and spread through the soil, strengthening, pushing stones aside, slowly, slowly reaching down to the heart of the earth, thickening over thousands of years to become the petrified roots of the ancestors of now venerable trees. Land on which food would always grow, where people would always be sustained; perpetual, unassailable, beloved place of her survival, guardian of her children's children and their children, preserver of her own mortality.

Then she visualized the boy. Worthless and transient. One dot among millions, soon to vanish as though he had never been. She saw his superficial good looks which would disappear under wrinkles and toothlessness, height which would shrink, muscles which would turn to flab and then disintegrate under hanging folds of skin, flat belly which would grow paunchy and then collapse into an empty bag, youth which would age in a few brief years and die. She saw his weak mouth and his sidelong glance and heard his silly drunken chortle and was incensed and unwillingly moved, because he was still her son.

Rachel Jedder and the attorney in Cross Street spoke for a long time. He was a shrewd man and might even have been a pleasant one had it not been for his antisocial odor and grotesque obesity. Despite his surprise and almost moral disapproval at her refusal to dispose of her assets to pay her son's debts, he recognized the decision as practical and saw that it was worth retaining this extraordinary client, who doubtless had further to go and many more legal matters that would require his services.

However, in this instance, he could offer only his own presence to represent Joel Blackaller at the hearing. This in itself was a most unusual action at a time when criminals were expected to defend themselves. Almost as an afterthought, he also offered one piece of advice.

Jelinger Were sprawled in a carved armchair in his library, his gaze on that weasel-faced woman heading her family at the far end of the room. He ignored Joel Blackaller, who had been brought in chains from Barnstaple gaol, and waved aside the fat sapscull of a lawyer's protests about his own vested interest in the case. Then he jerked upright and felt his blood pressure leap at the news that there was to be no offer to pay the outstanding sum. The woman was returning his stare dispassionately. It had cost him considerably more than three hundred pounds to arrange the finance and buy up the notes to create this situation in the certainty that her land would fall to him—yet she was still refusing to sell.

He stood up, knocking over the tripod wine table at his elbow, his face swollen and hot with rage.

"Sentenced to hard labor until the debt is paid in full, or for the rest of his natural life," he heard himself shout.

"Us chooses to join the Navy," Joel gabbled, throwing a nervous squint at Jonathan Palfriman, the lawyer.

"What's this?" Jelinger Were stared.

The lawyer spoke swiftly. "Your Honor, the prisoner elects to join the Royal Navy."

"The prisoner elects!" Jelinger Were could not believe his ears. "What nonsense is this, man?"

"A debtor may elect to join the Royal Navy rather than serve the sentence of the Court in prison," Palfriman replied coolly. "And this man chooses so to do."

" 'Tain't true! I will not have it!" All the magistrate's frustration came out in a bellow. "The prisoner is gaoled for life."

"The law of the land gives all debtors the right to join the Navy as matelots in place of such sentence," the lawyer insisted. "It is easily verified, Your Honor."

The cheer from the brothers was hastily repressed by his frown. Jelinger Were twisted to face his clerk, who confirmed the words with a nod and hands spread obsequiously. The squire turned back to confront the row of leering bumpkins with unconcealed hatred.

"Take him away!" He swung an angry arm in the direction of Joel Blackaller and his warder. "And clear the room."

His men began to herd the little band through the door.

"Mistress Blackaller!" he called.

Rachel stopped.

"Come here!"

She walked up, no taller at her full height than he sitting once more in his chair.

"You may think ye have won this day, woman," he said softly. "But ye shall rue it."

Her look of contempt traveled unhurriedly from his head down to his slumped body and spread legs, to his buckled shoes and back again, and then she walked away.

Outside, the family was hallooing and jumping about, and Joel, being led off on a pack pony, was looking back at them and jangling his chains idiotically like a dancing bear. Only John greeted his mother solemnly.

"Do you know what 'tis like for a man in the Navy?" he asked, accompanying her to her horse.

"Aye," she answered.

" 'Tis said to be worse by far than any gaol," he went on. "With floggings and hangings and men rotten with scurvy and pox and all manner of sicknesses, typhoid, cholera and the like, and only maggot-ridden ship's biscuit, salt meat and meal for rations."

Gathering the reins in one hand, she confronted him squarely.

"John—there were no other way. Joel is no boy of spirit to rebel and be flogged or such. He could die as easy from disease in prison, and maggots is no doubt better than no vittles at all. 'Tis a life in the open air and if he do learn to work, he can better himself. This were the only way and I'll hear no more on it."

She placed her small foot firmly into his outstretched hand, mounted and cantered on ahead of the rest down the drive and out of the park gates and on to Yellaton.

A week later, she went alone to Plymouth and watched the seamen boarding the *Niger*. It had taken nearly a day to discover that the thousand-ton frigate was bound for the West Indies to defend the wealth of the sugar plantations against the French. It was a campaign which was to cost England the lives of forty thousand men, mainly through disease rather than battle.

The ship creaked in the water. Its figurehead of an ugly woman with breasts like cannon shot heaved warningly. Matelots hung like flies in the web of ratlines from its three masts, and its sails, wrapped as though around corpses, lay supine along every spar.

The port was teeming with mariners and dock workers unloading barrels and mighty, cloth-wrapped loads and wooden boxes, some the size of houses, from merchant ships. And there was a black man, tall and shiny-skinned, with huge, dark eyes, striding loosely along the quay, arms relaxed, moving easily from the hips in a way she had never seen a man walk, like a confident black cat. He saw her and smiled, teeth displayed white and suddenly, so that she started. Had she expected him to have black teeth, too?

Then the throng was roughly parted by armed militia and a double line of men, shackled together, shuffled through the gap toward the ship. The woman beside Rachel shrieked, rushed forward and flung herself on a skeletal, pallid prisoner. She was shoved aside and to the ground by a guard, and tears rolled down the convict's face. A united wail arose from the onlookers as men and women wept aloud and cried to those they were seeing for the last time, and Rachel saw her son, Joel Blackaller, on the far side of the two rows. An armed man barred her from breaking through and running to him.

"Joel! Joel!" she screamed.

He turned and grinned, raising a manacled hand. A soldier cuffed him with the stock of a musket and he shook his head after the crack and ambled on, still grinning, like a young, friendly dog.

Up the gangplank, bare feet scuffing, chains clanking, men bawling orders, striking blows, the crowd ululating with grief.

Nothing more happened for over two hours. The prisoners had disappeared from sight into the unimaginable bowels of the vessel. One or two naval officers in smart uniforms stood idly on board, watching crew members go about their enigmatic tasks. On shore, the families watched and waited in tense silence.

Then the ship's bell rang twice and there was a shout. "Hands to the capstan! Loblolly boys!"

And then another. "Hands make sail!"

Sailors seethed up the rigging, topmen leaning out at spinning height, and the bows eased away from the land. The forestay and topsail yards bloomed with sail, petals of canvas unfurling and filling with the breeze, and the ship lifted like a tumescent, spumy cloud and glided, faster than seemed possible, across the water: past the island of St. Nicholas and soundless into Plymouth Sound. And the *Niger* was gone.

All the way home Rachel told herself he had been no good, feeble and a wastrel, influenced by any man with a loud manner and a gold-topped cane, following his own whims and fancies without thought to their consequences, always seduced by worthless flamboyance. She reminded herself in the pitching post chaise from Plymouth to Exeter of his deceit and unhelpfulness, and through each sleepless hour of the overnight stay at the Black Lion Inn she recalled the troublesome episodes of his infancy and adolescence, and on the long ride back to Beara the following day she assured herself over and over that no other action could have been taken without sacrificing the entire family.

But beneath the frantic tumble of her thoughts lay a bleak and constant ache, and the picture of his naive last wave and smile kept returning to her mind. She pushed it away again and again, and desolately wanted him back.

Jane Clarke came frequently to Yellaton over the next weeks and her presence soothed in the exclusive way of an old familiar friend. She brought her sewing and sat quietly by the parlor window during the light evenings and Rachel could talk to her as to no one else. Jane listened as she detailed the whole unhappy affair again and again, each time reaching the same conclusion—that she could not have sold the land.

"You did right, Rachel," Jane said. "There were no other way. You did right."

"My children do not think so," Rachel pointed out, tears beginning to shine.

Jane leaned across the small table and took her hand. "They be young and have forgot how hard it was. But we know, Rachel. No vittles and no coppers and no prospect. You and me have been without, and known the fearsomeness of it. Do not keep chastising yourself, my dear. You did right."

Rachel looked at her friend gratefully, remembering all the times they had shared since their first sight of each other in High Chilham church; the secrets they had exchanged, giggling, as young girls, and the deeper confidences of later years; the comfort they had given each other in times of trouble. Jane had cared for Rachel after the birth of each child and Rachel had eased Jane's penury whenever her own circumstances allowed. All her loves and tragedies had been revealed to Jane and no one on earth knew her better.

"You be a good friend to me and no mistake," she said. "And I'll find a way to repay you for all you've done one day."

Jane grinned. "Just give me a fine gentleman wi' a powdered wig and silver buckles as my reward, thank 'ee kindly."

Rachel squeezed her hand tightly and managed to smile too.

"That's better," said the other, and carefully folded her work away.

On the moor, the land was discipline. Rachel roused household and workers and sent them stumbling into the dusk before dawn to begin work, and day after day she joined them to plow and harrow, to weed the corn and roll the grass, to pull lambs from ewes and calves from cows, to hoe, long, backbreaking afternoons, between the turnip plants, to cut and stack the hay. She worked them all until their clothes were wet through with sweat, until they were too exhausted to speak, had barely the strength to eat and could just manage to crawl to their beds and fall into heavy, dreamless anesthesia. Then, as light died each night, she would force her punished body to the window and frown grimly over Yellaton and Lutterell and Arnwood, as though daring the land to betray her.

It was the biggest harvest ever reaped. Men, women and children from the village gathered it in under the blazing August sun, reaping and binding, the horses staggering under their overburdened wagons. The barn filled, and yet more loads kept rolling into the yard. Rachel Jedder looked at the abundance of it without pleasure. She thought of the cost and wondered where the boy was now and whether he still lived.

Jedder Wolcot was ambushed, arrested and charged with highway robbery on the other side of South Molton, not far from the cottage of Mistress Margaret Cole, a deserted woman with whom he often kept company. Later, she was seen dressed in a fine gown and with gold to spend on market day.

This time Jelinger Were made no mistakes. The case was transferred to Exeter and the prisoner sent there to be kept in gaol until the next Assizes, when he was brought before judge and jury, several of whom were known to the squire and had received a case each of the finest French brandy only that morning.

Squire Whidbourne and one of his farm servants, Jelinger Were and two of his men, and a constable from South Molton gave evidence that, acting upon anonymous information received, they had waited the night in a thicket close to where the Chulmleigh road was narrowed by the drop to a valley on one side and a steeply wooden incline on the other.

Just before first light, when the post from Exeter was due, Jedder Wolcot had arrived and concealed himself and his horse in the fringe of trees. When the mail coach-and-four came into view, he had ridden out, masked and with a pair of pistols in his hands, ordered it to a halt and its passengers to surrender their valuables. At that, Jelinger Were and his company had sprung forward, their guns cocked, and taken him.

"Excellent. Excellent," the judge murmured, audibly. "You are to be congratulated on bringing such a rogue to justice."

As the jury returned, after taking less than ten minutes to reach its verdict, he glared round the oak-lined room. The pause, as the twelve men shuffled into place, seemed hours long. Fear galloped in Rachel's throat and beads of ice-cold sweat broke out on her forehead. She stared at each in turn, willing him, willing them with all her might to free her son. She fixed her mind and her strange eyes, which seemed so full of occult power, on the foreman as he stepped forward and, without being conscious of it, she stopped breathing.

John leaned over the rail of the gallery. Jedder, by the bar of the Court, looked straight ahead. There was a restless shifting of documents by the clerk at the desk behind the judge. The foreman spoke.

"Guilty, m'lord."

The judge rapped for attention and turned to glower at the prisoner.

"Jedder Tresider Wolcot. This Court finds you guilty as charged of highway robbery, the sentence for which is that you return to the prison from whence you came; from thence you must be drawn to the place of execution; when you come there you must be hanged by the neck until you are dead. And God Almighty be merciful to your soul."

At the words, Jedder went white, but did not move. Rachel felt her heart halt and her blood take a mercurial plunge as the room went dark before her eyes and she swayed into John's arm. By the time her vision cleared, Jedder had gone and the fat attorney from Barnstaple was no longer nearby.

Breaking from John's hold, she rushed from the courtroom and down the stairs to the hall of the building, searching the groups of people for the lawyer as she ran. Jelinger Were, surrounded by his cronies, saw her and shouldered his way to her side.

"Did I not tell ye, ye would rue making an enemy of me, Mistress Blackaller?" he said. "And I am not done yet. Thy precious boys will be picked off one by one until ye give up that land."

But she did not hear him, for she had caught sight of the lawyer and was already straining to him.

"Maister Palfriman! Maister Palfriman! What's to be done? You got to save him! You cannot let him die!" She caught his arm.

The man looked down with embarrassed pity, his kerchief flapping in agitation, the stink of his sweat increased by his discomfort.

"There is nothing more I can do, Mistress Blackaller. The Court has passed judgment."

He tried to disengage himself, but she hung on and howled.

"No! No! You got to do summat. You cannot let it happen. He is my son. My best son."

People stopped and looked. Jelinger Were nudged Squire Whidbourn and laughed aloud. John reached her and drew her into the shelter of his greatcoat and led her sobbing away.

Each day for the next week they visited Jedder in Exeter Castle gaol, taking him hot food and sitting near the barred window to escape the stench of the soiled and crowded cell, trying to say normal and cheerful things, but pressed down by the unendurable knowledge that each minute was numbered, so that their words came slowly and there were long pauses between each subject.

"I've writ to the King hisself, with John here's aid," she told him. "I've writ what a fine son you be and how you be needed to work the farm and how you never done no hurt to no one. I've begged His Majesty's mercy."

It was the final day. The following afternoon he would be taken through the city to the gibbet at Heavitree.

"The King will surely grant a pardon. Just wait you and see. The Governor will receive his command and order a stop to it." She was babbling.

Jedder put a hand on hers and asked, "Have you the pearls with thee, Mother?"

"Yes," she whispered.

"Wear them for me tomorrow and be bold."

Rachel broke down against him and he stroked her head for a moment, repeating desperately, "Be bold. Be bold."

Feeling ashamed, she took control of herself and raised her head, forcing a smile, and saw relief cross his features. John shook his brother's hand with odd formality and then, quickly and unexpectedly, embraced him, and Rachel kept the smile on, like a polished bronze mask, until the prison door clanged shut behind them and they were in the street once more. Then she allowed John to help her back to the inn, where she went straight to her room, locked the door and sat on the plain wooden chair facing the view over the town.

At daybreak she was still there, awake and wide-eyed. As the cocks began to crow in the backyards of the houses, she stood up without stretching, poured icy water from the ewer into the basin and splashed her cheeks. She dressed with special care, checking each fastening, arranging each ruffle and ribbon on the plum-dark gown. The veil from the matching hat misted her disciplined expression as she lifted the choker of pearls from its case and clipped it on. In the old silvered looking glass, through the net of the veil, the circlet of precious beads looked like a shining scar around her neck.

The cart rumbled through the prison gates, led by a closed carriage carrying a parson, the sheriff and two sheriff's officers. Jedder, flanked by a pair of warders, did not seem to see his mother and brother following on foot behind. People joined them on the way, greeting and nudging and pushing each other; men arm-in-arm with their wives, women hurrying their children; merry, as though on a holiday, to join the crush at the site itself.

The scaffold had been erected the previous day. Its timbers looked pale and soft, as though encased in antler velvet, and the resin scent of the freshly cut wood filled the air like a forest.

The cart was backed under it. Jedder, hands secured in a halter and carrying the nosegay given to those about to be "turned off," was pulled straight beneath the rope. The parson descended, black-robed and reluctant, from the coach.

"You, prisoner, who for wickedness and sin, after many mercies shown you, are now appointed to die . . ."

Rachel's son jerked his chin, as though dismissing a beggar, and turned his face defiantly away from the proffered blindfold.

The crowd, grown excited, bawled jokes.

"Next shake will send his head toppling."

" 'Twill nod off!"

"Which comes of being caught napping!"

" 'Tis enough to put a man off his sleep for life!"

The hangman asked the traditional pardon of the victim, was granted it brusquely, and brought the loop of cord over his head. Jedder's deep brown eyes gazed down and met those of his mother and he smiled Will's smile at her.

The horse was whipped. The cart lurched forward. The rope jerked. The man's neck broke at right angles to his body, which twitched and writhed like a hooked fish meeting air. The mob yodeled and huzzahed, mouths full of broken teeth open wide with glee. Rachel Jedder watched, unblinking, until the death throes ceased and only the light wind moved the remains of her boy gently to and fro. Then she turned and left the place.

John wiped the blood from the back of his hand where her nails had cut in, looked up to his dead brother and spoke an unheard farewell, then followed her.

Twenty-four hours later he was to return to the gallows in a hired wagon and watch while a couple of young workmen cut the rope and let his brother's rigid body fall to hit the ground with an echoing crack of breaking bone. Lifting it tenderly, he laid it on the floor of the cart. Rigor mortis had set the head at its horrible angle of death. For Rachel's sake, John forced it into a more natural position and pulled the lids down over the wild, glazed eyes and tried to push the swollen tongue back into the mouth, but the blackened skin could not be disguised, and finally he shook his head sadly and covered the corpse with a linen sheet.

The thirty-four-mile journey to Yellaton took all the next day and was completed without speech. In fact, Rachel Jedder had not spoken since her last prison visit to Jedder. She was not even aware of the body in the cart behind her, for her soul was trapped by time in the last moments of his life. Within herself, the unendurable image of her adored son on the scaffold was indelible, the scene of his dying replaying over and over again. She saw nothing else.

The coffin, made by Jack Clarke, the local carpenter and undertaker, had been delivered to the house, together with a carved wooden cross, and the family on foot followed them back to the village and the grave-yard.

The coffin was lowered. The rector said a few words and prayed. The earth rattled onto its surface from the shovel. The cross was erected.

"Here lieth Jedder Tresider Wolcot, beloved son of Rachel. 1767–1796."

Autumn-brown leaves fluttered in their hundreds from overhead to cover the mound, and Rachel left the little group and walked back to her home alone.

Beara, ever bleak, shrugged the wind from its back and rolled on to the horizon. Created before time in a chaos of warring magnetic fields, every inhospitable fold of its surface formed by ancient, transcendental catas-trophes of scission and collision, heat and ice and flood and eruption, it was eternally indifferent. Mankind could destroy itself. The insects could inherit and reign and consume every remaining particle of animal and vegetable and then cannibalize themselves to extinction. Another perdur-ably long cycle of the dividing single cell would begin and grow to original, monstrous life forms, unimaginable parasites succeeding to temporary rule and self-annihilation, over and over, again and again. But the moor, rooted to the core of the earth, would revolve infinitely through space, reducing all tragedy to meaninglessness.

For days after the death of her dearest son, Rachel lay on her bed without moving or speaking. She refused all food and ignored all at-tempts to persuade her to return to activity. It was as though her soul had died with him and she was in suspension somewhere between life and death. Occasionally tears would well up and trickle to the pillow, un-noticed and without causing any spasm of sorrow to shatter her expres-sion of unseeing composure.

In the dark, thick mud of grief, she saw all her struggles as having been pointless, her achievements as just gaudy reeds covering a quick-sand of destruction, her existence as being without reason.

Another October blazed, making the land hot with colors, as though celebrating its own fruitfulness and the glory of its harvest with balloons and streamers and confetti and the wind like a noisy street band. As it invaded her senses through the open windows, Rachel Jedder felt betrayed.

For the first time, she questioned her own purpose and found no satisfactory answer. She herself could survive comfortably in a hut on a single acre, keeping poultry and a goat and growing sufficient vegetables and a patch of wheat for flour, so what had the accruing of farms and stock and gold been for? The land had cost her lover and sons. All her adult years had been spent in hard and serious sacrifice to its demands. Yet there was no one who might not simply dispose of it or neglect it after her death. Her adoration of it had brought only the malice and envy of her own kind; but, if it were not to share and enjoy with another, a fellow human being, where was the reason to it?

Will and Robert and Jedder, the three she loved most, had gone. Outside, the land, in its eternal guardianship of birth and death, flaunted the fulfillment of its role. Rachel felt full of hatred and decided, at last, to sell.

John relayed her resolution to Jelinger Were and made arrangements with the solicitor, Jonathan Palfriman, for the necessary contracts to be drawn up and the finance agreed. Rachel stayed in her room, aloof.

Isolated and increasingly lonely, she was locked into the past, haunted by memories of Will and Robert and Jedder, who had each understood and motivated her so well. Now, there was no one left to confide in and no one to give advice. Confusion mixed up her thoughts, and whole days passed without her being aware that they had come and gone. After a lifetime of toil and stress, she felt tired and wasted and wished simply to die herself.

"Mother, are you awake?" John was bending over her. " 'Tis time to rise. Today, we be going to Barnstaple to sign the parchments. Would you have Emma help 'ee, or lill' Jane?"

Rachel shook her head and he went away quietly, leaving her staring with pinpoint pupils into the ray-filled, blinding east. A half hour passed.

Suddenly she arose, holding tightly to the bedpost as the quickness of the movement made her feel dizzy. Then she dressed in old working clothes, went down the stairs, opened the front door and hurried toward Yellaton copse.

"Mother! Mother! Where be 'ee to?" John called after her. " 'Tis time we departed for town."

At the sound she broke into a stumbling trot, which took her to the damp path with its slippery leaves and enclosed fungal smell. The bushes needed cutting back, she noticed automatically, as they caught in her skirt, slowing her down. Then she was on Beara and crossing where the gray dog had loomed from the fog and frightened off Walter Riddaway and Matthew Claggett so long before.

240

On to Great Wood to follow the meandering stream, reflectively pausing to peer through its trailing weeds to see a shoal of minnows motionless against the brown stone bed, she came to the reach of the lake, at last. A compulsion made her return to the clearing in the shrubs by the inlet where she had first soaked her blistered feet and seen Squire Waddon on his fine horse, cantering across Braddon Park.

Leaning over the bank, she saw her own face made young again in the still, black water, and, on impulse, she discarded all her clothes and slid back into its ice-cold womb. As she was enveloped, the whole of her early life returned to her consciousness with pristine clarity: the brutal childhood years in the workhouse, and later at Wame's farm, half-starved and grossly overworked, unloved, unrewarded and without hope, until the gift of Jedder's land. She remembered every detail of the long journey and the indescribable revelation of her own destiny as she scratched up the first handful of earth from the running foot of the hare's-leg field.

Emerging from the lake, she lay on the ivy-covered ground to dry, full of thought, not noticing the cold, pressed into the musky leafmold, and when at last she dressed again, the mien of shut-in despair had been replaced by an old familiar look of tenacity and intent.

Rachel Jedder climbed the moor once more, but instead of returning to Yellaton, she turned south and walked more than a mile to where Great Wood tapered off to a straggle of saplings and the heath was unexpectedly split by a rock-strewn gully. This she traced to where it fanned without warning into a sheltered, fenced-off plot surrounding a one-roomed cottage.

This garden had been most assiduously cultivated, and although part of it had been set aside for the usual growing of vegetables, the weed-free clumps of plants in the rest were quite different from those normally found outside country dwellings. Many were unfamiliar even to Rachel, although she recognized borage and woodruff and hyssop, feather-leaved fennel and the umbrella seed heads of angelica. Her fingers absently picked a leaf of mint, crushed it and pressed the clean scent to her nose.

Hieritha Delve was great-aunt to eleven-year-old Jake Delve, who had been hanged by Jelinger Were for running away from his apprenticeship and taking five pounds of his master's money with him. She had seen Rachel from the web-curtained window and came to the door to beckon her inside. The shadowed interior was hung with bunches of drying plants and every surface covered with clay dishes of seeds and leaves. The smell cut into the nostrils with a saw-toothed edge.

The two sat by the burning log fire, Rachel talking and the old woman mumbling over cups of elderberry wine. She was toothless and almost bald, the last wisps of white hair like strands of mist round her skull, her hands knotted like twigs.

241

Folk came to her for remedies and ancient knowledge. John bought many of his veterinary supplies from her. Her speech seemed to make little sense most of the time, yet she could make barren women fertile and stop the arrival of unwanted babies. Young Roger Babb, whose new wife had publicly laughed at him after their wedding night, had been seen coming from her cottage and Annie Babb had not laughed again, but proved a remarkably docile girl thereafter. The village pondered over whether the potion had improved his virility or subdued her critical faculties, and Roger had taken to strutting.

Rachel spoke earnestly and long, making a restraining gesture each time the old woman shook her head and began to stand up. She felt in the small cloth drawbag at her waist for coins and held them out, but still the herbalist refused.

Finally, she crossed to whisper fiercely in her ear, "Did you see your young Jake dangle? He were just a child, but he be a corpse now, like my Jedder. Don't 'ee want to pay off new squire for such foulness? 'Twere murder, Hieritha Delve."

The faded eyes met her scrutiny and sharpened and the arthritic hands shook. Then the crone stood and trailed, hunchbacked, to the dresser to take out a little silver box. Opening it carefully, she spooned a portion of the powder it contained into a twist of oiled rag. Thrusting this at Rachel Jedder with a lot of muttering, she pushed her out into the garden and slammed the door quickly behind her.

Rachel did not go straight home. She returned to Great Wood instead and from its badger-haunted glades collected purple berries and red-spotted toadstools and fringed leaves of yew into her gathered skirt.

The family was grouped worriedly in the kitchen when she returned.

"I changed my mind. There will be no sale," she said, before they had time to question.

Emma and Jane cheered and hugged each other at the news. Dick Blackaller, who had never looked at her without brooding resentment since Joel's conviction, went out to the yard without comment, and John put his arm around her, expressed how pleased he was that she had left her bed, and agreed that she was right to keep the farms. The two apprentices giggled with relief in the corner and she managed to smile on them before clearing everyone from the room and instructing them not to come back until summoned.

Her oldest cooking pot was a round black cauldron, its iron so pitted and rusted with age that it was now used only for boiling up peelings and vegetable waste for the hogs and the fowl. She half filled it with water, tipped in the contents of her skirt and hooked it onto the chimney crane. The fire was burning well, but she blew on its embers with the bellows until the water boiled, when, very carefully, she added the powder obtained from the herbalist.

The steam became thick and blue. It made her eyes sting and run, and

242

her mouth go dry, and her lips itch and swell. For an hour the pot simmered, until all the berries, leaves and fungi were broken down and the liquid reduced, and then Rachel emptied it into a muslin to strain into an old wooden bucket with a fitted lid.

Leaving the house by its front entrance once more, she secreted the bucket under a whin bush to be collected again after dark. The muslin and old cooking pot were carried to the farthest end of the kitchen garden, where she buried them in an unused corner and covered the disturbed earth with brambles.

The night was unusually quiet, without wind or owl screech and the sounds of her footsteps were magnified by the overall stillness so that they brushed and crunched through the heather, and her own breath followed her like a stranger. The full autumn moon, massive and almost blood-red, gored out the way. In the three miles over heath and common, she did not hear the scuffle of another creature or the far-off gnar of a fox or the rustle of leaves.

Then the barking clanged and grated against the silence, mauling it to pieces, and Rachel, shrinking into the blackness behind the great house, threw a couple of mutton bones, brought for the purpose, toward the furor, which diminished into snarling and growling and a final yelp.

There was little time. Gentlemen went to bed after midnight. Servants arose before five A. M. She must do the deed and be home and abed unseen. It was the eye of the night.

The latch on the grooms' door to the courtyard clicked like an explosion, and an ever wakeful horse looked curiously from a loose-box and snorted noisily. She reached the well and leaned over its wall.

Far below, the ominous red moon was perfectly reflected in the water. She tipped out the thick liquid from her bucket. There was a little pause and then the reflection shattered into a thousand blood-soaked fragments in a distant splash.

The newborn son, his heir, suddenly had convulsions and died almost instantaneously. No one knew the reason, for the babe was still at the breast. The mother, Jelinger Were's second wife, and half his age, complained pettishly of the taste of the food, and then she, too, died. A dozen hogs died next, and even the strongest in the household went down with stomach cramps and sickness and the most violent headaches.

As was proper, the whole village went to the funerals of the squire's lady and son. Rachel Jedder watched the boxes drop into the earth and pictured again her favorite son's coffin and felt neither pity nor guilt. The man's tear-veined eyes met hers and held the look until he knew that it was she who had caused his bereavement, and his face crumpled.

Jelinger Were was an iron man, a man whose ambition and ability to recognize and seize opportunity had brought him wealth; a man who had exploited the new industrial patents and cheap labor of the north to the full; a self-made man.

The pleas of the weak and the sick had moved him only to contempt, and the sight of half-starved children laboring in his mills had aroused nothing but impatience at their clumsiness. But his marriage to the spoiled twenty-three-year-old daughter of minor county gentry had been the highlight of his life.

Her fastidious ways, her high, petulant voice, and her closets full of luxurious robes and petticoats of lace and lawn had continually enchanted him. Nothing had been too good for her. Her every whim had been satisfied, and for her he had moved from the harshly certain north to the soft-bellied south, to the fitting setting of the elegant house and estate of Braddon and his position as squire. When she had given birth to a son, Jelinger Were had known he was invincible. Riches, power and glory would come to this boy, and he was going to ensure it.

Now they were both gone, his lady and his heir, the symbols of his achievement, and he, a shadow of his former self, was standing on a dank, alien plot surrounded by half-witted bumpkins who had never accepted him. Not one aristocratic family of Devon was represented among the mourners. They had excluded him from their society long before. He was an outsider, hated and alone, and somehow that witch-woman Jedder had brought it all about. Tears of self-pity gushed, and he turned away.

Almost two weeks passed before the trouble at Braddon Manor was traced to the contaminated well. By that time, Jelinger Were had packed up and returned to the north, a heartbroken man. The well was filled in and a new one sunk and the whole estate was put on the market, for sale as one lot or as separate farms.

Rachel Jedder took the stage to Bristol and went to the house of a man her dead son had once mentioned, and there she sold all the jewelry he had given her except the choker and bracelet of pearls. With the money and the savings in the Cornish tin box, she went to the sale.

Seth Bartle and Amos Clarke managed to buy back their old holdings and Stephen Pincombe returned to Kingford. Sir Thomas Carew bought all the rest of the Braddon property except for Dadland, a three-hundred-and-fifty-acre farm, with grazing rights on the Beara side of High Chilham. That became Jedder's land.

John rode with her to take possession and they admired the buildings and the quality of the soil. There was a charming house, which she gave to Emma, newly married to Peter Spurway. Fresh water was in good supply and there was mature woodland for timber.

All was in excellent order and yet she did not feel the elation and sense of achievement which had marked the acquisition of every other plot in the past. The gorse-bound slope beside Arnwood, Arnwood itself and the valley, Lutterell's and, above all, Moses Bottom, her very first purchase—each had induced the orgasmic peaks in her life. This time, it was a mere business deal, an investment. She felt nothing, not even the satisfaction of revenge. It was a victory without joy.

Rachel, once such a high-spirited girl, was now a woman who rarely smiled. The early losses of Will Tresider and Robert Wolcot had caused almost frenzied misery, but could not be compared with the anguish she felt over Jedder's death. It seemed to run in her veins so that her whole body ached, and even the touch of a draft made her skin creep; her stomach could accept barely enough food to keep her alive, and her lungs were so constricted that they could draw only the shallowest breaths. She lost weight alarmingly and her hair combed out in handfuls when dressed each morning. Her extraordinary eyes seemed to have become even larger, so that they dominated her appearance and were full of such agony that others could not look into them.

She went about the daily running of the farms systematically, working with young Jane, who had been taught to read, write and count, on the accounts, reassuring the farm laborers at Dadland Farm that they would be kept on, supervising the winter threshing and storing of the corn in three barns. Yet the tasks, usually so absorbing, were dull, and her concentration was so poor that nothing held her attention. It was as though there was a distance between herself and everything she did, as though she were no longer truly involved.

Although their chatter was irksome, she tried to surround herself with people and immerse herself in detail. It was the only way to pass the time, and she was relieved if half an hour went by without acute consciousness of her bereavement, although the undercurrent of woe never stopped flowing. She longed for the days to lengthen so that they could be filled with activity and the sad, wakeful nights reduced to brief spells of exhausted oblivion.

Her regular ride of inspection was always postponed until the last possible moment. The total area she now owned was too large to be covered daily and so she looked over each of the four sections in turn and the area of moorland grazed by Jedder stock on the fifth day of each week. But these hours spent alone on horseback always intensified her wretchedness. They offered too much opportunity to be melancholy, and the more ordered and promising the land became toward spring, the more confused and ambivalent she felt.

Slowly she realized that, throughout her entire life, she herself had been the source of strength in all her relationships. Even as a young girl, she had been the one to take the initiative, to decide and guide, to plan and deal. In their most poverty-stricken years, her children had known they would never be allowed to starve or be without the security of home. Will Tresider and Robert Wolcot had been inspired and encouraged by her, and she had survived and destroyed Harry Blackaller.

Now, all the feelings of bewilderment and sorrow were reduced to a simple need to be received into warm arms, to be sheltered by the stability of someone else, loved and protected by another's certainty, to be supported by a lover, dependent upon a brother, to lean on a father.

The family had their own lives to lead. John was a good and conscientious son, but he and Urith walked out together during all his free time in their seemingly endless engagement. Emma was completely obsessed by her new husband, Peter, about whom she talked compulsively. Richard had become a bitter and malevolent man and kept to himself, working on the holdings sullenly and clearing off to follow his own pursuits whenever possible. Jane, at fifteen, was still dependent. Although she had a dear friend and confidante in Jane Clarke, there was no one with whom Rachel could wholly share either adversity or happiness.

Lost in thought and unaware that her face was wet again with tears, she rode, slumped in the saddle, along the edge of the beautiful Arn valley. The snowdrops were out as frail, white dew beneath the bare-branched trees, and a dormouse took sleepy advantage of the mild day to visit its store of seeds. A mistle thrush sang its song, but she did not notice.

Nor did she see, at first, the bundle of rags heaped in a hollow under the hedge. Had not the horse shied from it, almost throwing her, she would have ridden straight past. The rags moved and turned into the startled figure of a vagrant, who sat up and stared at her. His clothes were in tatters and the sole of one boot had parted from its upper, exposing a blistered foot. His features were obscured by a thick, red beard and by his tangled red hair, which was shoulder length. He staggered to his feet, and despite his being very thin, he was seen to be a big-boned, well-built man.

"What you doing here?" The woman, surprised out of her reverie and slightly unnerved by his unkempt aspect, spoke sharply. "This be private land. Be off with 'ee."

"Rachel Jedder," the tramp said, "do you not know me?"

His accent was not that of a laborer, although it had a local ring, and the voice was familiar. He stepped forward and she looked at him more closely. Then her hand flew to her mouth in shock.

"Squire? Squire? Is it you? Squire. Squire Waddon!"

246

CHAPTER FIFTEEN

It was inconceivable that Beara's leading landowner, with his proud bearing and flamboyant ways, could have been reduced to this bedraggled, humble tramp. Rachel stared with unconcealed dismay, blatantly comparing him with her memory of the man, leonine and muscular in velvets and costly lace, and unable to believe what she saw.

He looked back at her warily, ready to back away at the first hint of rejection, like a dog not sure of its welcome.

There was a silence before she blurted out, "Mercy on us! How did you come to this, Squire? What's become of all the money from Braddon?"

In her amazement, Rachel had forgotten good manners and tact.

Charles Waddon shrugged. "Games o' chance and creditors," he grinned, spreading his hands in a carefree gesture.

Her quick eyes saw beyond the nonchalance to the lines of strain and the way the cheekbones now angled his once full face and how his broad shoulders were bent. He swayed a little as he stood.

"Could not your wife's family have helped?" she wondered.

He shook his head. "Lady Ann died over a year ago."

"When did you last eat?" was her next question, and, as he shrugged again, she patted the space behind the saddle on the horse's back and instructed, "Climb on and we'll return to Yellaton and put some beef into you."

He hesitated, eyebrows beetling in a frown and his head turning away.

"Be you ashamed folk will see you? Or ashamed to eat in my house?" she goaded, with purposeful cruelty.

"Neither, Rachel Jedder, but it seems you have troubles enough." He had had time to look at her properly and see the skin blotched from weeping.

"Perhaps we could both do with a bite of good red meat inside us. The world always looks better then."

She had to help him up behind her, and before long they were both sitting over platters piled high with hot food and tankards filled with cider, and there was little talk until he leaned back in his chair and belched with loud satisfaction.

She viewed him with a mixture of pride and sympathy. It was oddly pleasing to have him at her table. After all, even though he had been reduced to such destitution, he was still Squire Waddon.

"It is good to see you again," she said, beckoning him to warm himself in the inglenook.

His clothes steamed as she told how disappointed she had been to miss bidding him farewell on his departure from Braddon, and then, without intention, the whole report of the three direful years of Jelinger Were's control over the district was spilling out and she heard herself talking openly of Joel's sentence and the death of her beloved Jedder for the first time.

Charles Waddon listened and nodded, his senses dizzy from the sudden intake of alcohol and nutrition and the heat from the logs. Then she was kneeling beside him, crying into his lap, and he put down a weak hand and stroked her black hair, vaguely surprised to see a few gray hairs, for he could not imagine her growing old.

It was as though her prayer had been answered and she had been given refuge. She crept into the crook of his arm and curled against the damp jacket and mumbled and sobbed, releasing all the sorrow and tension and malignity at last. His voice murmured comfort, and the fire eased and melted their limbs into relaxed and tender twining and his head came to rest on hers, and in the end, they both fell asleep.

When Emma came in for family supper with Peter Spurway a couple of hours later, she was humiliated to find her mother lying so brazenly in the embrace of a dirty tramp. As the girl tried to hustle her husband from the kitchen, Rachel awoke, but Charles Waddon, exhausted from neglect and cold winter months spent in the open, lolled back against the wall without waking.

"Fetch Dick and give him a hand to put this man to bed," Rachel directed her son-in-law, ignoring her daughter's vexed protests.

The squire did not even stir as the two men carted his tall, lightweight frame up the narrow stairs and deposited it on the nearest bed.

"Take them old rags off and make him comfortable," Rachel insisted, and watched while the two reluctantly did as they were bid.

When they had gone, she fetched a pair of scissors and gently snipped at the straggling beard until it was short and neatly shaped and then she stood and looked down at him affectionately.

"A long time ago, you saved a starveling pauper maid and come to her aid often enough after," she said softly. "Now 'tis time you were repaid, Charles Waddon. You won't never want again."

There was an empty cottage on Lutterell farm and she took him to it the next morning. Downstairs it had a main room with a tiny kitchen and pantry off, and a single bedroom upstairs. As she showed them to him, she recalled the great paneled hall and the drawing room with its high, ornate ceiling at Braddon and was embarrassed.

" 'Tisn't much, Squire," she muttered, blushing. "Not for a gentleman like yourself."

He had bathed and she had trimmed his hair and given him Jedder's best velvet jacket and white breeches and a shirt with ruffles, and silver-buckled shoes which were too small, although he did not say so. Now, it was his turn to feel awkward.

"I am no squire any longer, Rachel. And how can I accept such an offer when I have no gold and cannot pay my way?"

"You will always be squire to me," she replied quickly. "And I ain't never forgot that but for you, I would have hanged long since. I got land aplenty now and 'tis much due to you. 'Twould favor me greatly if you would stay on here as my neighbor and friend."

"I cannot live off you, Rachel Jedder," he insisted.

"Oh, but you ain't going to. I thought of that," she answered pertly. "John has his business and makes his own way. Young Jane is almost growed and will no doubt wed afore long, and, with so much stock and the three farms, someone is needed to keep the accounts and such. You'll earn your keep all right, Charles Waddon."

"Done!" He roared with laughter and slapped her bottom in a return to his former manner. "Though I might have guessed there'd be a catch to it."

"I don't hold with idlers," she responded, smiling. "You can start to-morrow, Squire."

It was an arrangement which worked remarkably well. Charles Waddon, now a much wiser man than the rake who had dissipated home, family and fortune, treated his part of the bargain seriously.

He made a complete and detailed inventory and valuation of all the Jedder property, and his accurate calculations of future grain and stock requirements were to increase efficiency in the running of the farms. He opened and kept, with immaculate precision, a new set of books, so that it was possible to tell at a glance all the outgoings and incomings and to compare current with previous market prices. He paid out the wages and advised Rachel on the price of extra labor, and eventually took over hiring the teams of men and women for haysel and harvest.

At noon each day, he came to Yellaton and ate with the family, given pride of place at the opposite end of the table from the mistress of the house, when John was not there. Most evenings, he returned to talk over the day's affairs, and gradually these discussions began to include not merely farm matters but Rachel's personal confidences, her plans and hopes for the land and her children.

As the better weather came, once the tilling was done the two would sometimes ride off together across the moors, and they were seen at inns along the coast, with her laughing until her eyes brimmed at his jokes and him ebullient and sociable and generously buying ale for all, just like

249

his old self, except that he no longer visited the gaming rooms or took part in wagers.

People seeing them together exchanged looks, and later, words, reminding each other of how she had enjoyed his protection while he owned Braddon and that there had "allus been summat 'twixt they two, since her had taken Matthew Claggett's smallholding." It became common knowledge that they would soon marry.

Another summer of hot, industrious days and balmy evenings, brilliant with stars, and they stopped on the return from market to sit in the dark for a while by the River Taw and enjoy the tranquillity and marvel at the purity of the sky. Rachel took off her boots and sat with her head on his shoulder and her feet playing in the running water.

"I am minded to give a little push and turn you into a mermaiden I once found in my lake many years ago," he threatened mischievously.

She giggled and gripped his arm tightly. "Don't 'ee dare, Charles Waddon, or you'll come in with me."

" 'Twould be worth the wetting, if the ending were the same." He tipped her head and kissed her, almost flippantly at first and then with more pressure and gradually rising passion, both his arms tightening around her.

Rachel felt her body tense and her back arch, and as his hand moved upward from her waist, her breast lifted to fill his palm. The delicious heat fired her belly and her legs stirred. It was so long since she had made love, or even thought about it, and yet, at the man's touch, the familiar, driving need returned and surprised her with its power.

Shaken, she drew back, breathing fast and smiling self-consciously. Twigs snapped as an animal moved through the thicket behind them.

"Folk will think us a pair of foolish young things," she murmured, her eyes downcast.

"No matter," he replied and raised her to her feet with a quizzical look.

As they rode home, she screened herself with nervous chatter, to which he listened with tolerance. After the brutal years with Harry Blackaller, even the idea of physical contact had disgusted her, and, on reaching middle age, although she had still enjoyed male company, she never imagined the possibility of such desire reawakening. It took her unawares and was as forceful as the first ardent response to Jack Greenslade, the acrobat, in her girlhood.

Charles Waddon was clean-shaven and dressed with elegance again. He had put on weight and still rode with the unmistakable style and poise of a gentleman. Although landless and penniless and actually in her employ, to Rachel he was the squire, and his attention was complimentary. The blending of fascination and flattery confused her. As they clattered through High Chilham, she passed on rural news, to disguise her indecision.

250

"Stephen Pincombe was wanting to know about our tegs. Seems he might buy some to build up the new flock on Kingford; so I told him to talk to 'ee. And Seth Bartle wants twenty-five pound for that gray. 'Tis a fine beast, but too fine a price to my thinking and we have always kept mares, though we could carry a stallion now, I suppose."

"Without doubt," he could not resist agreeing roguishly, and he chuckled as she flushed and pushed her horse on ahead, keeping distance until they reached his cottage.

"Well, Rachel Jedder?" he asked, dismounting and preparing to help her.

She sighed pensively and considered him, her head on one side. It would be so easy to be lifted down and carried through the door and up the narrow staircase to the small whitewashed room.

"A woman like you should not be alone," he said earnestly. "And after all the years we've known each other, would it not be agreeable to settle down?"

She felt herself waiting and did not answer.

"We are not growing any younger," he continued. "Running the farms will become an increasing burden for you and one which should be shared."

Her mind became very still and alert, almost as though she were holding a mental breath.

"It is shared already," she answered, slowly. "I share it with you."

He took her hand and kissed it and then his hearty face beamed up.

"I shall wed you forthwith, next month, next week, tomorrow! But we won't wait until then," he said happily, holding out both arms. "Come! 'Tis time a good man tumbled you again, Mistress Jedder."

"You mistake me!" she protested.

"Never!" he enthused. "You have not changed, wench."

"Do you love me, Charles Waddon?" she asked, without leaning toward him.

"What a question! When you know I have always had the greatest fondness for you."

" 'Tis not what I asked," she pointed out, still ignoring his arms, which dropped back to his side.

"We would be very content as husband and wife. We know each other well and like each other. We are not too old to have a romp and you would no longer have to bother your head about the land. What more could we ask, at our age?"

"Much more," she replied with certainty. "Oh, I know as you means well, but I ain't ready to retire yet, and I ain't never going to wed again, though 'tis an honor that you have offered for me." She shook her head over him and went on, "I values your friendship above all, Squire, and hopes to keep it for the rest of my life, but it wouldn't do that friendship no good for me to come to your bed."

251

"Rachel," he pleaded, "you need someone to look after you, to care about you. If you are concerned that there would be talk, there's no need. People have seen us keeping company and they expect us to be churched."

"Do they, indeed?" Her eyebrows raised. "Well, they'll be disappointed. I have looked after myself for nigh on forty-seven year and 'tis how I intend to continue."

"I have expressed myself poorly. Damme, I never was good with words," he blurted, downcast.

"No, dear Charles," she responded, kindly, ruffling his hair with affection. "You be an honest man and you spoke it exactly the right way."

There were voices raised in the kitchen. They could be heard from the stable as she bedded down the horse. John's voice was unusually adamant and Dick Blackaller's carried clearly.

"I tell you, they was kissing and cuddling by the river down Umberleigh. I seen it with my own eyes."

"I'll not stand by while 'ee talks of our mother thus," John thundered. "We'll hear no more of such calumnies."

"Where think you her is now then, brother?" the other taunted. "She's coupled with him in that hovel she give him and, if we doesn't do summat quick, they'll be wed."

"My! What a stir if Mother should marry Squire! Some folks up High Chilham would be that envious," Emma burbled, a-twitter with excitement. "I don't know what you're troubling about, Dick. There don't seem naught amiss with the notion."

"You pea-brained drab! That begging old tramp is getting his hands on our land, all we worked for, our inheritance, and you don't see naught amiss!"

Rachel had walked silently across the yard to listen by the side of the window. John's response to his half-brother sounded more controlled.

"Don't take on so, Dick. Mother will provide well for all of us, and what if her do wed with Squire Waddon? He has mended his bad ways. He do live soberly now and, to my mind, would make her a fine companion."

"Squire Waddon! Squire Waddon!" Richard sneered. "He bain't no squire no more. He be no more than a pauper and our mother ain't going to be wed to no pauper. You can all think 'tis no matter, but I bain't going to let it rest, take my word on it."

"If they be set on it, I don't see how you can stop 'un," John pointed out reasonably. "You know how 'tis, once Mother determines on summat."

"Be sure I'll stop them and be rid of that trickster Waddon, once and for all," Richard vowed.

Rachel heard his feet stamp across the flagstone floor and she drew back into the shadows as the back door slammed and he strode past her toward the cart shed. She waited for about ten minutes and then entered the house, greeting the family without giving any sign of having overheard.

Almost two weeks later, she noticed the top drawer of her bedroom tallboy was slightly ajar. Trinkets and a few mementos were kept there, and the key, hidden in a shoe-shaped snuffbox on the table, was rarely used. She checked the contents carefully.

The wooden French fan given to her by Will Tresider was there, its lacquered flowers chipped with age. A cheap pillbox containing a lock of Will's hair; the lamb's-head walnut spoon Robert Wolcot had carved for John; one of Joel's cravats; a small pearl-and-enamel pendant, a surprising gift from John; a set of Jedder's silver buttons, a pair of his silver buckles and a miniature likeness painted by an Exeter artist on ivory and also framed in silver—all were there. She handled them one by one. Lastly she opened the slim box and turned pale. The satin lining was bare. The precious pearl choker and bracelet had gone.

Strangely, her first feeling was one of relief. They were an unbearable reminder of the day her son was hanged, and they had not been worn since.

She crossed to the window and gazed to the clouded south, wondering who, with access to the room, could have stolen them.

Most days Jane Clarke came up from Lutterell, where she now cooked and kept house for the farm workers, to see her daughter, Meg, who lived and worked at Yellaton, but it was unthinkable that either of them would have done such a thing. None of the laborers or their wives could have had the opportunity. Little Robin, the workhouse stableboy, who slept in the house, would not have dared, although it was just possible that young Lucy, the dairymaid, might have found them pretty and taken them to try on thinking they would not be missed for a while.

The woman went to the girl's room over the old shippen and quickly searched its bare surfaces and beneath the straw pallet, knowing she was wasting her time, but realizing that this left only the members of her own family to suspect.

John would no more have stolen from his mother than pocketed church gold, and Emma had neither the nerve nor the wit to dream of such a crime, nor would Jane have touched another's belongings, but Richard Blackaller had both gall and brains, and plenty of opportunity to dispose of jewelry through his disreputable acquaintances across the county.

Rachel went resolutely to his room, which had been used to store apples and bunches of dried herbs many years ago and still retained their sweet and earthy smell. His cupboard contained good clothes, though mostly stained with ale and spilled food, and in one drawer, a bundle of soiled linen had been pushed to the back, where the girls would not have found it to take away and wash. There were packs of cards and a half-empty bottle of brandy, and, in the wooden chest under the window, a rope, inexplicably knotted at intervals, a curious, five-thonged whip, a pair of fetters such as those used to manacle prisoners, and several crude drawings of naked women, the like of which Rachel had never seen and which she found both shocking and intriguing.

It was while she was looking at these that he came in, swiftly and without warning, just as his father had done on the morning she had been secretly counting out the last of her savings. Rachel dropped the sketches instinctively, and blushed, and her son flushed, too, when he saw them.

"My pearls is gone, Richard Blackaller. What do you know of them?" She went straight into attack.

He glowered and slammed the lid down on the chest before wheeling to face her.

"Whenever there's summat up, 'tis always I as gets the blame, ain't it, Mother? Blame for Mary Lutterell, blame for Joel, and now I am supposed to be thieving from you. Well, I ain't and I don't know nothing of it and there be a dozen or more paupers and servants around here who could have done it."

"I've already searched the room of the only other person who might have took them," Rachel said coldly. "But to no avail."

"And what of the vagabond?" he sneered. "What of Waddon? I'll wager a few oyster stones washed up on his beach would be more than welcome, or think you he be too high-and-mighty to stoop to what you believe of your own son?"

"I do, indeed, boy," she answered with contempt. "Squire Waddon may have been profligate in his day, but he is a gentleman and has always behaved with honor."

"He has chance aplenty to creep about up here, seeing as how he be always in this house." Richard Blackaller's voice rose to a pitch of jealousy. "And if you can search through what's mine, you can search his cottage, and I demands it."

It was a clumsy trap and Rachel, remembering the conversation in the kitchen, perceived it and considered him for a moment.

"Very well," she agreed icily. "But you will accompany me."

She led the way downstairs and watched while he saddled the horses, then rode beside him in silence.

Dick Blackaller was jaunty, spurring on and jagging back his horse, so that it danced nervously, confused by the conflicting directions, and Rachel felt her irritation increase. She knew this son would never have made such a bold accusation without being absolutely certain of its accuracy. Somehow he had found a way to implicate her friend. The problem was going to be how to disprove Charles Waddon's guilt once the pearls were discovered in his possession. Her mouth tightened as she anticipated the discomfiting scene and could think of no way to avoid it.

254

The path to Lutterell, which had been so overgrown the first time she broke through it after the old man's suicide, was now cut back to a wide, well-used slope, and as they started down, they saw a rider begin to climb toward them from the far end.

Squire Waddon waved, called out and fumbled in his greatcoat. As they met halfway, he held out a handful of pearls.

"Rachel, these were in my pocket and, 'pon oath, I am at a loss to explain how they came there," he declared, his round face open with bewilderment. "I recall you wore them to Braddon, but I ain't seen them since, until this day. 'Tis devilish mystifying, but 'twould seem someone is having a jest."

"There!" yelled Dick Blackaller. "What did I tell you? I knew the rogue would have 'em and I was right."

Rachel ignored him and took the choker, letting it dangle carelessly from her hold, where it clicked like a scold's tongue. " 'Tis no matter, Squire," she said with obvious embarrassment. "I'm just sorry you've been troubled."

"Troubled! What mean you? That villain's a thief, a felon!" Richard screamed. "And if you won't have him collared and hung, then I will."

Waddon let out a roar and raised his cane and charged forward.

"Stop!" Rachel Jedder ordered, and twisted to confront her son. "There is a thief and a felon here, but it is not the squire. 'Tis you, Richard Blackaller. You thought I would wed with Charles Waddon and sought to put a stop to it by having him arrested and put to death for stealing."

" 'Tis a lie!"

"No good denying it. I heard you swear to be rid of Squire in front of John and Emma more than a week past," she rasped, her face stiff with outrage. "But now 'tis you we'll be rid of, for I'll not have you in my house no longer. You been wicked since the day you was born, always plotting and scheming, cheating and telling falsehoods, and this time you have gone beyond my forgiveness. This night, you pack your bags and begone and I don't never want to set eyes on you more. You done your last evil here."

He carried a portmanteau and two saddlebags to the stables and found her waiting. He looked at her with something akin to a plea in his eyes, but her expression was set with contrived indifference.

"Take the brown mare," she said. "And call at the offices of Jonathan Palfriman in Cross Street seven days from now. I shall have made over a settlement by then. It will be what I think you are worth, and, understand this, not a farthing more will follow upon my death. You wished for your entitlement and you shall have it all, now."

He answered with a look of unqualified malevolence which would have quelled a weaker woman, but Rachel turned her back and would not watch him leave.

The family was subdued by Richard Blackaller's departure, and after the expected appeal on his behalf by John, his name was not spoken. Sometimes, when they sat to eat together, it seemed to the woman that the room was full of the wraiths of her lost sons, whose invisible presence at the table held even more reality than those actually there. For months a brooding heaviness hung about the house again.

Gradually, however, the marching calendar, with its ruthless demands, monopolized time and energy, and they all became absorbed in the never-ending tasks of rural life once more.

After being engaged to Urith Luckbreast for three years, cautious John finally set a date for their marriage, and Rachel and the girls, thankful for the diversion, plunged into the weeks of preparation with zest.

The house was scrubbed from top to bottom. The apprentices were moved out and their two vacated rooms were decorated and furnished anew for the couple, who intended living at Yellaton. The barn was cleared for the celebrations and its cob exterior painted white, along with that of the house and courtyard walls.

When John protested at the fuss, Rachel merely smiled and chased him off, resolved that her last remaining son would have the grandest wedding seen in the village since the celebrations for Squire Waddon's own to Lady Ann.

The Luckbreast clan was the largest in High Chilham, eighteen children in all and connected by marriage to every other family, so all had to be invited, and it took Jane and Meg Clarke, young Jane Jedder, Emma, the dairymaid Lucy, Urith, herself, and Rachel two full weeks to cook enough for the feast. There were salmon, hams, roast fowl, venison, partridges and cold tongues; plum pudding and apple tarts, rich raisin pudding and syllabubs, with punch, wine, beer, cider and Madeira to drink.

Rachel and Jane Clarke baked the cake with a bushel of flour, 6 pounds of butter, 28 pounds of currants, six quarts of thick cream, four pounds of sugar, six pints of ale, eight ounces of cinnamon, two ounces of ginger, four ounces of nutmeg, and yeast. Then eight pounds of sugar were heated with rosewater and the resulting white candy poured over the whole to set as icing.

Musicians were booked and fireworks bought and a bonfire built and lanterns hung. Finally, John and his bride, looking thoroughly bemused at being the center of so much attention and glamour, led the guests into a night of country dances and reels to the accompaniment of four violins, a bass viol, taber and pipe.

Charles Waddon had given Rachel a copy of *The Lady's Magazine*, to her awed delight, and her ball gown was based on one of its fashion plates. Cut low across the bosom and high-waisted, it was made of fine, spotted muslin, and it caused a sensation. The panniers and corsets of the past had been discarded, along with the rich materials, and the garment was flimsy enough to be scandalous. Rachel, fully aware of the effect, stuck two ostrich plumes in her hair and determined to enjoy herself.

At first, she fussed around the guests, pressing them to eat and drink, seeing that every young girl had a partner and that the old were comfortable, talking to each in turn, ensuring that no one was left out. Sipping Madeira, she moved through the crowd, admiring wives and flattering husbands with her eyes, letting the atmosphere of hearty revelry gust like a merry breeze and whirl away all the cares and joylessness which had hung, like a great cobweb, over Yellaton for so long.

It was refreshing to be surrounded by friends and good folk, to see them all freed for a while from the labors of the land, happy and celebrating. The sweet wine frolicked through her, unlocking her spirits. All which had happened was over. Not tears nor prayers would bring them back. The past was gone. It was time to release herself.

Seth Bartle came and bowed with self-conscious clumsiness and she took his outstretched hand, gladly. The musicians tossed back their hair and wiped their brows and closed their eyes and set to with a will. The music tumbled and capered from their deft bows, pursued by the quavering echo of dancers humming the familiar tune.

Rachel felt herself lifted and carried down the line. The pied-piper rhythm of the reel led her on and her body created a beat of its own, alive and excited as a young maid again, and she danced until her dressed hair came unpinned and swirled round her shoulders and her face was damp and flushed with the exercise and she ached all over, exquisitely, and the morning sent its first light into the great barn. And she and Squire Waddon were the last on their feet. It was the best time she had had for years.

Although John's wedding did not mark the end of her mourning, she seemed more able to accept the disappointments and losses of the past after it. The nagging hollowness in her heart did not refill, but she found herself able to laugh again and take part in family festivals and activities with pleasure.

John and Urith were a sensible couple and, together with the squire, ran the business, farms and house smoothly. Each day dawned free from anxiety and even the unpredictable weather and its variable impression on the crops ceased to preoccupy her.

At first it was like a holiday, the only one she had ever had, and she reveled in it, sleeping late in the morning and taking long rides across the moors and excursions to the coast, where she sat on the floury white sands and watched the breakers roll in from America, or paddled in the shallow waters letting ripples drench her skirts. She went to town and bought clothes and even some jewelry—an ornamental watch hung on a delicately wrought chain for wearing around her waist, a gold ring set with emeralds, a gold-worked necklace and another of garnets. She gave presents, brooches to the girls and fob watches to the men, sating herself with spending.

The harvest light illuminated the earth once more. Acre after acre turned butter-yellow and shone as though electrified. The wheat stalks became brittle and polished, their heads fat with kernels. Like skeins of wild geese, the men swung their reaping hooks behind their leader, cutting down the waist-high corn to V-shaped clearings of stubble, and the women, following in rhythmic waves, bound the swathes with twists of straw and turned them into stooks. Lastly, the flock of children bobbed and darted in their wake, catching every ear left overlooked on the ground. From a distance they could have been performing a ritual dance, moving across the land as though to music.

To Rachel, shielding her eyes against the sun and enraptured by the sight, as she was every year, Jedder's land appeared as an arc of gold, curving in a wide semicircle from east to west behind the old house. She was reminded of the night spent in the ring of monoliths on Salisbury Plain so long before, and suddenly she was able to translate the dream. The man and the boy, Will and Jedder Tresider, lost behind the running fire of grain. The flight of stone steps to the brass-studded oak door.

Hurrying indoors to fetch paper, ink and one of Charles Waddon's quill pens, she went to the desk in the study off the kitchen and, with many blotches and smudged lines, drew a plan.

"Is there money enough?" she asked him that evening.

" 'Twill be a costly project," he replied doubtfully.

" 'Tis how I want Yellaton to be, built longer and the entrance moved to the center and stone pillars and a porch," she insisted.

"Like Braddon." He gave her a knowing look.

She lifted her chin and corrected, "Like the vision I had afore I come here. And there's to be a stone terrace and a wall of smaller pillars."

"A balustrade."

"What you will. And wide steps to the garden."

"What garden?"

"The garden I shall make."

"But, Rachel, you're no gardener," he said, exasperated. "You're a farmer, and, besides, the wind won't permit flowers and lawns to flourish in front of this house. 'Tis moorland here."

"I will become a gardener, Charles Waddon," she announced. "And drains and a double hedge of beech planted all round will give shelter and excellent conditions for flowers. And there will be a high wall to the west, and gates."

"Gates! What ever for? No one ever approaches the farm from that direction."

"They will in future. In order to come through the gates." Her logic was irrefutable.

258

" 'Tis a foolhardy scheme and thought up because you have too little to occupy you, Rachel." He was annoyed.

"Fath! But how you have altered, Squire," she teased. "What of your own squandering at Braddon?"

"And look where it landed me, woman!"

"Well, I shall not finish up there, never fear," she retorted. "But I will have this house made fit for the one to come."

"Who is coming?"

"That is none of your concern," she replied enigmatically, and would give no further information.

The enterprise occupied the winter. A builder was brought in to draw up workable designs from her rough sketches and she took to riding to see the great houses in the area and steal ideas from their architecture: the Chichester's Arlington and Youlston, on the other side of Barnstaple, Heanton Court, Mr. Hole's Ebberly and Rolle's Hudscot.

At home there were discussions and arguments and alterations, but eventually it was decided that Yellaton would be extended on each side to give two more main bedrooms, making seven in all, and the building enlarged behind to incorporate the old shippen, creating a box room above, a breakfast room, a dining room, a small winter sitting room and a larger study below. An entrance hall would be made behind the new front door with a sweep of oak stairs leading from it, and the original parlor would be lengthened to become a drawing room. She would have larger windows to let in more light, and last, the thatch was to be lifted to allow for servants' attics and replaced by a roof of richly textured local slate of graduated widths, the broadest at the eaves and the smallest at the ridge, which would silver with time and gleam in the sun and be a landmark for miles.

"This will bankrupt you, madam," Squire Waddon warned, affronted that all his advice was ignored and seeing what he felt was his own achievement in framing solid financial security for her thrown away.

"Fiddlesticks!" She dismissed the gloom. "This will be the sign of our prosperity for all to see and 'twill draw more wealth and more land to us, Charles. There will be Jedders here in a hundred, two hundred year, because of this house. With the place as it is, us can't never be no more than plain yeomen, but a mansion of substance will make this a family of position and influence."

"My position and influence was not preserved by Braddon," he emphasized again.

"That were because you was *maized*, Waddon," she discounted him autocratically. "But I am not. I knows what I be doing. Why think you Buller has put up New Place at Kings Nympton and Peirce rebuilt Annery at Landcross?"

"They are rich men, Rachel Jedder."

"And making themselves richer."

259

There was no answering her.

The materials were ordered and men hired, and as soon as the snows cleared and the drying winds blew away the last frosts, the regular farm servants were boarded out, the family moved down to Lutterell, and work was begun.

Each day, waking in a state of pulsing excitement, she could not wait to see what progress had been made; though, as she was last to leave and first to arrive at the site, nothing further could have been completed overnight. But she inspected the wooden scaffolding and scrutinized every joint and chivvied the men and bullied the builder and made a general nuisance of herself. She was alarmed when the old house seemed, at one point, to have been reduced to a shell yet only a few weeks later, she was marveling at its impressive expanse.

John and Urith and Emma and Peter Spurway and the squire and young Jane had to take it in turns to go with her, regardless of their other duties, and make suitably favorable comments and, in fact, they were all impressed, if also apprehensive.

It was while she and Jane Jedder were admiring the house from the hillock above the Bideford road that a young man rode up and greeted them with familiarity.

Rachel looked at him questioningly, but his eyes were already on Jane, who went pink and ducked her head. Her mother frowned and tapped her crop impatiently on the saddle pommel.

"I heard how fine Yellaton is become and wished to view it. 'Tis magnificent, indeed," he said, and then noticed her expression. "You do not know me, Mistress Jedder?"

"I believe not."

"Forgive me. I had thought you would remember. Henry Wellington of Wrey." He bowed politely and smiled as Rachel's face cleared. "Father sent me to my aunt and uncle in London when Mother died and I suppose I must have altered somewhat since then."

"Most certainly. You were but a sprig when last we seen you." She took in his bearing and manner with approval, but his gaze had already returned to her adopted daughter, and within minutes he was eagerly accepting an invitation to call on them.

"What did I tell you, Squire?" Rachel was brimful of the news that night. "Wrey be the best property 'twixt here and Cranford Moor, and Wellington be a splendid young gentleman and the only son, most fitting for our Jane. Did I not say as fortune would come to the new Yellaton?"

" 'Tis not like you to matchmake," he grinned, unaware of the way she had played Emma and Peter Spurway to the altar. "And are you not a trifle cocksure? The boy has barely stolen a glance at Jane."

"But I seen the glance and how her a-glanced back," she replied smugly. "There'll be no stopping they two."

He shook his head. Rachel was becoming thoroughly eccentric, and he sometimes wished her back in the fields with less time to meddle and indulge these mad fancies.

But once again she proved right. Jane, at nineteen, was a tall, slender young woman, rather serious and with a natural dignity which had kept even the most impudent village lads at bay. Her smile was unexpected and sweet, accompanied by a light in her eyes which revealed a strong sense of the ridiculous. She was accomplished and intelligent, often losing Rachel in her knowledgeable conversations, but providing a quick foil for Charles Waddon, who saw his dead sister in her more each day.

Henry Wellington, a few years Jane's senior, was amazed to find such perfection in the depths of rural England, where he had expected to miss the saucy city beauties and to be bored by buxom, slow-witted wenches or long-toothed, neighing horsewomen.

They fell in love with each other instantly. His father, who would once have disapproved of such an alliance, was persuaded by Yellaton's fresh Georgian elegance and the spread of its land to agree that his son might seek permission to pay the girl attention. Rachel, her own attention firmly fixed on Wrey's four hundred acres, gave it gladly, and prayed.

The two walked and rode together daily. Rachel would see them from the window, drifting through the heather, or chasing along the tracks, or cantering to meet each other, or lingering hand in hand over their nightly farewells, and felt her heart twist, almost sadly, memories whispering so that she had to turn away.

It was late one afternoon when she took a detour to examine the state of the ditches feeding Moses pond that she came upon them making love.

They did not hear her and she stood back in the thicket and saw Jane's hand stroke his head and pull him to her mouth. They were already half undressed and he moved to her and she received him in a way that showed it was not the first time. Rachel saw the girl's loose chestnut hair spread over the fallen yellow leaves and heard the sounds of her pleasure and watched his blind, ecstatic face and how tenderly he cradled her afterward, as though trying to keep her as an indivisible part of himself, and murmuring love; and she caught her breath at the intolerable invasion of sorrow and longing and stole away.

On reaching her room, she slid the bolt and slowly took off her clothes. She had put on weight since cutting down the physical work; suckling infants had eventually developed her breasts to a limited but acceptable fullness and her waist was still clearly defined. Her stomach was no longer hard and flat, but a raised mound with a tracery of pearly stretch marks from bearing six children. The tops of her arms were heavier, although in the long glass she could see that narrow shoulders and a good skin had left her with the slender, sinuous back of a girl. It was still a shapely body, probably more likely to be appreciated than the bony frame of her youth, but nevertheless it was a middle-aged body. There

261

were lines on her neck and her elbows were coarse and her hands rough and swollen. She was less flexible. She was middle-aged, some might even have said old. And yet she felt the same. Had darling Will walked in, the same desperate fervor would have consumed her, the same emotion transported her to wild and weeping submission, and she would have responded with a lust made even more fierce by the awareness of her own mortality which only comes with years.

She lay on the bed and absently fingered her nipples, which puckered and rose to the touch. She closed her eyes, imagining Charles Waddon exploring and rousing her again, but it was the wrong image, and, sighing, she opened her eyes and got up.

The young were marrying and mating. Everywhere she went she saw their mooning looks and tightly clasped hands and the way they constantly strained to be close. Urith was already huge and due to give birth, and after a two-year wait, Emma was pregnant at last. Rachel knew if she dressed and went to Charles Waddon he would welcome her into his bed and soothe her, but that was not what she wanted. It was not enough. How long before she shrank and wizened to total sexlessness? How long had she left to live? Anger made her wrench the brush through her tangled hair until her tear ducts smarted.

In the weeks which followed, she was short-tempered with everyone and hypercritical, finding fault with everything. The men on the farms learned to avoid her or, at least, not to be discovered resting on their spades when she came by, and the family grimaced behind her back, while paying lip service when in her company.

Urith gave birth to a fat, large-headed, unattractive son, and Rachel looked into the cradle at her first grandchild and promptly lost interest, although she had the grace to make a few congratulatory noises before fleeing from her daughter-in-law's suffocating maternalism.

It was a disappointment that the baby had not captivated her. Although motherhood and children had never held much attraction, she had presumed, unreasonably, that this child would enchant her, fill her days and be the focal point of her plans. Now she simply felt bored and restless and thoroughly irritable.

It was Barnstaple Fair week. Rachel had not visited it for twenty-six years, not since little Sarah and Robert Wolcot had caught measles from the gingerbread seller. But she had nothing to do and the atmosphere at home was, though of her own making, uncomfortable; so, refusing half-hearted offers of company, she set out down the steep track to Langleys Ford, through to Chapelton and on to the town.

At first, pushed here and there by the enthusiastic crowds, she could only think miserably of her long-dead baby, and she decided to return to the livery stables and leave. But then she found herself at the front of a standing audience before a Punch-and-Judy show, laughing and talking to her neighbors, and then the procession and music and comedians took over.

She rode on a wooden wheel which whirled her high in the air and went into a booth to see moving waxworks and then to see a fire-eater. She bought sweetmeats and ate them in the street, wandering from stall to stall, delighted by the jugglers and a dancing dog and the bright colors and raucous bands. She was drawn into a dance by the river; passed from hand to hand, she was bowed to by both gentlemen and wagoners, twirled between grand ladies and dairymaids and carried along to where the horse sale was being held by half the tinkers and dealers in the land.

There were piebalds and skewbalds being sold by gypsies, and ponies, summer-fat from Exmoor and Dartmoor, and nags with spavins and cow hocks and ewe necks and hard mouths and broken winds, ancient geldings pepped up with a dawn feed of oats and old mares with marks burned into the table of their teeth to make them seem years younger. There were bolters and rearers and kickers and biters with their ears back and tails twitching. No one in his right mind bought a horse here, and yet, full of ale and cider and bonhomie, hard headed countrymen were handing over handfuls of coins and making off with beasts a donkey boy would have rejected.

She walked aimlessly among them, enjoying the atmosphere of trickery and barter; then she stopped. An old farmer and a dark-haired man were arguing about the price of a big, showy chestnut. The yeoman was shaking his head and pointing out some invisible fault in the animal, and the owner, who had his back to her, straightened his shoulders stubbornly and tightened his hold on the reins. The horse jerked its head and champed on its bits, stamping a slim hind leg and sidling round behind its master.

Rachel skirted them until she could see his face. He was about twenty-five years old and neither a tinker nor a known dealer. His accent was familiar, but not local.

"How much do you want for 'ee?" she demanded.

The two men stopped their exchange and looked at her in surprise.

"He's no lady's ride, mistress," the younger man replied with remarkable honesty.

"How much?" she asked again.

"Fifty sovereign." It was too much, and he looked down at her tolerantly, as though humoring a child.

"Done!" she heard herself say.

"Now, look'ee here, mistress," the old farmer protested. "Us was about to slap hands on it."

"Aye, but you hasn't." She waved him aside.

The horse seller held up his hand, grinning widely.

She slapped it and felt the sting smack against her palm.

"And I has."

"Right enough, ma'am." The young man nodded appreciatively. She tilted her head back to hold his attention in the cinnamon-and-herbal smoke rings of her eyes and saw his own brown eyes widen.

263

He moved to check the bridle unnecessarily and asked, "Do you want the horse taken to stables, or shall I tether him here till you collect him?"

The animal was to be delivered to Lutterell's farm, not earlier than 2 P. M. and not later than 4 P. M. the following afternoon, she instructed.

"But that be out of my way!" he protested.

"Not if 'ee wants payment." She gave a small, wicked smile and walked away, conscious that he watched until the corner of a house hid her from sight.

Rachel Jedder went straight to the Three Tuns Tavern and drank two brandies in quick succession before calling for her mare and starting for home.

Once out in the country, she shouted and sang with exhilaration, urging her mount to gallop until its neck was damp with sweat and white flecks lathered its shoulders and flanks and she herself was too breathless to continue.

That night she told scandalous tales and jokes over the supper table until the whole family was weak with laughter. Walter Tucker, the head stockman, was invited in and plied with ale as a bribe to play his fiddle, and she danced with her son and then her son-in-law, and finally with Squire Waddon, hypnotizing him with spells and the temptations of unspoken promises until he could not resist pulling her close and whispering persuasions of love hoarsely in her ear, but she only laughed and broke loose to catch her fat grandson from his cradle, whirl him around the room and dump him, bawling, in his mother's lap. At last she sat down, panting and gleeful, and let the others continue the party.

"What you up to, Rachel?" Jane Clarke came to sit next to her.

"Whatever do you mean?" she responded innocently.

"We've known each other too long, friend, and 'tis clear you're up to no good," Jane persisted. "I ain't seen you like this in years, but 'tis a mood we haven't forgot, for it always led to some transgression."

"Not at all, Jane Clarke." Rachel pretended to be ruffled. "Can a family not have a night's merriment without such silly talk?"

"Say what 'ee likes, but I knows better." Jane, unperturbed, nudged her in the ribs. "And whoever he be, he becomes you. Why, you looks all of twenty again."

"True enough. You could be no older than the day we met." Charles Waddon drew up another chair and took her hand and Rachel engaged once more in the delicious pastime of flirting.

Despite dancing to exhaustion, she could not sleep, but lay in the four-poster bed hugging herself and letting her fantasy loose until daybreak.

She spent the morning bathing and washing her hair and was unable to eat breakfast or the midday meal. Then she changed into a smart new riding dress of scarlet velvet. The voluminous skirt was longer in front that it should flow gracefully over the saddle pommels and sweep down over her legs and feet. She wore soft leather boots and a saucy matching jockey cap with ribbons and a peak, beneath which her face was framed by short, free curls. After that, with nothing left to do, she paced up and down her room until John knocked on the door.

"There be a fellow here wi' a horse, Mother. We told him he be mistook, but he will have it that you bought the beast at the fair."

She snatched up her gloves and hunting crop and pushed past him, slowing only just before opening the front door and stepping into the open. The horse seller was seated on a black gelding and leading the chestnut. Rachel Jedder deliberately stood her ground instead of going to the mounting block, so that he had to bring the horses over.

"You shall accompany me while I try the animal out," she commanded.

The stable boy tightened the girth on the sidesaddle and was sent away. The horse seller dismounted and put out a broad hand into which she placed her small foot and was up in a trice. The chestnut bent its hocks and plunged sideways, but she was already in control. Together they clattered over the cobblestones to the bridle path leading along the edge of the farm, through the woods and out to Abbot's Hill.

Rachel dug in her heel and felt the powerful muscles bunch under her as the new horse sprang forward and his red mane whipped back across her face. There was a shout from behind, but she took no notice except to race the faster, and the high hedge alongside seemed to change into a green dragon fleeing in the opposite direction, and a hare leaped ahead as though setting course for hounds, and her cap bowled off like a rolling stone, and the horse seller was easily outdistanced.

Leaves crackled like fireworks under the hooves and then the horse cleared the boundary brook, without breaking stride, and beat onto the open moor. She steered him into the wind, on to where the stream spilled in a waterfall over a rocky ledge, and drew up by Quicks Pool.

"You set a goodly pace, mistress," the horse seller grumbled, as he reined in beside her. "He's only a young beast, and I thought for a time he'd run off with you."

"That would have troubled you, would it?" she asked.

"Well, he's a good animal and I would not like to see him come to harm," the man said earnestly.

Rachel laughed with pleasure at his lack of guile and said, "Help me down."

The speed had colored her cheeks and lit her eyes and freed her hair in a shower of sparks, and when he lifted her to the ground, close to him, neither of them moved, but looked at each other for a waiting, silent moment.

He saw a diminutive, disturbing woman, amused and challenging, whose extraordinary gaze knew everything. Her hair was thick and long and smelled of spice, her nearness candent, and he was bewitched.

She saw dark, tousled hair, brilliant eyes and the lightening burn of

265

his smile. Suddenly she reached up, wound a finger into one of his curls and licked his top lip with a quick, catlike tongue, and then there were only rushing impressions of his mouth and hands and shining skin and the incense of autumn in the air, and she tasted pollen and crystals as she came gladly and willingly to the bittersweet pain.

"Yes," she whispered. "More."

The moss bed by the brook felt like goose down and the water made the sound of pouring wine, and when it was over, he lay back and she grazed from his stomach to his chest with gentle teeth and came to rest at last, at last, in the hollow of his shoulder with her arm relaxed over the curve of his ribs and her belly against his hip, where she had always been. The place she had never left.

Now, she asked the question. "What do they call you?"

"Tom," he answered sleepily. "Tom Tresider."

"And what do you know of Will Tresider?"

"My father's name is Will," he looked surprised. "Why? Are you acquainted?"

"A long time ago. You are very like him," she murmured, and sighed the deep sigh of pure fulfillment.

They lay close, his hand tenderly stroking her arm and her back, her fingers moving over his resting body in repeated caresses of drowsy love.

"Where do you live, Tom Tresider?"

"In Kent. My father has an orchard there and raises horses, too."

She remembered how Will would carry her under the little blossom-covered apple trees at Yellaton, and she tucked her head into the young lover's shoulder.

"And have you family? Brothers and sisters?"

"We are five. Three sisters, and William and myself. I am the oldest."

Six, she wanted to confess. There was another brother. Jedder. Will Tresider had six children. But she kissed his smooth neck instead and said nothing.

She tried to imagine them all at home and bit back a hundred impossible questions. What did he look like now? Was his hair as black? Was he happy? Did he ever think of her? Her fingers were quite still and her position no longer relaxed, but the boy, unaware, rolled onto his side to hug her to him.

There was a pause and she closed her eyes tightly before venturing, "And your mother? Tell me of her."

He grinned affectionately. "Mother's little, about your height, and she laughs a lot. She puts up with us all, somehow, and makes the best umble pie in Kent."

Rachel asked no more. She emptied her mind and let his nearness engulf her and provoke the delightful, indulgent feelings of desire again until her skin crept and tingled and her lips bloomed with lust, and, although she did not move, he knew.

Rachel Jedder and Will's son made love again and the sky grew somber and rain began and he held her closer and loved her more, and, finally, they could no longer see, could only sense each other out with cold, wet kisses and fingertips like ice.

"I won't return home," he vowed. "I shall stay on and see you tomorrow and every day after that."

"No," she decided regretfully. "You must ride tonight and not return."

"But I want you," he persisted.

"I am not for you, but I shall remember you, Tom Tresider." She gave her word. "And you will remember me."

They parted at the outer limit of her land and the rain fell as it had when she parted from Will, setting free the muscadine seduction of the earth and reminding her of why she had stayed behind.

"Where did this horse come from?" she wanted to know before he left.

"My father bred him. He had a chestnut stallion once and the line goes back to him."

Rachel Jedder rode back to Lutterell farmhouse in a daze. The years separating her from Will had been spanned at last. She was one with him again. The agony of Jedder's death, the regrets and disappointments, the restlessness of the past months, all were soothed and she was totally at peace with herself.

The next weeks passed euphorically and became months, and family and workers basked in her approval. She ceased to bully the builders and was unusually patient with the apprentices. The plan for the garden at Yellaton became more elaborate, and stone was delivered for the wall which was to protect it from the Atlantic gales.

In early spring, Emma's child, a girl, was born. Rachel went to visit them at Dadland as soon as the news arrived. Her daughter was still sobbing from the exertion but seemed none the worse for the experience. The bundle in the wooden cradle by the bed was so completely swathed that no sign of its content was visible.

Rachel unbound the top wrapping and a furious little face glared up, screwed up and screamed with rage, tiny fists clenched and feet kicking.

Rachel beamed at her first granddaughter.

"There you are! What a time you've taken!" she said. "I have been waiting for thee."

CHAPTER SIXTEEN

Radigan Jedder Spurway shrieked and squalled without stopping from that day for the next two years. She seemed to require no sleep, but was perpetually hungry, scratching and biting at Emma's breasts, and later, cramming milk sops into her mouth before hurling the dregs across the room. Her eyes, which had been almost navy blue, changed with the development of sight and became particolored reflections of Rachel's own—inner buds of green in calyxes of brown.

Almost from birth she struggled to sit up, turning puce in the face and howling with rage at her own helplessness. As soon as she could sit, she bellowed to crawl and then to stand, and at ten months she was already walking, and she soon acquired a forceful vocabulary, which she used with piercing arrogance, to obtain her basic requirements of mother, food and objects. Everything within her reach was smashed or used as a swinging weapon to clout dogs and adults alike. Earthenware platters were broken and pewter dented and knitting unraveled and clothes used as dusters and the cats sat on. No night passed undisturbed.

Her father, Peter Spurway, tired after twelve-hour-long working days in Torrington, grew bearish and truculent from lack of rest and blamed his wife and took to spending his evenings in the Black Horse to postpone the journey home. Flustered Emma, already pregnant again, wept and worried about barmaids and eyed her rumbustious child with disbelief and eventually with fear. Her friends from the village clucked of goblins, changelings and spirit possession and suggested remedies which ranged from herbs and dead toads to straight gin, which Emma herself swallowed, although it would have made more sense to dose the infant.

Only Rachel Jedder found her granddaughter wholly laudable and thought her fiendish exploits diverting, even encouraging them surreptitiously by lifting her to within reach of tempting articles, or showing what fun it was to send a full bucket of water swilling across the yard so that the pecking hens fluttered through the air in squawking panic, or bringing gifts of noisy toys—bells and drums, and whistles made from notched ash sticks stripped of their bark and with the pith blown out.

When she was not visiting the child or watching progress on the house at Yellaton, she spent time with the young chestnut horse bought from Tom Tresider. The animal was high-strung and had obviously barely been trained to the saddle, and never to the sidesaddle. John, who had never understood why she had bought him in the first place, argued that, at over sixteen hands high, the crittur was far too big for his mother, and wanted him sent to Seth Bartle for breaking, but she would not hear of it or allow anyone to handle the beast but herself.

Each morning she would lead him on a lunge rope to the hare's-leg field and there teach him to walk, trot and canter in a circle around her on command. Later, he learned to change direction and then to halt at a word. After the session, she fed him a carrot and released him, watching with pleasure as he galloped and kicked up his heels in relief at being unbridled.

All her life, Rachel had judged her animals by their ability to produce wool, milk, meat and progeny and by their cash value in the marketplace. Fat hams, an abundant udder, a fleshy rump or hand-deep, cloud-thick fleeces had gained her admiration. Legs had to be strong and square to carry the maximum amount of brawn or growing embryos. Bright eyes and glossy coats pleased her because they indicated health and were evidence of efficiency.

Horses were for traction and transport and needed broad chests and hard muscles, and she had chosen the largest draught horses for the farms, and stocky, trusty cobs to carry her, without tiring, all day on the land.

However, this was a completely different kind of animal, elegant and fastidious, with a lightness and quality not found in any of her previous mounts. A farmer should not have given time or stable room to such a frivolous, spindly, skittering brute, but Rachel found herself unexpectedly moved by his extraordinary grace.

The small, dished head, large eyes and high-set flowing tail told of Arab ancestors. His neck was curved and slender, like an illuminated Celtic symbol, and his long sloping shoulders ensured the easy, floating action of a thoroughbred. His back was sound, his frame well sprung with plenty of lung space. He was fast, agile and intelligent, and, as he came to know his mistress better, he grew playful, galloping flat out across the field, aiming straight at her until he was near enough to shake the ground beneath her, then swerving aside, so close that his warm, grassy breath misted her face; nudging her with his nose from behind; searching her hands and clothes for hidden tidbits, shying at imaginary stirrings in the verges and scattering leaves and fleeing mice and shrews when they went out together.

It did not matter that he would not plod patiently to the village under a load of full panniers, or that he could not draw a trap or pull a plow. He did not have to be useful to justify his existence, for to ride him was to become part of a wild, free magic. He faced the Devon hedges with courage and skimmed the moors like a bird. He was flawless, moving like a swift tide, burnished as a red-gold chalice and shaped in the divine mold of legends.

Seeing the horse through new eyes, which recognized such excellence for the first time, changed Rachel Jedder's whole outlook. The immaculacy of the land and tolling seasons and the mystic cycle of birth, reproduction and death had always held her willingly in thrall, but a life of service to the majestic order had manufactured no compass to measure the relationship of shades and movements and patterns each to each other. Her love of nature had been instinctive and accepting.

Now there was time, time to watch the young chestnut horse and from him to discover that form, color and motion could be appreciated in themselves and not just as the random side effects of the great whole. Her tastes refined and became more sophisticated.

The alterations at Yellaton were almost completed before she understood that they involved more than the simple addition of more rooms to the house. The balance of its intimacy with Beara Moor had been shifted and she went to examine it anxiously, in case she had made a mistake. But although the rebuilding had been extensive, the symmetry and steadfastness of the basic design had preserved its character. The extensions were constructed of cob to match the original, the mud and straw trodden down in layers by the mason, as a laborer threw on the mixture and another pared off the excess, and a carpenter fitted the lintels. Later, the spaces for doors and windows had been cut out of the finished walls, which were then left several months to dry out before being smoothed and plastered. The result was a large white house the rough and undulated surfaces of which gave the impression that it had stood there for a hundred years.

Viewing it critically, Rachel decided to dispense with the stone balustrade bordering the paved terrace and settled instead for a wide flight of steps set into a plain turf bank dropping to the garden.

Next, searching Barnstaple and Exeter, she fussed over fixtures and draperies. In the beginning, unsure of herself, she consulted Charles Waddon constantly. Never having been involved in such domestic matters, he proved to be of little help, having more knowledge of tack rooms than breakfast rooms. Eventually, forced to trust her own judgment, she discarded solid, weighty country craftsmanship in favor of the latest sinuous town furniture: mahogany chairs with tapering, carved legs and oval backs, an upholstered sofa with a curving back, a chaise longue, a charming oval table supported on a central pillar and four outward-curving claws, and chests of drawers with serpentine fronts for the extra bedrooms. Wine-red velvet curtains were hung in the long drawing room because she could not resist the luxurious feel and sight of them.

At last, nearly two years after the start of the work, Yellaton was finished, decorated and stylishly fitted out, and Rachel, John and Urith and their son, Robert, moved back up from Lutterell's.

Jane's spring wedding to Henry Wellington took place within the month, the celebrations providing a suitable excuse to invite the entire neighborhood to feast, dance and compliment. Everyone, out of pure curiosity, accepted.

Rachel, queenly in royal purple, greeted friends, neighbors and rivals alike with a beatific smile, absorbing their exclamations and whispers of envious admiration into her pores like scented oils. The bridegroom's parents, Henry Wellington, Esquire, and his wife, stood at her side. The stolidly affluent Spurway parents arrived impressively and in discomfort in a landau from Torrington. Squire Waddon was bowing to the bride.

The presence of the well-connected Wellingtons and Sir Thomas Carew, new owner of Braddon, ensured the arrival of a number of the county families, Lord Fortescue from Filleigh, the Hamlyns of Clovelly Court, the Reverend Mr. Turner from Garwood and even Sir Benjamin Wreys from Beer Charter and his formidable aunts, the Misses Wreys of Prexford Barton. Their carriages rattled up, bespattered with mud from the open moorland roads, and they emerged, righting their wigs and smoothing their gowns to accept Rachel's welcome graciously before making stately haste to view Squire Waddon, in whom they all took an inordinate interest. The tale of his being discovered as a vagrant and how he now lived in a cottage, managing this strange Jedder woman's land, had reached and intrigued them all.

Before long, Sir Benjamin and Charles Waddon were singing rude songs, their arms about each other, and Mistress Hamlyn was giving Rachel the name of her favorite seamstress, and the Reverend Turner had buxom Meg Clarke pinned, giggling, in a corner, and Lord Fortescue gave a loud belch before slumping, unconscious, onto the new chaise longue, the glass of port and brandy rolling from his hand. Only the Misses Wreys remained stiffly upright, like a pair of silk-dressed wax dolls on a sofa. The triumph of all Rachel's tears and fears and years on Jedder's land was grand and undeniable.

She took the yawling Radigan from Emma's exhausted charge and summoned a flute player. As the notes floated around, the child stopped screeching and clutched at them as though they were visible, like bubbles, and when the musician stopped playing, she waved a demanding arm and drew an imperious breath in preparation for another outburst, and his fingers quivered and the air trilled again.

"She's impossible, Mother." Emma bumbled about like a pasty white dumpling. "We can't do nothing with her."

" 'Tis naught. Just high spirits," Rachel defended protectively. "Shows she's going to be a maid what knows her own mind and that's no bad thing."

"Well, I can't be putting up with no more of it, I tell you straight." Her daughter was close to tears again.

Rachel sighed and glanced round at her guests, hoping no one would notice. Emma sank into a chair and ominously drew a lace-trimmed kerchief from her bosom. From being a buxom, pretty wench, she had plumped into proportions which would have been outsize even without pregnancy.

Radigan pulled her grandmother's hair vigorously to the accompaniment of a rising caterwaul, and in retaliation Rachel tweaked her nose sharply so that the howl was cut off midway and the infant's banded eyes stared into her own with owl-like annoyance before the small mouth shut and turned down.

"No one else has a cheel like her," Emma was wailing. "All we wants is a nice lill' maid."

Radigan gave her opinion of this in a rudely vibrating noise and Rachel, remembering her own cumbersome months-in-waiting, looked at her inflated daughter with unusual sympathy.

"I expect you could do with a rest," she agreed. "So how say you if I keeps the bantling here till after your time?"

Radigan Jedder Spurway never returned to Dadland Farm and her natural parents. Yellaton became her home, and only her grandmother could really control her, though rarely exercised her power to do so.

Strangely, this child gave Rachel more gladness than any of her own had done. Jedder had been beloved and her joy, but she had not felt as much affinity with him as with this granddaughter, upon whom she looked and saw herself. They shared the same volatile temperament, the same fighting instinct, the same will. The woman considered the luxurious surroundings of the new house and the protective presence of the family and the daily covering of table and sideboard with food, and wondered what more she might have achieved had her own life started out in such circumstances.

She dandled the little girl on her knee and told of her extraordinary journey across England to reach Jedder's land, and how Will Tresider had found the flock of sheep, and of the birth of the first calf and the buying of Moses Bottom and the Arn valley. Often she talked of things the infant could not understand, but she made them sound like exciting adventures, which all ended in success and happiness.

The very smallness of the child was endearing, her neat, round head, her diminutive hands and feet, her little, striving body, her snub nose and pouting, elfin mouth. The features of all children, which had not affected Rachel before, touched her now, as though she realized, at last, that the extremity of her youth and the burdens of the homestead had denied her many of the rewards of motherhood. She had been so busy ensuring their survival that there had been no time just to sit and enjoy her own children, to share their ways and watch them grow.

The two played games and giggled over jokes and exchanged secrets. Antics which would have caused irritation years before were viewed with amused tolerance, and a lot of naughtiness was positively encouraged.

The lost children had ceaselessly tugged at their mother's memory. No day had passed without their darting, one after another, through her mind, led always by Jedder and followed by Sarah and then Joel, and finally even Richard Blackaller. Each remembered image mimed its heart-twisting part: her favorite son, aged about ten, winking and holding out coppers earned from ratting; the baby shaking golden curls; lanky Joel horsing about with his sisters and Dick running up with a hatful of broken eggs. Rachel had had to tighten her lips, swallow hard and deliberately involve herself in some task to escape.

Now Radigan became compensation for them all and for her own deprived childhood. Radigan would want for nothing. Radigan would have everything she wanted—and much more. So she showered presents on the child; impractical dresses of silk and satin, a porcelain figure of Harlequin (soon broken), a wooden doll with jointed arms, and a rag doll, and, most splendid of all, a baby house commissioned from a local carpenter. It was a perfect miniature of Yellaton House, the whole front elevation swinging open to reveal an interior identical to the one in which she and her granddaughter lived, including the furniture.

Even Squire Waddon remonstrated at such an extravagant gift to a two-year-old child, but when he pointed out that Radigan was being disastrously spoiled, his old friend left the room, refusing to listen.

When she was not with Radigan or the young horse, Rachel supervised and worked in the new garden. An eight-foot-high stone wall had been built along the west boundary to take the brunt of the weather, and a bank, topped by thorn, had been raised around the south and east borders with a path running under it, edged by beech, so that a double hedge was growing as an almost impenetrable screen.

As with everything she tackled, she took this latest hobby very seriously and, since the conception of the alterations to Yellaton, had been gathering expertise and considering all the parks and gardens she had seen, as well as some of the small patches kept by old couples outside their cottages, and the tidy staidness of the rectory garden. She consulted Charles Waddon and gardeners now employed by Sir Thomas Carew at Braddon Manor, and asked endless questions of old Ben Beare, who had actually been one of King George III's undergardeners at Hampton Court, and of Hieritha Delve, the ancient wisewoman in the herb-bound hovel below Great Wood.

She learned to prune fruit trees into cordons and fans, and to train and cut shrubs into shapes, and how to cultivate purely decorative plants of the kind which had not interested her before. Her ideas began to flow and she wanted something of everything. She would have labyrinths and fountains, topiary and an arboretum, drives and walks, spaciousness and massed shrubs, all in an acre.

Much time was spent mapping out designs, to be rejected upon re-examination. Eventually she was forced to restrict the scheme to four gardens, and after that, it was a matter of deciding her own preferences out of the many alternatives—conclusions which took several more weeks to reach.

Meanwhile, quince and peach trees were planted to be trained against the wall and a wide, straight avenue was cut and lined with holm oak to run from the wrought-iron gates to a stone sundial set in a circular bed below the terrace steps.

To his satisfaction, old Dave Bartle, now unfit for heavy farm work, was drafted to help his mistress, along with a ten-year-old pauper boy, young Robin.

To the left of the avenue they made an intricate knot garden of convoluted beds edged by low box hedges and filled with colorful ground cover. Narrow paved paths curled between, as though through a maze. This garden was echoed on the opposite side of the drive by another, slightly less elaborate parterre of five beds sown with culinary and medicinal herbs. Phillyrea, intended for topiary, punctuated the corners of both patterns.

A juniper-trimmed aisle divided the herb garden from a formal oblong pool, filled with water lilies and containing a central stone figure spouting water. It was overlooked by a trelliswork arbor bordered by moisture-loving plants, hostas and ferns, irises and lily of the valley.

But the place which was to become Rachel's favorite lay below the ornamental knot garden and was approached through a shaded walk, beneath a pergola covered with honeysuckle, wisteria and climbing red roses.

She had always visualized the rose garden with absolute clarity, imagining herself emerging into its heady perfumes and sitting for sunny June afternoons surrounded by its incomparable blooms. In its planting, she let herself go, at last, ignoring the rigid rules followed in the other three gardens and greedily cramming in as many different species as could be obtained: Damask and Alba, the roses of Lancashire and Yorkshire, were grown so close that they intertwined. The single, creamy flowers of the musk rose hung among the pink-and-white-striped clusters of Rosa Mundi. A moss rose, multipetaled, fragrant and pale pink, grew beside the deep black-red Rosa Gallica, and the new Rosa Rugosa and the cinnamon and burnet roses were randomly grouped together. Full-bloomed romantic heart-red cabbage roses were everywhere.

It would take beyond her lifetime for the holm oaks to reach their final evergreen fullness, and several years before the knot gardens grew into their planned motif, but the rose shrubs stretched and thickened rapidly, and Rachel and Radigan soon spent many hours playing around them and gathering bouquets of flowers and basketfuls of petals, which were added to cloves and lavender, dried and left in open bowls to scent the bedrooms.

Here, in the almost hidden gazebo, the child would often fall asleep on her grandmother's knee. The sable feathering of lashes against the peach down of her cheeks was enchanting, and Rachel, half surprised at herself, would place the dimpled hand in her own callused palm and marvel, appreciating at last the miracle of human youth.

Two more boys were born, John, who looked very like his dead Uncle Jedder, and Joseph, brother to Radigan. But, although their grandmother saw in them the future muscle of Jedder's land and treated them with amiable approval, her real love was reserved for the girl.

For this child's third birthday, she gave her a small dun-colored Exmoor pony, bought a year earlier at Bampton Fair and carefully trained to be shockproof by Seth Bartle and herself.

Radigan, lifted into a saddle for the first time, took the reins and drummed her feet against the pony's side, urging it forward. The animal obediently moved straight from a standstill to a trot, breaking free from Emma's unprepared hold. After a few paces, the child toppled to the ground. As the two women started forward in dismay, she stood up, red-faced with anger, ran to her mount, which had stopped, and began to try to climb back on without aid.

Rachel, absolutely delighted, swung her in the air, kissed her enthusiastically and seated her firmly in the saddle again.

"Did ever you see such a brave maid?" she cried to Emma. "Ain't no fear there. Why, she'll have outgrown this little horse in a twelve-month!"

Emma shook her head dismally. " 'Tisn't no good for a girl to be that wayward, Mother. How's she going to settle later, with you egging her on?"

"Don't 'ee take on so, daughter. She'll settle when her's a mind to."

As soon as the child became old enough and competent, it became their custom for the two to make the daily tour of inspection around the estate together. Everything the woman stopped to look at and every discussion she had with the farm servants was explained in words the small girl could understand.

"That bit of guttering will have to be fixed or the water will soak through the wall and do the cob no good."

She would point out necessary repairs, and then make for the red Devon herd grazing on Lutterell.

"See that string o' stuff hanging under her tail?" She indicated a bellowing cow in the corner of the field. "Well, that and her hollering be signs that she's ready for the bull. 'Tis time young Ben brought him up here."

The two helped with the lambing, Radigan being shown how to check a posterior birth by reaching into the ewe to confirm the hocks, hindquarters and tail of the lamb.

"The feet may look upside down, but that don't mean the lamb is coming out backwards. It could be because the crittur hisself is wrong way up."

The child began to comment and report and question during their

275

excursions, noticing that certain overgrown hedges were restricting the horses' progress and wondering why part of Moses meadow lay under a film of water when it had been dry the week before.

"That's because the old drains should have been checked and made new," her grandmother answered, annoyed by the sight. "And, if 'tis not done now, the pasture will be spoilt."

The temperature dropped quickly, and in the early mornings the child would climb into Rachel's warm feather bed and watch the smoke signals of their breath collide in the chill air. Later in the day they would have snowball fights with her brother and cousins, or test the strength of the ice on the oblong pool before skating and falling across its surface, or take wooden trays from the kitchen to toboggan down the white slopes of the moor. Radigan was just seven years old and these were her last months of complete freedom.

After much argument within the family, the following spring she was sent to school in South Molton, a distance which meant that she had to board and could only return home at weekends.

John and her parents argued that there was a dame in High Chilham who could have taught her the catechism and to dabble with paints and sing and stitch and such matters fit for females; but Rachel was adamant. Radigan Jedder Spurway would not be burdened with illiteracy, as she had been. The child was to be taught to read and write and count, and then be given books.

"Books! But there's no need for it. Her's got family. I will show the boys all that kind of thing and they can handle them matters later on." John had sounded exasperated. " 'Tisn't proper to fill a maid's head wi' learning."

"Jane be well learnt," Rachel pointed out.

"Her be different," Peter Spurway replied. "More docile by nature than our Radigan."

" 'Twill just make her discontented, Mother," Emma had put in.

"Aye, and who'll wed her, if her knows too much?" asked her father. "What man will want her?"

Rachel had snorted with annoyance and refused to continue the discussion, and then felt her eyes moisten at the sight of her pet being deposited, with her box of clothes, outside the forbidding-looking house in the center of the busy town.

The following morning, the schoolmaster himself rode all the way to Yellaton, his face creased with anxiety and his eyes shifty.

Rachel saw him from the window and felt her throat constrict and sheer terror clamp around her like an iron case.

Radigan had disappeared, the man stuttered, and she flew at him, screeching and clawing. Charles Waddon pulled her back into his arms, and listened over her shaking body to the report of how the child had been fed and put to sleep, seeming to settle easily; but at dawn the schoolmaster and his wife had found the bed empty and cold.

"Not another, not this child," Rachel whispered. "I cannot lose this child."

Every man on the farms was taken from work and sent across the country, those on foot searching to just beyond the village and those on horseback covering the ten miles from that boundary to the market town. Rachel sat with her head in her hands, rocking and moaning, picturing every danger, from exposure on the moors to murder, and believing in death.

One by one, the men returned, dispirited and tired, until only the child's father and uncle and Squire Waddon hunted on, and night drew in.

Rachel abandoned hope. It was the way of her life that happiness was no sooner reached than it was snatched away. Her granddaughter, her darling, her chosen heir was gone.

Carriage wheels crunched up the avenue. There was a loud rapping on the front door and Sir Thomas Carew walked in, followed by Urith.

"My keeper caught a young rabbit of yours in the park," he said, beaming at Rachel, who gazed back without understanding. "I thought it should be brought to you."

And Radigan ran into the room.

"Us didn't like school, so us come home," she announced and took a cake from the tray of uneaten food on the table by her grandmother's chair.

The woman stared, sat up and slapped her hand so hard that the cake fell on the floor. The child flinched and looked resentful.

"Put her to bed," Rachel told Urith, before thanking her neighbor politely and wishing him goodnight.

Day was no more than a pale stroke in the east when she roused her errant granddaughter next morning. Ignoring the complaints of sleepiness and sore feet, she made her dress in a coarse linen smock and heavy boots, which had been stored in a chest since Emma's own childhood.

Without speaking, she took her to the kitchen and pointed to the big fireplace full of ashes and the last corners of partly burned logs.

"Clean that out, and all the other fires, and reset them," she ordered.

"That's Lucy's job," the child said crossly.

"Oh, no, 'tis your task now," Rachel told her.

"Why?" demanded Radigan.

"Because today is the day you starts work, like every poor child in the country."

" 'Tis early and us be tired. Nobody else is up and us doesn't want to work," the little girl whined.

"Children as doesn't go to school must work in the house and on the land."

"No!" The child sat down on the floor and glared her challenge.

Rachel picked her up, carried her to the nearest chair, placed her over her knee, lifted her skirt and spanked her bare bottom without restraint, ignoring the screams of temper and the kitchen door bursting open as Urith, John and Meg Clarke ran in. She waved them back and returned her tearful granddaughter to the floor.

"Now!" The order was given in a voice which allowed no rebellion. "Work!"

When she had completed the task and swept the kitchen floor and helped Lucy carry the buckets of milk from cowshed to dairy, Radigan was given a piece of dry bread and half a cup of milk for breakfast.

Then all the farm workers were called to the courtyard and Rachel propelled the child before them.

"All these grown men hunted many hours for you, Radigan Spurway," she said. "No labor was done on our farms. Time and money was lost. When money is lost, folk cannot be paid, then they cannot buy vittles and their own children go hungry. For showing so little concern for their welfare, you will ask the pardon of them."

The child, blushing with shame, went to each man and, under her grandmother's direction, muttered, "I beg pardon for the trouble I have caused."

"Now," said the woman, as they reached the end of the line, "you're to go to Lutterell and pick stones, to help make up the work neglected yesterday through your folly."

It rained steadily all that week, and Rachel would sometimes go stealthily to see her small granddaughter, sheltered only by a piece of sacking, clearing stones from the fields. She remembered the backbreaking relentlessness of the task and wanted to hurry her indoors and wrap her in warm shawls and hug her close again. Deliberately steeling herself, she would turn away.

"Don't 'ee think she's had punishment enough?" John ventured on the fifth day.

" 'Tis a merciless world, as you know, son, and our family is remarkable well off in it, but only through hard work and some good fortune," Rachel answered. "I bin lax too long. 'Tis all too easy to slip back to pauperdom, and Radigan has to learn her duty to them as labors here for us. She needs to find out what 'tis like to be without comforts and feel the pain of toil."

On the sixth day, she had a cob saddled and rode the three miles to High Chilham with the child trudging alongside. She visited Jedder's grave and then called in at the blacksmith's with an order, and finally tethered the horse by the village pump and walked to the long, bleak building off the square.

A very fat woman, her neck hidden beneath a scarf of chins, greeted her without enthusiasm.

"Us can take on another wench at Yellaton," Rachel said and was ushered inside.

Holding Radigan firmly, she stepped over a thin child of about five years old, scrubbing the floor, and passed two tots scraping clean a mountain of platters with a bucket of dirty water.

As the beadle's wife opened a door, the sound of sobbing and whimpering within stopped, as though the waifs there did not dare to breathe in her presence.

"Alice Pope!" she shouted.

A girl with running nose and eyes sidled up to stand in front of them, staring at the ground.

" 'Tis no more than a cold, mistress," the fat woman assured Rachel.

The girl's arms and legs were almost fleshless, just bony appendages to a hollow, undersized body.

"How old be 'ee?" Rachel asked.

" 'Bout seven year, mistress."

"Will you work hard for me?"

There was the beginning of life in the child's look.

"Yes, mistress."

"Milk cows and scrub, shift in logs and pick stones in the fields?" Rachel pressed.

"If it please 'ee, mistress." The pauper, sensing escape from the poorhouse, was eager now.

"Just you give her a good beating if her don't," advised the fat wife. "They learns soon enough from leather."

Rachel glanced down at her granddaughter, whose eyes were wide with fright, then she took Alice's hand kindly and walked both children out into the sunlight, sat them on the horse and led them home.

That night, she asked John and Emma to join her in the drawing room over a dish of mulled ale.

" 'Tis time you knew what provision I have made for you and your families, the contents of my will." Rachel was straightforward, ignoring Emma's protesting twitter and John's expression of distaste.

"The land is not to be divided," she went on. "You, John, is to have the right to the house at Lutterell and one sixth of all the income from the three farms until you die. After that, your family will be paid the full value of the whole of Lutterell farm by the estate.

"Emma, having a husband to provide for her, is to have the use of Dadland house throughout her lifetime, and the value of that will be paid to her family upon her death. As you know, Jane was given her portion as dowry on her marriage to Henry Wellington. My good friend, Jane Clarke, is to have my gold-worked necklace and the sum of fifty pound, and, John, you will be expected to give her shelter for the rest of her days. If Joel ever returns from the sea, he is to be given the same settlement as Richard received, one third of which to be afforded by each farm on the estate.

"Think you this be fair and proper? Will you be content with it?"

The two nodded, Emma without fully understanding and John appreciating that the value of Lutterell farm would secure his children's future.

"Yellaton House and its lands and the lands of Lutterell and Dadland and Arnwood and Arn valley are to go to Radigan," Rachel concluded.

Her son nodded again, confirming that he had already guessed this, but Emma's mouth dropped open.

"We knows you wish the land kept as one piece, Mother, but she's a bit of a girl. Why not have one of the boys to farm it?"

"There be plenty coming to your two boys from the Spurway trade. They won't never go hungry. And I've made sure as John and Urith's children will have shelter to grow in and gold when he's gone," Rachel pointed out. "But Radigan Spurway has a particular purpose. She will do more than farm this place, daughter. Wealth and position will come to her and, through her, much more will be added to Jedder's land. 'Tis her fate, and I have known of it since long afore her were born, and afore you were born, too."

On the seventh day, the Exmoor pony and the big chestnut were brought out and Rachel and her granddaughter rode off early together. The child was very subdued.

"Watch the path we take, maid," the woman instructed. "Take heed of where we go and everything we pass, because I want you to remember it all."

They went down the side of Yellaton coppice, round the hare's leg, Yonder Plat and Brindley and on to Moses Bottom, up the steep incline to Arnwood and down the other side to the valley.

It was a soft, gray day, quiet and without a breeze, the uniform cloud cover slanting to an indistinct horizon, the spring colors muted by the pall to an almost summer fading. As they reached each section of Jedder's land, Rachel repeated its history and how it had been obtained, as she had done so often before to the girl.

They cut back over the hill again to ride around Dadland. The fields were seamed to each other by tidy hedges and their pattern crazy-paved over mounds and slopes all the way to the lower end of Lutterell.

"In the beginning, all this were moor and woodland. Men and women and little children lived and died to clear this land and make it fit to grow corn and raise beasts," Rachel said. "See that great tree? Well, they rooted out hundreds of trees as big as that, and bigger, first axing through the trunks, then chopping and sawing the branches, then digging out and hacking the roots and, when all that were done, dragging out the remains of the boles with teams of sweating oxen.

"The men cut out each of these fields, strip by strip, from the wilderness, year by year, from the time of their boyhood to their old age, and their sons after them, and the sons of those sons after that, on and on, like all them names the parson reads out of the Old Testament, until they come to us. And my grandfather, Penuel Jedder, did his share, and my

280

mother helped with harvest, and I plowed the fields of Yellaton, and your own mother picked stones when her were half your age, because nature soon takes back what we leave uncared for."

At noon they dismounted, and Rachel took two stone bottles of cider, a loaf of granary bread, some sliced raw onion and cheese from her saddlebag and they sat on a bank amid a scattering of small wild daffodils to eat. The day was so still that it would have made a disturbance to talk. Even the sheep and cattle were motionless and gave the landscape an air of unreality, like a painting.

Then they rode on to Lutterell, over each pasture and through each spinney there before returning up the hill to Yellaton. At the top, Rachel stopped again. It was the one place from which almost the entire spread of her property could be seen.

"One day, all that land might be yours, Radigan Spurway." She indicated the span with a sweep of her arm. "What would you do with it?"

The child looked at her, tongue-tied.

"It has taken us near a day to ride around it. If you lived alone and plowed and tilled and reaped without rest every single day for fifty year, could you keep it clean and fruitful as it is now?"

The child shook her head.

"No, you could not. For 'tis too much for one pair o' hands and needs many folk to make it prosper," Rachel agreed. "And the one as it all belongs to must keep and feed and pay those workers and needs know more than plain farming to do it. The mistress of an estate this size *must* know reading and writing and figurework, so you can understand prices and costs and such and make sure you be not cheated, and so's the world knows you ain't a simpleton as can be fooled."

The woman scrutinized her granddaughter and offered her the choice. "You can go back to the fields and labor alongside the others, Radigan Spurway, or you can go back to school and become a proper lady and learn what be necessary to make you fit to be landowner here. Now, which will it be?"

Radigan returned to South Molton the next day and Rachel took up again the habits she had gradually formed during the years they had spent together. She passed much time in the garden, energetically digging and planting and weeding, until every bare patch of soil was covered with foliage and flowers. At her instruction another two acres of trees were added to Yellaton Wood.

She began to draw, and obtained some paints. The dame who ran the village classroom taught her a little of colors, and her fear of the blank white paper and her embarrassment at the clumsy marks she made upon it gradually gave way to concentration. Her hand became more certain and her eye began to see beyond the superficial appearance of objects and surroundings, and some of her efforts were surprisingly agreeable.

Each May and June, she kept watch on the orchards for bees swarm-

281

ing. Although the first swarm from a colony was sometimes large, it contained an old queen and was not as valuable as the second, more restless, swarm, with its young virgin queen. As the cloud of insects rolled through the air, she would follow it, banging noisily on a piece of tin with a hammer, until it swooped to hang roaring on the branch of an apple tree.

Then, swathed in veils and heavy clothes and gloves, she would place a straw skep upside down on the ground below, give the branch a very sharp shake, whereupon the bulk of the swarm would drop into the skep, which was then turned the right way up. Bees from the fringe dived at her in outraged confusion but within minutes discovered the entrance to the skep and joined the others, to be moved at nightfall to their proper position in the apiary.

A few weeks later, the first bees to hatch from the new queen's brood would appear in the heat of the day to dance their first flight in front of the skep before starting work on the purpose of their lives, the collection of nectar and pollen.

In late summer, Rachel would return with sulphur smoke and a knife to rob the oldest colonies, leaving the youngest to live on through winter to provide for the next year.

Then the combs would be cut up, crushed and pressed through muslin, the honey gluing fingers and lips and gumming her long hair into tangles. It flowed into the tubs like apricot wine and the family spread it on malted brown bread, and dropped it into cake mixtures, and stirred in water and yeast with the sticky residue to make mead, and washed the wax clean to make sweet-scented candles to be lit at Christmas. And the house and outbuildings were filled with the sultry, golden, racy smell, which made the women seem more voluptuous and teased the men and gave the rooms a bawdy air.

Time passed quickly. In the mornings, her youngest grandchildren toddled around her like a litter of piglets, different small faces appearing each year, the oldest going on to school. Every weekend, Radigan, growing taller and more graceful, came home and recited all she had learned.

Hot summer days seduced Rachel to drowse among the roses. The sounds of farm and moor carried to her there, the bells of her flock, the whistle of the shepherd and the barking of his dogs, distant men shouting to each other, Meg Clarke singing in the house, the creaking, laden haywain passing alongside the hedge with grumbling wheels and the cushioned thud of hooves.

Incidents and crises which had once so inflamed or alarmed her now seemed comparatively unimportant. If the corn harvest was poor, then the fruit or potatoes had probably been good, and in any case there was always next season. Quarrels within the family were soon over. Dramas in the village provided light entertainment, fascinating for a day or two and then forgotten. The need for fleeting thrills had gone. Serene at last, she could look back and appreciate the fullness of her life. She had done nothing in small measure, held nothing back in love and hatred, friendship and sorrow. Her successes and her sins had been full-blooded and she had few regrets. The Jedder estate was established, its future decided, and there were still the years ahead to be spent in mellow contentment.

John brought her a young dog, the first since the gray dog. It was a rangy, disgraceful creature and ran with the chestnut horse on her rides, which now fared beyond the farms to the crannies of Beara and became a daily exploration and celebration of that remote and secret triangle of land between the two great rivers of North Devon. Relaxed and at ease within herself, Rachel drew closer to that which had always been her inspiration, the rhapsody of the countryside, with its ever-changing spectacle and the pendulum of its annual swing from seed to harvest.

So suddenly that it caught Rachel unawares, Radigan Spurway was fourteen years old and finished with lessons. She was taller and prettier than her grandmother had been. No hunger had drained the blush from her skin, nor deprivation sapped with expression from her strange eyes, which still shone with challenge and verve. She had acquired bearing along with her education, and Rachel, watching her descend from the carriage in a blue outdoor pelisse and matching silk bonnet, her black hair set in ringlets, was well satisfied.

"I got a gift for 'ee, my lovely," she said, after embracing her. "Change out of them soft shoes and come with me."

They went into the courtyard and she clapped her hands. The stable boy led out a small, purebred Arab mare, gray with dappled hindquarters and perfect conformation. Charles Waddon had studied *Messrs. Weatherby's General Stud Book* in detail to find the correct breeding and the Prophet's Thumbmark whirl of hair on the crest of her neck confirmed his choice.

Radigan forgot the restraint demanded by etiquette and hugged her grandmother sturdily, and then, after taking a moment to introduce herself, hugged the horse as well.

"The hunt meets at the Golden Lion in High Chilham tomorrow," Rachel told her. "Try her out then. We can go together."

The first frost of winter had come down upon Beara during the night, and, as the two horses clattered out from Yellaton, the northern and western sides of the hedgerows were still crisp with hoar, which also lay in wide, silver paths in the shadows. The ground steamed where the sun had shone since its rising and the rime was melting into a clear glaze on the leaves. At the touch of the frost, the soft-stemmed plants had instantly rotted, their broad, rain-catching foliage shriveled and blackened, and the last roses had died in bud.

Exmoor, ethereal as an Oriental print, was swathed in mists. The forests of the Taw Valley had drowned in a lake of white cloud, the highest treetops forming a fleet of sails over which the birds hovered in lost bewilderment. The floor of the woods, still overhung by papery autumn leaves, was white and hard as marble.

About thirty riders had already gathered by the time Rachel and Radigan reached the meet. The landlord of the inn was serving toddy, which peppered the air and licked the stomach like a flame. The hounds were enlivened, as though having run through an icy waterfall on waking. They rolled on the brittle grass and pursued each other boisterously, sterns waving like a bed of reeds. From the water-silk sky, a pale-gold sun stirred a direct beam of warmth into the chill morning and the atmosphere fizzed.

There was some jostling for position as they moved off to draw the covert at Glebeland, although, despite all the nudging for position, the field would soon divide itself into "the forward, the cunning and the useless." People joined the hunt for many reasons: to be seen, or to see, or to boast their exploits that night at dinner, or simply for the sport. The men eyed each other jealously, determined to prove their hardiness and the courage of their mounts. The horses, gingered up by the cold, tossed their heads and snorted, excited by the sound of the horn and the familiar prospect of the chase.

For minutes, the hounds silently searched the wood and the followers waited with quiet impatience. The acorns had fallen and the birds had picked off the last of the filberts, but the trees were decorated with color, mottled, green-veined oak and mustard-yellow hazel, scarlet rose hips against the time-fingered ash, and everywhere the polished parchment of the beech.

Rachel raised her gloved hand to neighboring farmers and was joined by Squire Waddon and young Jane's husband, Henry Wellington. Radigan sat a little apart, stylish and slender on her smart new mare, and caught many an eye, which caused her grandmother to smile with some smugness.

As they were about to move on, the girl came up, pointing her whip and asking, "That is where our land adjoins Braddon, is it not?"

Rachel nodded. "Of course, maid."

"Don't it seem a shame to stop there, Grandmother?" Radigan gave her a mischievous look and cantered off.

The hounds dived into Great Wood and gave tongue almost at once. A figure on a rise to the east raised his hat.

"View halloo!"

The pack streamed from the trees, fastened on a line and set a hard pace. The frost had stiffened the soft earth, and the riders, following in a bunch, took the first low hedge with ease. Along the headland of the next ten acres, gaps opened up between them as the better horsemen got away and over the fence and the more timid slowed to open and pass through the gate. Rachel, scanning the field, saw her granddaughter already well ahead, riding almost stirrup to stirrup with William, eldest son of Sir Thomas Carew.

"The minx!" she thought to herself and then whooped with glee.

The big chestnut plunged forward and the champagne air splashed into her face and the music of the hounds made the hair at the nape of her neck rise. The last of the surface rime had melted, and the moor, its bracken like beaten copper, opened before her. Rachel had never felt better, and her pulse raced as she passed Jack Hooper and Ben Morrish and careered downhill to gallop through Tiddy Water in jets of spray.

The horse needed no urging. His strong hocks rocked him up the other side of the combe and, as they reached the top, she saw Radigan and William Carew leap the stone wall outlining Yellaton, like a pair of dolphins.

She heard herself laughing with sheer pleasure and raced after them. The chestnut horse rose to the wall in a surge of power, and Rachel, in that split second of flight, saw all the vivid beauty of her homeland at once: the fine house, shining white on the brow of the hill, its gardens stretching before it, sprinkled by the fountain and last, lingering petals; the two mighty rivers winding to meet and mingle in the distant Atlantic; verdant meadows and plowed acres, like islands in the Beara sea, which swelled to where the fortification of Exmoor secured North Devon from the rest of England.

The bank beneath the well dropped sharply to a gully. The big horse, his eyes fixed on the hounds ahead, miscalculated the landing and fell, hard, arcing over in a somersault and flinging off his lightweight mistress, to come down on an outgrowth of rocks.

Other riders galloped to her, Squire Waddon frenziedly beating his way through them, shouting her name and pitching from his mount to her side. He snatched up the inert body, gripping too tightly, and blundered blindly over the uneven border of the moor and the long drive to Yellaton, to lay her on a couch. She did not move. Observed by round-eyed grandchildren, he put his head to her heart and then his watch case to her mouth. No pulse throbbed into his hearing. No breath misted the silver. Charles Waddon pulled her limp form into his arms with a great sob. Rachel Jedder was dead.

Jack Clarke made Rachel's coffin of yew, as he had made those of Robert Wolcot and little Sarah and her favorite son, Jedder. At the insistence of John and Squire Waddon, she was to be buried at Yellaton. The village, old friends and enemies alike, attended the funeral; farmers and their wives traveled from South Molton and Barnstaple to be there; strangers came up from the coast and the Bideford taverns. They came on horse and foot, by carriage and by wagon, many setting off at dawn to arrive in time.

Some came from curiosity, to see who else was there, and some came simply to be present at a historic local event. Not a few came without knowing why and were astonished at the throng, and others, without much love for her, came and found their eyes filling. The Wellingtons and Carews and Barlingtons and Rolles were only a few of the landowning families who bowed their heads at the graveside.

The winter sun was already descending when all were gathered, and the shadow of the ancient beech spread, dark and protective, over Rachel as the flock, brought close that the shepherds might attend, murmured its plaintive chant. Her family and close friends stood on the right of the grave, with the gentry positioned to the left, and behind them, in a packed circle, the people of the moors and coast heard the rector speak the words that would round off all their lives.

Emma wailed and tears rolled down John's face and Jane Clarke leaned, pale and silent, on her daughter's arm as the clear air grew chill and the grass damp with dusk.

Squire Waddon told again of Rachel Jedder's epic journey across England and her arrival at Yellaton as a penniless waif. He reminded them of the tragedies she had faced and the hardships she had survived and the triumphs of her life. He wept without shame, and all were acutely aware of the loss of her powerful presence among them.

Then, finally, John threw a handful of earth, like the one she had first gathered, from Jedder's land onto the coffin and led his crying wife away. The rest of the family slowly followed and the crowd dispersed, whispering and solemn. Only Radigan remained, staring down at where her grandmother lay under the great tree. William Carew came to her and put a gentle hand on her arm.

Again the leaves came down in pattering drops, and Radigan Spurway made the vow she would never break, and received the message through the sound: that the wooden case would crumble and its lining shred and the rains would wash Rachel free, to become part of the earth at last, part of Jedder's land.